EXPIRATION DATE

EXPIRATION DATE

A NOVEL

ERIC WILSON

Author of *Dark to Mortal Eyes*

WATERBROOK
PRESS

Expiration Date
Published by WaterBrook Press
2375 Telstar Drive, Suite 160
Colorado Springs, Colorado 80920
A division of Random House, Inc.

The characters and events in this book are fictional, and any resemblance to actual persons or events is coincidental.

ISBN 0-7394-5370-X

In cherished memory of
Alistair MacLean *(The Guns of Navarone)*
and Nathaniel Hawthorne *(The House of the Seven Gables)*

———

Dedicated to:
Carolyn Rose,
your soothing voice convinces me to never stop feeling;
Cassie Rose and Jackie Renee,
your fashion and music tips remind your dad to stay in touch.

Author's Note

Life is a coin toss, flipping us end over end. Some believe we come down on the side of free will, able to choose our own futures. Others think we land on the side of fate, filling our roles in a sovereign scheme. But what if, in a divine twist, we find ourselves balanced on the edge of the coin? In *Expiration Date,* I want to explore earth's tension between heaven and hell. Fiction is a tool. With it, I hope to climb high, to dig deep. Join me in this adventure. Together let's uncover hidden things.

> I will open my mouth in parables,
> I will utter hidden things.
>
> PSALM 78:2, NIV

The Devil's Work

Russian-Finnish Border, August 1917

A curse? He rejected the notion.

As the train lurched through the night, the revolutionary scraped his finger along the object in his pocket. Like skin clawed from an enemy's throat, sooty residue peeled from the oak tube and pushed beneath his thumbnail.

He smiled. By finding it, his agents had defied all superstitions.

This tube and its contents had once belonged to that lecherous priest, Rasputin. After conniving his way into the Russian Tsars' graces with promises to heal their hemophiliac son, Rasputin had died last December. Poisoned with potassium cyanide, shot by a Browning revolver, he'd risen demonlike from the cellar floor of Moika Palace and chased his attackers outside. They had overpowered him. Shot him again. Then shoved his body through a hole in the frozen Neva River.

Yet his lunacy continues to guide the Tsars! The weak fools.

The locomotive ascended a steep grade. The bulbous smokestack angled upward, and moonlight slid down the gleaming ironworks.

"Feed the fire," the engineer yelled at him.

He pushed the tube deeper into his pocket. "Of course. *Da.*"

With stout arms, he lugged wood from the tender car to the boiler. Flames raged and steam howled in stark contrast to the icy air at his back.

More firewood… *Grrunt.*

Sparks… *Pa-hissh!*

Trees thickened alongside the railway, and the revolutionary imagined they were fellow conspirators gathering to conceal him. He hated to leave St. Petersburg, but it was a necessary detour. Since 1914, German bullets and bayonets had killed Russians by the thousands, and recent government documents had put his own life in jeopardy by calling him a traitor, an agent of the kaiser. Wisdom dictated that he cross the frontier into Finland. From hiding, he would rebuild his base of Bolshevik support and reconfirm his allegiance to Mother Russia.

The revolutionary hefted another armload of wood... *Grrunt.*

Soon he would return to this place... *Pa-hissh!*

And then he'd hammer the final nail into the coffin of imperialism. For too long, the Romanovs had trusted in icons and artifacts while peasants and paupers starved. The revolutionary's own brother, Sasha, had resisted such injustice and later swung from a noose at Schlisselburg Fortress for his assassination attempt on a Tsar.

You will not have died in vain, Sasha. This I promise you.

"*Astergaisya...* Beware!" The engineer's gestures broke through his thoughts.

"What is it, comrade? We're at the border already?"

"Da. Please...*pozhaluista.* Keep yourself busy."

"Of course." The revolutionary adjusted his stoker cap. "I'm a worker, simply doing my job. We must trust the disguise." Underneath, he wore a blond wig to hide the thinning red hair of Konstantin Petrovich Ivanov—his name according to his forged factory pass.

"Well then, get back to work."

As the engineer turned away, the revolutionary slipped the tube from his pocket. He could not risk its detection in the event he was searched; it held the key to relics and riches. He poked the object into a crevice between brass and iron, swiped a finger through grease at the base of the tender box, then molded the sludge over the hiding spot.

He examined his work. Adequate for now.

Brakes screeched, and the engine belched smoke as it dragged its load between Belo-Ostrov's barbed wire and guard stations. Beneath light bulbs wearing misty halos, soldiers approached with hand signals and shouts.

"Stay back," the engineer said, "as I perform my duties."

The revolutionary nodded, pressing himself into the shadows while the engineer uncoupled the locomotive and guided them to a water tower. The tower's belly burbled as it emptied into the boiler tanks. The revolutionary felt a matching uneasiness in his own gut, an atypical show of nerves.

Again, he thought of Rasputin's occultism and the alleged curse on those who tampered with the tube: "misfortune and grief to all but the innocent."

He snorted. Such nonsense still infested the Romanovs' minds.

"Papers!" A militiaman clomped up the steps and cast a hard eye at him. Slung over the shoulder of the wool uniform, a rifle pointed at the star-studded sky.

"Here." The revolutionary relinquished his pass. "The night is cold, *nyet?*"

"Comrade Ivanov, you are a factory worker?"

"At Sestroretsk, sir."

"Why then are you here? You're also a stoker?"

"I stay warm and get paid. I cannot complain."

The militiaman studied his smudged face, then returned the papers.

The revolutionary pocketed them. "Thank you...*spahseebah.*" He watched the soldier stride toward the station. He waited, expecting a group of guards to rush him.

"Vladimir llyich Lenin!" they would call out. "You are under arrest!"

Yet five minutes later the locomotive was chugging into Finland.

Without further incident, the night passage led to Terijoki Station, where the train slowed to a halt beside a pine-planked platform. The engineer bid Vladimir Lenin farewell and surrendered him to a cluster of woodsmen, who clambered aboard to greet their leader with bearlike embraces and alcohol-scented kisses.

Lenin pretended the fanfare was an annoyance, but allowed himself to be manhandled good-naturedly toward packhorses tethered among the trees. His comrades' whispers of a local tavern hinted at the source of their ebullience.

Behind them, the locomotive gathered steam and proceeded on its way.

"The engine car. Oh no!"

One of the woodsmen turned in his saddle. "What is it you say?"

"Foolishness!" Lenin reined his mount to a halt. "I'm not thinking straight."

"What's wrong, comrade?"

Lenin squinted, but the woods blocked the station from view and muffled the clattering of the train's huge wheels. "This is not good, not at all."

"It can wait, I'm sure. Tell us up ahead in the pub."

"But it's already too late!"

"In your country, perhaps. Bah. Not here. Never too late for a drink."

"Don't you understand? If you hadn't rushed me, if you—"

"Come, old man. Take it slow. The night is patient with our bucolic ways."

Vladimir Lenin raised a fist skyward, a gesture which only multiplied his frustration. Why blame a god whose existence he denied? He shifted his vitriol to the woodsman. "I let fear and excitement distract me. I let you distract me! I left something behind on that train."

"A woman, no doubt. What was her name?"

"Nyet. Far more important."

"If it can't keep you warm at night, it's of no concern. As for vodka and women, they're always in demand." The woodsman pointed through the trees. The tavern's light was coy and golden, tiptoeing over the snow to meet them.

"You miss my point. On that train engine, I hid an object that'd make Rasputin turn in his grave."

"Bah. Let the old devil rest in peace."

"You think the devil's work is done?" Lenin hesitated, disturbed by the idea that the curse might be to blame for his loss of the wooden tube. "This is a plague on the mind!" he bellowed. "Nicholas and Alexandra Romanov cling to Rasputin's mysticism while we freeze. They refuse to see that electricity's the new god."

"Soon they'll understand." The woodsman's gloved hand thumped against Lenin's back. "With or without your object, you'll return to St. Petersburg and clear the entire *ektenia* from this path of revolution. Am I wrong?"

Lenin knew the ektenia well. Listing the entire Romanov family, it was prayed over weekly in Russian Orthodox services.

"Their blood will be upon my hands," he vowed.

"Then relax. For one night at least, the local spirits can ease your mind."

PART ONE

This strange man...
was making himself at home...after so long an absence,
that the dead people...would have had more right to be at home.

Ethan Brand, Nathaniel Hawthorne

He bought a ticket...
hoping that by going away to the west
he could escape.

Jonah 1:3

1

Haunted

Enough with the melodrama. He'd had his fill.

Clay Ryker crossed his arms, pressed his forehead to the window of the Greyhound bus, tried to think of anything other than his wife of ten years and his nine-year-old son. Heaven had slipped through his fingers, and hell crouched on the outskirts of his approaching hometown.

This town. Junction City…

Like it or not, the place was in his system. Twelve years ago, it'd fashioned him, emboldened him, sent him off a hero. The graduation accolades, the city paper headlines, even the coach of his basketball rivals had lifted him on wings of destiny. With a full scholarship, he'd headed off for the University of Wyoming. He was going places, doing things. He would change the world.

And it was all a lie. I can't even change my wife.

One head thud against the glass.

Ex-wife. Or soon to be.

Thud.

"Hey." A voice made Clay turn. "Yeah, you. I'm trying to sleep back here."

"Oh."

"If you don't mind."

"Sorry."

Clay leaned back and imagined Jenni's face: blond hair and green eyes; freckles dotting a thin nose; a slight indentation in the center of her lips. She'd filed the divorce papers months ago. Would she drop his name too?

He tilted his head and watched grass seed swirl in the wake of the passing bus. During his senior year in Wyoming, a season-long slump had soured the interest of NBA scouts and ended his athletic dreams. Nevertheless, he'd earned his diploma, moved Jenni and Jason from Laramie to Cheyenne, started his own business, worked seventy-hour weeks, took on a second mortgage to keep afloat—and lost everything in the process.

Here he was, back where he'd started. Moving in with Mom and Dad at the age of twenty-nine.

On the window, Clay's breath blossomed in random patterns, like Rorschach inkblots from his counselor's office. *What do I see, Dr. Gerringer? I see a dollar bill all wadded up and stuffed through a wedding ring. Oh, and it's on fire... The next one?* Pause. *Nope, just a mess of ink. What do you want me to do? Lie?*

In fact, he had lied; he had seen something.

A face along a riverbank. Bloated and wet, with sightless eyes.

Clay relived the nightmare from twelve years ago. One impulsive act, followed by whispers and suspicion. The memory of that day still lingered, a specter of guilt that had haunted his endeavors and pried at the seams of his marriage.

Clay Ryker would never forget. Above all, he could never tell.

———

"You having a pity party?"

"A what?"

A boy wearing jeans tucked into stubby boots crawled into the seat beside Clay, stared up with big blue eyes. "Pity party. That's what my grandpa calls it when I put my head against the window and pout. Am I bugging you? Grandpa said not to bug anyone." The kid looked back at a snoozing elderly man.

"You're fine," Clay said.

"Nothing to do on this bus. I hope we stop soon. You're tall, aren't you?"

"For a grownup."

The kid smiled. "Over six feet?"

"Six three. Hundred and ninety-nine pounds."

"Wow! Two hundred pounds."

"One ninety-nine," Clay underscored. Occasional drinks had softened his washboard stomach, but it was nothing he couldn't remedy in the gym.

Ripped abs, corded arms, legs like tree trunks—he was only weeks from regaining his former glory.

"Maybe one ninety-eight," he heard himself say.

"I'm big, too," the kid boasted. "I'm seven and a half. My name's Bobby."

"Hi, I'm Clay."

Bobby kicked at the metal footrest. "Are you married? My mom and dad're divorced, but Grandpa says it's not my fault. Says grownups get confused and make mistakes."

"You have a smart grandpa."

"Grandpa's divorced too."

"Oh." Clay looked down at Bobby. "I can see why you'd be upset."

"I'm not upset." The kid sniffed, then punched his fist into the seat between his legs. "Don't you know anything? Boys aren't s'posed to cry." With eyebrows knotted, he moved down the aisle and flopped from sight at the back of the Greyhound.

Clay stayed put, ears ringing with his own son's words from four months ago: *Why'd you make Mommy cry?*

Jason and Jenni now lived in a two-bedroom condo on the outskirts of Cheyenne, supported by Jenni's new job as a sports massage therapist. She'd been screening calls, ignoring Clay's messages. A few weeks ago when a male picked up, Clay had stared at the receiver before slowly setting it down. After a stint at the bar, he'd found himself on Jenni's doorstep, belligerent and unsteady. The intensity of his voice had brought neighbors to their windows. City police converged on the scene. Corralled into a patrol car, Clay festered with rage.

He realized in that moment he was capable of things he'd regret—things against his wife, against himself. Hadn't he studied and worked hard? For what? He'd put almost ten years into his marriage. A decade.

Sounded too much like *decayed*.

Since that night a judge had granted temporary orders to Jenni's attorney, restricting Clay's time with his son and requiring monthly support payments.

Now, with the bus humming along Highway 99, Clay told himself this change of location would do him good. Better to get away, to shut down and succumb to the numbness. He let his forehead hit the window, then gave a laconic laugh.

I feel no pain.
Thud.
I feel nothing at all.

———

Asgoth knew he was homely and misjudged. Even feared. Outfitted in tan trousers, a pale yellow shirt, an argyle vest and matching socks, he skulked across Holly Street toward Founder's Park. With a stiff finger, he scratched at his head.

Looks are deceiving, he consoled himself.

At least he no longer wore the plain black robes and that golden cross.

Along the park's perimeter, Asgoth found leafy refuge behind a tree and watched two tall women stroll along a path in hip-hugging jeans and belly shirts.

Mylisha and Summer. Black and white versions of one another. They spent their waking hours oblivious to his existence in their small community.

This town. Junction City…

Like it or not, there was no getting rid of him. For twelve years, its citizens had avoided, teased, and toyed with him. They'd foiled his plans and brought him low in the eyes of the Consortium. Quaint churches marred every other block, and Scandinavian families worked the land. Despite its name, this place was but a dot on the map. A dead end.

Junction City sorely needed new blood. Spilled blood.

Asgoth crept back across the street, climbed uneven steps to his second-story apartment. A neighbor, descending, looked right through him. They all did. He'd learned to live with it, to let it fuel his determination.

He had barely passed through his door when cold fingers locked on to his neck and thrust him against the wall. He resisted. Ineffectively. Brute strength had never been his to claim, but with the intellect at his disposal he deduced that this threat was nothing of a permanent nature; bare hands rarely served as premeditated murder weapons.

Plus, these hands were unusual. He knew their odor of incense and sweat.

He stopped struggling. "Why're you here?" he gasped.

"This is my last visit." A set of eyes floated into view, gray pupils matching the calm strength in the intruder's voice. "The Consortium's tired of you, A.G. We've tried to sustain you here, but you've given back so little."

"I've had some bad luck. You know that."

"Luck? Success comes to the ones who work the hardest on the smartest schemes. You and Mr. Clay Ryker've got some history between you, which I suggest you clear up. Otherwise, your presence in this town becomes a liability."

"What do you want me to do?"

"Be persuasive but discreet. He needs to remove himself from the picture."

"A self-sacrifice?"

"Either him or you," the intruder concurred. "And we'd like a down payment, to prove you're serious about your efforts here. The free ride's over."

"I've been trying."

"Forget it. This town's barely worth the effort."

"Tonight"—Asgoth forced the words from his strangled throat—"it'll change."

The intruder snickered. "Sorry, A.G. You're dead in the water."

"One more chance. Please."

"Cold hard cash. We'll take one hundred thousand dollars, nothing less."

"Okay. I can get it."

"By when? We need a date."

"The second weekend in August."

"During the Scandinavian Festival?" The color in the intruder's eyes seemed to coil like smoke. "This time it'd better work, or you're gone. We can't let you keep stumbling around town, raising questions that're better left unanswered."

The fingers snapped free from Asgoth's neck. Before he'd dropped to the carpet, the intruder was gone—a vapor woven into the shadows.

Asgoth dragged himself to the apartment's window. He pulled himself up and peered through a gap in the curtains at the ladies still pacing the park. Shortly, Clay Ryker would arrive on the Greyhound, and one of these women would trigger the necessary chain of events.

Yes. The one with the strawberry blond hair: Summer Svenson.

Asgoth would save Mylisha for later.

A Part to Play

"Junction City, next stop." The driver closed the door behind the late arrivals.

Clay watched as a thin woman used a sandaled foot to scoot her carpet-bag down the aisle. She passed up the empty seat in row seven, stopped at nine.

"Taken?"

"Nope, all yours," Clay said. What would it hurt? He had only one more stop.

Bracelets jangled on the woman's sun-dried arms as she raised her bag into the overhead storage. A fringed maroon shawl wafted about her shoulders.

"Here, let me help…"

"Too late," she said, punctuating the words with a grunt. "Or maybe you intended it that way." She curtailed his explanation with a wave of the hand and folded herself into the aisle seat.

Okaaay then. Clay found diversion reading road signs.

"Signs, huh?"

"Excuse me?"

"You're reading signs," she said. "What's your sign?"

"Uh, as in astrology? Capricorn, I think. Born in early January. But I don't really go for all that."

The woman took hold of his hand. He stiffened in astonishment as she uncurled his fist and traced fingertips along his palm. A shiver ran up his arm; it'd been months since a woman had touched him in any intimate fashion. Her scent of oregano was a refreshing touch of individuality, and her hair was loose and long. One of her bleached strands clung to the fabric of his University of Oregon sweatshirt.

He pulled his hand away.

"Forgive my forwardness. My name," she said, "is Henna."

"Hannah?"

"Henna. As in the plant."

"Oh, my bad." He had no intention of offering his name in return.

She withdrew her ring-adorned fingers, twined them in her shawl, and considered him with wide eyes. "You…you are a man with many burdens."

He shrugged. "Aren't we all?"

"Men? No, not all of us."

"What I meant was—"

"Don't worry, I understood."

"You caught me off guard, grabbing my hand like that."

"Do I look like I bite?" She clicked her tongue. "You sure know how to make a lady feel good about herself, don't you?"

"Guess it's just a gift."

Henna's voice lost its warmth. "Every gift comes at a price."

What was this lady's deal? Clay scanned the bus where passengers dozed, read paperbacks, or dipped with rhythmic monotony into noisy potato-chip bags. Bobby was curled up with his head on his grandfather's lap. Ahead, the setting sun fixed the driver in silhouette.

"My stop's coming up," Clay told Henna. "Window's all yours when I go."

"I've already seen all I need to see, but you don't—"

"My stuff's up there," he went on, rising to his feet.

"But you don't want to hear it, do you? Not into palm reading, I suppose."

"Don't see much use for it, that's all. Nothing personal. I was raised with your basic teachings from the Bible. Guess that means I'm narrow minded, right?"

"Would it be narrow minded of me to agree?"

He gave a laugh. Dropped back into his seat.

Henna said, "Do you want to know why things are falling apart for you?"

"I'm dying to know."

"Why you lost your grandfather's money? Why your business collapsed?"

"Hold on! How do you know about that?"

"Why your wife left you? Why your son rarely speaks with you?"

Clay's hands began shaking. He touched his wedding band, then clamped fingers into his knees. He turned to face Henna. Why was she pestering him? What else did she know about his life? Although he wished she could be swept away in an undertow of her own superstition and navel gazing, he was snared by her words. She seemed to be onto something. Maybe she could help.

"Okay, I've got a few minutes. What're you trying to tell me?"

She clutched his hand again, and this time he opened it to her tracing finger.

"Perhaps," she said, "I've been sent to put things right, back to the way they should've been. God works in many different ways, you know."

"Go on."

"You're a man with high expectations," she said. "You're disappointed in yourself, yet you're only human. A man. A child of the earth…Clay."

He cut his eyes to hers. Did she know his name? Or was it coincidence?

"Clay's a beautiful thing, malleable and full of possibility. If it gets hard, though, it easily breaks." Transfixed by the contours of his palm, Henna's face twitched. Her fingernail came to a stop. Dug into his skin. A tic started at the corner of her lips, and she dropped his hand into his lap.

"What?" he asked. "What's wrong?"

"My apologies." She looked away. "But I believe this is your stop."

The bus was slowing, turning left from Highway 99 onto a side street. He surveyed the familiar backdrop…the sidewalks where he'd learned to skate, the old water tower, the fire station. This was his past; he needed a glimpse of the future.

"Tell me, Henna. Was it something good or bad?"

"These things are meant to be discovered on their own."

"I admit I mocked you at first, but I'd really like to know what you…felt."

She nodded out the window. "This is your stop."

"I'm serious. I need to know."

She seized his hand a final time. "You're sure you're ready to embrace it?"

With her skin hot against his own, Clay glanced at the other passengers. Embrace what? What'd she have in mind? He heard himself say, "I'm sure."

"It will come," she said. "You'll begin to know things. You'll feel them."

"Excuse me?"

"Remember, though. In the Garden of Eden, knowledge was the first seduction."

Seduction... Delivered in a whisper, the word seemed to reverberate through the shell of the bus, and Clay felt glances shift his way. Beside him, Henna laid her head back with eyes closed.

He cleared his throat. "Thanks for the advice, but, uh, I need to be going."

Henna said nothing. When he tried to pass into the aisle, her legs resisted him with the stubbornness of a rusty gate.

———

Summer Svenson sensed movement to her right. Was she being watched? She peered through the trees of Founder's Park, saw nothing, shrugged away her uneasiness. She and Mylisha continued pacing the walkway. Within minutes the bus would bring Clay Ryker back into their lives.

"You seem nervous."

"Me?" Summer pursed her lips. "Little edgy, that's all. What about you? It's been years since you've seen Clay. You think he'll still look the same?"

"I sure hope so, girl."

"Aha, you *do* have feelings for him."

"Some."

"Teenage romances die hard. Better watch out," Summer kidded, "or I might steal him away. You know you're no match for my long legs." She pretended to model, stretching first one leg, then the other.

"Put those things away before you blind someone."

Summer laughed, turning to examine her friend. They'd met almost thirteen years ago while playing high school basketball. On the court, they'd been aggressive and unstoppable; off court, giggly and girlish. Things had changed for them, in early '92. Human nature had shown its darker side.

Summer nudged her friend's leg with her own. "Don't try to deny it, Mylisha."

"Deny what?"

"I know you. You've been missing Clay since the day he left for college."

"Maybe. But," Mylisha clarified, "I've no intention of stirring things up again. He's a married man."

"Ah-ah-ah. Correction. A man going through a breakup."

"So we've been told, but you know the kind of stories that spin through this place." Mylisha stood and moved toward the park's fenced display.

"I say he's all yours for the taking, Mylisha."

"A man on the rebound? No thank you. Last thing I need's sloppy seconds."

Again Summer felt a predatory heat—as though some lecherous old man were watching her from the shadows. She thought of mentioning it, then joined her friend in perusing the bronze plate's description of the freshly painted train before them.

The 1904 Finnish locomotive was a throwback to the railroad's glory days. Sent to Oregon as a gift between countries, she'd found a place of honor in Junction City. A survivor of four separate wars, and one of only two such remaining engines, this beast of burden had played its role in the Bolshevik Revolution.

The Bolshe-what?

Summer reached through the fence to touch the machinery, realized it was as cold as the history it represented.

So what if she didn't know world events? She knew things about good ol' JC, things that'd make your hair stand on end. Five thousand people, give or take, and she had dirt on a fair percentage of them.

Secrets were her cash in the bank. A little blackmail could go a long way.

Mylisha seemed fascinated by the train. She said, "We studied the revolution in one of my college courses. Did you know the word *tsar* comes from the Latin word *Caesar*? You think about it, Summer, and it's kinda crazy. Lenin escaped from Russia on an engine like this."

"Hellooo? Since when have I cared?"

"Don't you think it's…mysterious? Lenin could've been on this very engine."

"I thought Lennon was from England. From Liverpool."

"Girl. Tell me you're not that stupid."

"Just messin' with you." Summer shrugged. "But I mean, honestly, you're talking about some Russian dude who lived, what, seventy, eighty years ago. Why should I care?"

"Because history's full of lessons. My people've taught me that."

"What's the lesson here? I guess I *am* stupid."

Mylisha checked her watch. "The lesson is that an air of mystery is a good thing. I say we head home and forget surprising Clay. No use in seeming desperate."

"Hey, let's face it. We're not getting any younger."

"That doesn't mean I'm desperate." Mylisha set a hand on her hip. "Oh no you didn't… I know you didn't just roll your eyes at me. Anyway, I say we let Clay make the first move."

"You're just scared."

"Since when?"

Summer wanted to say: since you broke up with Clay, since your younger sister got the UCLA athletic scholarship you wanted and then squandered it on drugs and no-good losers, since you got promoted into Safeway management and stopped dating.

"Mylisha." She brushed a coil of hair from her friend's face. "Years ago I lost my sister and my parents, so I know what it's like to feel alone and afraid. Please, though, tell me you're not just trying to avoid the past."

"I'm not scared," Mylisha insisted. "Come on, let's jet."

———

Asgoth paced the apartment, alone with the old plumbing's creaks. It'd been like drawing blood to get a place of his own, even one this humble. Dank and mildewed, the space was stained by ceiling leaks and the former occupant's splatters on the kitchen walls.

"I cannot fail," he whispered into the darkness.

If he did, he would lose his last vestige of hope. He'd be banished—for a third time. An exile, wandering the isolated deserts of his own mind.

He checked the wall clock, cracked and askew. "Where are you, Monde?"

In reply the door flung open, and Asgoth darted behind a curtain. Mr. Monde marched in, an angular creature with a long nose and a knife slash of a mouth. Beneath feathered black hair and onyx eyes, he wore a corduroy jacket that softened his angles. Despite the failed project which had separated them years ago, Monde still exuded arrogance like imported cologne.

"Are you here, A.G.? Are you prepared to join forces again?"

"You're late." Asgoth slid into view. "I guess old habits die hard."

"Aren't you the ever-impertinent one? You summon me, then spit out ridicule." Monde wagged a finger. "Last time we worked together, it was your insubordination that cost us. Your indulgences attracted unnecessary attention."

Asgoth breathed into the man's face. "Here, the past has no bearing."

"You still have the Consortium's six other members to convince of that."

"I'm moving forward. Soon they'll have no choice but to accept me."

"A town this size holds little interest to them."

"I know, they're still capitalizing on Eugene's moral ambiguities and anarchist sympathies. Since my relocation here, I've watched them build fortunes on the sex and drug industries. They've infiltrated the campuses and, even more impressively, the fringe religious groups."

"While remaining faceless and anonymous, I might add."

"We cannot be apprehended, if we seem not to exist." Asgoth verbalized the axiom which long ago had been pounded into his thinking. He despised it. He was tired of being ignored. He wanted to be seen, to be feared. "Junction City has potential, Monde. I have a secret or two that'll change the Consortium's thinking."

"They want tangible results."

"They will have them...and sooner than they suspect. The Consortium's strategy is to erode the establishment's base, but mine's more straightforward —bring the structure down with one well-placed explosive."

"And Junction City's the place for it?"

"It's perfect. It's so mundane."

"So...rural."

"Exactly. No one would expect it here."

"Are we speaking of a literal bomb?"

"If one comes in handy," Asgoth responded. "Though I meant it figuratively. Fear is a weapon unto itself. It could shatter the idyllic pretenses of this town."

"Fear." Mr. Monde widened his eyes, stepped closer, then threw out both arms like a great bird swooping down on its prey.

Asgoth stumbled back, chafed by Monde's laughter. "You think it's funny?"

"I think you're fortunate to have me at your side. I'm not too modest to remind you of my own recent success. You read the newspapers, so you know the things I accomplished in Corvallis and in the coastal region. With a bit of help I manipulated one particular family and helped locate a lost inheritance."

"But it's now out of your reach, isn't it?" Asgoth watched his partner blink. "That's why you answered my summons, that's why we're stuck together again as partners. We must pool our energies to show our value."

Monde squared his shoulders. "Admittedly, my stint at the coast was tinged with…regrets. Let it be noted, though, I won't allow you to belittle me before the others. At the end of the day, what do I have if not my pride?"

"My sentiments exactly. Which is why we'll have to trust each other."

"I suppose. Tell me, does Mr. Clay Ryker have a part to play in this?"

"That's a strange thing to ask."

"Is it? You're certain you've no personal ax to grind?"

"And what if I do? What business is it of yours?"

"Does he even know of your presence here?"

Asgoth scoffed, "He has no idea."

Dirty Little Secrets

Clay's mother met him at the curbside, wearing low heels, a tailored cream dress, and a purse over her arm. Clay had always admired her classic looks; for the first time, however, he noticed wrinkles around her eyes and lips, and he was reminded she would not be around forever.

Della pulled back her shoulders, studying him from beneath waxed brows. "You made it in one piece, dollface. How was the trip?"

"I should've flown. You meet a whole different element on the bus."

"We did offer to cover the airfare. You know that you could've—"

"Mom, I don't want to spend the rest of my life in your debt. You and Dad've done enough already…you know, with everything that's going on right now."

A reference to his insolvent business and escalating debt. At three hundred bucks an hour, his lawyer fees alone were enough to do him in.

Clay's mother led him to a sparkling white Dodge truck, which he was certain she'd pressured his old man into buying. She climbed behind the wheel. Clay dropped his suitcase and sack on the truck's bed, then joined her in the cab.

"Nice."

"A gift from your father."

Bingo.

"Here." Della dangled a set of keys. "He and I agreed you can use the Duster while you're reestablishing yourself."

"That thing still runs?"

"It's at the house, but you'll have to fill the tank."

"Mom, I don't need to be spoon-fed. I'll be okay."

"Don't be ridiculous, doll. Take what's offered you." Della's lips formed an obstinate line, and she pushed the keys his way. As she lifted her chin and tossed styled black hair, Clay recalled how his mother had often used such gestures to solicit sympathy and compliance.

"Okay," he heard himself give in. "Thanks, Mom. I appreciate it."

He reached for the keys, his hand brushing hers. A jolt shot across his skin, and miniature chisels of heat carved through his nerve endings. Numbers. Six of them. Etched like tattoos into his palm.

1.2.2.5.2.1...

He yanked away. Staring down, his eyes denied the sensation.

"Clay? What is it?"

"Did you feel that?"

"Feel what?"

"Your skin."

"Why, thanks for noticing." She patted his leg the way she had when he was a child. "Your father hasn't even said a word. It's a new moisturizing lotion I bought at our Avon meeting last week. I'm sure you remember Mrs. Dixon? She's my consultant, and she says the medicated formula does wonders."

Numerals. Still throbbing on Clay's palm. Each number, like hot wax poured into a mold, sloshed and burned and hardened into irrefutable shape.

1.2.2.5.2.1...

Were they products of his imagination? Or something more?

He rubbed his hand against his leg, and the apparition began to fade. On his sweatshirt he noticed a strand of Henna's hair. He wound the bleached fiber around his ring finger while the lady's voice penetrated his thoughts once more.

It will come... You'll begin to know things. You'll feel them.

Feel what? This was crazy.

God works in many different ways...

Beneath the barrage of recent events, Clay felt his faith in such notions crumbling. If, indeed, God was involved in daily existence, did he work through palm-reading, herb-scented women named after plants?

At this point Clay would believe just about anything.

———

The red Honda Prelude zipped through the narrow streets. At the wheel, Summer paid no attention to her friend's tightened knuckles on the door handle.

"You really think Clay'll call you?"

"I have no clue," Mylisha said. "Before he ran off to college and got married, he never gave much reason for breaking things off. He turned real quiet, like he was guarding something. A hard one to read, that boy. Who knows what he'll do?"

"But you do have a glimmer of hope."

"Maybe. Just a little. I say, let the boy be a man about this."

"Got that right." Summer flashed a ravenous smile. "And I bet every inch of him is just *starving* for attention. Men. They're so predictable."

"Shush." Mylisha slapped at Summer's forearm. "Clay and I are just friends. That's all we can be, all we should be."

"You don't mean the racial thing, do you? People need to grow up."

"No, I'm talking about right and wrong. He's still legally married, Summer."

"Oh yeah, you're stuck on that." Although Summer Svenson poked fun at Mylisha's resolve, she wished she had some of her friend's moral fortitude. The girl passed up a lot of opportunities for the sake of her beliefs. Hard to understand, but harder to begrudge. Summer, on the other hand, took what came her way. "Listen, I've been meaning to talk to you about something."

Mylisha's bright mahogany eyes turned her way. "What?"

"I respect your views on religion, I hope you know that, but it seems like you let God rob you of your happiness. I mean, look at you. You never get out, you have no serious relationships, and we both know you work *way* too many hours."

"It's called responsibility. Can't just up and leave when I feel like it."

"Isn't there anything you do just for yourself these days?"

"Of course there is."

"Like what?"

"My classes at LCC."

"Oh, you're the real party animal, racking up credits at Last Chance College—"

"Lane Community."

"Whatever. You deserve to have a little fun, that's all I'm saying. Half the time, you're watching after your sister's kids. Time to stop living like a prisoner."

"A prisoner?" Mylisha's voice grew husky. "That is so unfair. What about you? Your world spins around whoever happens to be the hottie of the week."

"Wait. Don't *even* put on your self-righteous attitude with me."

"We've all got our problems, Summer. I'm the first to admit it."

"Well, that's mighty white of you."

"Very funny. Girl, why are we even discussing this?"

"Because friends take care of each other, and somebody's gotta tell you…"

"Tell me what?"

"You've changed, Mylisha. You're getting—I don't know how else to put it—*boring*. Time to break loose."

"And set aside my beliefs? My heritage?"

"Sure. Break a rule here and there. There's freedom outside the box." Summer slowed the car at an intersection. "Just think about it, that's all. Are we cool?"

"Tell me my ears didn't lie. Did you say I was boring?"

"Maybe that's too strong a word."

"Even worse than the other *b* word."

"Just trying to do you a favor." Summer looked both ways, then accelerated. "Promise me you'll think about it?"

In her peripheral vision, she saw Mylisha fold her arms and stare off.

Fine. The girl could go on living in a religious bubble, but Summer wasn't about to pass up a chance to contact Clay Ryker. Officially, this was the first day of summer—her day. Would Clay remember her? The odds were in her favor. They'd been in high school together, during the early nineties. Like, *where* had the time gone?

Plus, now that he was back in town, he needed to know a few things. Time to spill one of her closely guarded secrets.

———

Beaming, Summer felt heat touch her cheeks. "You're sure it's no bother?"

"Not at all," Clay's voice assured through her neon-colored cell phone.

"Good. I'd love to talk with you."

"Why not? It'll be nice to see you all grown up. Last time I remember, you were one of those pesky high school sophomores. Thanks for catching me up on the latest. Almost forgot how gossip makes this town go round."

"Better to *create* some commotion than admit we don't have any, right?"

"I guess so. You know where my parents live, out on Cox Butte Road?"

"Like I'd forget."

"In a little while, then," Clay said.

By obtaining his permission, Summer felt acquitted of any wrongdoing. What further excuse did she need? She'd always been attracted to Clay's lean, mean physique. He was a missed opportunity.

Sorry, Mylisha, but you took your stance. Now I get a turn.

Summer drove slowly to maintain a facade of nonchalance. The way to the Rykers' led across croplands before rising to the crest of a wooded knoll. Her headlights played through dust and pollen kicked up by the day's farm equipment. As she pulled into the driveway, stars winked with hints of romance. The night was on her side.

She made adjustments in the mirror. With a finger still touched to her lips, she noticed a figure watching from the porch. She'd been caught in the act of primping.

Oh, well. Let him stare.

She stepped from the car, tossed her hair.

"Summer." Clay's voice sounded deeper than on the phone. Warmer too. Leaning against the rail, he looked bulkier than she remembered. A grown man.

She twirled once for inspection. "It's me, the same little girl from JC."

"It's you, all right." He took a long, miscalculated stride that bypassed the steps and dropped him on the path before her. He caught himself. "Been waiting for you out here, waiting for an excuse to get out of this place. Parents." He threw a thumb over his shoulder. "They never let go, do they?"

"Well, you *are* back in their house. How's it feel, being in town?"

"Claustrophobic. Hardly anything's changed."

She noticed Clay's words were slurred. "What about you? You found work yet?"

"I'll do some job hunting tomorrow, but no more tree trimming or pipe laying. Did enough of that as a teenager."

"You'll find something. I know you will."

"Starting over." He turned to stare at his childhood home. "What a concept. Never thought I'd be here again, closing in on the big three-o."

"Life can get pretty crazy."

"Don't know if I can handle it. Being in someone else's house, eating someone else's food. You should see the fridge. My mom's got V8 juice and yogurt stuffed between Dad's six-packs of Miller Lite."

"Free drinks? Bonus."

"Rock on," Clay agreed with false cheer. "Really, I didn't expect to end up like this. Things just came apart piece by piece."

"You and Jennifer?"

"Jenni." His voice caressed the name.

"And you were such a sweet couple." She waved away his questioning look. "Remember a couple years back? You were in town on summer vacation, I think, and I ran into you guys at the Scandinavian Festival."

"Okay. Yeah. In the beer garden, right?"

"What a night. All huddled under the tent while it poured down rain."

Clay gripped a porch post. "I'm taking my son to the festival this year. According to our temporary visitation agreement, he'll be with me most of August."

"He'll love it. Just wait till he eats his first Finnish funnel cake. Or an *aebelskiver* with powdered sugar. Those're the best."

Clay's eyes turned glassy with nostalgia.

"Listen," she said, "you can't let one person's opinion define who you are. Sometimes things just don't work out."

"It's not that," he said a little too quickly. "It just doesn't make sense. I mean, up till last October, Jenni was still writing me little love notes."

"How sweet."

"She even carved our names into a pumpkin."

"Sounds adorable."

"With a capital *A*." He swayed, then hugged the post. "*A* as in 'All the Way Out in Wyoming.'"

"Is she still there?"

"It's where Jason was born. He's nine now. Good little ballplayer." Clay rubbed his forehead. "The sheriff served me papers on December 18. 'Merry Christmas, Mr. Ryker. Ho-ho-ho.' Here's the thing, Summer. I'm a guy, so I admit I don't have relationships all figured out." He plopped down on the wooden steps. "But it doesn't make sense. Even my therapist can't pinpoint where things went wrong."

"Have you told the therapist everything?"

"Whaddya mean?"

"Have you held anything back?"

He tried to level his chin, to look her in the eyes. "Why're you asking?"

"We all have histories, don't we? Our dirty little secrets."

With his fist, Clay covered a burp, then lowered his head.

Summer had to ask. "Clay? How many beers have you had?"

"A."

"Eight?"

"A," he repeated. "As in 'All of Them.'"

She tried to join in with his raspy laughter, but she could think only of Mylisha and Jenni. To take advantage of this good and lonely man before her would be to encroach on others' territory. An empty victory at best.

See, Mylisha, my world doesn't revolve around every guy I meet.

As for the other thing Summer wanted to tell him? Maybe she should pass it on and let Mylisha become the bearer of secrets, since Mylisha also had been scarred by the injustice. She owed that much to her friend.

"Pathetic, isn't it?" Clay commented. "I don't even like Miller Lite. Can't even have a pity party the right way."

"Pity party? Whoever put that idea in your head?" Summer turned so that the moonlight could play along her lip gloss. She'd let Clay enjoy the view at least. "You have every right to think about yourself a little. Work it, baby, work it."

"That's right." He slapped his hand onto the rail and pulled himself back up. "So you wanna go into town? Maybe shoot some pool?"

"I'd *love* to, Clay, but I can't. No matter how much I'd like to say yes."

He cocked his head as though her answer hadn't registered.

"I can't," she reiterated. "Not tonight."

"Gonna tell me why? It's an innocent request, you know."

"I know it is. It's Mylisha I'm thinking of. She's missed you and hasn't even been serious with anyone else since you left. She should be the one to share a night out with you. Am I wrong?" Summer slipped a hand into his and squeezed.

He flinched. Jerked away.

The reaction made something inside her hurt. "I shouldn't have come," she said. Turning her face up to his, she was caught by his dark green eyes, dilated and full of fear. "Clay, are you all right?"

He wobbled.

"What happened? You feeling sick?"

"No." He scrubbed his hand on his jeans. "Nope, I'm fine."

"You want me to help you back inside?" She reached for him.

"Stay back! I can do it myself."

"Okay, I'm sorry. I was only trying to… I didn't mean anything by it. You're right anyway. It's getting late, and I should head back. Thanks for talking, Clay."

"You betcha."

"You know, maybe I could take a rain check." She shrugged one shoulder. "I might have some free time in the next week or two."

"Sure."

"I'll keep in touch."

"In touch?" His eyes shifted to his palm. "That might not be the best idea." With overwrought focus, he turned and worked his way up the steps into the house.

———

Summer's Prelude carried her back down the hill. Vying for her attention, the look in Clay's eyes continued to trouble her. He'd been unquestionably shaken.

She sighed. *Oh, what might've been.*

Her red car sped through the curves until the road broadened once more onto the flatlands. She refused to live her life victimized by fear. Her sister, Milly, had died in an auto collision, and Summer often found herself tempting fate.

Before her, night clouds stretched over the smattering of town lights, and she wondered what Mylisha was up to. Nothing much, probably. What made her friend tick? Would she be ready to carry the weight of a secret or two?

Summer knew she'd been hard on Mylisha earlier. A peace offering was in order, an apology card.

After a detour into a corner market, Summer headed for her friend's apartment on the south end of town. A semitruck rumbled by. A sports car wearing a coat of gray primer purred alongside, long enough for the driver to try to catch her eye.

Get a clue, jerk!

On Maple Street she edged to the curb. Pushing ten o'clock already. Was it too late for Mylisha? Hard to tell anymore.

Summer's left hand opened the car door, and her right clutched for—

"Omigosh!"

On the sidewalk a man was facing her with a lewd fire in his eyes.

She thought of slamming the door and hitting the locks, imagined peeling away. Then, thinking of Mylisha alone in the apartments behind this stranger, she chose to face him. She would put on her game face. As if to confirm her decision, a cone of light washed over the man's form and revealed ugly tan pants and an argyle vest.

So much for his cloak of intimidation. *Hellooo? What a loser!*

Now he was wearing a secretive grin, and she flung the door wide, rising to meet this challenge.

"Listen, buddy, what's *your* problem?"

Screeching rubber and a revved motor were all she knew of the vehicle that caught her from behind. She felt something snap as her arms were thrust over the door. With disembodied, fading vision, she rode the torn metal panel through the air, her head careening toward a picket fence in the yard that became her resting place.

4

The Envelope

Despite disquieting memories and a boozy heaviness slogging through his head, Clay woke early. The noise of a lawn mower grew louder outside his window. His father, no doubt: *Up and at 'em. No sleeping in around here, Son.*

Mumbling, Clay found his way to the bathroom.

Splash of water. Excedrin. A towel to dry off his face.

Funny thing. Last night the alcohol had helped him forget, whereas here in the piercing light of morning it only deepened his gloom. Back in Cheyenne, as a concession to Jenni, he had once upon a time attended an AA meeting. Some in the room had been a mess. Screwed up in a big way. He knew he was different, though. He didn't drink all that often; he just used an occasional buzz to take off the edge.

And to forget. Mostly to forget.

He combed a hand through his short brown hair. Even his scalp felt bruised.

This time he ran both hands over his head, facing his discomfort head-on. This was a new day, a fresh set of circumstances. Time to get on with life.

Of course, a job and a paycheck would help in a big way.

In socks and boxers, he fetched the *Register-Guard* from the paper box on the porch and spread it on the table tucked into the dining nook. As coffee percolated, he ran a finger down the classified columns.

Déjà vu. At this same table, scanning the same subscription who knew how many years ago, he'd sought out his first real job. He'd landed three summers' worth of work with the Junction City Parks Department and climbed his way to crew supervisor.

Yep, I was a working machine.

With his mom's Avon scented pen, he began circling job possibilities.

Gerald Ryker burst through the back door, grass clinging to his boots, sweat staining the T-shirt beneath his overalls. "Clay, you're home."

"Hi, Dad."

"You get in last night? You have a safe trip?"

"Uneventful." Clay knew anything more would be a waste of breath.

"The lawn mower wake you up?"

"What lawn mower?"

"Never mind."

Clay tried not to smile at this subtle victory. *Score one for the Claymeister.*

"You get the coffee brewing, Son?"

"In the pot."

"Good. Back under my roof, I expect you to do your part."

Gerald Ryker hefted his omnipresent blue travel mug. To the trained eye, it functioned as a barometer of the man's disposition, and its present configuration boded well for Clay. Empty, with the lid off: partial clearing, chance of sun.

Seconds passed while a torrent of caffeine filled the container.

Clay said, "Cream's here on the table."

Gerald snapped the lid into place and stood rigidly in the middle of the kitchen.

"Hold on, Dad. You drink it straight up, don't you?"

Clay braced himself for an admonition or, more likely, a sound bite from the past: *Black for me, Son—same way I like my women.* The phrase had been monumentally offensive to Clay in high school when he'd started dating Mylisha French. With nervous defiance, he'd introduced her to Gerald, expecting a reaction. Instead, he'd received stony silence on the subject.

Here in the Ryker residence, silence was a language of its own.

"You looking for a job?" Gerald ignored the creamer, hooked a chair with his foot to join Clay at the table. "Tell you right now, you're wasting your time."

"Huh?"

"Did I mumble, Son?" Gerald took a long slurp from his mug. "Forget the classifieds. You got work all laid out for you. Stan Blomberg's expecting you."

"Blomberg?"

"Used to work with me in the lumberyard. Heavyset, red hair, a real religious fanatic. He left the lumberyard to manage things over at the monument company. Blomberg's a character, but we've stayed in contact over the years."

"Did you say monuments? You mean tombstones?"

"Now's no time to be picky, Son. Pay's not bad starting off." Gerald set a fist atop the blue mug and elaborated. "Ten and a half an hour. Could go up at your ninety-day review. If I remember right, insurance and 401(k) will kick in too. You'll have to ask Blomberg. One judgmental son of a gun, but he'll lay it all out for you."

"And I'll be doing what exactly?"

"Like I said, you'll have to ask him."

Clay tried not to react. This was his parents' house, so it was only natural they'd nose into his decisions. He folded the half-read newspaper and pushed it across the table to his father.

In handling the newsprint, he realized he'd smudged his fingers with ink. He gazed at the stains, felt a quiver of foreboding, the same sensation he'd had after last night's encounter with Summer.

She'd taken hold of his hand, and he'd felt indentations throb beneath his skin. Cryptic numbers. Ephemeral, yet undeniable.

6.2.1.0.4...

Just like the incident with his mother...*1.2.2.5.2.1...*

He forced the sequences from his mind like a bad dream.

"So, Dad, Blomberg's open to this idea? He's expecting me?"

"This Monday morning, the twenty-first. Eight o'clock."

"And you didn't think to ask me about it?"

"Job's a job, Son."

"Guess you've got it all mapped out for me."

"Man's gotta go out and make things happen. The least I can do."

"The least." Clay crossed his arms. "You know, maybe next time you could run it by me first. I'm not a kid anymore."

Gerald looked up over the newspaper. "This your way of saying thanks?"

"It's my way of letting you know I'll be making my own decisions." Clay pushed away from the table, wishing Jenni could hear this newfound candor. She'd said he couldn't verbalize his feelings? Well, try this on for size.

"Listen," Gerald said. "For the time being, you're under my roof."

"I understand that, but—"

"Good! I don't need you to come in and tell me how to live my life."

"Funny thing, Dad. I was trying to make the same point."

Gerald's fingers, white at the knuckles, twisted around the travel mug with the strength of a man who worked daily to the point of exhaustion— though the exhaustion was nowhere to be found in his flashing eyes. He coughed, spit twice into a handkerchief, which he returned to his pocket, then opened the sports section.

End of discussion.

Flashbacks of adolescence clouded Clay's view of his father's immobile form. The man meant well. Clay could almost hear Dr. Gerringer expounding the need for maturity: *Ironically, self-preservation finds its greatest ally in the survival of the social unit. You become a whole individual by becoming part of something larger than yourself...* And blah-dee-blah.

Clay cleared his throat. "Early Monday morning, Dad? I'll be there."

"Good."

"Thanks. For trying to help. For finding me a job."

"Here." Gerald slapped the paper down on the table. "Take your stuff."

Clay looked down. There between sports pages four and five, a generic white envelope bore his name in black block letters.

———

Mylisha was exhausted. She couldn't believe she'd caved in again, staying at her sister's place in Eugene. She'd done it for her niece and nephew. She'd slept fitfully on the couch, wondering about Clay, waiting for Shanique.

At five thirty in the morning, Shanique had plunked down on the cushions.

She reeked of smoke and perspiration. She sounded cheery, bragging about a group of businessmen who'd wandered over from the Hilton. "They's in town for some convention." A sharp laugh. "And some sightseeing. These boys was throwin' down the benjamins, you know what I'm saying."

Mylisha sat up, pulled on her shoes. "The kids fell asleep around midnight," she said, "and both got baths. Tyrone wouldn't eat a bite of dinner though."

"Yeah, he be like that sometimes. Never can tell wit' dat one."

"Shanique?"

"I know, I shoulda been home sooner."

"Tyrone asked about you."

"Me?"

" 'What kind of work does my mama do? Where she go?' he wanted to know. 'Ain't no stores open in da middle of da night, not dat I seen.' I couldn't do it, couldn't lie to him. I told him he'd have to talk to you."

"Mylisha, baby, you don't gotta cover for your li'l sister."

"He's six. He's a smart kid."

"Don't you worry 'bout nothin'."

"Why would I worry?" Mylisha gathered her college books and home-work, tried to keep bitterness from seeping into her words. "Things'll work out for you, Shanique. They always do."

"I know *dat's* right. The Good Lord takes care of his own."

As Mylisha headed back to Junction City, she mulled over Summer's words, Clay's presence in town, Shanique's situation. She turned onto Maple Street. Along the curb, between two police cars and an unmarked vehicle, a tow truck was hefting a red Honda Prelude with a missing door. Dark stains dotted the pavement underneath.

———

Missed. Missed again.

Man, what's wrong with me? That stupid envelope's throwing me off.

Still wearing his boxers, Clay Ryker found his mark at the free throw line in the driveway. With exaggerated patience, he bounced the basketball once more, bent his knees and cradled the ball, felt its leathery surface on his fin-gertips. Fixing his eyes on the back of the rim, he let the energy climb through his legs and shoulders and hands, then propelled the ball in a graceful arc toward the red metal hoop.

Ka-lunk-ah-thunka-thunk… Denied again.

He was out of practice, true, but he never missed free throws. Certainly not three in a row.

Where had the envelope come from? Who had sent it? The Rykers' property was on the outskirts of town, but the sender must've been on the premises this very morning, slipping the note between the newspaper's pages. Gerald had been up and about, but maybe it'd happened while he was mowing.

Regardless, someone had been out here. Someone who knew Clay's secret. How was that possible?

Clay tore the envelope from the elastic at the back of his shorts and once more read the hand-scrawled message.

You like to push your secrets down, don't you?
But this is one bill you can't run away from!

Fear punched Clay in the chest. He wanted to discount the handwritten words, but they touched on the truth. Someone *knew*. He *had* pushed down his "secrets"—literally. He *had* run from that "one bill"—all the way to Wyoming.

Here he was back in JC, and the past had resurrected.

Or maybe it had never really died.

Moving to the side of the garage, he shredded the note and then shoved it deep into the garbage can full of lawn clippings. Burying his sins. It was what he did best.

A Stubborn Leech

Clay watched a man with a hand truck browse through blank headstones. Monday morning at Glenleaf Monument Company. Compared to Clay's satellite mapping business in Cheyenne, this place was hopping. If the gravel lot was a desk, the stacks of stones were reams of paper, ready for appropriate data, waiting to be filed into the graveyard for safekeeping.

Another life. Another death. Sinners and saints.

"You catching all this?" Stan Blomberg asked. "Think you can handle the job?"

"Yes, Mr. Blomberg."

He followed his new boss into a corrugated metal building where black marble slabs and white crosses rolled over chest-high runners toward a sand-blasting chamber. Annoyed by the interruption, two men and a woman looked up, steel hooks and rollers poised in canvas-gloved hands.

When Blomberg explained that Clay would be joining the team, the woman's look changed into a shy smile. Clay shook hands with the male workers, then gave a sharp nod.

He issued a softer nod to the lady. She could read into it what she wanted.

"Then after the lettering's been etched," Blomberg was explaining, "and the stones've been sent through the sandblaster, they come here to be brushed and sealed. It's vital that we get the lettering peeled correctly. Our work around here is as unto the Lord. A sacred task. Now see this right here? This is what happens when we get rushed. Are you guys getting paid to cost me money?" he barked. "You gonna show Ryker here how it's done, or do I have to come back and show him myself? For the life of me! See that nick? That's where the blaster found their mistake. You think the grieving parents want that on their little one's stone?"

The words tugged at Clay. Jason's face swam into focus.

"You with me, Ryker? You grasping the nature of this job?"

"More than you know."

"Glad to hear it. Because," Blomberg prattled on, "when mistakes like this happen, we gotta start all over again. A stone wasted. Money dribbled down the drain. And if that happens too often that means less for me. And when there's less for me, I become a real bear…which is no picnic, let me warn you now. Instead of smiling and throwing you a bone for a job well done, I start breathing down your neck. If that doesn't do the trick, I kick your can through the front gate, and you find yourself hoping and praying you don't stumble into me in the Bi-Mart parking lot anytime soon."

Clay gave a laugh, recognizing humor's ability to communicate a point.

Blomberg stared at him.

"I get your meaning, sir."

"I hope so. You're Gerald Ryker's son, and I'm bringing you on 'cause I owe him a favor. Your qualifications have diddly to do with it. Warning you now that if you let me down, you'll let your old man down. I'll show no mercy. You gonna laugh again?"

"No sir."

"Good thing, because I'm serious as a heart attack."

"I'm here to work. Show me what to do, and I'll do it."

Blomberg weighed this riposte, pursed his lips, then clapped a hand on Clay's shoulder. "Get to it. What're you standing around for?" He pointed back along the runners. "Digs…he's the guy with the fuzzy ears. He'll show you the way we do things around here."

"Digs?"

"He's been called that as long as I can remember. He can tell you the story if he wants. No loitering though, not on my clock, not on my payroll. You got that?"

"Your time is precious. Got it, Mr. Blomberg."

———

"Please, A.G., be seated."

"You first."

Exerting his authority, Asgoth placed a hand on his partner's shoulder and guided him through the Burlington Depot toward a corner table. All around, townsfolk conversed over hotcakes and sausage links. Monde slid into a seat, craned his neck for a view through the window. On the opposite street corner, the Finnish locomotive stood on display, freshly painted yet largely overlooked.

"Engine 418." Monde whistled. "Quite a specimen, I must say."

Asgoth nodded, afraid his voice would betray his obsession with the train. The fact he had stumbled upon it here, halfway around the world, suggested an appointment with destiny.

The Consortium demanded of him a hundred thousand dollars. Based on time-tested formulas, this meant two thousand per citizen or ten percent of Junction City's average annual income.

Seed money for turned eyes and deaf ears.

If the tales were true, this train held the key to riches far beyond that. Enough to sow corruption throughout the entire county—perhaps the entire state.

"Is it true, A.G., that the train is cursed?"

Asgoth snapped his head around. "How do you—"

"Don't look so shocked. For quite some time, I've known of her link to our past, but I've kept the information to myself. Here and there, I've heard whispers that ancient forces stand watch over her secrets."

"Misfortune and grief to all but the innocent."

Monde seemed riveted by the recitation of the curse.

"More than a few times I've tried to go on board," Asgoth said.

"The result being?"

"It's impossible, as if it reads your intentions. It's like being impaled on a fence crafted from spears of fire. But listen, Monde, take a crack at it. If pain's your thing, you'll enjoy every second."

"I tried this morning," Monde confessed. "It hurt like hell."

"Which means we have to find someone innocent enough to help."

"Innocence is a misnomer. It doesn't exist."

"Not in the way most think, but I may've found a young boy who fits the bill."

"Let's hope he doesn't meet the fate of your earlier failures."

"I...I don't know what you mean, Monde."

"Oh, but you have no reason to hide it. We've all lost a friend or two."

"You mean William? He was my best friend. My only friend at the time."

"And you let him die a premature death."

"Are you implying I was at fault?"

"Merely stating the obvious."

A waitress approached the table with place settings in hand.

Asgoth erupted. "What does it take to get some privacy here?"

She never even looked at him. The dishes clattered in her hands, and she hurried off, spooked by the outburst.

Monde crossed one leg over the other, then rested his wrists together on his knee. "Are you trying to convince me you shared no blame in William's death? Are you going to tell me you were the victim? In fact, you should've prevented it."

This was absurd. Why should he, Asgoth, need to explain himself? Yes, he was the victim; even the Consortium had acknowledged so after their investigation.

In a rush the memories came back…

Twelve years ago along the riverbank. A face with sightless eyes.

Only one other person knew all that had transpired that day, and once Clay Ryker understood the weight of his obligation, once his darkest sin was exposed, he would have no choice but to offer himself as a sacrifice.

"Listen, Monde, let's stay focused on what's ahead."

The black-haired agent tilted his head in agreement. "I'm listening."

"Here it is, a list of my most promising contacts. This is where you fit in, with your ability to uncover the human psyche's frailties. Your job will be to identity their most exploitable faults."

"A rewarding task." Monde perused the list. "Let's see, this first name here…Mitchell Coates. Is this correct, that he's sixty-eight years old?"

"Is that a problem?"

"A problem? No. A challenge? Certainly. It's quite the paradox, isn't it, that the elderly ones often show the least weakness of all."

Asgoth smirked. "His wife's still alive. I'm sure she could play a role."

The bin of Molly bolts was depleted. Just his luck. Done with his first week on the job, Clay meant to grab a few supplies at the hardware store on his way home. Rather than compete with his old man for the remote, he'd wall-mount a TV in his old bedroom. A little weekend entertainment. First, he needed the items to secure the set.

"Can I help you find anything?"

Clay shook his head.

The lady in the Ace Hardware uniform informed him the store would be closing in five minutes. "I'll be able to ring you up at the front register."

"Ready to call it a day?"

"Definitely. My feet're aching."

"I'll make it quick."

Clay turned to scan another row of fasteners, stumbled, and almost ran into a portly man in a buttoned shirt and sagging canvas pants. In an effort to catch himself, he grabbed at the man's hairy forearm while uttering an apology. Then, as he withdrew his fingers, he felt it again.

Numbers. *7.2.0.4...*

Defined and burned into his palm.

The sensation's clarity was startling, like a branding iron seared into his nerve endings. He wanted to quiz the man for information, wanted to study the guy's skin so he could put the questions to rest, but he knew he'd only look like some head case. The numbers were real—he was sure of it—yet invisible, numinous. Beyond proof.

Proved one thing only, that he was losing his mind.

"Might wanna watch where you're going, big fella," the gentleman said. Above his chest pocket his name was stitched in white thread: *Mitchell Coates.*

"Should pay better attention," Clay agreed. "You okay, uh, Mr. Coates?"

"Think I'll survive." The man gave a sage nod. "Hope you find what you're looking for."

"A couple of Molly bolts, that's all I need."

"Tried goin' down to Jerry's yet?"

"Not yet. Thanks for the suggestion."

"Glad to help."

Clay rubbed his hand against his shirt and continued browsing. He nudged up to the register a few minutes later, but as he set down brackets and a laminated shelf, he noted that the numbers continued to linger on his skin. He ran a brief self-exam and found nothing obvious to the eye, but they persisted, hardwired directly to his brain.

7.2.0.4… What was their meaning?

"You find whatcha needed?" The woman was back in her retail rhythm.

"For now," Clay said.

The bell rang over the door. He turned to see Mr. Coates heading out to a van at the curb. The man heaved a yellow container through the side door, swiped his hands against his overalls, then let the rust-pocked vehicle carry him away.

———

After dinner Clay nabbed a cold can of Coke and followed his father into the living room. He settled into the couch, glad to take the pressure off his feet. He felt drowsy. His muscles were tight from lifting gravestones, proof that he needed to chisel his body back into shape. Tomorrow he'd take a solo day hike along Alsea Falls.

"Blomberg says you're slow."

Clay sighed. "Good to see you too, Dad."

"You're unmotivated. Those're his words."

"Since when?" Clay took a gulp.

"Just relaying the message."

Armed with travel mug and remote control, Gerald was facing the TV. Draped over his recliner like a hero's cape, a throw blanket declared the supremacy of the New York Jets. From this spot, Gerald had harangued his son about those mythical football greats: *Look at Joe Namath. He'd stand in the pocket till the last second, then launch that pigskin. There's a guy who could teach you something, Son. Man's man, lady's man…the guy had it all. Just don't make 'em like they used to, do they?*

Amazing how a father's words stuck in a kid's head. Like flaming darts.

"Got something to say?" Gerald demanded. "Or you gonna just sit there?"

A defensive tone clogged Clay's throat. "I just started the job, Dad."

"First impressions, Clay. First impressions."

"Don't worry. A couple more days and I'll have Mr. Blomberg converted."

"Converted? If you mean religion, you'll be preaching to the choir."

"Do I look like a preacher?"

"Blomberg's already got religion up the wazoo. You just remember, Son, your beliefs are a personal matter. You leave it at that. Your mother told me how you and Jenni got real involved in that church in Cheyenne. Well, look at how things turned out. Not quite the miracle cure you thought it'd be, was it?"

Anger tightened like a cinch around his ribs at the memories. The obscenities and denials that rushed to his lips remained unspoken as sitcom laughter filled the room. He went to the kitchen and yanked open the cupboard over the hooded stove. Into his Coke, he splashed some rum from a bottle his mom stored for cooking.

A long swallow. Fortification.

"Jenni," Clay said, returning to the living room. "Is she what this is about?"

"You still yakking? I'm trying to look at some TV."

"You never did like her. You wanted me and Jenni to fail so that you'd come out looking like the successful family man."

Gerald changed the channel, changed it back.

"Admit it," Clay insisted. "You never liked her. Am I right?"

"Never liked any of your girlfriends," Gerald corrected. His finger flicked the lid of his mug. "Never could figure you out. Blond bimbos, punk rockers, that black girl..."

"Mylisha."

"My-leee-sha. Sounds like a cough medicine. I mean, who names these kids?"

The cinch grew tighter. Clay's head was pounding, his blood pumping.

"Truth is," said Gerald, "Jenni's your wife and none of my business. I can't take the blame for your mistakes. You gotta own up to them on your own. Be a man."

"Least I didn't let her run our household," Clay reacted. Jenni had avoided control actually, even begging Clay to be more assertive in his role. Still, this was perfect ammo for fighting back against his father.

"Son, I'm going to pretend you never said that."

"Well, let's face it. You let Mom call all the shots. What she says, goes."

"I keep the peace! That's a secret you should've learned."

"Oh, you think? Maybe Jenni wanted more than just peace."

"This oughta be good."

"Yeah, maybe she wanted an actual friend, someone to talk with. Maybe that's all Mom's ever wanted!"

Gerald clenched the remote. Inadvertently he pressed the mute button, and the TV fell silent as though Clay's statement had shocked it into submission. Clay had to ask himself, though: What kind of friend had he been to Jenni? A meager provider, a distracted lover, certainly not much of one for communication. Jokes and shoptalk, sure. Deeper connection? Nope, too vulnerable.

He could still see the tears in her eyes that he wished he had wiped away.

The TV blared back to life, yet in that moment of shared stillness Clay sensed comprehension pass between father and son. They were two of a kind, more than either dared admit.

As quickly as the moment came, it passed.

Gerald lost himself in the sordid details of a prime-time exposé, and Clay retreated to his bedroom.

———

Clay anchored the TV stand in the upper corner. As he tightened the brackets with a screw gun, his mind played over the past few days. Things had turned strange. He tried to shake the sets of numbers from his head.

1.2.2.5.2.1…6.2.1.0.4…7.2.0.4.

Was there a pattern? A purpose?

Six numbers, then five, then four. Each set incorporated the numeral 2.

He connected the TV plug, flopped on the bed, hit the remote. He was midway into his second hour of mindless entertainment when an idea crawled its way out of his vegetating gray matter. It clung there, like a stubborn leech waiting to be recognized.

Clay snapped alert, suddenly aware of the leech's presence. His peripheral logic plucked at the idea and examined it. Could this theory be true? Could it explain the pattern behind the numbers?

Come on, Claymeister, do your math. Okay, this is creepy!

Counting on his fingers, he confirmed that each set of numbers totaled unlucky thirteen.

6

Dying Breed

Scritchh, scritchh, scritchh…

Eve Coates heard the sound in the dead of a Thursday night, and her eyes sprang open. Normally she would've been snuggled like a spoon in a drawer with her husband of forty-seven years, but now her body turned stiff beneath the toasty eiderdown. Her fluffy pillows gave little comfort.

Tonight she was alone. Mr. Coates had traveled north to Silverton.

Scritchh, scritchh…

Probably one of them critters, she told herself. If it weren't for them in the first place, she wouldn't be in this predicament.

Rats, field mice, possums… Whatever they were, they'd been messing with the crops, and her husband, Mitchell, was fed up. Couldn't blame him after the years of attention he'd given this property. Built their family a little slice of heaven here on the edge of Junction City.

Problem was, he couldn't rid the place of these pests.

Aggravated, he'd picked up a container of poison at Ace Hardware a couple of days ago, then spread it around the farm as the label instructed. This morning she'd been at his side while he checked the barn and the fence line, but he'd found nothing. None of the little beasts. No sign that the stuff was doing its job.

Mitchell said it was the final straw—and when he said it, he meant it. He'd decided to go north to see his brother for some advice, said he'd be back by sundown.

Three hours ago he had called with the bad news.

"Eve, I might not make it home tonight," he told her. "Van's gone belly up. Could be the fuel injection, could be somethin' simple. We'll try to get her fixed up so I can head back soon as possible."

"What about supper? You gonna sleep there at Donny's?"

"I'll be just fine, darlin'. Good news is, Donny's got some chemicals for me to use, swears they'll do the trick. Mean stuff, downright nasty. When I'm done, those buggers won't know what hit 'em. Stuff's so powerful you hafta wear a mask while spraying it."

"Sounds dangerous. You be careful, Mitchell."

"Don't you worry. I won't start glowing in the bedroom or nothin'."

At that, she heard Donny's distinctive hooting in the background. Not a bad guy for a brother-in-law, though he did have his quirks. As for Mitchell, he was a good man. Almost fifty years since their wedding at First Presbyterian on a warm spring day.

Mr. and Mrs. Mitchell Coates...

She still liked the sound of it. Did that make her a hopeless romantic? Well, why not? Sure, the grandkids puckered their little faces and squirmed when Gramps and Grams got snuggly, but they found reassurance in the farm's atmosphere, and Eve took pleasure in that. Families didn't always stay together like they used to. Had to hold on to the old ways.

A plain fact: she and her man, they were a dying breed.

"You don't worry about a thing," Mitchell had told her before ending the phone call. "I'll be home before you know it."

That was just it, though. She was worried. There was that sound again.

Scritchh, scritchh...krr-thump!

What were the critters doing, having a party out there? She smiled at the thought, but her fears stayed close by. Her mind flashed to the loaded shot-gun her husband kept stowed in the corner of the closet. No sir, that was just silly. A last-ditch option. Sure, with a little prompting from her man, she'd fired the thing a time or two, but she hadn't enjoyed it, not one bit. Thing could blow a hole in a concrete wall.

She settled for an alternative.

In a flurry of movement, she flicked the clock radio to FM jazz oldies, then burrowed herself under a mound of pillows and covers. Creating an opening with her elbow, she inhaled cool air. With the muffled sounds of Duke Ellington lulling her to sleep, she curved her body into the space her husband usually occupied.

She missed having his little potbelly to wrap her arms around—two spoons in a drawer. Life really wasn't all that complicated; people just liked to make it that way.

In her billowy cocoon, Eve began to snore.

———

Through the lace curtains, Asgoth saw the still form beneath the eiderdown. The inactivity confused him. Hadn't the woman heard his noisemaking? Was she a hard sleeper? This was supposed to be easy. He'd coordinated events flawlessly thus far, and his friends in Silverton had waylaid Mr. Coates without a hitch.

Now it was a matter of executing the rest of the plan. If he failed to placate the Consortium's members, he had little doubt as to his next destination. Hell...

Under another name perhaps—Fresno, Salem, Olympia—but hell all the same. He ground his teeth at the thought of further isolation.

After midnight, a set of lights sliced through the rows of corn at his back, then stabbed at the side of the barn. Mr. Coates had arrived. After the necessary delay, the boys in Silverton had carried out Asgoth's orders by getting the man's rattletrap van back on the highway.

The vehicle now wobbled from view around the far side of the barn, the lights went out, and springs creaked as the driver disembarked. Mitchell Coates entered the barn with a large canister and gas mask in hand.

Asgoth grinned. Time to wake the lady. To let fear become a weapon.

He dropped an object into the potting soil, then with a gnarled branch, clawed at the siding along the bedroom window.

———

Clay stepped into the kitchen. His mother was fluttering about, excited about the newest cookware she'd purchased at her ladies' gathering this evening. Gerald, set into action by her presence, was tying off a garbage bag and marching out to the garage. His sporadic grunts were all the response Della needed to continue her exuberant chatter.

Clay moaned. High school revisited. Mom and the old man deep in denial, coping with their relational flaws by gorging on activity, by heading separate directions in the name of calendars and commitments and kids. Long reign codependency.

See, Dr. Gerringer, I'm beginning to recognize the symptoms.

As Clay tried to slip down the hall, his mother's voice caught him halfway.

"Oh, Clay, you're home."

"Yep."

"Did you see the baking stone I…"

Clay elbowed the door closed, dropped a rented Xbox game on the bed.

Della came to check on him, as though she held a lifetime pass into his privacy.

"Whaddya want?" he barked at the door.

"Your day go well?"

"Yeah, sure." Stretched on the bed, toes hanging off the end, he felt infantile and foolish. "Not exactly the job I would've picked, but it pays. As usual, the old man has my life mapped out for me."

"It's his way, you know that. He wants the world for you."

"I'd rather he just butted out."

"He's trying to help. He sees the difficulties you've faced in the past year, and it upsets him that he can't fix everything for you."

"I've never asked him to."

"Been quite some time since we all lived under the same roof, Clay. We all have adjustments to make. You'll have to give me some leeway and Gerald, too."

Not *Dad*, but *Gerald*. Della had always recognized the rift between father and son. At certain moments Clay believed his mother alone had the ability to fathom his inner conflicts. She understood. She'd seen his toddler hands reaching out for the father who shunned contact; she'd heard the oft-repeated manifesto: "Gotta be a man's man. You got that, Son?"

"Now," she said, "why don't you come sit at the dining table. I'll reheat the supper I made for you. I bet you've missed your mother's cooking."

Della could stray so far off the path that Clay questioned her altogether. "Actually," he snarled into his pillow, "I've missed Jenni's cooking."

"You coming?" Della said through the closed door.

"Coming."

"Dollface?"

"Coming!"

"By the way," she said as he shoved into the hall, "you got a phone call earlier on. I thought I might mention it while out of earshot of your father."

"Don't tell me."

"It was Mylisha. Mylisha French."

"I said, don't tell me! As if I don't have enough to think about already."

———

Eve Coates bolted up this time. The torturous scratching was only feet away. *Behind the wall, right there!*

She dropped to her knees at the bedside and waited until the scratching repeated. This time it was further down the house, and she thought she heard heavy footsteps. From the radio, a rich tenor voice continued serenading the night.

She decided she couldn't just sit here until some unknown attacker came for her. She had to put her panic aside and deal with this. That's what Mitchell would tell her.

Eve whispered, "Oh, Mitchell, where are you? Why tonight of all nights?"

On hands and knees, she scurried to the closet and slid back the door. Her fingers felt along the metal runner in the carpet, the roll of wrapping paper, the shoes and boots and her only pair of high heels—which, she reflected, she hadn't worn since brother-in-law Donny's latest wedding in the lodge at Odell Lake.

The polished stock of the shotgun renewed her confidence. A little, at least.

She inched up the wall into a standing position, weapon at her side. She could do this. Her arm brushed against a picture frame on the wall. In the photo, Mitchell stood proudly beside that train engine downtown, the one he'd helped repaint.

Now don't do nothin' silly, she told herself. *Be ready!*

She cocked the gun the way her husband had shown her and moved into the hallway. She wondered if the intruder had entered the house. If it was an intruder at all. Maybe a big animal. Had she left a window open? What about the cat's door? The last cougar to kill a person in Oregon had been only a couple of miles from here.

Past the parlor and into the kitchen, she crept. With the shotgun's barrel resting on the counter, she picked up the phone and dialed 911. A woman answered. Her steady voice encouraged Eve to collect her thoughts.

"Need to report an intruder on our property," Eve said. "A thief, I think."

"Are you at your home? On Dane Lane?"

"Oh my goodness, I can hear 'em moving around outside."

"Ma'am, you'll have to speak up."

"They're outside. I'm afraid they…they might hear me."

"Can you see, is it a person? Could it be a dog or a cat? Maybe a raccoon?"

"Reckon so," she said. "Could be just about anything. Please, what do I do?"

"Take it easy now, and tell me your name. To whom am I speaking?"

"Eve. Eve Coates. My husband, he's—"

"Okay, Mrs. Coates, I want you to breathe deeply and stay calm. I'll dispatch an officer to your home. You sit tight, and everything'll be fine. He should be there within ten minutes."

Lights were moving inside the barn, throwing pale spears into the dirt and compost pile outside. Someone was out there. Maybe more than one of them. What did they want anyway? Unspeakable answers spun through her head.

Ten minutes? That's much too long. That's forever!

"By then it might be too late," she said, feeling indignant and alone.

"Ma'am, it'd be best if—"

She pushed the phone back onto its hook. She couldn't sit here like a trapped animal. She had to act. She hadn't survived raising three boys without a little fire in these bones, no sir. If this intruder thought she'd be a defenseless little old lady waiting for trouble, he was wrong. Eve Coates was mad, and she'd let him know it.

With the barrel pointed at the ground ahead of her, she unlatched the front door and took a knee-buckling step. Out here in the moonlight she felt so small. Couldn't turn back now. Best to keep on. The July air was mild, the sky dark and clear.

Sweaty-palmed, she marched across the yard, straightened her spine, and faced the cracked barn door. Lifted the shotgun, felt it tremble in her hands.

What to do now? Go in? Wait? Or—

A figure thrust open the door. With the light at his back, the creature appeared larger than life. In his hand he was aiming something her direction. Long and narrow, it looked like the barrel of a gun. His hand was on the trigger.

She fired first.

The gun leaped in her arms, bruising her shoulder, knocking her back a step. The intruder gave a hollow shout as the blast slugged him ten feet the other direction onto the straw-strewn floor. Torn open by pellets, the hand-pumped canister in his grip sprayed pressurized liquid in all directions.

"Eve!" The voice ripped through the chaos.

Mitchell? My Mitchell!

The horror was indescribable. That was her husband's voice coming from the masked victim on the straw. What had she done? The consequence of the moment squeezed tears from her eyes, huge hot drops that spilled down her nightgown like a broken strand of rosary beads.

She forced aside the violence of the scene and let her love for him take over. She collapsed over her dying husband. Slipped the mask back off his forehead. Begged forgiveness from this man who meant everything to her.

"I thought you were... I didn't know you'd come back, Mitchell."

"The chemicals. Watch out for the—"

"Why didn't you come straight to bed? I was afraid. I heard noises and thought someone was out here and...and..." A wave of emotion swept over her.

"I was gonna do some sprayin'. Without you here. It's dangerous stuff."

"Oh, Mitchell. Forgive me."

"S'okay, darlin'."

"I didn't hear the van."

"S'okay. Hush, it's okay." His voice was fading.

"I'll getcha some help. We'll getcha fixed up."

"No." He had hold of her arm. "Too late for that."

"I'm so sorry. I thought—"

"Eve, I love you. Listen. We've had a...a good life, haven't we?"

"Of course we have. I love you too."

"A good life," he repeated in a whisper. His hand tightened. His body sagged.

She sobbed over him, racked with grief. She called out to nobody in particular. To God specifically. She snuggled beside her husband, gasping. Her tongue grew thick and coppery, her cheeks burned where tears had run dry, and her skin became increasingly itchy.

This must be what guilt feels like, she thought. *It's what evil does to a person. The chemicals from the canister...*

She realized they were all over her clothes, filling her chest and snatching her breath away. She hardly cared; in fact, she knew she deserved it. Quick justice. For that, she was thankful.

"Hail Mary, mother of..."

Losing consciousness and control of her bodily functions, she caught an image of argyle socks stepping close to her head. Tan pants, too. She tried to look up, but her muscles would not respond. The chemicals were corroding her nasal passages, coursing into her lungs. Too late now.

With concentric rings of red and black pulsing before her eyes, with a vise constricting her muscles, she hugged her husband's neck and let herself drift away. If Mitchell was going, Eve wanted to go away with him.

Mr. and Mrs. Coates. Forty-seven years and still together.

Wrestling with Angels

By the end of his second week on the job, Clay was finding artistic enjoyment in the crafting of the grave markers. Although they stabbed at his secrets, they inflicted a good sort of suffering. Penitent pain. Beneath his fingers the markers grew from relatives' chosen templates into expressions of love. Some communicated with pristine lettering, others with grandiose poems, nature scenes, even photographs.

The dates, however, were cold hard facts. Written in stone.

"You're gettin' the hang of it," Digs told him that morning.

"Not bad for my first few days."

"Seventeen years for me," Digs stated. His fingernails, thick and grooved, tapped against a slab of marble. "Seen friends and family go through here."

"No kidding?" Clay looked up. "You've worked on your own relatives' markers?"

Digs brushed at a white tuft sprouting from his ear. "You do what you're paid to do. S'okay, until you're peelin' the letters of your own mother's name. By any measure, that's a bad day on the job."

"Oh, man!"

"But my mom died givin' birth to me, so I wouldn't know."

"Oh."

"It's a joke. Lighten up, Ryker."

"Not exactly something to joke about." He was uncertain which part had been in jest, if not all of it, but he didn't press for details.

"Believe me. In a place like this, all day kickin' out headstones, you gotta laugh to keep it from gettin' to you. Give it a couple of weeks, and you'll be jaded like the rest of us. Just don't let Mr. Blomberg catch you makin' jokes. He takes dyin' very seriously." Digs couldn't suppress a series of giggles.

"He takes everything too seriously. If I started joking, he'd probably kill me."

"Ha-ha! Attaboy, Ryker. You're already catchin' on. Couple of weeks, and you'll be a regular ham, guaranteed."

Wendy, shapeless in her baggy work pants and matching blue shirt, lifted a grin for Clay's attention. "And we'll all be tickled to death," she said, joining the dark humor. At that, she and Digs burst out laughing.

Brent remained on task. He was the burly one who'd been operating the hand truck on Clay's first day. Without a hint of amusement, Brent said, "You two are twisted, you know that? Twisted. You think I'd let them talk about you that way, Ryker, you think? Huh?" He dropped his tool on the workbench. "Over my dead body."

The trio of co-workers were rubbing tears of mirth from their eyes by the time Clay forced out a laugh. For no apparent reason, his mind shot back to the numbers he'd discovered on his mother's arm. And the other sets—on Summer, on the older guy at the hardware store. They'd seemed so real.

Were the sum totals of thirteen the sole connection? Was there any point?

He resumed his work on a rose-colored headstone.

———

Asgoth brushed a hand over his shirt. Despite the years, the musky sweetness of pot smoke still clung to the material. On the left sleeve, scratch marks and dots of dried blood hinted at savage events.

He had endured so much. Time now to let his experiences produce results.

A clawing sound brought him back to the physical confines of the apartment. He hurried into the living room, prepared for confrontation. To his chagrin, Mr. Monde and a squat female companion came through the front door, unannounced, uninvited.

"Who's this?" Asgoth demanded. "Why're you here?"

Though debonair as always, Monde couldn't conceal the slight flaring of his nostrils. "Forgive the intrusion, A.G. This is Pristi, the Consortium's seventh and newest addition. She comes to us from a larger network that stretches across the country."

"An impressive network, at that." Pristi nodded her large head. "If only you knew the details, the subtleties, the intricacies it encompasses. Mind-boggling, actually. Imagine the wonderful cooperation required to maintain such a—"

"Why're you here?"

"Your manners, A.G." Monde placed an arm over his guest's shoulders. "This woman's visit is an honor, proof that the Consortium supports our objectives."

Asgoth suspected the motives were less noble, but he eased up. "Pristi, you caught me by surprise. Glad to have you. Would you like a seat?"

She steepled her hands beneath her chin. "No need for formalities. I'm in a hurry, on the go, in a rush. We know you intend to culminate your plans during the upcoming Scandinavian Festival, but have you planned the acquisition of funds yet? One hundred thousand is not so much, but here it'll present a challenge."

"Don't worry, you'll get your money. I've got an idea."

"Engine 418?" Pristi ventured.

Asgoth turned stone faced. How did she know of that?

"Your secret's safe with me." Pristi winked. "As of yet, no one else in the Consortium knows. Being quite the history buff, I was intrigued by a recent article in which a Finnish historian mentioned a Bolshevik journal dating back to the First World War. A fellow revolutionary wrote of Lenin's consternation over an item he'd left on a particular train engine. A Finnish locomotive. Engine 418."

"This is public information?"

"Why so appalled? I'm sure you'll devise a way to reach it before your rivals."

"Rivals? But who else could understand the significance of—"

"Who else but those connected to Rasputin," Monde said.

"The Brotherhood of Tobolsk?"

"None other," Pristi corroborated. "Boris Soloviev was the first to lead them. Although raised within the Russian Orthodox Church, he was versed in hypnotism and the occult. He was married to Rasputin's daughter, a match made in hell. He discovered things known to only a handful and let selfish ambition take over. This Brotherhood was established to protect the Tsars, but—"

"They failed. They disbanded."

"Or so we believed." Pristi closed her wide eyes. "A new faction has arisen, and they are committed, dedicated, religiously devoted to their task."

"Which is?"

Her eyes popped open. "Is it so difficult to discern? I suggest you move quickly. They want the treasure, just as you do."

———

Dmitri Derevenko weighed the cell phone in his wide palm and, from the back of a taxi, watched the streets of Orlando slide by. This vast country, this American union of states, irritated him. For over two centuries she had held herself together. If a place of such debauchery could manage this, surely Russia could rise again.

The Brotherhood of Tobolsk endeavored to make it so.

With heat hanging between the palm trees and sidewalks, the morning was already stifling. Dmitri longed for Ekaterinburg's cool summer breezes, for the days of leisure along the shores of Shartash Lake.

Those days were over.

He rested his left hand on his hip, where European-cut trousers hid his scar. All those who pledged loyalty to the Brotherhood bore it, a slim hot-knifed incision in the shape of an angel's wing.

The mark commemorated Jacob's wrestling with the angel on the riverbank. Jacob had grappled with God and prevailed. The Brotherhood would do likewise.

After paying the driver, Dmitri bore his laptop case between dilapidated apartment buildings, past a pool of green-tinged water, up warped wooden steps. His firm knock brought to the door a tan, stocky man with a shaved head, wearing a white tank top. Juan's gold wristband flashed as he reached out in greeting.

Dmitri bristled. In his country it was bad luck to shake hands over the threshold of a home; it was proper to meet in unity on one side of an issue, never in between.

"How's life treating you, *mi hermano*?" the man said. "Everything good?"

"I'm breathing, da. But my soul is heavy."

Juan laughed. "Are you always so dramatic?" He led the way into a living room where bamboo blinds covered windows and an air conditioner rattled without zeal. "You act like you carry the world on your shoulders."

"Russian men have a need for greatness. We are born with this."

"In Cuba"—the man puffed his chest and grabbed his crotch—"we are born with other needs." He guffawed, dropping into the overstuffed couch. He tapped a cigarette from a pack on the cushion beside him, lit up with extravagant pleasure. "So, amigo, I have found the information you asked for. The man you are seeking, he lives in Fort Lauderdale. I'm sure, at his age, he wishes only to be left in peace."

"Peace. Everyone wants peace."

"It's a noble thing. We have enough trouble in this world, *sí*?"

"It's a false peace if it comes without cost."

Juan's chuckle turned into a cough. He waved through the cigarette smoke, as if this could cure his congestion. "Do you want the man's information? *Aquí...* Here. Does this satisfy your request? If so, we have money to exchange."

Dmitri took the offered CD. At the corner table he made space for his laptop by shoving aside a stack of local newspapers and a half-eaten bag of Cheetos. He opened the only file on the disk, scanned the contents, felt a surge of triumph.

"So," Juan said from the couch, "I think you owe me another five thousand dollars. American greenbacks, of course. None of your Russian play money."

Play money? He mocks my motherland.

Dmitri folded his laptop. "Da. You've done an excellent job. Speak to my partner to arrange the payment, and he'll tell you where to go." He pretended to place a call, then stretched his phone toward Juan. Aimed it toward his ear.

"Hermano, I thought that you—"

"You can go to your grave!"

With a thumb pressed over the keypad and an index finger on the power button, Dmitri Derevenko triggered a hidden mechanism. At close range, a .22-caliber bullet exploded from its chamber, slammed through the Cuban's shaved skull. His eyes went blank even as his head keeled to the side. A final burst of brain activity brought his arm to his mouth, thus crushing the cigarette against his lips. The burning object popped free from his fingers. Landed on the cushions.

Beside the glowing ember, Dmitri set a copy of the *Orlando Sentinel.* When tongues of flame began licking at the corpse's baggy black jeans, the Russian stepped into the hall to remove the smoke detector's battery. He shook his head.

Arson. A dead illegal alien. Another botched drug deal, or so it would seem.

Nothing more than a footnote in Orlando's unsolved case files.

———

With the quiet of a passing ghost, Asgoth floated down the apartment stairway. Midnight was behind him, the cold morning hours moving in to oversee this undertaking.

He crossed the empty street. Faced the fenced locomotive.

Misfortune and grief to all but the innocent.

The decades-old curse hissed in his thoughts, reminded him of the other times he'd tried without success to strip this train of its wealth. Concerns about any Brotherhood involvement fanned the fire of this latest endeavor. He was convinced the treasure should belong to him; by rights, it was his to possess.

Rasputin in his travels had accumulated relics from the Holy Land, religious objects capable of stirring the Romanovs' fervor. After the priest's murder, whispers of a hidden chamber swelled and then faded as zealots and treasure seekers failed, one by one, to turn up any evidence that such a hoard existed.

The lost chamber became known as Tmu Tarakan.

In Russian the name referred to any place of desolation.

"Which is where I am now," Asgoth spoke to the silent park. "And the key to the chamber is on this train."

He took a step toward the mechanical monster. In the moonlight the antique Finnish headlamp was a glowing eye filled with malevolent warning; the front grate was an iron mouth set firmly against any intrusion.

Asgoth circled to the back where the tender car hooked to the engine. He felt safer here, out of the headlamp's line of vision. All around, the park was hushed and motionless, as though the trees had become spectators at a gladiator event.

Don't hesitate. Take advantage of this moment!

Asgoth threw himself onto the bars, gripped the metal with desperate fingers. He slithered up and over, oblivious to any physical danger. Within a breath he was inside the fence.

Engine 418 sat high upon a pair of displayed railroad tracks, glistening. Asgoth hated that an old man like Mr. Coates had been able to coat this beast lovingly in fresh paint; he despised those who touched her in wide-eyed ignorance and curiosity. And Summer Svenson had been no better than the other violators.

Of course, those who knew of the train's contents became susceptible to the curse's scourge.

Misfortune and grief…

Asgoth planted his foot on the engine car. He was nearly on board.

Before him, fiery sentinels of dark orange and blue seemed to spring into position. Heat raced through rivets and metal to engulf his trespassing limb. Pain blossomed around him. Blinding. Disorienting.

It's only superstition, he tried to convince himself. *Nothing more.*

An explosion of light lofted him through the air so that he found himself skidding across grass and gravel outside the fence's perimeter. Flames whipped through the bars, crackled at his feet. He scrambled upright and dashed to the refuge of his apartment across the street.

Why had he thought this night would be different from any other?

Asgoth sputtered in rage. He felt like a child. He barely knew his own father, and as one of a number of illegitimate offspring, he'd always felt driven to validate himself. To gain respect. And honor.

The Consortium had become his surrogate parent.

He vowed that at any cost he would win back their approval.

A Basic Slab

"Baby, you 'bout done in there?"

Mylisha downed a pill with a glass of water. "Don't you ever sleep, Shanique? You been up all night."

"It's mornin'. Best start hoppin', or you'll be late for work."

Mylisha had forty minutes to be at Safeway. After another late night here at her sister's, she could find little to inspire her in the bathroom mirror. Her hair needed another perm; her bright brown eyes had turned dark and brooding; her full lips were dry, devoid of sensual appeal.

As a woman of faith, was she wrong to rely on antidepressants?

Summer Svenson's death had shaken her to the core. She was still trying to wrap her thoughts around this new reality. Soon, very soon, Summer would call or ring the doorbell or visit during a lunch break, and things would return to normal.

Where was God's hand in the accident that had killed her friend of thirteen years? Mylisha had heard the pat answers, the clichés: "At least she felt no pain." "Must've been her time to go." "She's in a better place." Yet none of them eased her loss. Summer, at the age of twenty-seven, was gone for good.

Even worse, Mylisha had no assurance her friend would be waiting inside heaven's gates. Not that Mylisha deserved any better; her only hope was in the Bible's promises. She believed that faith, not good works, would lead her through that narrow gate. Jesus was the door, the only way to God.

What about my friend then?

The Friday newspaper scudded beneath the bathroom door. "You gotta read dis," Shanique urged. "For real. You see it? Your horoscope, there in da middle."

Wonderful. Some head-wrapped floozy telling me how to live my life.

"Says to expand your boundaries. If you don't, dey become your barriers."

Mylisha snatched up the paper, rolled her eyes, found herself matching her birth date with the zodiac signs. She was a Pisces? This tidbit piqued her interest. Shanique always said if God was the maker of the moon and stars, then he surely could guide his children in this manner. Maybe the girl had a point. Despite her years of shaky decision making, Shanique was still full of smiles, with cash in her pockets and two beautiful children.

Mylisha spread the newspaper on the sink's edge, massaged hand cream into her skin as she weighed the words for the day. Curiosity skirted her faith, flitting through her head and poking at her fears.

"It's good advice, that's all," she whispered. "Nothing wrong with that."

"Gotta think about yourself," Shanique cajoled. "You help plenty with the kids, sure 'nuff. And I'm grateful. But look at you, Mylisha. You ain't get-tin' any younger. You think I don't know whatcha done for me? In high school? At the district meet?"

A twitch tugged at Mylisha's lower eyelid.

"You was the sports *goddess*," cooed Shanique. "Basketball, softball, high hurdles—you did it all. But you gave me dat last race. You let me win."

"Shanique! Why would you say such a thing?"

"You know it's da truth. Mama's tried awful hard to teach me, but I never was no good at no schoolwork. You was just tryin' to help, givin' your li'l sis-ter a chance."

"Why do you insist on sounded uneducated? You're not stupid."

"Maybe no, maybe so."

"We both know better."

"I done learned to survive my own way, okay?"

"There's so much more you could do if you'd set your mind to it."

"Ain't got it in me, baby. I wasted my scholarship, *your* scholarship. I let you down. You think I don't know dat? Was I s'posta keep turnin' to you for handouts? No, I had to figure things out myself. Day I got back from UCLA I thought you was gonna kill me for sure. I woulda deserved it, for real, for real."

"I didn't let you win."

"Deny it all you want, but I know whatcha did. Guess I owe you a thanks."

Protected by the locked bathroom door, Mylisha faced her reflection in the glass. When she blinked, tears streaked her cheeks like raindrops on tilled earth, silver droplets spilling from her lips, from her chin.

"I didn't let you win," she repeated. This time she was speaking to herself.

———

The phone was a concrete slab in his hand. Clay had sped home on his lunch break, hoping to save a few bucks on lunch, hoping to get through to Jenni who worked from her condo on Fridays, billing clients. When she failed to answer, he listened to her message machine and issued a quick hello.

"Hope things're going good for you guys. Love you, Jason, little buddy. Can't wait for you to come visit. Give me a call if either of you feel like it, okay? Have a good weekend."

The one-sided exchange left him empty.

He stood holding the phone in one hand, the refrigerator door in the other. Longnecks called to him from the lower shelf, but the condenser kicked in, interrupting, and he settled for bean and cheese burritos. Anything else required kitchen skills.

While the microwave hummed, he wondered if his son had been listening at the phone? Had Jenni been standing there, insisting he ignore the call?

Or was she somewhere else? With someone else?

If only I could go back and...

"Stop beating yourself up," a church deacon had told him a month ago.

"It's my fault though, a good majority of it. The stuff between Jenni and me, that's bad enough, but now Jason has to pay for my mistakes."

"God's sovereign," came the flat reply.

"You mean God wants this to happen? He doesn't mind if my family falls apart?"

The deacon spread his arms over two of the chairs lining the Cheyenne chapel. "He has a reason for these things. It's not our place to ask why. I hear you're going back to Oregon, is that true? Well, it's the right decision, Clay, and it keeps the sickness from touching others in the congregation. Trust God's plan, and move on."

"The sickness?"

"God hates divorce. You know what I'm saying."

No, Clay didn't know. Was *he* the sickness? Didn't God cure sickness? The memory of the interaction stoked his fury. So what was the plan? If anyone was listening up there, it'd sure be nice to get an answer.

Ding! Vittles for the ex-husband.

He peeled the tortillas open to let them cool. The first bite filled his mouth with steam-laced cheese, gave way to still-frozen bean paste.

Oh, wasn't this fun? The bland ingredients went limp in his hand. Was this what Bachelor Boy had to look forward to? Years of nuked nutrition?

He dropped the burritos into the garbage.

Clay had been back in JC for less than two weeks, and he'd done little more than work, eat, sleep. Besides the sports section, he avoided the depressing content of the newspaper. As for Summer Svenson, she'd never called again—surprise, surprise—and he had been avoiding contact with old friends for the simple reason that he didn't feel like rehashing his marital flaws for every busybody in town.

He'd also been skipping church. Didn't want to spread *the sickness.*

Of course, there was also that issue of the numbers.

The less skin-to-skin contact the better. At the grocery market, the gas station, the video store, he kept his hands to himself. At least the bare skin of his elbows and shoulders had conjured nothing out of the ordinary.

His hands. They were the lone culprits.

Has Ryker Lost His Touch?

The irony of it all. If only those Wyoming sportswriters could see him now.

He poured himself a glass of pulpy Minute Maid, then brought the phone to his ear again. He had a dial tone. Seven little digits, that's all it'd take.

Mylisha French had called a few night backs. For what reason? What'd they have to discuss? During his last year of high school he'd shuffled her aside as scholarship offers poured in; he'd let his hopes for the future relegate her to the past.

Don't dwell on it, Clay. You're the man.

His hand turned damp as he began to dial.

What about Jenni? He loved her, no matter what her idiot lawyer assumed.

Plus, they were still married. Technically speaking. He dropped the concrete slab onto the counter, drained the rest of the juice, and felt the pulp stick in his throat.

All his relationships seemed to go down like the OJ.

Tasty at first? *Check.* Then lumpy and hard to swallow? *Check, check.*

———

"Gotta hand it to you, Ryker. You're getting the hang of this." Mr. Blomberg pounded a hand into Clay's shoulder blade. "Didn't think you'd amount to much, way you dragged your feet around the first couple of days, like you were afraid to touch death. It's our job, though. You know that now, don't you?"

"Yes sir."

"Day in, day out, important business we do here, smoothing the details for bereaved loved ones. Can't take that too lightly. Each stone's a way of re-affirming that individuals do matter in the grand scheme of things." A meaty finger poked Clay in the chest. "You know God's up there, right? You think he's got a master plan?"

Clay floundered, unaccustomed to this side of Mr. Blomberg.

From the other end of the warehouse runner, Digs and Wendy focused on their work orders. Brent twisted his mouth in scorn, threw Clay a look that said to shut his trap and let the bossman move on. These co-workers had warned him, and his father had told tales of Blomberg's religious invective.

What do I care? Bring it on. I'm in the mood for a tussle.

"God?" Clay said. "Yep, I think he exists. Not so sure about a master plan."

With the pomposity of a man rarely challenged, Blomberg flattened back a lock of red hair. "Now tell me, how does that make an iota of sense? You take the safe route and agree there's a God, but you won't buy into the idea of a master plan. How can he be God if he can't form a plan?"

"Beats me." Clay's thoughts raced to Jenni, to Jason. Were they part of the plan? Let the small-town boy find love, then let his family fall apart. Some plan. "I think we're all gonna die, Mr. Blomberg."

"And?"

"That's my theory, start to finish. Birth. Pain. Suffering. Death."

"And?"

"Oh, and sickness. Can't forget that. Gotta keep the sickness from spreading." Clay fingered his wedding ring. It wasn't coming off, not until the divorce was official.

Till death do us part, Jenni. That was the deal.

Blomberg inquired, "So the good things in life—they're just accidents?"

"Accidents, mistakes. Call them what you like."

"This theory of yours, you pick that up from your heathen professors in your secular college education? You dealing with facts here or personal experience?"

"You want facts?" Clay dropped his wood-handled pick and turned to confront his bulky antagonist. "Or you want me to work?"

Digs chipped in. "Hey, Mr. Blomberg, the kid's goin' through a divorce. Might wanna cut him some slack, let him work things out before you ride his case."

"Is that true, Ryker? Hometown hero leaves his wife behind?"

"She filed," Clay said through gritted teeth. "All part of the great master plan."

"Oh, now I see. If things're good, you take the credit and give yourself a pat on the back. But once things start to slide? Suddenly it's all God's fault. You slap him in the face with your failures and decide life's just one huge cosmic joke."

"Nobody's laughin'," Digs said. "Let him be, Mr. Blomberg."

Brent cut in. "Bossman's got a point. People use religion like some magic cure-all. My opinion? Greed—that's the name of the game. All about the dinero."

"Hey, can't throw the baby out with the bathwater," Wendy said. "Right, Digs?"

Digs tugged at his lip. "People won't take the counterfeit 'less they think it's the real thing. That's the way I see it. Can't have one without the other."

"Hold on. What if we haven't found the real thing yet?"

"Good question, Ryker," said Blomberg. "That's the bottom line. Because if you go around saying you believe in a God, then you gotta believe in his plan."

"Maybe he's just dropped us here to fend for ourselves."

"An unfeeling, distant God?"

"You nailed it."

"What about the God of justice and righteousness?"

"Justice, huh? What about the woman hit by a stray bullet the day before her wedding? Or the innocent kid run over by a drunk driver?"

Blomberg's eyes narrowed. "You can't question God's judgments."

"His judgments?" Clay carved the tip of his pick into his maple workbench. "See, that's what I mean. How can we be so sure that he's a loving, personal God involved in every aspect of life?"

"You've tossed him aside. Is that it, Ryker?"

Digs, with his eyes on an order, was shaking his head as if to indicate he would not be an accomplice to Blomberg's pious display. But Clay knew the boss was right; he was slipping away, losing his hold. Losing his religion—like the classic REM song.

"I just can't accept," Clay said, "that he's an uncaring God. That's not the God I knew, not the one I grew up believing in."

"Then what do you believe, if you can tell us that much?"

"Mr. Blomberg, I don't think this is the time or the place."

"You're on my time, at my place." Blomberg spread his hands. "Let's hear it."

"I believe..."

"That's a start."

"I'd rather believe God doesn't exist than believe he doesn't care!"

"Ah! The prodigal shows his true colors." The big man gesticulated as though victory had been won. "Well, good, that settles that. World's full of fence-riders, and we certainly don't need another one."

Clay clenched his jaw, gave extra attention to the job at his fingertips.

Wearing a self-congratulatory expression, Blomberg stood in the center of the warehouse. He clapped his hands once, told everyone to get back to work, then spun his wide frame toward the exit.

———

Crammed into a rental car en route to Fort Lauderdale, Dmitri felt his short hair grate against the roof. Never mind. His car in Ekaterinburg was smaller still. Three weeks ago, he had squashed into the dusty Prada on his way from the Ural Mountains to Moscow. He had stood outside the Kremlin, in Red Square, where throngs once paid homage at Lenin's Tomb.

Vladimir Lenin. Marx and Stalin.

Their ideas had crushed a nation's spirit; their methods had scarred bodies and countless souls.

Dmitri believed the land could be restored. Reared in the warm glow of glasnost, he and his comrades had been convinced their country would be free at last, ready to regain her place of honor. Instead, Mother Russia had foundered, falling prey to organized crime and freewheeling religious pretenders. She had thrown morals aside and become a patchwork of ideologies and revolt.

Now it was every man for himself, as it was in the West. What a sham.

Recently Chechen rebels had thumbed their noses again at President Putin when an explosion in a Grozny stadium killed the Kremlin's puppet ruler. And why not? When leaders were less than honorable, less honor was deserved.

Still an hour from his destination, Dmitri Derevenko pulled into a rest area. These thoughts tired him, and Florida's humidity drained his energy.

He stretched, relieved himself in the men's room. He dug through an ice chest in the car's trunk to retrieve a container of cucumber-tomato salad. Sour cream and dill sauce played along his taste buds, nourishing his body, reviving his mind.

He snapped the container's lid shut and shoved himself back in the driver's seat.

For decades, the coals of the Brotherhood had smoldered beneath the ashes of Imperial ruin. Feeble. Flickering. Forgotten. Like all good Russian stock, the Brothers had faced tragedy but refused defeat. Recent discoveries had rekindled the flames, and a new gathering of Brothers had formed an eternal pact.

They would not rest until a Tsar regained the helm of their great land.

No easy task. It would require vast wealth and irrefutable proof of an heir's identity. The rest, as always, would remain in God's hands.

May our destiny be realized. May the Brotherhood succeed!

He merged the car back onto Interstate 95. In Fort Lauderdale he would find an old man basking in anonymity on a government pension, a man with a time-softened German accent and a head full of secrets from Hitler's regime.

Dmitri secured his cell phone to his belt.

Modified in Croatia with Maksalov VI components, loaded with four small-caliber bullets, the device was armed and ready to place another call.

—

Clay did not look up, did not acknowledge his fellow workers. He closed his mind to Blomberg's sanctimonious display, slid a finished headstone down the line, and drew the next project closer. Best thing to do now was let the job take over.

He smoothed the printed order and read the headstone's specifications—name, date, and epitaph. A basic slab. He'd whip through this one and move on to the next, squeezing solace from routine.

June 21, 2004.

Like a fist in his gut, the date stole away his breath. He knew these numbers.

6.2.1.0.4...

His vision turned fuzzy. He refocused. Stenciled there on gray stone, the letters spelled the name of his visitor from a few weeks ago.

Summer Lee Svenson.

9

Another Note

Time to deliver the papers. Kenny Preston loved this part of the morning. His clothes were right where he'd left them, so that he didn't even have to turn on the lights to get dressed.

He moved through his basement room with a working man's sense of responsibility. He was thirteen now. This newspaper courier job put extra cash in his pockets, which lightened his mom's load. She was a good mother, doing it on her own, deserving every penny he could give to help out. Recently she'd even gone so far as to find him a pet.

On the stairs Kenny felt warmth brush against his leg. A creature stirred, roused by his alarm clock and fumbling preparation.

"Hey, girl." He reached down to pet soft fur. "How'd you get all the way down here, huh? Missed me already? Missed you too."

The puppy's firm, small body wagged beneath his affection.

"So what'm I gonna name you? Mom says it's up to me."

The puppy's nose pressed against his hand, tiny teeth nipping at his pinky. She was the cuddliest little thing. Kenny tugged at her ear, eliciting an amateur snarl that sounded like Mr. Gustafson's car trying to start up on a cold morning.

"Gussy," he said. "That's what I'll call you. Gussy. You like it?"

He cradled his dog, carried her to his mother's room on the backside of the kitchen. After words of adoration, he propped Gussy on the carpet and pulled the door shut before her tiny nose could poke through. The whines that followed him down the corridor made him wish he could skip today's paper delivery.

Uh-uh, I've got a job to do.

Kenny Preston put on his bike helmet. With the dual-pouched bag slung over his shoulders, he guided his mountain bike through the side door of the garage and found the bundled papers stored inside the gate.

Fog was thick, dampening his hair and draping a blanket over the block. Already his hands were growing numb, but he was used to it. His mom would have hot chocolate and marshmallows ready when he returned fifty-five minutes from now. Maybe less, if he pushed for a record.

For you, Gussy. I'll hurry for you, little girl.

His left hand steered the bike while his right launched the *Register-Guard* toward front steps and porches. Passing Gustafson's place, he rode through a plume of exhaust from the car warming in the drive.

Could he shave five minutes from his record? For Gussy?

The route was straightforward. He knew Junction City was built on a grid, numbered streets running south to north, alphabetized streets east to west. He was up off the seat churning the pedals when an apparition stepped into his path.

Kenny plied the brakes and skidded along the sidewalk, then righted himself with a wheel-stuttering maneuver that saved his knees at the expense of a few papers.

"Going a bit fast, weren't you?" said a female figure in charcoal gray sweats.

"Didn't see you. Sorry." Kenny collected the dropped papers, brushed away leaves and dirt.

"No harm done. Listen, kid, I need your help."

"I didn't hit you, did I? I said I was sorry."

The woman gave a light chuckle. She toyed with a bracelet on her wrist. "I'm speaking of a small errand. You're pretty nifty on that bike, and I—"

"I'm in a hurry. Got papers to deliver."

"You must be trying to earn some money, huh? This morning, you could make a lot more. A little detour—that's all I'm asking."

Kenny was suspicious; his mother had warned him against such things. He had his hands on the bars, a foot ready to shove off. "How much?"

"Twenty dollars."

In a show of disdain, Kenny started to move forward.

"I'll double it. Does forty sound better?"

Kenny lowered his chin, smiling at his own ingenuity. Forty bucks could go a long way—wood, nails, and paint to start a doghouse in the backyard. "Okay, tell me what I have to do. I need to hurry. Need to finish my route."

"It's summer, no school. You have lots of time."

"Not much. I have a deadline. And if I don't get back, my, uh...my dad'll come looking for me." The fib seemed justified. He fought back a rippling chill.

"Well, it shouldn't take too long. See this envelope?" The woman brushed a strand of hair from her face, fixed serious eyes on him. "You need to deliver it to that address and tuck it into the sports page of today's newspaper."

Kenny leaned forward to read the black lettering.

"Cox Butte Road? That's not my route."

"Forty dollars. If it takes an extra twenty minutes, that's two dollars a minute."

"Is it anything illegal?"

The lady grinned. "Of course not." She laid the cash atop the envelope, then handed it over. "What're you waiting for? We don't want your...dad to get worried."

Did she know he was lying? Why didn't she take this to Cox Butte herself?

The crisp currency tantalized Kenny, and before she could withdraw the offer, he pocketed everything. Maybe there was a romantic note enclosed or a humongous bill. What'd it matter? He had the money, and the job sounded harmless enough.

"It'll get it there," he told the woman.

He set off as fast as his thirteen-year-old legs would pedal.

———

"He's a kid," Asgoth's female friend said.

"You already knew that, Henna."

"You promise he won't get hurt?" Sitting on the floor, Henna dropped her head into her hands. "There's a line I don't believe we should cross."

"I won't touch him," Asgoth vowed.

Earlier here in the apartment's shadows they had concluded a morning session with Mr. Monde and the other contacts. Henna had chosen to stay after, to be alone with Asgoth. He knew he must assuage her concerns. His fingers settled over her blond hair, and she tensed before melting under his ministrations.

"Thanks for your reassurance, A.G.," she said. "I needed to hear you say that."

"Are you having doubts?"

"I don't think so."

"I won't lay a finger on him," Asgoth reiterated. "He'll serve another purpose."

With eyes half-closed, the woman leaned back into his massaging touch. "I admit, I was a little worried. I'd be dishonest to tell you otherwise. When I heard how Mr. and Mrs. Coates died, I thought we might've let things go too far."

"And you have the right to point a finger?"

"No. I just... I don't know what went through my mind."

"An unfortunate accident—that's all it was. She thought he was a burglar."

"I know, I know. Forgive me."

"Don't speak of forgiveness. Love means never having to say you're sorry, isn't that so? You should know that by now. Come on, relax and let the tension go."

As she surrendered to his touch, Asgoth stole a view through the window blinds. With its bulging smokestack and conical nose, the Finnish locomotive taunted him from the park. "You can look," it seemed to say, "but you can't touch."

Asgoth felt perturbation flood his veins. Through his arms, sparks of electric energy dredged up yesterday's memories. Had Rasputin actually reached from his grave to cast a spell over the iron beast?

Asgoth needed an accomplice. An innocent child.

Kenny Preston was suited for the task.

"Ouch!" Henna shrank beneath his fingers. "That's too deep."

He backed off, then cursed this timorous response. Why let a woman dictate his actions? "No," he told her. "If I ease into it, you'll see I can go much deeper."

The road slithered upward into the mist, and Kenny feared he'd never reach his destination. This uphill portion was a killer. Only one more mailbox to go, and he'd be at the Ryker address.

Forty dollars…Gussy's doghouse…forty dollars…

He counted it in his head as his tires whirred over slick road. Shifting through gears, he fought his way to the hilltop. The wreath of fog gave way to a yellow L-shaped home with a cream-colored railing around the porch and a pair of white oak trees at the corner. A basketball hoop was fixed over the garage doors.

Could this envelope be for some kid his own age?

"Clay Ryker"? Uh-uh. It's not anyone I know.

Breathless, Kenny braced his mountain bike against a fence post and measured the distance to the front porch. He'd read front-page news about drug deals gone bad, where people got beat up and even shot. What if this was a criminal transaction? He had no idea what was in this envelope.

It gave him a brief thrill.

He stooped behind his bike, watching. No movement at this early hour. Twenty seconds, he judged. He could get to the paper box, feed the envelope into the Saturday morning paper, then rush back here for his escape.

Mom…Gussy. What'm I thinking? I shoulda told the lady to forget it.

Kenny weighed the envelope, held it up to the gray light from the clouds. It contained a piece of folded paper. A check maybe or a note. Nothing against the law as far as he could tell. Nothing explosive.

In a low crouch, he sprinted across the grass, slipped, regained speed, and lunged up the stairs. He tugged at the box's lid, tried to locate the sports section.

The envelope fluttered from his fingers to the porch.

His blood was burning at the back of his neck, his muscles tightening in his legs. He picked up the fallen item but fumbled it again.

Cli-cli-clakkk!

A deadbolt was turning. The front door was opening.

"I see you, kid." The door opened. "Been watching you through the hole."

Although Kenny's pounding heart told him to make a dash for it, the mild-mannered words stiffened like concrete around his feet. He should escape; he knew that. But who was this guy? What was this all about?

"Please don't run." The man was tall and wearing a plaid bathrobe.

"I wasn't doing nothing wrong, mister, just delivering the paper."

"Are you the usual paperboy?"

"This isn't even my route." Kenny extended the plain envelope, then stepped back as the man pushed open the screen door. "I don't know what's in it," he said.

"Neither do I."

"You don't?"

"You're sure it's for me? Where'd you get it? Who gave it to you?"

"Seriously, mister, I'm just doing a favor for some lady." Kenny paused, wondering if he should admit he'd been paid. No, that might get him in trouble. That money had a purpose now, and he wouldn't risk losing it. "I don't even know who she is. She said to bring it out here and put it with your newspaper. That's all she told me."

"Have you done this before?"

"No!" Kenny backed up. "Never."

"You didn't deliver another envelope a few weeks ago?"

"No way, not me. Am I in trouble? I didn't mean nothing—"

"You're not in trouble. Can you tell me where the lady lives, anything like that? I need to know who's sending me these notes. What's she look like?"

"She had sorta blondish hair, I guess. She's older, like my mom's age."

"Did you see her car?"

"No, she was walking. And wearing gray sweats."

"Hmm."

"You're Clay, aren't you? Like it says on the envelope."

"That's me. What's your name?"

Kenny felt panic grip his throat. This guy was setting him up, getting him to relax so he could fish for information. Clay's green eyes seemed nice, and he wasn't exactly scary looking. But he was very tall, which was bad enough.

Kenny thought about his mom and his puppy and his responsibility as the man of the house. The envelope was delivered, and the cash was in his pocket.

Time to get outta here.

In a single movement, he spun and leaped from the porch. He considered himself a fast runner, a regular champ at tag, and he knew he had the element of surprise. He pumped his arms and legs. He thought of how he'd grab his bike, toss a leg over, and rocket down the hill.

Forty dollars…forty dollars. Cold gulp of air. *Forty dollars.*

Clay caught him halfway across the grass. The man's jumbo hand clamped onto his shoulder and whipped him around. Kenny resisted, shrugging free of his jacket, but the man's other hand latched onto his bare arm. He'd been caught. Running had only made him look guilty, and now he was done for. Dead meat.

Suddenly, to his amazement, he was free again.

"Dang it!"

Clay had dropped Kenny's arm and was staring down at his own skin. He shook his hand in the air like a man warding off a swarm of bees, stomped his foot, then wiped his palm against the bathrobe. "What's going on! Did I ask for this? Arrhhh!"

Baffled by the man's behavior, Kenny took the opportunity to rush to the bike and speed away. His feet could barely keep up with the spinning pedals. The tires skidded, and his heart thumped in his neck and his ears. He was free.

What would he tell Mom about his jacket, though? The money couldn't even buy him a replacement. So much for a doghouse.

That's what I get. Stupid me! Never shoulda even talked to that woman.

One good thing. At least that Clay guy had never found out his name.

———

Bathrobe-clad, Clay stood rooted in the middle of the yard. The unidentified kid on the bike had vanished down the road, leaving him here with a jacket, an envelope in hand, and a series of numerals burning along his nerve endings.

7.1.1.0.4…

Each digit carved its presence. The sum total, once again, was thirteen.

He knew he shouldn't be surprised; in fact, he should be used to it. He had to admit, Summer's passing had shaken him. Sure, he'd known her only casually, yet he'd seen her, spoken with her, touched her.

And she had died soon after, her numbers matching those on her tombstone.

A blue Escort zipped by, and Clay realized how ridiculous he must look out here in his plaid robe. He shuffled back to the porch, wincing at a sliver that poked through his dew-soaked socks.

7.1.1.0.4...

That would be July 11, 2004. A week from tomorrow.

Hopping on one leg, he picked out the sliver, but his mind was on the paperboy. Was the kid in danger? Were the numbers a dire omen? If the dates could be matched up like this, what about that old guy in the hardware store? His numbers would've translated to July 2. The day before yesterday.

Clay was relieved that his mother's numbers implied a date years away.

He tamped the thought down, convinced his imagination was getting out of hand. He couldn't be responsible for every stranger he met. Maybe this was all part of his need to punish himself, his drive to pay for the death at the riverbank.

"I'm trying to start fresh," Clay told himself. "I refuse to do this to myself."

He tore the envelope, doubled it, started to tear again. Wait. Maybe he'd be better off saving these clues for later. He collected the pieces and stuffed them into a pocket.

———

Guilt was a blade at his throat, holding him hostage, forcing him back to this momentous spot. Clay brought the Duster to a stop on rutted mud and pebbles, then set the hand brake. The engine idled, ready for a getaway.

He glared at the ripped envelope on the seat, contemplating a reaction.

Here at the riverside, the blade pressed deeper, sharpened by the view of these waters. At this place one nightmarish incident had stripped him of his golden-boy aura, disturbed the course of his career, bled into his marriage.

For Clay, returning to JC had been an effort to regain his confidence, to rediscover his potential. Instead, he felt inadequate—as he had in college. A jump shooter who had lost his touch.

Except now I have more touch than I want!

Still in his robe, Clay leaned over the steering wheel and stared up at the railroad bridge. The sun was drilling through the fog, skipping along the river's surface, and riveting the girders with refracted sparkles. This is where it had happened.

Up there. Clay flicked his eyes. And down there.

He hated what he had done, hated that someone was now throwing it back in his face. The mysterious author of the notes had an ax to grind, no doubt about that, but Clay wouldn't just roll over and die. If only he could uncover this person's identity.

"It's not gonna work," he told the river. "I'm not giving in that easy."

Near the bank the daylight pointed out a knotted stump caught in an eddy. The misshapen wood, bleached by water and sun, brought back to mind a spine-tingling sight. There, not ten yards from the stump's present position, Clay had stood over his friend's body—bloodied, naked, facedown in the water.

10

Bad News

"Gonna be late for work, Son."

"I'm not going."

"Thought you worked Saturdays."

"Not today."

"Does Blomberg know this?"

"I'll call right now." Clay brushed past his father's place at the dining nook and dialed from the kitchen phone. He left a curt message on Mr. Blomberg's voice mail.

Although Gerald's censure went unspoken, he ripped the lid from his blue travel mug and downed the coffee. Storm brewing; small craft advisories. With the urgency of a yachtsman trimming his sails and battening down the hatches, Gerald gathered the front section of the newspaper, then stalked to his bedroom at the end of the hall.

Watching the storm pass, Clay knew his mother would discern the source of shifting weather and come to check on him.

Sure, he desired comfort after the past few days' events—preferably, though, from others of the female persuasion. Such as Jenni. Or Mylisha.

On the table the regional section of the *Guard* offered distraction. Clay moved back his father's bowl with its residual Cream of Wheat ring. In respect for Summer's death, he scanned the obituaries, but he was sure he was a few days late. At the job site, Mr. Blomberg had been the one to tell the particulars of the hit and run, how Summer's head had struck a fence, how she'd died after a few comatose days in the hospital.

The culprit was yet to be apprehended.

How many people had been at her funeral? he wondered. Was she buried on the hillside by her parents and her sister Milly? No wonder she'd never called again.

Now Mylisha's call made sense; she must've been crushed by this loss.

Trying to shake off depression, he panned to the section's quaint back page where local yokels could see their names in lights, where years ago his future exploits had been bandied about with such confidence.

Human interest, they called it. Hometown heroes. Sports stars. Little old ladies with the courage to face down intruders.

Today's picture did show an elderly woman. Smile lines creased her cheeks, underscoring the contentment she felt at her husband's side. Mr. and Mrs. Coates, the story stated, had farmed acreage on Dane Lane and served the community as man and wife for nearly five decades before the tragic events of July 2.

"Mr. Coates sustained gunshot wounds to the chest..."

Clay studied the photo, bug-eyed.

July 2, 2004...7.2.0.4.

"No! Tell me this is a joke."

He choked on the details, shoved the paper away. His father's bowl teetered at the table's edge before crashing into pieces on the floor. Deaf to the rush of feet from the hallway, Clay bolted from his chair and tried to block out the image of Mr. Coates. The man from Ace Hardware. Hairy forearms. Canvas pants and work shirt.

This couldn't be right. It was impossible!

In two separate cases now, the sets of numbers coincided with dates of death.

———

"I'm being punished."

On his bed Clay ground his face into his hands until sparks of light exploded behind his eyelids, yet the terror of the newspaper column remained. Were the numbers intentional or accidental? Was this somebody's idea of a joke?

"What the hell is going on?"

He groaned. *Hell... That's exactly what this is. The penalty for my sins.*

With palms opened before his eyes, he studied the unique whorls, the individual scars and lines, the epidermal layer. He flexed his fingers. Somehow, here at his fingertips, he could discern numbers.

Expiration dates.

This was more information than he wanted. He touched his fingers to his own skin, waiting for the branding iron to sizzle the newest numerals into place.

Nothing.

Apparently he was numb to his own demise. Not that he really wanted to know. What had the lady on the bus said? "God works in many different ways…" Had Henna passed this gift on to him? The newfound ability felt more like a curse.

"Clay."

Motionless, he let his mother assume he was napping.

"Doll, you have a phone call."

Probably Mr. Blomberg. Or the credit-card people catching up with him.

Della lowered her voice. "It's a woman, dear. Her voice was so full of melancholy, I told her you'd take the call."

———

"Hi, Clay. Guess who?" Mylisha sat up against her headboard. She'd been mourning Summer's death and now felt the pillow's sogginess under her thighs. "I can't believe you're here, back in JC."

"Me neither. It's been a couple of years."

"Please tell me you haven't gone bald and pudgy."

"Who me? White men can't do bald. Least not the tall, skinny ones."

She chortled. "You wouldn't look right. Dat's for real."

"I heard you called a few nights ago. Things okay?"

"Do I need an excuse?" She tried to block out Summer's face. "Would've called back sooner, but I've been busy with work and my classes at LCC."

"Didn't even know you were going to school again. What're you taking?"

"Guess."

"Filmmaking. Like you always talked about doing."

"You think you're pretty sharp, boy." She closed her eyes. "Actually, I'm working on business management credits."

"If you say so."

"It's more interesting than it sounds." She pulled back. Why should she explain herself? She'd already caved by calling him first, so now she'd wait for him to take the lead in the conversation. Mr. Ryker's turn.

"Sounds like you're staying busy." He cleared his throat. "Man, Mylisha, it's good to hear from you. Sorry I haven't kept in contact. After I got married, it just seemed like a line I shouldn't cross. Jenni wouldn't have minded. She's pretty mature about that kind of stuff. Just felt strange. Does that make any sense?"

"I stopped trying to make sense of you the day you left."

"Yeah, I was stuck in my own fantasy world. Had nothing to do with you."

"Apparently not."

"No, Mylisha. I mean, it wasn't your fault. I was an idiot in high school, pretty self-centered. You're probably glad I didn't go all the way to the pros with basketball. Serves me right, huh?"

"That's just stupid talk."

"Turned out to be human after all."

"Always were human, one of your best attributes. What're you goin' on about? I wanted you to make it, Clay, wanted you to reach your dreams. That's all I ever wanted for you."

"Well, I've made a mess of things now. Ruined my marriage, lost my business, got bills piled higher than MJ can jump."

"MJ's retired."

"Cut me some slack here."

Mylisha sighed. "You moved on. That was your choice. No need to explain. You had your opportunities and ran after them. Can't blame you. Not like I've sat around cryin' over the tall, fine point guard who got away. I do have a life."

"Fine?" Clay's pleasure was evident. "That sounds so...old-fashioned."

"I'm old school, getting set in my ways now that I'm all grown up. My girl Summer, she said I was boring. You believe that?"

"Summer Svenson." Clay seemed to catch his breath. "You know, Mylisha,

I can still see the two of you working the ball downcourt. You were smooth on those fast breaks. Practically unstoppable. Did you still hang together after high school?"

"Mm-hmm, for the most part."

"Mylisha, I'm sorry. I heard what happened. Not that it helps any, but I've been thinking about you, about what you must be going through."

"Why weren't you at her memorial service?" Mylisha's tone turned harsh.

"I didn't even know till yesterday," he said. "No one told me."

"Don't blame me. Just like the old days, you never called back."

"I've been completely out of touch. Had to get the facts from my boss over at Glenleaf Monument, where I've been working. A hit and run, right? He said she probably felt no pain, probably went into a coma the moment she hit her head."

"She never came out of it." Mylisha felt her voice falter.

"I don't even want to think about it," Clay said. "I first found out about it when they handed me Summer's work order."

"Her what?"

"I did her headstone."

"Clay! That's horrible."

"Tell me about it." He paused. "There's something else, Mylee."

The affectionate nickname silenced her. She bit her lip, dropped her chin against her chest. In the dresser beneath the window, their old cards and notes still filled a shoebox that she knew she should've dumped years ago.

"Sorry, my bad," he said. "It just slipped out."

"Mm-hmm."

"Do you think we could meet up somewhere, maybe hang together awhile? I need to talk to someone. Been experiencing some crazy stuff."

"I hear dat."

"I already called in to take the day off. Whaddya think?"

"Skipping work? That's not like you. You sure you're okay?"

"I don't know."

"Oh, so now you don't know. Tell me the truth, boy, are you feeling sick, or are you just playing for my sympathy? If I catch you milking the situation…"

"I'm fine." He emitted a weak chuckle. "Or so you say."

Mylisha imagined a goofy grin twisting his mouth, pushing dimples into his chiseled cheeks. His sense of humor, his carefree attitude, had attracted her from the beginning. During the last year of high school, however, things had shifted. They'd both made mistakes. They'd both pulled away. Eventually he'd started flashing his grin again, but she knew him too well to miss the minor differences. After that accident at the river, a part of him had gone into hiding.

"Clay, today won't work. I'm one of the managers down at Safeway, and I'm scheduled to go in. Final inventory, paperwork—that sort of stuff."

"It's important, Mylee." He apologized. "Mylisha."

"Ooh," she said. "I knew you coming back to town was bad news."

"If only you knew."

"Aren't you still married? People around here'll talk. You know they will. Wonderful JC, the rumor capital of the world."

"Hey, it's not our problem. We're adults now. We know where things stand."

Mylisha knotted her fingers in her comforter, and her college handbook flopped from the bed onto the carpet. Well, good for him. She was glad he had it all figured out. In her own heart, emotions were still swirling, dredged up by the sound of his voice. By the ache of his rejection. She'd climbed the corporate ladder, made a stab at an education.

As for her real dreams and desires? She'd laid them aside. Locked them away for safekeeping.

Was she ready to see all six feet three inches of him? What would happen when he turned his dark green eyes upon her? Could she deal with that?

Summer was right. I am scared.

"So today won't work," Clay conceded. "What about tomorrow? We could hike out to Alsea Falls, get some exercise and fresh air, leave this place behind."

"Back for two weeks and you're already trying to get away?"

"Trying to make sense of things. Need some distance, that's all."

"Boy, haven't you had enough distance?" She felt herself begin to unravel. "You expect to come sauntering back into town and have everything grind to a halt for you? We do have lives, you know. It's not as if we've sat around waiting for Mr. Ryker's grand return. You hear what I'm sayin'? What do you want from me?"

"Hey, you're the one who called. Guess I just need someone to talk to."

"Until Jenni comes back?" Mylisha bit down on her lip, drew in a breath. "Clay, I'm not up for this. Probably be best if we drop any plans to get together."

"What plans?"

"That's exactly what I mean. Good-bye."

11

Discoveries and Decoys

With a raw sound, the postcard scraped beneath his door. Customarily, his mother delivered his mail in person with her artless self-promotion: "You're welcome, Clay. It's no problem. Whatever your mother can do to help." Had to give it to her, though; she knew to alter course when his mood swings loomed.

Clay lent the card a suspicious eye. He pulled himself into an upright position on the bed's edge, bumping an empty can onto the carpet where a trickle of beer formed a yeast-scented stain.

So what was this, another message? Another secret revealed? Another bill?

Speaking of bills, they had tracked him down in the last week. According to the temporary court orders, Clay was solely responsible for his restructured business debts under Chapter 13 bankruptcy, and he'd been burying the paper mines beneath dirty laundry around the room, awaiting the inevitable explosions.

Boom! There goes your credit.

Boom! Thought you paid that one off? Think again, sucker!

Boom! Take a trip to the back of the line. What? Oh, you wanted to finance that economy pack of boxers? Too bad, Mr. Ryker—you flunked the credit check. A whoppin' F for you. F for financial flunky. F for failed family man.

Clay scanned the floor and conjured an image of cleared carpet. Couple more paychecks and maybe, just maybe, he could come through with the minesweepers. Find space to walk again. Prove to the world—meaning Gerald and Jenni and Jason—that with some hard-earned cash this boy could fly.

Back to the postcard…

Was it from Jenni? He missed his wife and the simple pleasure of sitting in a room together while she read one of her latest legal thrillers and he scanned the paper's box scores. Early in their marriage, they'd taken treks into the Wyoming wilderness, packing Jason along until he was old enough to walk.

Man, those pint-sized khaki shorts and his little hiking boots...

The boots were worth fifty bucks for the memory alone.

Clay wiped at his eyes. Standing, he felt his head spin. He steadied himself against the pitching of alcohol in his system, then fetched the postcard. The photo showed Old Faithful doing its thing. Yellowstone.

The handwriting on the back was uneven, yet legible.

Daddy, I want you to come home. Mommy works to hard and reads and won't play Xbox with me. I don't think she knows how. She hugs me real hard. Why did you hafta move? I don't want you to. Can you bring the bus back? I love you. Jason

The second time Clay read it, his throat tightened, and the words ran like ink underwater. Jason still called him Daddy. Clay held the postcard to his chest, and his shoulders shook. He made not a sound. In his mind, the image of Jason's nine-year-old face popped up, dirty and full of wonder the day he'd carried in a beetle for his momma's inspection. Jenni had jumped, dropping a can opener. Clay and Jason had laughed, a male moment of bonding.

Concern now swelled through Clay's chest. His son seemed so far away.

Then he thought of the paperboy on the porch early this morning.

7.1.1.0.4... A warning?

Clay took a drink from a half-empty container on his nightstand. He had one week to find and safeguard the paperboy. Yes, this is what he would do. Since Jason was a few states away, Clay would channel his concern toward this newly threatened child. He would serve as protector. Perhaps he could do this one thing right.

One thing, just one thing...

When the sunlight roused him on Sunday morning, he was stretched out on the bed with his clothes wrinkled about his body, the overhead light glaring, the postcard still clutched between his fingers.

"Kenny?" His mom's voice carried thinly from her twin bed.

"I'm going to do the paper."

"Be careful out there. You know cars have a hard time seeing you."

"I know, I know." He ruffled Gussy's ears, then kissed his mom on the cheek. "Love ya, Mom. Be back soon."

Kenny Preston took his usual path through the garage's side door. Stuffed with inserts, the Sunday papers were the hardest, often overflowing his shoulder bags. Today's date was stamped clearly: July 4, 2004. Independence Day.

He couldn't wait for tonight's fireworks display in Harrisburg.

The morning wind was light, the sky streaked with violet, and Kenny felt invigorated by the smell of fresh-cut grass and hay. On Juniper Street, a resident had asked that his paper be brought each day to the welcome mat on the back porch. This morning Kenny found a tip folded there beneath a pack of gum.

Koolerz. My favorite. And five dollars!

While his jaws worked the gum, his legs pistoned him forward so that he was able to complete the Sunday route before seven o'clock.

Which gave him a few minutes to kill.

He rolled the five-dollar bill in his hand. His mom was right that the world wasn't such a bad place if you knew the right people. Actually, she had said, "...if you know the right person." Meaning God.

Kenny had come to understand this a few months back. In a Sunday school class, the teacher explained that Jesus was a real man who came and lived on earth. "Even though he was God and could've stayed in heaven, he humbled himself so we humans would know how much he loved us. He went through struggles just like we do. He was tempted but never sinned. He was a spotless lamb, sacrificing himself for the sins of the world. His death brought each of us life."

The words touched Kenny. In his heart he believed, and in his head it made a strange sort of sense. At the teacher's invitation, he raised his hand. Yes, he'd done things wrong, which separated him from his Father God. Yes, he wanted Jesus to make things right.

Kenny Preston was born again, saved, baptized—the whole deal.

Yep. I know the right person.

The traffic was minimal this early, but his mother's warnings played through his head. He looked both directions. Blocks away, near the Dairy Queen, he saw a panel van waggling around a corner.

Ivy Street was Junction City's main thoroughfare, a segment of Highway 99 that ran up and down through the state. If Kenny followed it, he knew it'd take him to Portland, where he could visit the IMAX theater and the old submarine at the Oregon Museum of Science and Industry. His last visit to OMSI had been on a field trip.

A hundred miles away. He could do that. One big adventure.

Of course, his mom would freak. Always an entertaining thought.

Kenny cut across Ivy, through a parking lot and an alley, then bunny hopped a curb so that he was on the smooth path running through Founder's Park. This was the site of the locomotive. He loved this train with its hints of intrigue and spies, battles and mystery. Supposedly, some famous Russian guy had escaped on this thing.

Kenny was ready to explore. The morning was young, locking the park in shadow. The coast was clear.

He laid his bike behind a bush, then shimmied over the gate that guarded Engine 418. The machinery was huge and dark. New paint fumes and the smells of wood, smoke, and grease floated about. He had to jump to reach the first step. At the rear, the tender car was a reminder of the work required to make this monster move.

Dude! And I thought the Sunday paper was bad.

Kenny heard a voice, low and feeble in the dawn.

He wedged himself back into the engine's cabin. Okay, he was trespassing, but he meant no harm. A little exploration, that's all. Why did people these days try to discourage a kid if he used his imagination to let off some steam?

Maybe because of school shootings, Kenny thought. Kids weren't just kids anymore; they were potential criminals.

Well, I'm not! I'm thirteen just trying to have some fun.

The voice passed from his left to his right. Kenny gripped the metal, flattened his back against the rough surface to assure he would not be detected. Hopping the fence hadn't been the brightest idea.

He was losing his balance. With tight fingers, he clawed the cold iron at his feet.

Caked grease—oooh!—coming right up between his fingernails.

Scurrr-tinkkk!

The texture changed beneath his touch. In the corner, where floor and partition met, his finger exposed a wooden object amid flakes of grime and curled black residue. An old piece of kindling from the tender box? A twig blown here by the wind?

Or maybe it's a war relic.

Kenny's mind kicked into high gear. He'd seen newspaper stories about children in Florida who came upon pirate treasures or farm boys here in Oregon who plowed up old army munitions. This could be his chance at something big.

"What're you doing in there?"

His muscles jerked at the sudden nearness of his accuser.

"Get out of there before I call the police, you hear me?"

His eyes crept to the partition to assess the threat.

"What's your name, young man? You tell me this instant." The woman was hunched in a brown wool coat, leading a shaved and shivering Chihuahua on a leash.

"Kenny Preston," he said. Stupid, stupid. What made him open his mouth?

"Well, get out. Must I repeat myself?" Eyes full of admonition, she picked up the dog as though arming herself for confrontation. Kenny couldn't help but notice her chin had more white hairs than the pooch's. Had she heard of razors?

"I'm going," he said. "Wasn't doing nothin' wrong."

With leery eyes glued to Kenny, the woman grumbled into her Chihuahua's ear.

Kenny scaled the fence and grabbed his bike. He could always return tomorrow or the next day for this latest find. Was it important? Probably not, but he'd be back.

Asgoth scratched his elbow, then rolled up the sleeves of his pale yellow shirt. This was a workday. For others, Sunday might be a day of reverence or recreation, a day to catch up. Not for him. Not anymore.

He thought back to his golden years.

Though his stint as a high schooler had never brought him popularity, he had celebrated his own social triumphs. He'd spent most summer weekends at Fern Ridge Reservoir, exploring the benefits of pot and ecstasy with his peers. He'd coerced and been coerced into all sorts of wayward activity.

Anything to fit in and feel accepted. To feel human.

Then the risks had gone too far.

Like countless others before him, Asgoth had learned the hard way—one act of stupid pride, one slip-up. The Consortium had moved in to mop up his mess, and in so doing they'd built lucrative careers.

Asgoth was still scraping by. Still fighting for respect.

And I hold you responsible, Mr. Clay Ryker!

Asgoth paced the sidewalk, searching for Monde. How long must he wait? Down the street he saw an elderly woman shuffling along with a lap dog on a leash. Then, spotting a kid on a bike, he forgot his impatience.

Kenny Preston. The boy hopped the curb and entered the park.

"My apologies," Monde offered, appearing out of nowhere. "I've seen Pristi off, and the Consortium's scheduled us for review after the Scandinavian Festival."

"The Scandi-Fest. We still have a few weeks to work with."

"Which necessitates our haste, yes. Already, we know the Brotherhood's topnotch personnel are targeting this location." Monde lifted his beaklike nose, sniffed at the air. "The trick will be to misdirect them or perhaps leave a substitute...a decoy."

Across the way, Kenny was climbing the train's iron fence.

"Do you remember me mentioning an innocent young boy? Take a look over there." Asgoth gloated. "He's the one."

Gussy sniffled at the door, alerted to Kenny's presence in the garage.

"Hey, girl."

Kenny parked his bike, then scooped his darling into his hand as he swept into the house. From the kitchen, the smell of melted cheese and bacon tantalized his growing body. He could hear his mother's slippers scuffing along the tiles. He wondered if this was what it was like to be a grownup, to come home to your space, to feel as though the world was shut out from the confines of your castle.

Won't be long. Mom already calls me the man of the house.

Kenny's father, the other Mr. Preston, was in Alaska. He'd left when Kenny was three, spewing vows to Mrs. Preston that he would return with a bundle of cash and a new lease on life. Whatever that meant.

Mr. Preston had sent one check. And two letters. He'd never come back.

A spike of pain tore through Kenny's chest.

"Gussy!" He pushed her down onto the living room's throw rug. The silly dog had latched on to his skin through his shirt. "Bad girl, Gussy. Don't bite!"

"Kenny, you okay?"

"She bit me. No big deal."

"Ready for breakfast? You have two minutes to get washed up."

Brrngg-brrngg... From down the hall, the phone chirped. Kenny yelled that he had it, then made a dash, sliding on his socks, trying to beat the second ring.

Brrn—

He snagged the receiver, awarding himself half credit. "Hi."

"Good morning. Is this the Preston residence?"

"Um, yeah. Who's this?"

The baritone voice said, "Need to speak to Kenny Preston, if I could. Is that you? Please don't hang up. It's important."

"No thanks. We don't wanna buy anything."

"Hold on, Kenny. I'm not a telemarketer. Sorry if I'm scaring you, calling up like this, but I need to...need to warn you about something."

Static hissed from the receiver as Kenny carried it into the front room, where he peeked through the curtains. Like clockwork, Mrs. Larsen was trudging around her flower beds with gloves on, clippers in hand, a bag of weeds and roots trailing behind her. She was about the nicest person Kenny knew. In the light of dawn, her crown of white hair looked radioactive. Her husband, Mr. Larsen, was gone—a victim of cancer. Apostate…or something like that. No one would give Kenny the details, but he knew it had to do with *down there.*

Which made him nervous.

What if he died? What would his mom do? Would Gussy even remember him? Sometimes he worried about his own body. Things were changing. Maybe *he* had apostate cancer.

"You still there? Kenny? Don't hang up, I beg you. I know this sounds bizarre, but if you'll give me a minute, I'll try to explain. Will you let me do that?"

Kenny let the curtains fall back into place. "First tell me your name."

"Clay."

Clay? The dude's tracked me down. I should never have—

"Are you still there, Kenny? I promise I'm trying to help you."

"Sorry. Can't talk. My mom's calling me for breakfast."

"How about later? I could meet you and your mom together, if that'd be better."

Kenny balked at the thought of dragging his mother into this. She had reasons for keeping an unlisted phone number, and he was here to protect her. He wanted to know, "How'd you get my number?"

"Got it from the *Register-Guard.* I said I wanted to pass on a message to my newspaper carrier, and I gave your description."

"Do you know where I live?" Kenny inquired.

"Nope, they only gave me your phone number. By the way, I have your—"

Kenny disconnected.

12

No Turning Back

Clay fought off panic. He stared at the dead phone in his hand and reminded himself he had nearly a week. Would Kenny Preston end up as an unsuspecting victim, another weight on his conscience?

It would be more than he could handle.

The jacket under his arm took on new significance; surely he could use it to track down the kid. Overriding his sense of propriety, he riffled through the pockets and found nothing but lint and a sticky glob of chewing gum. He thought he was out of luck, then noticed the small slit of an inner pocket.

Inside: an orange plastic card with a magnetic strip.

"Nickel's Arcade." A local address and number.

Tomorrow, Clay decided, he would visit the downtown hangout, poke around, ask if anyone knew the person to whom the coat belonged. He called and found out the place would be open from 10 a.m. to 10 p.m.

For the heck of it, he perused the local directory and confirmed that Kenny Preston's phone number failed to match any of the Prestons listed. No number. No address. Nothing. With all the mixed families these days, the kid could have a different last name than his parents. His mom could be single or a divorcée who had dropped her married name.

Against his will, Clay's thoughts jumped to Jenni—her freckled cheeks and smiling eyes. Last year he'd begun to see her first hints of laugh lines. He'd planned on watching them deepen.

What did he have instead? An uncertain future.

A judge would decide his fair share of marital property, while lawyers argued both sides of spousal and child-support payments. Clay didn't mind helping his family. He did mind the courts stipulating when, where, and how much; he did mind having no say in how it was spent.

He slammed his bedroom door on the way out.

Della, whipping from the kitchen, almost collided with him. "Breakfast is served," she said. "There on the table."

In this house he'd heard the same phrase every Sunday since he could remember. He recognized it as a compromise between his parents, a weekend arrangement. Della always cooked up sausage, peppery hash browns, and scrambled eggs with cheese; Gerald always joined her for Mass at St. Helen.

Clay felt a sudden, palpable affection for his mother.

"Mom." He took hold of her arms, bare below the sleeves of her cornflower blue dress. He needed contact. He already knew her numbers, knew they indicated a date far off—though not far enough. Regardless, he could let down his guard.

"What is it, Clay?"

"Thank you."

"For?"

"Just thank you. For everything." He thought of her years of hard work, child rearing, the constant shuttling, and her ubiquitous smile.

"Oh, don't be silly. Go eat while it's hot."

"Really, Mom. Thanks."

Della's eyes softened beneath her shield of Avon cosmetics and Gloria Delaney hair products. "You're a doll."

"Yeah, yeah." Clay gave an affable squeeze, then let go. "So you've told me."

Later from the dining nook, he watched his parents depart in the gleaming Dodge pickup. Gerald took the wheel: *No woman's gonna drive me around.* He looked forlorn and bitter behind the windscreen.

Alone in the house, Clay delved into his robe and removed the shredded pieces of yesterday's envelope. He nabbed a roll of tape from the drawer beneath the phone. Setting the pieces on the kitchen counter, he smoothed the torn edges with his fingers and assembled them with strips of tape.

The message was uneven, but clear enough.

You thought you'd get off scott-free, but you were wrong.
How many must die to pay for your sin? Sacrifice yourself so others
might live!

Who knew? Who'd been there at the river? The wording was too specific: "one bill you can't run away from…" "thought you'd get off scott-free…"

Bill Scott.

Dead at age seventeen.

Bill and Clay had been alone that day. Spring break of their senior year. A great day to be at the river if you could handle the Willamette's temperature. Of course, the beer helped with that, pilfered from the cooler in the Scotts' garage. After the investigation, the alcohol in Bill's system was no secret and was widely blamed for his death. A lesson to all good boys and girls.

A lesson Clay had elected to forget.

Now the incident rose from his memory's muddied waters, insisting he replay the events and set aside guilt and anger long enough to search for clues among the details.

———

Friday, March 13, 1992.

A canopy of clouds. Filtered sunlight. A slight breeze ruffling the Willamette River's deceptive waters. A bridge of aging, gunmetal gray.

"You sure it's safe?"

"Sure," Clay said. "We've done it feet first. Let's go headfirst."

"How deep is it?"

"Deep enough."

"What about stuff floating beneath the—"

"Hey, if you're afraid, just say so. Stop making excuses." Clay mounted the railing. "I'm gonna do it."

Bill Scott shrugged. "Whatever, man. Go for it."

Clay looked down past his toes on the rusted metal girder. To intensify the thrill of the activity, he and his companion had rolled their clothes up on the shore and tackled the structure in the buff. Bolstered by the six-pack now discarded in the bushes, they had convinced themselves they were invincible. They'd completed two flailing, yelling, posturing descents into the dark pool. The water was chilly. Murky, too. The distance between the river and the lower section of the structure was a minimum of fifteen feet, twenty-plus feet to their perch on the girder.

"Having second thoughts?" Bill gibed.

With his stomach backflipping into his throat, Clay gripped the metal with one hand and leaned out over the impact zone. The water toyed with a group of leaves, spinning them in a lazy circle. A moving target.

Don't think. Just do it. Do it!

Letting go was the worst part. Once airborne, there was no turning back. Stretched out over the river, unencumbered, Clay felt the rush.

His lungs became a combustion chamber, and his adrenaline exploded into a primal yell. He tucked his head between overlapped forearms, knifed into the water, then carved rudderlike hands upward to alter speed and direction. For a moment, he was floating in the cold darkness, arching back to the surface.

He came up with a kick. Let out a war whoop of exultation.

"That is awesome!" He climbed up the bank, crossed to the middle of the bridge, and reached the railing again. "Completely radical!"

"I'll take your word."

"Oh, come on. You gotta try it."

Withstanding Clay's heckling, Bill took his place at the girder, his body tight against the brace. His right leg started quivering.

"You gonna do it?"

"Shut up. I'm thinking."

"You can't think. You just do it. Just jump."

"Shut up, Ryker!"

Clay emitted a clucking sound. Despite the charade of kidding around, he felt annoyed. He could hear his dad's voice: *Gotta be a man's man.*

Honestly, what was Bill so afraid of? They'd talked before about going bungee jumping or skydiving. Even sketched out plans for a summer-long hike on the Pacific Crest Trail, braving bears, cougars, the weather, and other humans. This was nothing in comparison.

Not to mention that Bill had done enough other things that implied he had no fear—stupid, meanspirited things.

"Is it gonna hurt when I hit?" Bill asked. "Looks a lot higher from up here."

He curled his hands behind him, clamped on to the metal. He eased out over the water, trying to stare down the danger. Intense and self-absorbed, he seemed not to notice Clay's approach. He started to let go the same instant Clay gave him some encouragement.

A prod...a push...a shove.

They were all really the same, weren't they? Sure they were. Sure.

Bill flailed through the air and hit the water in a contorted dive. His thighs slapped the surface. His toes followed his body down. He was a blur in the water, a phantom moving through the netherworld.

The specter came to an abrupt stop. Then shrank into the black depths. He was gone.

Clay released a nervous chuckle. Seconds ticked away. Slowly the enormity of his action struck him. He had pushed Bill from that precipice, and he was not rising to the surface; he was not coming up.

Clay stepped back, stunned and unsure, then darted across the bridge and slid down the slope, blaring his friend's name, surveying the river and the shorelines for any glimpse of sandy hair and a squat torso. He waded into the water, dove beneath the surface. Visibility was nil. No sign of his companion.

Minutes later Bill Scott made his appearance...

Facedown, lifeless, his body nudged against the riverbank.

Clay turned him over, then shrank from the clammy skin, the touch of death. He saw a wound on the skull where it had collided with a hidden object, floating or fixed, beneath the roiling surface. He gagged and retched into the water. He called out, yelled, looked around. He would have to go for assistance; he'd have to tell someone.

The solitude that had been so exhilarating now collapsed about him—a blanket of icy detachment. Nobody to help. Nobody in the vicinity.

Also no witnesses.

Or so I thought, until these notes started showing up.

Although authorities had questioned him and others after that horrible day, no one else claimed to have seen a thing. Two kids; a few drinks; a blunt object floating beneath the surface... The cops concluded that it was a tragic accident.

Obviously, though, someone *had* seen. Someone *had* been there.

For reasons unspecified, this person had come back to torment him.

———

Upright in seat 14B of a commercial jetliner headed for Portland, Dmitri Derevenko gazed down on the Columbia River. Wending its way to the Pacific, the water was a blue green thread stitching together Oregon and Washington. On either side, towering rocks and stretches of trees formed a tapestry of tan and green, rust and ocher.

How could a land so stunning produce such debauchery?

He sipped at his mineral water and pressed his head back in his seat.

Unbridled freedoms and relativism had blinded Mother Russia. Black marketeers, swindlers, peddlers of superstition—they had swept in and taken advantage. Even his own countrymen had turned into capitalistic cannibals.

Who could restore Russia to greatness? Who but a descendant of the Tsars?

Enter the Brotherhood of St. John of Tobolsk.

"Sir, we'll be landing shortly," a flight attendant informed Dmitri. "You'll need to fasten your seat belt and return your tray to the upright position."

He dipped his head. "Thanks for the warning."

The flight attendant smiled, gave him a wink. He'd been pleased to find that his square jaw and bright blue eyes held sway over women even here in this land of the "beautiful people." This was a talent, a tool. He would use it when necessary.

All for the Brotherhood. For the sake of the Almighty.

His father, his grandfather, his great-grandfather connected him in an unbroken line to the original band of Brothers. Formed in 1918, named by Empress Alexandra in honor of the town's saint, the group had consisted of Tsarists who wished to see the Romanovs returned to power. Lenin's revolution had ousted the once-mighty Romanov family, thrusting them into exile where they faced a dubious future under house arrest. The newly formed Brotherhood hoped to rectify the problem.

The solution, however, was far from easy. With Lenin's revolutionaries in power, terror was ripping the country asunder. Famine threatened; religious freedom withered; godless men did godless acts.

The Brotherhood understood they needed to take action, but it would require adequate funding and clever coordination. They needed a leader.

Boris Soloviev claimed he could meet the challenge.

Indeed, Soloviev proved to be a shrewd man. A dichotomy of loyalties. Trained in Berlin, raised in the Orthodox Church, he was also an in-law to Rasputin and well versed in the occult. He molded people to his will, securing finances from baronesses, clergymen, peasants, and nuns. He instilled in the Brotherhood a sense of purpose. Rumors prevailed that three hundred officers of the Brotherhood were standing by, disguised and ready to rescue the Imperial Romanov family. They were the "good Russian men," awaiting Soloviev's signal.

But the signal never came.

As a young boy, Dmitri heard his great-grandfather tell the tale with tears in cataract-clouded eyes. The old man relived the proud dreams over bowls of cabbage soup and heels of black bread. With bottles of vodka, he faced the demons.

Dmitri cinched his seat belt. Ran his hand along the hidden scar on his hip. He swirled the last of his mineral water over his teeth, then crushed the plastic cup in his fist as he recalled Soloviev's treachery.

Curse the man! Curse his mysticism and greed.

Conveniently, the Bolsheviks had arrested Soloviev even while Red Guards whisked off the Romanovs to the Ipatiev house in Ekaterinburg. The pointless detainment provided Soloviev an alibi for his failure to procure the family's freedom—and in this manner he escaped punishment.

Whereas the Tsars did not.

On July 16, 1918, the storied family was gathered in a basement. With a volley of gunfire and stabbing bayonets, guards brought the Tsars' centuries-old dynasty to an ignoble end. Reports leaked out that the Romanovs were dead.

Only a handful understood the nuances of this deception.

Clay dropped into a seat at the breakfast nook and forced the memory back beneath the surface—down, down, down where it belonged. A freshwater leviathan constrained by sheer force of will.

Yes, I know, Dr. Gerringer…a coping mechanism. And thank goodness!

Just as he feared, the memories left him still clueless as to the identity of his tormentor. He scanned the message's ominous words, traced the letters with his fingers, a blind man trying to read nonexistent Braille. Blowing out a sigh of frustration, he buried his face in cupped hands and sent up a prayer for help.

Please, Lord, I need a sign here. Not that I deserve one, but—

A distinct scent interrupted his desire to start bargaining.

An aroma…like vanilla and cherries. Like his mom's Avon pen.

Clay sniffed at his fingers, ran his nose along the reassembled paper of the message. No doubt about it. The words had been penned with scented ink, with an Avon pen if he were to venture a guess.

It was a tangible clue. Wasn't much, but it was a start.

PART TWO

...how pale his features! and how like a shroud
the sheet was wound about his frame!
Yes; it was a corpse, in its burial clothes.

The White Old Maid, Nathaniel Hawthorne

I sank down
to the very roots of the mountains...
imprisoned in the land of the dead.

Jonah 2:6

13

The Deception

On Monday, graveyard humor prevailed at the monument company.

Most everyone had stayed up late for Fourth of July celebrations, hangovers were in evidence, and Mr. Blomberg was away on business—or so his secretary claimed. Rumors had him on a flight to Hawaii.

Brent seemed to consider it his duty to keep the crew on task, although he lagged behind Digs in seniority. Clay kidded Digs and Wendy. They slung jokes back and forth. In light of recent happenings, Clay found this to be an outlet, a means of putting things in perspective.

Or a means of denial.

Either way, the neck muscles that had cramped in his fitful sleep last night began to loosen, and he even worked through an entire fifteen-minute period without considering the numbers he'd been detecting on others' skin.

During lunch break, Wendy pulled out a timeworn riddle. "D'ya hear about the little Egyptian boy who got lost in the pyramids?"

Brent and Digs groaned. Clay waited for the answer.

"He was trying to find his mummy."

In his mind Clay saw Jason. He headed back to his workbench.

What about the paperboy? Kenny Preston.

7.1.1.0.4... Only six days away.

At closing time Digs took Clay aside to ask what was troubling him. Clay remained stoic, turning down an invitation to grab some buffalo wings at the Raven, a nearby tavern. He thought it sounded too Poe-ish, too grim.

"Maybe next time, Digs. Appreciate the offer."

"Can't carry it all on your own," Digs admonished. "Something's eatin' at ya. Ain't no weakness in asking for help."

"I have an errand to run. Sorry. Gotta go."

After a belch of smoke, the Duster took him to Nickel's Arcade downtown. He questioned clients and teenage employees for details about a kid named Kenny Preston. A few recognized the jacket. Nobody knew where he lived.

"Whaddya want him for anyway?"

"Like I said, I want to make sure he gets his stuff back."

"Try back later." The speaker was a chubby teen in a schoolgirl's skirt, a black Disturbed T-shirt, and a chain connecting the piercings in her ear. "He's a skinny little runt. Comes in coupla nights a week, hogging the games, scrounging tokens."

"You think he might be in later tonight?"

She shrugged. "He's too young for me, so what do I care?"

———

"You're sure you want to do this?"

"Anything for you, Mom."

And anything to keep an eye on your Avon partygoers.

"You really don't have to." Della's motherly line was baited with guilt.

"It's fine," Clay assured. "I've been busy with work, but if I take you to the party, at least we'll have a few minutes together, right?" He set a kiss on her cheek.

"You're welcome to drive the Dodge," she offered in reward. "We'll need to leave soon, though, since I'm expected to help Mrs. Dixon with refreshments. How will you occupy yourself while waiting at her place?"

"Actually, I've got some reading to catch up on."

"Reading? You've never been much of one for books."

"People change," he mumbled. "At least, outside of Junction City."

Della ran a hand over her arm, back and forth, as though soothing her nerves. She said, "Stability does have its good points, dear. Some people use change as an excuse to run away."

Clay had no response.

As Della went to fetch her purse, he grabbed an old Stephen Lawhead novel from a shelf in the hall, then tucked a written draft of a divorce agreement between the pages. The paperwork had arrived in today's mail. A formality.

As if some fat-cat lawyers can decide the outcome of my marriage.

Twenty-five minutes later Clay dropped his mother at the Dixons' front door. He stationed the Dodge truck between the three-car garage and a fermenting burn pile and remained vigilant as vehicles began turning from Lovelake Road up the meandering drive. He felt confident strapped to the powerful diesel engine.

All part of the plan. If he spotted his target, he'd be ready for pursuit.

He counted the arrivals. *Twelve, thirteen, fourteen…*

Would he find his tormentor here? He mulled over the few clues he'd obtained. Apparently, the note writer had been using a scented Avon pen, and judging by the paperboy's description, she was an adult woman with blond hair.

The fifteenth guest parked along the Dixons' lawn. She was a young Hispanic mother, nudging along a toddler in a pink dress, fussing over every ruffle.

Clay knew his own mother enjoyed these Avon parties. Friendship. Connection. All the things she lacked at home in the churlish weather systems Gerald generated.

Clay thought of his wife, Jenni. Of her Bunko nights with the gals.

Had she been crying out for something deeper?

Although inconvenient, he'd always viewed those Monday evenings as his opportunity to hang out with Jason, order pizza, stay up late playing Xbox together.

Rarely, though, had he given Jenni the same amount of attention. Time had become scarce, particularly as Satellite Mapping Elite nosedived, gobbling up his grandfather's investment and bringing a lien against his and Jenni's home. Some nights, paralyzed by inadequacy, he had shrugged off Jenni's attempts to woo him to bed, opting for the couch and the remote. With business not performing as hoped, he feared failure might show itself in other areas of their marriage.

Of course, Jenni's disappointment only intensified his shame.

Bunko… Even the name felt like a slap in the face.

Shifting in the truck seat, Clay lifted his eyes as another guest—*let's see…that's number sixteen*—stopped a Subaru near the front entryway. The sinking sun drenched the woman in copper hues as she strolled to the door. Thin, wearing sandals and a shawl, with blond hair. Mid to late twenties.

She smoothed her shawl, then turned her face his way.

Henna? The lady from the Greyhound?

Electricity jolted through Clay's hands, up his arms, to the roots of his hair. Each follicle was a needle on a seismograph, registering his suspicions. She was here. Now. He knew with all certainty this lady was involved in his recent turmoil. Did she recognize him as well? Or was he shadowed by the sun at his back?

Henna entered the house without knocking.

———

Asgoth shuffled his feet through the apartment's gold shag carpet. He stopped at the window, where mold ringed the glass like a black weather seal. He could see warped roofing and tarpaper spanning the causeway below. On the roof's surface, empty beer cans glinted in the sun, and a curled magazine flashed suggestive images as leaves ballet danced over the filth.

He despised this pitiful existence.

From the beginning of time, the unscrupulous had found profit in the sex and drug trades, and he'd been told that the others in the Consortium enjoyed places regal and palatial. His home was nothing but a washroom to them.

Well, that'd change. He'd peel this town open, revealing once and for all the dark core of even the smallest of communities.

Earlier in the day Asgoth had met with his circle of recruits. They came with open minds, eager to establish a presence in Junction City, trusting in the finances he planned to tap—although he provided no details of Engine 418. With enthusiasm, they'd agreed to start things off with a bang.

Yet they were unaware of his ultimate, much more intimate, goal.

A goal spawned by a memory…

Cold water. Dragging him down. Open wounds pumping into the river's current. Knots in his stomach as death reached in and twisted his internal organs. Staring out through luminous eyes. Fading. Sinking into black depths. The end at hand.

Or so everyone thought! But I've never left this place.

In five weeks, at the Scandi-Fest, his deception would be revealed. Each of his victims would be another timecard punched for compensation—one fat paycheck, signed in Clay Ryker's blood.

———

As Clay stepped down from the Dodge, he let the door rest against its latch. He moseyed toward Henna's car, stretched his legs. Gave the house a casual glance.

Thin curtains filtered the living room's light onto the rhododendrons outside, and laughter escaped through the picture window. Motion-activated porch and garage lights clicked on simultaneously.

Clay knelt on the Subaru coupe's far side. Tested the passenger door.

Ti-shtikkk… He was in.

Keeping an eye on the house, he ran a hand through the glove box. He found a pouch of registration and insurance papers, which listed an address on…Lovelake Road? He ran his gaze from the paper to the numbers beneath the porch light. They matched. He verified the name of the vehicle's owner: *Hannah Dixon.*

Had Hannah chosen "Henna" as a nickname?

Not unlikely. A fashionably Oregonian thing to do—in honor of mother nature.

As he thought about it, he remembered the Dixons had two daughters who had been underclassmen in his high school—gangly, dark-haired girls. Time and hair coloring must've worked wonders. He could barely put faces to them, and as far as he knew, he had no ties to them, no deep dark history.

So the Subaru's owner was Henna. Hannah Dixon.

No wonder she had approached him on the bus. To her, he was no stranger. She knew his name; the circumstances of his marriage and business were readily available within the circle of small-town gossip. Nothing mystical about it. When he'd failed to recognize her, she had used the encounter to her advantage.

Clay slapped away a fly, his mind full of new questions.

Sure, Henna could be the one writing the notes. Mrs. Dixon could provide her daughter enough scented pens to keep her tormenting him for years.

But what was the motivation? How'd she know about that day at the river?

He recalled images of Henna and Bill Scott together at a football game. For a time, they'd been seen hanging together. They'd even showed hints of a romance—or something more likely attributable to raging hormones.

With the sun blurring his vision, Clay turned back to the truck, caught a hint of movement there at the driver's side. He heard the door click shut. Who was out here? In a flash, his legs were eating up the distance. He caromed around the hood, scanned the truck bed, dipped to peer under the chassis. He raced around the entire vehicle, but the intruder had disappeared.

Through the window, he spotted a generic white envelope.

He grabbed it and ran toward the house. The front door was unlocked. He slammed his way through and arrived breathlessly in the middle of the living room with multiple sets of eyes trained upon him. These ladies could think what they wanted, but he was determined to solve this mystery.

"Where is she?" he barked out. "Why is she doing this to me?"

Della stood with one hand raised. "Clay, what's taken over you?" She looked about at the Avon guests. Through an archway, women moved in and out with glasses of punch and small plates of sliced cheese and crackers.

"Where is she?"

"Who?"

"Henna." Clay's tone was incriminating. "Henna Dixon."

"Why, she's right behind you, doll."

Clay turned, following his mother's gaze, and found Henna settled into the sofa beneath the picture window. He saw her lips twitch. "You," he said. "You were on the bus. In the seat next to me. You tried to...tell me things."

"Is that a crime?"

He held up the envelope. "Why'd you put this in the truck?"

"What is it?"

"Oh, come on! I know you were just out there."

"She hasn't moved from that seat since she arrived," Della said. "Honestly, Clay, what's this all about?"

Henna flashed a benign smile. "If I'd known you liked Avon so much, I would've sent you your own invitation to my mother's party."

Peals of laughter followed her statement, easing the room's tension, and Clay muttered apologies on his way back to the truck. Had he turned into a head case? What was going on? He opened the envelope and found another note addressed to him.

You tried to bury your bill, but I have pressed on.
Get on board, and go to the end of the line!

14

Spymaster

Kenny Preston was eager to return to Engine 418. Monday his mom had dragged him into Eugene for his doctor's visit and for her appointment to reapply for food stamps. Today she'd given him a list of chores, which included removing Gussy's "attempts to revitalize the back lawn."

He frowned at the memory. Why not just call it what it was?

Doodie duty. How disgusting.

By a quarter to twelve, the day was already sunny and hot. Mom thanked him for his help, "rehydrated" him with a glass of cran-raspberry juice, and told him he could go play arcade games at Nickel's as long as he returned for lunch around one.

Although he'd lost his game card along with his jacket, he knew there had only been five or six credits left. No big deal. For an hour he was free.

On his way to the arcade, Kenny stopped at the locomotive. Huddled in the engine's cab, he felt an apprehension brought on by the large, menacing machinery.

He chose to slip into his imaginary role as a secret agent.

I'm a shadow, a spy on a mission. No fear.

Spymaster Kenny ran his hand along the cab floor, dredging black sludge before detecting once again that piece of carved wood. He blew out a sigh, surprised at how concerned he'd been that the object would be gone. With his pocketknife jabbing and slicing—almost into his own skin—he freed the thin tube.

Kinda disappointing. Grungy and stained, it didn't look like anything special.

Never could tell, though. With a little washing up…

The spymaster stuffed it into his front pocket before vaulting back over the fence. In a crouch he darted to the rosebush and threw his leg over the bike that now had become a Nazi motorcycle, stolen with the help of a young maiden for his clandestine escape. Roaring through occupied territory, the spy extraordinaire headed for Allied lines with his secret bundle intact.

Was he being tailed? Had the lovely maiden betrayed him?

Throwing glances over his shoulder, Kenny stood on the pedals and raced along Sixth Street, then cut through an alley that led to Nickel's Arcade. He saw no signs of a pursuer, but he had a growing sense he was being followed in real life.

The stronger the feeling, the more convinced Kenny became that he should keep his discovery to himself. Nobody would expect him to find something worthwhile, but what if he had? What would he do with it? Was there anyone he could trust?

Jesus, you're the smartest of anyone. Please give me a plan.

Just like that, as clear as a father telling his son how to read traffic signs, an idea entered Kenny's mind. He knew just where to go.

———

One after another, headstones completed their sober trek through Clay's work area, affecting him more deeply than he'd expected. Life was so transitory, death so arbitrary.

Along the riverbank…

It was not my fault. It wasn't! How could I have known what would happen?

The lunch bell rang. He punched out at the time clock—choosing to disregard the gloomy symbolism—and let Digs ride shotgun in the Duster down to the corner market. Clay bought a beer to accompany his lunch; Digs ate from a brown paper bag, patient and thoughtful, his manner communicating empathy with Clay's struggle.

"Been there, pal."

"Where?" Clay leaned against the store's outer wall. "I'm fine, Digs. Really."

"It's botherin' ya, plain to see. Nothing unusual about that."

"Everything's just dandy." Clay pulled one foot up and tilted back the drink.

"You sure that's a good idea on lunch hour?"

"I'm thirsty, okay? I don't even like the taste that much. You're right, though, about the job. People pass on. It's part of life, but you just never realize how persistent it is, one order after another. Tombstone after tombstone. You work at a place like Glenleaf, and you hope that maybe just once you'll have a slow day on the job."

"It's a busy place, that's a fact. No such thing as dead time."

"Funny. Ha, ha."

"Bad pun, I know. Really oughta stop jokin' about such grave concerns."

Clay moaned, swirled the bottle. The liquid foamed like peroxide on a wound.

"Hey, don't take it wrong, Ryker. Just my way of copin'. You know that."

"I'm not sure I can keep doing this work."

"Sure you can."

"I don't know. I've got other issues I'm dealing with." Clay emptied the beer and set it on the ground. With the toe of his shoe, he traced graffiti on the wall. "You should see my little boy, Jason. Brown hair, thick like mine. And his mother's big green eyes. I'd do anything to have him here right now."

"I had a son."

"Had?"

"Haven't seen him since he was, oh, four years old. His momma up and left."

"Sounds familiar."

"But she had her reasons. See, Ryker, I have a record. Did time—seven years at the state pen. Been cleaned up ever since, collectin' my paycheck and payin' off my land. Got a trailer, some good acres of rye, and a fine view of the sun when it crests over the Cascades. Got nothin' to complain about."

"What'd you do? I mean, not that it's any of—"

"You're right. Ain't none of your business."

"So you haven't heard from your son? Do you know where he is?"

Digs sucked in his cheeks as if trying to remember. "Nope. Haven't heard."

"That must be rough. Man, if something ever happened to Jason…"

"Know whatcha mean. It's probably best that we can't see into the future."

"What if we could change things? If we could intervene somehow?"

"No." Digs bent to pick up Clay's abandoned bottle, tossed it into a dented trash can. "We're only human, guaranteed to mess things up worse than we already have. Believe me, it's best not knowin'. Easier to take it one day at a time."

Clay was less certain. "We'd better head back. Lunch's almost over."

As he found his seat in the car, he couldn't shake Henna's words from the encounter on the Greyhound. Sure, knowledge could be seductive, but fore-knowledge could arm you against impending doom. Wouldn't it be better to have a little advance warning? Diseases could be averted, accidents avoided, lives spared…marriages saved.

Yep. Let Clay Ryker make the rules, and the world would be a safer place.

It sounded so simple.

"I'll drop you back at the shop," he told Digs. "Something I've gotta do."

The Mario Brothers clock over the counter warned Clay he was well past his lunch break, and he knew he'd take heat for it when Mr. Blomberg returned from his trip.

Right now, Kenny Preston was his focus.

Nickel's Arcade was a busy spot, with clusters of kids attached to the most popular games along the wall. Clay recognized a few of the games. Although he experienced a surge of adrenaline at the possibility of head-to-head com-petition, he saw nobody matching Kenny's appearance.

Maybe he should give it a few minutes. See if the kid showed.

Clay inserted a bill into the coin machine, purchasing a game card. He checked out his options, headed for a virtual motorcycle race.

"You like playing games, I see."

The female voice, cutting through the volley of human cheers and com-puterized noise, chafed at something inside him.

"I could say the same about you, Henna. Did you follow me in here?"

"Why do you treat me with such suspicion? So we grew up in the same town, we shared a bus ride, our mothers both like Avon... Is there something else I'm missing?"

"You're the one writing the notes."

"What notes?"

"You paid the paperboy to stick an envelope in my newspaper."

"Clay, don't flatter yourself." Henna chuckled and smoothed the front of her shawl. "If I wanted to write you a love letter, I'd send it through the mail. I'll admit I used to have a schoolgirl crush on you, but I'm a woman now. Or haven't you noticed? I was right about you. You're a man with many burdens."

"So you don't know about the notes? Or about Kenny Preston?"

"Kenny who?"

"Preston. Or as it says in the note, 'pressed on.' I'm not stupid, you know."

Henna tilted her head, gave him a condescending look. "You really should've listened to me on the bus. You've missed your opportunities, and now you're clamoring for direction."

"You still haven't explained what you're doing in this place."

A chubby girl with multiple ear piercings, the same girl Clay had met the previous night, latched on to Henna's arm. "What're you doing here, Mother? I thought you hated the noise. Oh, is this guy bugging you? He was here yesterday, nosin' around."

Henna etched her fingernail along Clay's arm. "Seems to be a habit of his."

Without another word, he watched them exit the arcade.

———

Kenny changed course, swerving around the bike rack in front of Nickel's, coasting along Front Road, then up and over the train tracks with a burst of acceleration. The sun's heat radiating from the rails was so hot he thought his tires would melt. Sweat popped out along his forehead, underneath his eyes.

Spymaster Kenny. Agent on assignment.

So as not to give anything away, he passed his destination and circled the block. Coming back around, he saw the coast was clear.

He hesitated at the edge of an embankment before plunging into the small ravine carved between housing developments on one side and the railroad on the other. Most of the year rain fed this brier-filled ravine, but the summer months dried it out for garter snakes, grasshoppers, and ants to explore.

Kenny loved it down here. His tires splayed dust and pebbles as the bike leveled out. He avoided a patch of broken glass, drove to the drainage pipe's mouth.

With the bike parked in weeds so tall they tickled his shirt sleeves, Kenny edged into the orifice. Although it would be easier to walk on his knees, rough stones and corrugated metal discouraged it. His shoes scraped over a pile of trash, kicking the sound down the tunnel and through the welded grate at the far end.

This tunnel used to be his hideout. His safe house. For years, Spymaster Kenny had used this spot to avoid school bullies, win games of hide-and-seek, flee frustrations at home. Here, in the coolness, he'd practiced saying all the things he wanted to say to his father—words he might never get to express face to face. He had also spoken to his heavenly Father, voicing fears he'd never admit to his mom. She needed him to be strong.

Be strong and courageous. Weren't those the words God spoke to Joshua before sending him to conquer Canaan?

Well, here I am, Jesus. Ready for any assignment.

Kenny dug the wooden tube from his shorts' pocket. Turning the grimy treasure in his fingers, he wondered if it was worth anything. So smooth and symmetrical. He rolled the object against the cuff of his shorts, smearing grease and gunk into the cloth.

Oops. He'd have to shove these shorts deep into the laundry pile and pray the stains washed out, otherwise his mom would kill him.

Something stirred outside the tunnel.

He froze. He could feel the low rumble of a vehicle passing overhead. Dirt spit from the tunnel's metal ribs into his hair. Time to scram, he decided. He'd conceal this thing and come back for it later.

He inched into the darkness. Was it still there? His secret hiding spot?

At eye level a bubble in the metal jutted into the earth. This manufacturing flaw provided a perfect spot for his secret objects, both real and imagined. He poked the wooden tube into the metal bubble. For now, the locomotive's treasure would remain the spymaster's secret.

15

Friends and Foes

He'd been told to rent a room here and wait. That'd been days ago.

Near the Portland airport, Dmitri Derevenko chewed on sunflower seeds while eying the ramshackle Val-U-Inn with a sign boasting Clean Towels, Hot Showers.

A humble step on his journey. He believed the Tsars' bloodline remained intact, as well as a portion of Rasputin's fortune, and he intended to find it. Once their coffers were filled, the Brotherhood would bolster an heir's rise to the throne.

In the last year others had become unwitting allies in this dream of national resurgence. Viktor Vekselberg, oil and aluminum magnate and one of the world's richest men, had acquired nine Fabergé eggs from the Forbes collection. He'd spent nearly a hundred million dollars to return Russia's treasures to her soil, and in May the eggs had gone on exhibit in the Kremlin's Patriarchal Palace.

Da, this is good for my people. We must never forget our past glory.

Dmitri slipped through the hotel room door and turned the deadbolt. In the mirror next to the TV, he ran a finger along the angel-wing scar on his hip. The failure in his great-grandfather's milky eyes still plagued him. Dmitri knew, like Jacob of the Bible, that his quest was far from over.

He must still wrestle with angels. And with demons, if need be.

He wondered when Fort Lauderdale detectives would discover his latest victim. Locating the .22-caliber bullet in the old man's brain would be easy; finding a ballistics match would be the challenge. His was no ordinary gun.

Dmitri plugged in his laptop, holstered his cell phone on his belt.

———

"Your sister's always scored poorly, Mylisha. She's a sweet child. We both know it's true. She has other concerns, though."

"I think she uses it as an excuse, Mama. That's what I think."

Cross-legged on a lime green beanbag, Mylisha held the phone against her ear while painting her fingernails metallic purple. On the stereo, Kanye West was singing "Jesus Walks," pleading for God to show him the way.

"That may be so," her mother continued. "Regardless, the Good Lord's put you there for a reason. He knows you both need each other. Sure, Shanique's made some poor choices. She's not walking in the ways we taught her, but that gives you no right to place yourself in judgment over her. You hear what I'm saying?"

"I hear you." Mylisha turned down the music. "I miss you and Dad."

"We miss you too, sweetie. When're you coming to visit again?"

Mylisha's parents lived and worked in Santa Monica. After their daughters had graduated, they'd moved from Oregon in search of less rain and more income. They'd found the first in southern Cal; they still sought the second.

"I'll try to get a few days off during my winter break from school."

"Let us know. You take care, Mylisha. You're in your mama's prayers."

Mylisha dropped the cell phone onto the beanbag. She finished her nails, capped the container, turned up the music until the bass shook her apartment.

Why did the troublesome ones always get the attention? At home, in college, on the job, it was always the same; the squeaky wheels got the grease. Ever since their older sister, TraVonda, had gone off to the University of Tennessee, Mylisha had tried to pick up the slack—studying hard, working long, following her parents' rules. Even on the track, she'd trained harder than her little sister. But no matter how much partying Shanique did the night before, she was always right there, neck and neck at the tape.

"You wore me down, girl," Mylisha admitted to her empty apartment.

It was true: she'd given her sister that last race. If Shanique had trained half as hard, she would've dominated the track anyway. Mylisha had simply tired of competing with Shanique and her talent, with Clay and his dreams.

In addition, during that last year of high school, she'd been threatened into leaving Clay Ryker alone. Angry and scared, she'd tried to work out a deal, but it had backfired. Clay had been hurt, and she'd let him go his way. Only Summer Svenson had known the full account of her troubles.

Mylisha readjusted in her beanbag, turned on the TV. She found distraction in a show called *Beyond the Stars*.

———

Clay was channel-surfing from his bed. A mind-bending variety of channels clicked past. He stopped. Okay, this could be entertaining.

Beyond the Stars...

A prime-time special dedicated to numerology, astrology, psychics, and reflexology. No doubt Henna Dixon ascribed to this sort of stuff.

Clay scooted back against his pillows. Typically he shunned superstition, figured it was bad luck even to talk about such stuff—a wry smile—but the numbers had forced him to reconsider. He could no longer disregard the phenomenon; the repercussions had become all too real, and he needed some rational answers.

Of course, there was an easy solution.

No human touch. A boycott on all contact.

Whether a blessing or curse, he could just wash his hands of this responsibility. Who would believe him anyway? He couldn't deny the numbers, yet neither could he prove their existence. Certain things in life had to be accepted blindly.

Which just might be the point of this show.

Clay raised the volume, settled back with a drink between his legs.

The first study proved amusing. A professor passed envelopes to his students and told them to read their personal horoscopes within. Afterward, he asked them to weigh the information objectively and raise their hands if they thought, beyond question, it fit their individual situations. A majority responded. "Amazing," they exclaimed. "Like, omigosh, my life to a T." Others thought it fit, albeit with small discrepancies. Only one student believed it to be totally inaccurate.

In conclusion, the professor instructed the class to exchange and read one another's horoscopes. Titters of embarrassment and disbelief filled the room as the students realized they had all been given the same exact horoscope.

Buncha gullible people, Clay thought. *Just goes to show you.*

In another study, however, when a famed TV psychic was put to the test, he passed with flying colors. Skeptics were unable to prove any coercion or tomfoolery, and the psychic's knowledge about the studio audience's deceased family members was confirmed by further research.

Knowledge...the first seduction.

Henna's warning echoed in Clay's ears. He could still see her face at the Avon party. So innocent. So smug.

Following a commercial break, *Beyond the Stars* concluded that charlatans did abound. Apparently, though, there were others with certifiable paranormal abilities. The show's closing statement encapsulated Clay's confusion.

"In a culture grounded on empirical facts and scientific data, the hunger for spiritual meaning continues to assert itself." The sweater-clad host set a hand on a globe. "Some claim there is no higher power, no afterlife, nothing outside of that which we define with our five senses. Others claim that we're all part of a collective consciousness, that we limit knowledge by restricting ourselves to finite physical definitions. Perhaps in the future, brave pioneers of science and spirituality will join hands, leading humanity one step further along the path of progress, one step closer to harmony with our vast and expanding universe."

Heat coiled on Clay's palms. In the background he thought he heard the doorbell, but he focused instead on Henna's statement from the bus.

You will begin to know things. You'll feel them.

He was feeling things, all right, but he still knew next to nothing. Certainly not how to redeem his marriage. Or his ruined financial portfolio. Or his—

"Son, you in there?" Gerald pounded on the door. "Turn down that blasted TV. You got someone here needs to talk at you."

He opened the door, found himself impaled by his father's glare.

"Clay, what sort of trouble have you brought back into this house?"

Uprooted from his command post in the recliner, Gerald clearly felt justified in venting at full volume. He brushed past his wife and rumbled down the hall on his way to the workbench in the garage, his usual escape route.

Della mouthed an apology to Clay before nodding toward the living room. "He's in there. Please, for our sakes, don't say anything foolish."

———

Asgoth and Mr. Monde rendezvoused at the Long Tom Grange. Made famous—or infamous, some might say—by a local scandal, the grange had played host in recent months to a group of lighthearted, scantily clad gentlemen. Their calendar was a hot seller, and the middle-aged male models had welcomed their corresponding nicknames: "Mr. March," "Mr. June," "Mr. July."

"Which would you be, Monde? Could they have captured you on film?"

"I find that inappropriate, A.G. Not the slightest bit funny."

"You're more sour than usual."

"And you're more...incorrigible."

Asgoth looked forward to making his next announcement. Monde and Pristi had surprised him with news of the Brotherhood's reemergence; this now was his chance to catch his partner off guard.

"What is it?" Monde inquired. "You're hiding something. That much is obvious."

"We have a new arrival in town."

"One of the Brotherhood? Already?"

"No," Asgoth said. He gazed past the tree-shaded grange and a row of daffodils. Over the rise, fields stretched toward a row of foothills. "I'm speaking of your feared nemesis."

Monde huffed. "I fear no man."

"Well, he's certainly not much to look at. He's lost some weight, but he's still a hefty fellow. Used to be a boxer in his childhood days. Have you figured it out?"

"Sergeant Vince Turney."

"None other."

Monde's black brows furrowed. "But why here? Why now?"

"I'd like an answer to that myself."

———

Clay stood tall, then moved to meet this newest complication. Passing through the kitchen, he snagged two glasses and a can of V8. Nothing like hearty vegetable juice to chase off the guests.

"Mr. Ryker? You mind if I call you Clay?"

"Been called worse."

"Name's Vince Turney." A stocky man rose from the couch. "Call me Sarge, if you like. Mmm. You sharin' the V8? I'll take a glass."

Okaaay, so much for that plan.

Clay poured the drinks and, with mild awe, watched Sergeant Turney gulp down the swill. The man had deep-set brown eyes, dark, buzzed hair, and remnants of a double chin that leaped with each gulp. His utter lack of pretension appealed to Clay. He seemed close in age and came across like a fishing buddy, one who could give and receive attention without demands.

"So, Sarge, what's this all about? I did have other plans for the evening."

"Good question. And I'm sorry to be a bother. See, I'm lending a hand to the local authorities—a pinch hitter, a freelancer. When the police run short on experts or manpower, they call in an investigative consultant such as myself. Mostly I keep my business within the tri-counties. Used to be a cop not long ago. In Corvallis."

"Let me guess. A sergeant?"

Sarge cocked a finger. "He's no slouch, this one."

"You're too young to retire. Why aren't you still doing the police thing?"

"That's a whole other story."

"Okay. What about now? Can you tell me the reason you're here?"

"Well, truth is, I'm investigating an incident that happened on the other side of town. You heard about the older couple, Mr. and Mrs. Coates? Tragic scene. We're trying to piece together that night's events. Let's see." Sarge fumbled with a notebook. "It was a Thursday night. Actual time of death was early Friday morning."

6.3.0.0.4...June 30, 2004.

"I didn't know them," Clay said. "Not sure what you want me to say."

"Just checkin' each angle. The Coateses' case isn't the only one I'm involved with. Two weeks ago there was a vehicular homicide, also here in JC."

6.2.1.0.4...June 21, 2004.

"Summer," Clay heard himself say.

"Yes sir. Summer Svenson. Guess she'd been out at your place that night."

"Now wait a minute. I had nothing to do with—"

"Whoa, no one's accusin' anyone. Ease off the pedal."

"Then why are you here, Sarge? What's this about?"

Sarge raised both hands. "Connectin' the dots, that's all. Gotta trust me, Clay. See, I've got a personal attachment. I knew Summer way back when. Hadn't seen her in quite some time, not since...well, not since her sister passed away."

"Her sister? Milly? From what I heard, Milly was killed in a head-on collision a few years back. Some idiot teenager was reaching for a CD and swerved."

Sarge coughed into his hand. "Milly was my fiancée."

Clay swallowed. The room seemed to shrink.

"Life just keeps on marchin'," Sarge said. His deep brown eyes seemed to melt. "God's brought a new woman into my life by the name of Josee. Best thing that's ever happened to me. But this mess with Summer Svenson has set my mind aspinnin'. Lotsa heartache and memories. As you can imagine, Josee wants it settled before we can move on. Says it's best if I deal with it now rather than later."

"You think it's wise to mix your work and personal life?"

"My experience tells me they're often one and the same."

Clay thought about the headstones on his workbench, about the macabre events since his return. This investigative consultant had a point.

"I'm just tryin' to make sense of all this and see that justice is served," Sarge assured him. "That's my job whether or not I've got personal stakes. Both our tempers could run hot here, but I'm hopin' you'll work through this with me."

Clay sipped the V8. Was he a suspect in these deaths? He'd done nothing wrong. Whispering through his mind, from beneath the river's surface, dead pale lips told him otherwise. He was guilty. A sinner on a pilgrimage, stumbling along this path of absolution, forcing others—such as Jenni and Jason—to shoulder his shame.

A sinner…sinner…sinner.

"Clay, you say you didn't know the Coateses. Had you ever talked with them, by chance? Bumped into them?"

"No, of course not." Clay exhaled. "Okay, wait. There was one time. I ran into the old guy at Ace Hardware." When Sarge nodded, Clay got the impression it was information the consultant already possessed.

"You been by the train engine recently?" Sarge asked.

"Excuse me?"

"Engine 418. The one parked down at Founder's Park. You seen it lately?"

"In passing. Not something I pay much attention to."

"Did you know Mr. Coates was involved in its repainting project?"

"Before he died?" Clay tried to catch the words, but they were out of his mouth. "Sorry. Stupid question."

Sarge studied his notepad, scraped fingers over his short hair. "You know, Summer Svenson also visited the train. She was there mere hours before you saw her. She was seen touching it."

Touching?

This conversation was irritating Clay, digging beneath his skin.

"I guess I'm missing the connection," he said. "Where do I fit in, Sarge? This is all fascinating, gotta admit. But I'm afraid you're barking up the wrong tree. I had nothing to do with either of their deaths. If I could've stopped them, I would have. You have to believe me on that."

"Sounds convincing, Clay." Sarge peered up from his scribbles. "I'm even inclined to buy your story. There is one other item to discuss, though. See, while we were running a perimeter check at the Coateses' place, we found something in the flower bed beneath their bedroom window."

Clay folded his arms. What a waste of his time. He had things he could be doing, such as trying to protect an innocent boy from… *From what?*

Five days left, and counting down fast.

"Okay, okay," he said. "I give. What'd you find?"

The consultant slipped a Polaroid across the table. The photo bore a freshly penned case number and showed an oval belt buckle with Clay's name scrolled in silver filigree. He recognized it. Indeed, the buckle belonged to him.

16

The Stone Figurine

Clay felt like a crash-test dummy, slammed into the wall, disjointed. Head lolling. Quartered yellow and black circles dotting his lank frame like cross hairs in a sniper's scope. He was being set up. They'd put him in the driver's seat and claimed he was to blame.

He looked across the coffee table into Sergeant Turney's eyes, then looked away.

Shoot, maybe I am a...sinner. I know what you'd say, Dr. Gerringer. You'd dismiss my guilt as some outdated code of morality, but I can't shrug this off.

"So you admit the buckle's yours," Sarge said.

"I haven't admitted to anything. My mind's a blur right now. In fact, I think we'd be better off talking about this later."

"You look as though you've been blindsided by a truck."

"I feel like it. I promise, I haven't seen that belt buckle in twelve years."

"Twelve years, hmm? And where was that?"

Clay had last seen the buckle the day he and Bill Scott packed their clothes in the riverside bushes. In his rush after finding Bill's body, Clay had missed the belt as he dressed to go for help. Later the authorities had roped off the scene and refused to let him search for the item. When he tried to explain that it should be near Bill's clothes, a gangly, bespectacled detective eyed him with suspicion. "Clothes? We've covered every inch of the bank. Lotsa trash and beer cans—the usual junk—but we have yet to find a shred of clothing. You wanna revise your story?"

Sarge was less accusatory. "You with me, Clay? Anything you need to tell me?"

"I'm just trying to—"

"Get lost! That's what he's trying to tell you."

Clay snapped up at his father's voice. Gerald was standing with boots apart, his fists cocked and loaded at his sides.

"You listen here, Sergeant What's Your Name. We had our share of grief when Clay's friend died. Cops poking around. Questions and suspicion. My family's name was smeared, and that's something I don't take lightly."

"A man's name is everything. I'm just—"

"Got that right! Now I'm only gonna say this once. Get off my property!"

Sarge's jaw muscles tensed. Standing, he placed a business card on the end table and looked Clay in the eye. "You think of anything, anything at all, you call me at that number."

———

Beyond the Long Tom Grange's silhouette, sunrays retreated through the hills and scratched with spiteful orange claws at concrete-colored clouds. The breeze was picking up over the Long Tom River, sweeping the day's warmth into cellars of dusk.

Asgoth breathed deeply. Evening time infused him with life.

Despite the attempts to snuff him out, he was not dead. He had risen from the depths. Once he mined the riches of Engine 418, he'd be able to pay off the Consortium, and they'd be unable to overlook his resilience and ingenuity. Even Sergeant Turney's arrival would not dampen his mood.

Monde, too, appeared to be relishing the dusk. He stretched his arms, let the wind play over him. "A.G., you might be interested to know that I have the next date arranged. This one's required a fair amount of psychological testing."

"You're sure it'll work? Will the sergeant cause you any trouble?"

"It's time to set your doubts aside, don't you think?"

"You're right, Monde. Absolutely. Do you mind sharing the specifics?"

"The woman's name is Rhea Deering."

"She works in the tavern, right?"

Monde nodded. "Her expiration date will be the twentieth of this month. If all goes as planned, Clay Ryker will cross her path and take on the burden of her approaching death. The human psyche's made to take only so much. Let's see how he handles it."

"We'll make sure he has few options."

Naturally, Clay would still have freedom to choose his course and stand firm against their schemes, but how long could he rack up guilt before col-lapsing beneath its weight? No doubt, the deaths of Summer Svenson and the Coates couple had been persuasive. A young boy, though. That would push Ryker to the limits.

At thirteen years of age, Kenny Preston was on the small side. Easy prey. They'd shadow his activities, applying pressure and fear, then draw him into a final trap.

———

Over Wednesday and Thursday, Kenny sensed he was being watched. He saw movement from the corner of his eye, heard scuffles on the sidewalk behind his bike and down alleyways. Was he making these things up? Creating some summer excitement?

This morning on his route Kenny heard a car growling at him through the fog.

Okay, that was just silly. Blame it on his overactive imagination; as the only child of a single mother, he relied on it for adventure. Of course, he hadn't forgotten about his latest treasure hidden in the drainpipe, but his mother had been keeping him on a short leash. As if she knew there were something bad out there, something waiting for him.

I'm not afraid. Spymaster Kenny's no stranger to danger.

Kenny had been spending most of his time with Gussy. The puppy grew bigger by the day, nibbling on everything. Dribbling too. Mom said Gussy could sleep on Kenny's bed once she was housebroken. Until then, it was best if she slept outside, which meant the little girl needed a doghouse.

Kenny gathered scrap plywood from the garage. He had a saw, a hammer, a Maxwell House can full of nails. And forty-five dollars saved up.

So he'd lost his jacket. It being summertime and all, he wouldn't need a new one till school started. Maybe Clay Ryker still had the old one. He hadn't seen or heard from Clay since Sunday's call. The dude was probably harmless. Still, better safe than sorry—that's what Kenny's mom always said.

"Mom, I need to grab some stuff from the hardware store."

"You know I don't like you going out at midday. The traffic."

"I'll be careful. I'll use the crosswalks."

"Can't it wait?" She was slicing onions and carrots, then stirring them into a pot of simmering chicken broth. "I could drive you down later."

"I'm a teenager, Mom. All my friends get to ride around by themselves."

"I can't control what other mothers let their kids do."

Kenny eased alongside her. He knew she'd clamp down if he let his attitude slide. Better to work together. Do a little sweet-talkin'.

"Promise to play Scrabble with you after dinner."

"Kenneth, are you trying to bribe me?"

"I just need a few things for Gussy's doghouse. Won't take long."

"Scrabble? You promise?"

He crossed his heart, wore his most sincere expression.

"You'll go there and straight back?"

"Is that a yes?"

She swatted his backside with a hand towel. "Go before I change my mind."

———

Clay couldn't believe his luck. Or was it divine intervention?

There was Kenny Preston, up on the pedals, riding through the crosswalk.

Calls to the newspaper, Internet searches, visits to Nickel's Arcade, talks with Oaklea school officials—every effort to track down Kenny had come up empty. He'd called Kenny's number twice more, but he was sure the Prestons had caller ID and refused to answer unknown callers.

Stuck at a red light at Sixth and Ivy, Clay stared through the windshield. *I'll spook him if he sees me. Maybe I'll catch him as he gets off the bike.*

Turning right, Clay moved to the curb on Sixth. He idled the car, watched the bike cross over train tracks, pass the U.S. Bank and small gift shops. He edged back into traffic in second gear, following until Kenny parked the bike outside Ace Hardware.

Please, not here again. I don't even want to think about old Mitchell Coates.

———

Kenny changed his mind. This was a perfect chance to check on his treasure. He threw a leg back over the mountain bike and sped from the hardware store over another set of tracks. Swishing down through dry grass, he startled a snake. He ditched the bike, looked around, crawled into the drainage pipe.

Pebbles bit into his knees. Flies buzzed around a dead salamander.

He reached his fingers into the hiding spot, the hollow bubble in the metal, and felt the wooden tube roll away. He tried again and gripped the smooth surface.

He had it.

Spymaster Kenny squatted near the iron grate. Fearless, he ignored the wind that rustled through the grass outside and eyed the cork plugging the tube's end.

Once and for all, he would reveal the awful secret.

The Nazis' cause would crumble, their horrors would be revealed, and his girlfriend in the Resistance would come running into his arms.

The cork resisted his fingernails. He turned to his pocketknife for help. After a small squeak, the cork popped free and released a dank odor. The upturned tube spilled a stone figurine into the spymaster's hand, unlike any he'd ever seen. He wiped it with his finger, noticed it was a king from a chessboard.

Regal, slender, and black. Topped by an ornate cross.

"Kenny."

He jolted. His eyes panned down the drainpipe and saw a shadow blocking his only way out. He pressed back against the grate.

"Kenny, I'm not trying to scare you." Clay Ryker's voice reverberated along the pipe's expanse. "Can we just talk?"

"What do you want? Why're you tracking me?"

"You were riding across the street. Am I supposed to ignore you?"

Kenny clutched the king in his hand. "I've heard that car following me in the mornings, heard it with my own ears. Sounds like a growl."

"I drive a tan Duster, and it barely even purrs."

Kenny smiled, despite his distrust. "Then whose car is it?"

"That's why we need to talk. I think you might be in danger. Do you know any reason someone would come after you? Any reason at all?"

Kenny's pulse pounded in his neck, and the stone chess piece felt like ice in his hand. He pried his fingers apart, stared down at the black figurine. Was someone after this? Had they seen him take it from the train? That mysterious old lady had tried to warn him away, as though she knew something he didn't.

"I found it fair and square."

"Found what?" Clay asked.

Kenny looked up. Why had he blurted that out?

"Is that a king you've got there? It's beautiful."

Kenny thought of throwing the object as far as possible or of shoving it back into the hiding spot. Instead, as he looked down the length of the drainpipe, he met Clay's eyes and found nothing but genuine concern. Only a few other men had given him such a look, and only his uncle who lived up the McKenzie River had done so more than once.

"Listen, I'll leave you alone," Clay said. "I'm going back out, but I'll wait for a minute in case you wanna talk. If nothing else, you can have your coat back. It's in my car."

"The one that purrs?"

Clay grinned. "That's the one. I'll be outside."

Alone for a moment, Kenny slipped the king back into the oak tube, plugged it with the cork, slipped it into his pants. He longed for the attention of a father. Sure, his mom went out of the way for him, but what would it be like to have a man around?

Kenny felt his Adam's apple jump, the first time he'd ever experienced such a thing. His Mom was right; he was getting older, maturing into a man—like Joshua in the Bible. And a man would deal with this situation head-on.

Time to be strong and courageous.

"Anyway, Mom's gonna freak if I don't get back soon," he whispered to himself. "May as well listen to what this dude's got to say."

———

On his way home, Kenny replayed Clay's morbid warnings. The man had tried to sound calm but couldn't hide the intensity in his voice. He meant every word. He wanted Kenny to stay home and do nothing unusual or risky, particularly on Sunday. He even asked permission to swing by on that day to check if everything was okay.

And for some reason, Kenny agreed. He bought into Clay's every word.

Why not? It was basic eighth-grade math. All Kenny had to do was add up the note he'd delivered to Clay, plus the thing he'd discovered on the train, then multiply that by this suspicion that he was being spied on.

As Kenny came in through the garage, little Gussy yapped at his ankles, and his mother chided him for being late. He said he was sorry. Tried to act normal. Played Scrabble with her that evening and even used his tiles on a triple-word score to spell *phantom*. Mom still won, but it was his highest score ever.

He ruined everything, though, when he overreacted to her suggestion.

"Kenny," she said, "you're a growing boy with lots of energy. I have an idea for this Sunday. Of course I'd expect you to be careful, but I already talked to Uncle Terry. What if we drove out to his place after church and went inner-tubing?"

"On the McKenzie?"

"It's only a stone's throw from his back door. You'd have a ball."

Under normal conditions, Kenny would've whooped and hollered, but with Clay's warnings stamped into his mind, his suspicions had come alive.

"Are you sure, Mom? Isn't it kinda dangerous out there?"

"Don't remind me. I know it's hard for you not having a man around, and I'm trying to be better about not always fretting over you."

"Maybe we should skip it. Maybe some other time."

"Kenny?" Tears shimmered in his mother's eyes. "I thought you'd be excited about this." She stared at him with a dumbfounded expression, then rose to the kitchen sink and started on a stack of dishes. Her back was turned to him, but Kenny thought he heard sniffling.

In a rush of guilt and sadness and anger, he hurried down to his room.

17

In the Wreckage

Clay obsessed about the paperboy's well-being to the point of losing sleep. Recently the old nightmares had been creeping back in, hosted by blank-eyed cadavers and watery ghosts.

He confiscated a bottle of Baileys Irish Cream from his mother's cabinet over the hooded range, slipped into the darkness on the back porch, and filled a shot glass.

Took a gratifying sip.

The liqueur coated his throat with creamy warmth, heightened his introspective tendencies. He turned the shot glass in his hand; he had picked it up as a souvenir while on a basketball road trip with the University of Wyoming.

His junior year. Back when he was shooting well, still had the touch.

They were in Nashville playing Vanderbilt's vaunted team. Vandy was pulling away. Early in the fourth quarter, Wyoming made a comeback. They battled to within seven points. Their center scored again, then blocked a shot on the other end and launched the ball downcourt for a fast break. Clay Ryker streaked to meet it, took it for an easy lay-up, and got fouled.

At the free throw line, he had a chance to cap off this remarkable turnaround. To pull them within two. A one-possession ball game. The ref blew the whistle, handed him the ball. The crowd jeered, but he had learned long ago to feed off this collegiate bedlam, to convert the negative energy into focused determination.

"C'mon, don't be afraid." The Vandy point guard was leaned down, hands on knees, taunting in low tones. "You can't think about it. Just do it."

Like an incantation, these words conjured memories of the bridge. Clay blinked. In the stands, the faces morphed into wide-eyed blobs. Voices mocked and accused. His knees weakened. To corral his nerves, he spun the ball and lined up his fingers on the rough leather surface. Looked down.

He was cradling the lifeless head of Bill Scott.

He dropped the ball and, after the ref handed it to him again with a reproachful look, his opportunity to convert the three-point play turned into a new sort of nightmare. The shot fell short, scarcely nicking the rim; the team's comeback failed; the ride home was the longest of his athletic career.

Rolling the souvenir shot glass between his palms, Clay wondered if there were connections between his high school guilt, his college disappointment, and his present conflicts.

So far, three sets of numbers, three dates. Three dead bodies.

He ran his finger along the glass, sucked the sweet droplets from his skin, then made a decision to drink no more tonight. He walked down the steps, poured the remaining liquid into the weeds along the foundation. In an act that felt symbolic, he stepped beneath a pair of white oaks and flung the glass into the blackness on the other side of his parents' fence.

God, if there's any hope of saving this Kenny kid, I'm gonna need some help.

The prayer imbued him with a giddy sense of purpose. The numbers did have significance. They were a gift, which he would use. He would reach out to save a life—and perhaps his own in the process.

———

As instructed, Dmitri Derevenko had been waiting at Portland's Val-U-Inn. His pulse quickened when the phone on his hotel nightstand rang.

"Hello?"

"*Brat* Dmitri...Brother Dmitri, is that you?"

Dmitri recognized Oleg's choirboy voice, and he was amused by the salutation. In their language, *brat* meant *brother,* yet in English it meant *pest.* Perhaps this was a coincidence, but it highlighted the differences between two cultures. One could view a relationship as a bond, while another could view it as a nuisance.

"Da. I've been here many days already. I think I'll rot in this place."

"Don't lose patience. We're on the right path, moving forward."

"Is it wise, Oleg, to speak of this on the telephone?"

Oleg's wry laugh bubbled through the receiver. "In this country they think only of their own glories today. They take no time to appreciate the sacrifices of the past. Our goals are nothing but foolish talk here. The dreams of fools."

Dmitri grunted at this sentiment.

"We're making progress," Oleg continued. "But the trail's old, very faint."

"And the information I got from the former Nazi? Is it helpful?" Dmitri hoped the details given by the old Fort Lauderdale man were accurate. Both he and the victim had been grateful when the torturous questioning ceased.

"Without it," Oleg said, "we'd be at a dead end. Instead, we have hope."

"But you still haven't found whom we seek?"

"Nyet."

"I can't wait any longer. Please...pozhaluista. I need a task, something to do."

"Of course, Dmitri. This is why I've called you. You'll go to Engine 418 and recover the hidden object. It may be nothing important, a waste of time. On the other hand, it could be a vital link for tracing the imperial treasure and their bloodline."

Dmitri envisioned himself in Ekaterinburg, at the recently consecrated Cathedral-of-the-Blood. Built upon the ruins of the Ipatiev house where the massacre of the Tsars had occurred, the grand cathedral stood to honor the end of the Romanov dynasty.

He contemplated what would happen if, weeks from now, the Brotherhood addressed the media from those same marble steps. Ekaterinburg had been named after Peter the Great's wife, making it a place of destiny in Russian minds. What if Dmitri proved the bloodline still pulsed in human veins? Would Mother Russia open her arms to her long-lost son, embracing again civic, artistic, and religious expression?

"A Tsar might yet live," he stated.

"Da. Our rightful ruler."

———

Mylisha closed out her register, locked the night deposit in the safe, and headed back to her apartment. She parked on the back end so that she had to cut across the grass to reach her stairway. Although this route was longer, it circumvented the still visible stains on Maple Street. Nevertheless, her eyes wandered in that direction.

Inside, she programmed her CD changer to alternate disks after each song. With a bowl of Lochmead ice cream in hand, she kicked off her work shoes, plopped into her beanbag, and savored the first spoonful of chocolate and cookie dough bits.

"Mmm." She sighed.

Music swooned from the speakers with romantic tenderness, then took the hand of a deeper groove and began a saucy jaunt around the room.

She took another bite. "Mmmmm."

But no matter how hard she focused on tastes and sounds, she could not erase the desire to pick up her cell phone and dial Clay Ryker's number. She wanted to believe it was something more significant, maybe more spiritual, than a simple desire to find closure with an old flame.

Licking ice cream from the upturned spoon, she stared at her purple phone with its luminescent numbers. She tapped at the keys. Played a game on the screen.

She didn't hear so much as feel the heavy footsteps coming up the stairs.

She had been nursing a suspicion that Summer Svenson's death had been more than a horrible accident, more than an act of violent irresponsibility. Someone had been aiming for Summer, Mylisha was sure of it.

This same fear now played tricks with her mind.

In a flash she was out of the beanbag, dropping her phone onto the floor, and tossed the spoon into the sink and the ice cream container into the freezer. She snatched a knife from the block on the kitchen bar. She peeked through the hole in the door, saw a white guy in his thirties, in dark canvas pants and a striped red and white polo shirt. The distorted image made him look like a cartoon character stuffed into a crystal ball.

"Who's there?"

"Sergeant Vince Turney. Investigative consultant."

"What do you want?" She saw the man fumble to produce an official-looking badge. "How do I know that's real? You can get ones just like it at the dollar store."

"Got a few questions for you, nothin' more. Won't take much of your time. Has to do with the vehicular homicide that happened right outside your building. I don't think it was an accident, and I'm hopin' you might be able to help me."

His confirmation of her suspicions prompted her to open the door.

He spread his hands in playful reaction to her weapon of choice. "Cut to the chase? Is that your point?"

She rolled her eyes and turned back into the living room. She lowered the music, kept the knife beside her on the couch, gestured him toward the beanbag. He considered it with apprehension, then surrendered to her wishes. His weight splayed the lime green material so that he ended up tilted backward, to the left.

The guy deserved a point or two for effort.

"Not much of one for beanbags," he said. "They work better for you skinny folk."

Mylisha laughed, and their eyes met. "I'm Mylisha."

"Glad to hear it, or I've gone through this trouble for nothing. Call me Sarge."

"Want something to drink, Sarge?"

"Sounds good, so long as it's not V8 juice. Don't mind the stuff, but I got more than my fill the other night."

"Bottled water or Pepsi work?"

"Sure thing."

"Which one?"

"Hmm. Let's go with Pepsi."

Mylisha returned with ice-filled Portland Trailblazer cups. She wondered if notepads were still in vogue. The one propped on Sergeant Turney's knee reminded her of those '70s detective shows, whereas she would've expected a Palm Pilot tucked into a shirt pocket.

Sarge scored another point for old-school charm.

"Ah, that is good stuff." He took another long sip, with eyes closed as though he was enjoying an infrequent pleasure. "Thanks, Mylisha. Now the reason I'm here, if you don't mind me takin' up a little of your time, is to discuss your good friend. And before you get your hackles up, let me tell you, she was also a friend of mine."

"And you got stuck on the case? That's not right."

"I requested this one," he explained. "I'm a consultant. They turned it over to me a few days ago. Truth is, the police don't have a whole lot to go on, so the case's slipped down the list of priorities. But to people like you and me"—he tapped his fist against his chest—"there's nothing more important."

"You got dat right."

"And somewhere, there's one other person interested in this."

"The one who did it!" Mylisha spit out the words.

"There were no skid marks at the scene, no sign that the driver tried to swerve away or hit the brakes. I'm thinkin' an angry boyfriend. Or an ex."

"Summer had lotsa relationships. None of them what you'd call serious."

"Anyone else who might've had a bone to pick with her?"

"Sure." Mylisha's mind flipped through a stack of local names. "She kept a mental catalog of JC's secrets, and some people avoided her because she was a threat. A potential embarrassment, you know what I'm sayin'?"

"Did she use blackmail?"

"Sarge, this is my friend you're talking about."

"And I'm tryin' to catch the person who took her from us. Which means we've gotta go where the truth leads us. However close. However far back."

For the next thirty minutes, Sergeant Turney explained some of the steps he was taking in his investigation—from a countywide search of wrecking yards and auto-body-repair shops, to the questioning of family and friends, to a visit with an insurance-claims adjuster who'd helped narrow the hit-and-run vehicle to a mid-'90s Ford based on blue paint chips found at the scene.

"There you go," Mylisha voiced. "You've got the murder weapon."

"Wish it were that easy. Using a list from the police computer, I'll be goin' house to house, to every place with a registered vehicle matching the description. Got a guess on how many Fords there are in Lane County alone?"

Mylisha shook her head. She just wanted her friend back.

"More than a couple," Sarge informed her. "And that's assuming the perp's a local."

They continued to discuss the details preceding and following Summer's accident. Summer hadn't died until four days later, which had given Mylisha time to sit with her in the hospital. Mylisha had hoped. Prayed. Wept.

"Still feels like I failed her somehow," she said.

"Know the feeling. I sat with Milly for a day and a half. Not a thing I could do."

Mylisha thought it was strange how life brought people together. She could hardly believe Sergeant Turney was the same guy who'd been engaged to Summer's sister, but she did vaguely remember meeting him in passing four years ago. He'd been thinner then, although he wasn't bad looking now. Beneath heavy brows, his eyes were the color of rich and creamy chocolate.

"Got something for you," he told her. "Picked it up at the station."

"Thought you didn't work there. You said you were a consultant."

"Freelance, that's right. Make my own hours, go where I please. Despite the good share of ribbin' they deal out, they still treat me like one of their own. Has its advantages." He flipped his notepad to the back, produced a baby blue envelope from between the pages. "This is yours. They found it in the glove compartment of Summer's Honda Prelude. Been sittin' in an evidence box all this time, but I figured you might like to have it since it's addressed to you."

"To me? From Summer?"

"I can only assume."

"It's been opened."

"They checked it for possible clues, figured it was harmless. It's private, so I haven't read it, but one of the officers said it might be of sentimental value to you."

"Oh no you don't." Mylisha waved a finger, chastising herself for the moisture now collecting on her eyelashes. She pulled the envelope to her stomach, as she would a cold pack to soothe a wound. "You mean to tell me it's been just sitting there all this time? In the wreckage?"

Sarge nodded.

Suddenly his eyes widened, cut through with dark swirls. "For the life of me! Why didn't I see it before? The wreckage."

Mylisha waited, but he did not elucidate; he, too, seemed plagued by unanswered questions and past mysteries. She wished she could say something to help. She was a comforter, a nurturer; she was no good if she wasn't looking out for others.

"Your glass is empty, Sarge. Want a refill on your Pepsi?"

"S'okay." He tried to rise from the beanbag.

"You can take the cup with you if you want."

"Thanks, Mylisha, but I best be movin' along. Some stuff I need to check on."

18

Under Pressure

The next set of numbers broke the rules.

On his way to work, Clay grabbed his lunch sack from the fridge, brushed past his father at the dining nook.

"It's Saturday. Actually puttin' your nose to the grindstone, eh?"

"Only missed one day so far, Dad."

"Blomberg's a hard one to please. Don't push your luck."

Gerald popped the lid from his blue travel mug, letting his morning java cool. Forecast: scattered showers with partial clearing. He turned his attention to the *Register-Guard*, said as an afterthought, "Your mail's by the phone, certified letter from Wyoming. Signed for it yesterday afternoon."

Clay trudged back into the kitchen. He'd already returned the last set of documents—with a few contested points. He tore at the flap as he headed outside, found a list of concessions and counterpoints from Jenni's lawyer, followed by a deadline for Clay's final response.

Warming up the Duster, he stared at the papers. He felt paralyzed by inadequacy, by pride and a sense of injustice. He had an urge to fly straight to Cheyenne.

Not that Jenni would soften if she heard his apologies or pleas for forgiveness.

Was there any hope of stopping this marital train wreck?

Clay knew better. His continual calls had elicited no replies. His son's postcard from Yellowstone was the lone strand tying him to all he held dear while these tedious legalities sawed away, severing the cords of his family. With all his might, Clay had swung the sword of human endeavor and found himself flailing forward when it bit into nothing of substance. Now he was falling upon his own blade.

Where's God in all this? Does he know I exist down here?

Clay warmed at the thought of seeing Jason in a month. Jenni was worried about letting their son ride the Greyhound or Amtrak alone, so Clay had split the cost of an airline ticket with her. Jason would fly into Eugene the second week of August, in time for the Scandi-Fest. He'd stay through the rest of the summer.

Clay fanned the court orders and let his fingers move down to his son's name.

You're a good kid, Jason Alan Ryker.

Hot and razor-sharp, the ink stabbed upward through Clay's skin. Touch receptors fired. His brain received signals that defied biological explanation.

8.1.0.0.4...

He yanked away, his fingertips aflame with the uninvited numerals.

That's a day before the festival starts. The day Jason arrives!

Was there no escape? Clay had come to accept these expiration dates on human skin—no matter how illogical—and he'd found ways of insulating himself against this knowledge. Here, though, the numbers were presenting themselves through an inanimate apparatus. Despite his efforts, the curse seemed determined to assert itself.

Or perhaps it was a gift. Could he, with this information, circumvent death's design and distract the Grim Reaper from helpless souls?

Tomorrow he would have his answer. With the paperboy.

———

"You all right there, Ryker?"

"Fine."

"Been awful quiet all day." Digs was picking at his ear, his finger buried in white tufts of hair. "Something to do with your wife or kid—that'd be my guess."

Clay moaned under the weight of a blank granite headstone. Stored against the wall at his back, it jutted into his path. As he shifted it toward the corner, a nub of his glove caught beneath the rough-hewn bottom and pulled away from his hand. He set his bare palm on the arched granite, tipped it to remove his glove, but it crashed back, cracking the surface of another stone and spraying jagged chips.

"Careful," Digs said. "Gotta stay tuned in or you're liable to hurt yourself."

Clay glanced at his arm. By cinching his sleeves to his elbows in the early afternoon heat, he'd left himself vulnerable to the rock shard now protruding from his skin. Blood, mixing with shop dust and dirt, formed a spongy gasket around the wound.

Without pain or emotion, he eased the shard from the gash.

This, however, was not his focus.

His fingers, once again, had extracted death dates from a lifeless object. On the blank granite, he had discovered a set of numerals without any apparent connection to an individual. Perhaps this stone would be assigned to an upcoming victim's grave.

Whoever it was, he or she would be breathing their last in ten days.

July 20, '04... Again, the digits reached the same total as the others.

"Better clean 'er up. Last thing you need's an infection."

"Be back in a few," Clay said.

He steered past Digs on his way to the first-aid kit in the bathroom. Mentally, he turned over the details at his fingertips. This was crazy. People did not die only on dates adding up to thirteen.

In horror movies, maybe. By design of some psychopath, possibly.

Not here in the real world.

He splashed water and disinfectant over his wound, ran his hands under the faucet until the heat became too much to handle. He could not burn away the latest numbers. They throbbed, more persistent with each pump of his heart. Neosporin and a Band-Aid provided physical solace, nothing more.

He leaned on the bathroom sink and stared into the mirror. A quick look at the facts: one, people were dying; two, he seemed to know beforehand; and, three, the narrow scope of dates indicated intelligent manipulation.

Maybe I'm to blame. I caused one person's death years ago. Why not others?

The notes were right; he had tried running from his guilt over Bill. Despite his hand in the death, he'd remained "scott-free," innocent in the eyes of the law.

The latest note had consisted of threats against Kenny Preston—"I have pressed on"—and used symbolism of trains and railways.

Engine 418. The old war-horse downtown.

How did it all tie together? Sergeant Turney had mentioned the engine's involvement in his investigation, and Kenny had found a lost object aboard, but Clay knew of no reason for a connection.

Speaking of which, how had his belt buckle ended up on the Coateses' property?

Clay returned to his workbench, snugged his gloves back on.

"Need some space to breathe, is that it, Ryker?" Digs studied him. "I know how it is, sharin' a roof with the old man. Gets to you after a while. You ever need a place to sack out, you're more 'n welcome at the Digs estate."

"Appreciate that, I really do. But I'm more trouble than you deserve."

———

Mylisha dropped groceries at Shanique's place, basked in the giggling hugs of her niece and nephew, gave her wild-haired and sleepy-eyed sister a kiss on the cheek, then headed down the street for a solitary walk in the Rose Gardens.

College kids tossed a Frisbee in the late afternoon sun. An ancient tree with knotted limbs so heavy they required bracing provided shade to a couple on a blanket. A gaggle of elderly ladies pointed and paused between rows of fragrant roses.

Mylisha smiled yet knew her pleasure was vicarious.

She found an unoccupied bench that faced the river. Across the wide waters, Valley River Center served as a shopping haven and mall-rat paradise.

In her hands the baby blue envelope addressed to her offered a link to her deceased friend. She'd left it unopened last night, denying its finality. Her heart still pulsed with hope that Summer would skip through a door and admit her death had been an elaborate hoax.

The greeting card made a shushing sound as Mylisha slid it out. Summer's handwriting looped across the paper, carefree and alive.

Girl, we've been together through thick and thin. Don't pay any attention to what I said about you in the park. You're not boring. You think
I'd still hang with you if you were? Hellooo!
    I stopped by Clay's tonight. Stupid idea, I know, but I've always

had a thing for that guy. Don't worry. Nothing happened. He's still twisted up over his marriage, and I got the idea you still mean a lot to him.

Pretty obvious that some people never wanted you two together. You know the things Bill Scott tried to do, but he wasn't alone. He had help from that freshman chick he was dating. What a freak! And from that older guy who kept hanging around, the one who worked down at the lumberyard.

Should've told you this earlier, I know. But it's not like it would've changed anything. I mean, who would've believed us? Seemed better to just keep my trap shut and not make any waves. Might be good for Clay to know. He'll be mad, but at least he won't feel as bad about what happened, if you know what I mean.

Mylisha, you should be the one to tell him. I think he needs to hear it from you.

Anyway, girlfriend, just wanted you to know that we're still…

Friends Forever,
Summer

Mylisha chewed on her bottom lip. These were matters best left alone.

Years ago, with God's healing and cleansing, she had managed to bury the fear. Once in a while though, it came back to whisper cruel threats in her ear, to reach violating hands into her thoughts. She owed it to Summer to consider the card's words, but it would be so much safer to ignore them altogether.

Mylisha tucked the envelope into her purse, strode back to her sister's place. Shanique was in bed. The kids were planted in front of the TV, laughing between bites of Cocoa Puffs.

They seemed content. Which irritated Mylisha.

Why had her sister's choices proven so successful? Mylisha had tried to walk the line, to do what was right, but she questioned whether God was even watching. Why was she the lonely one? Her soul bore wounds she could not understand.

She drove over the Jefferson Street Bridge to the mall at Valley River. She needed something new—or something ancient and tested. Why hesitate? This could be a return to her tribal roots. Since the beginning of time, mankind had consulted the skies for answers; they'd relied on signs in nature, in God's handiwork.

Was a horoscope or astrology chart any different? Mylisha ached for guidance and God's will. Maybe here at last she would discern answers for her life. She shoved aside doubts to the contrary.

———

Clay's workweek was over, but he wasn't ready to end it in seclusion at his parents' place. He'd had more than enough of his father's testosterone-heavy sneers and his mother's subtle conniving. He needed an evening out. Away.

Even if it meant risking contact with others.

Saturday night at the movies? He liked the sound of that.

He checked the Internet from the computer in the Glenleaf front office, found a listing for *Spiderman 2* playing at Valley River Center. He'd have just enough time to grab a bite at the food court.

Less than half an hour later he was in line for Sbarro's pizza. He found himself watching the mall's bevy of young women in hiphuggers. On high heels, they marched the walkways, an army of shoppers with loaded purses and credit cards slung over their shoulders.

Best-looking troops he'd ever hope to see. What would it be like to enter the battlefield once more? He missed the touch of a woman. How long had it been?

Get a grip, Claymeister. You've still got a ring and a beautiful wife.

With eyes down, he carried his pizza to a table and ate alone.

———

The mall provided Mylisha a diversion. She browsed clothing outlets, dreamed of new furniture arrangements, listened to demos of the latest CDs. She had a specific destination, though. The other stores were links of a chain, encircling and dragging her toward a place she'd long avoided.

Time to tap her soul's connection with earth, wind, and sky.

She scooted through the food court, eyes straight ahead on the tiled floor, determined to let nothing dilute her newfound resolve.

Wait up, girl. You should plant yourself in a seat and rethink this.

Mylisha lifted her chin and marched on.

———

This wouldn't be the final act, not even close. Nevertheless, it would be sweet.

Hidden in the darkness, Asgoth paced by the Preston home on Oak Street, enamored with the golden glow oozing through the curtains and the muted yelps of Kenny's puppy. A sadistic grin was carved across his lips. He wished he could knock on the front door and enter. He considered it but reminded himself it would be futile.

Asgoth pulled down on his argyle vest. He must wait.

Hours remained before the proper date rolled into position on the calendar. For a bit longer, that runt of a paperboy would be safe in his bed.

19

The Creature

The basement bounced the alarm clock's sounds back and forth over Kenny's head. This wasn't like him to wake up late. Grownups were always talking about being tired and stressed. Was this what they meant?

Sunday again. Big newspapers.

And big trouble, according to Clay. Kenny wanted to discount the warnings but couldn't shake them from his skull.

He shut off the alarm and stared into the darkness. He could feel moisture in the air, indicating it'd rained during the night. One of his favorite T-shirts said, "Oregonians don't tan. They rust."

Kenny loaded his shoulder bags and wheeled his bike through the side gate. In the drain from the roof gutter, water rumbled and sluiced onto the driveway, carrying leaves and worms and acorns. Junction City's streets glistened.

"Kenny."

"Clay. You sure you wanna do this? You don't have to, you know."

Clay wore a hooded sweatshirt over rain gear. He unloaded a ten-speed from the trunk of an old beater and pulled on a pair of biking gloves. "Would it seem strange if I said I think it'll be fun? Always wanted to have a paper route, but sports kept me too busy when I was a kid. My dad had me trying everything—basketball, baseball, football."

"My dad's in Alaska."

"For how long?"

Kenny adjusted his helmet. "He's been gone since I was little."

"Just you and your mom, huh?"

"And Gussy, my dog."

"Did you tell your mom about me?"

Kenny noticed Clay's furtive glances up and down the street. He knew this was the guy's real purpose in being here, to serve as a bodyguard. Not that Kenny needed it, but he wasn't going to complain, uh-uh. The streets did look a little spooky this early; plus it was nice to have a man who was concerned. Not to mention, he could use an extra hand with the Sunday editions.

"She'd freak if I told her. 'Don't talk to strangers,' and that sort of stuff."

"Good advice, Kenny. Especially today."

"You're serious about this, aren't you? Hafta admit it seems kinda wacko."

"What about the lady and the note she had you deliver? And that chess piece you found on the train engine? How do you explain those things?"

"Dunno." Kenny hefted a saddlebag for Clay's use. "Here. You can cover one side of the street, and I'll cover the other. I'll let you know which houses have special instructions. We get lucky, we might even find a tip."

"See? I knew this would be fun."

Clay's face did not match his words as they pedaled into the street.

———

On the back porch of a house on Juniper, Asgoth was nearly finished with his trap. At his side he knew Monde was fine-tuning his plan, a mechanic of the mind calibrating psychological tools for maximum effect.

Behind them, a dog growled. Claws raked along wooden gate slats.

Asgoth shivered. "I know he can't hurt us, but that thing scares me to death."

"No need to worry, A.G. As you've marvelously demonstrated, you're able to survive almost any danger."

"Absolutely. But there are some I'd rather not experience firsthand." Asgoth crouched near a welcome mat, adding last-minute details.

Monde rattled the fence, and the deep-throated beast went wild.

"Would you quit that?" Asgoth shook his head. "I already told you—"

A lock snapped like a branch in the morning calm, and the neighbor's back door slammed into vinyl siding as a stubble-faced man thrust his barrel chest outside. Windows quivered in their panes, and the light fixture over his back door plummeted to the cement pad in a burst of frosted glass.

"Shut up, you stupid dog! See whatcha made me do?"

A low snarl escalated into one sharp bark.

"Just won't listen, will you? Filthy, no-good mutt!"

Behind the wooden slats, the man appeared to move through time-lapse frames. He wore cowboy boots and no shirt. Curly chest hair sprouted with vigor around the straps of his coveralls. Cursing, he swung back a leg and shot the boot's toe into the animal's ribs. Did it twice more.

The dog slunk to the ground, growling, tail tucked—but eyes ablaze.

"That'll teach ya to shut your pie hole! I'm tryin' to get some sleep here."

Asgoth peered over at Monde. His partner was a statue of intense thought, black hair lacquered to his head, sharp nose pointed forward. One hand covered his mouth, but there was no shock or sympathy behind the gesture. Instead, for the first time since they had worked together, Asgoth heard Monde start to giggle—the sound of a bird, high pitched and mocking.

The irate neighbor was headed back indoors, grumbling all the way.

Monde grabbed at the gate. Rattled it.

Again the dog went berserk.

———

Dmitri Derevenko entered Junction City from the north. He passed a church with a Scandinavian windmill on display, then spotted Safeway and Papa Murphy's pizzeria.

These small towns amused him, wearing facades of respectability, while behind closed doors immorality played across plasma TV screens. No different than in Russia. Modern technology had paved new roads for age-old perversion.

He thought of the Cuban. And the old German.

His bullets had brought their lives to an end, but didn't the Scriptures make it clear there was a time to kill? For the common good, evil men must be removed.

I'm one of the good Russian men. The Brotherhood will do what it must.

Dmitri pressed his palm against his hip. The angel there, carved from flesh, accompanied him every step of his journey. She justified his actions, held his hand as his victims tried to inhabit his waking dreams. Although destiny wore him down at times, he felt comforted by the angel's presence.

Following MapQuest directions, he arrived at the site of Engine 418.

The tender car and cab gleamed beneath a fine mist while plumes of fog around the huge iron wheels gave the illusion of steam. Encircling the beast of burden, the fence seemed a grave injustice.

Dmitri parked his rental car and approached. He bowed once before attempting to scale the metal bars, but the bars turned to molten lava in his hands. He pulled back. Scorched.

He tried again at a different spot. Same reaction. Again.

Five minutes later he roared like a creature robbed of its prey.

———

"We're almost done, I hope."

"Couple of blocks left." With Clay looking to him for instruction, Kenny felt a glow of pride. "Here, let me show you how this house works. We gotta go to the back."

They propped up their bikes and went around to the back porch, where flowerpots lined the railing and wind chimes jingled. On the ground, a fuzzy mat welcomed them.

"Paper goes here?" Clay asked. "On the mat?"

Kenny nodded. "And look, we got our first tip of the day."

He lifted an edge of the mat to reveal a pack of watermelon Koolerz. At the same moment, he caught the shifting of a shape behind the wood slats next door, but he knew better than to let that Rottweiler scare him. The gate was always locked.

"Leave the gum alone," Clay said.

"These people're okay. They've left me stuff before."

"Don't touch it. Look at the powder around the edges."

Kenny frowned at the pink-tinted dust sprinkling the pack. Strange. Maybe his protector had a point. As he stood and turned, he bumped into an earthen pot that seemed intentionally placed in his way. It wobbled and then toppled from the rail. Shards of red pottery scattered over the walkway. In his attempt to catch the object, his head brushed a wind chime, and the metal tubes rang with chaotic frenzy.

The dog came unglued. Behind the fence, a territorial growl built into aggressive, fang-tipped barks. The Rottweiler's anger was unlike anything Kenny had seen. Jaws snapped; slobbering lips peeled back, ripe with rage; large paws backed by muscular shoulders pounded against the gate.

Ka-clickk...

In the moment before the gate crashed open and the animal rocketed into full view, the tinny sound of the releasing clasp swept over Kenny's arms, combed through his hair, shoved the breath back down his throat into his lungs.

Kenny stared in denial. "That gate's always locked."

Although he trusted Clay's intentions and enjoyed the male attention, he had resisted, until this second, the reality of any deadly danger.

"Get behind me," Clay ordered. "And run!"

———

Clay had already decided to protect Kenny Preston at any cost. To lose the kid would be to lose his own peace of mind. His past, his present, his foreboding future would collapse into one heap upon his head, crushing him.

But he'd never counted on a dog entering the fray.

On a logical level, Clay understood Rottweilers were not inherently evil. He could hear Dr. Gerringer explaining how the fear mechanism triggers a knee-jerk moral opposition to the source of one's fear—*if it scares you, it must be bad.* Clay also knew dogs' protective instincts were beneficial and often desired.

On a visceral level, however, this beast sent shudders through his limbs.

His senses went into overdrive: the taste of battery acid in his mouth; the touch of sweat droplets beneath his rain gear; the sound of cracking gate slats and grinding pottery beneath his feet; the smell of wet, musky fur, as the black and brown creature hurtled into the open...

And the sight of a rake poked down into the grass.

Clay scrambled across the wet lawn, slipped to one knee, got his fingers around the handle. The Rottweiler was charging, claws tearing up clods of mud.

Clay yanked on the garden implement, but the metal tines bit into the turf. Rebutted by his own strength, he was pulled forward and off balance. He landed hard. The rake's handle was underneath him. He rolled. Twisted the tool from the earth so that it lay atop his chest like a spine ripped from an enemy carcass.

The dog was upon him. Curved nails slammed into Clay's thigh, thrust through his weather gear by rock-solid canine muscle. Above his throat, ropes of saliva dangled from snarling jaws.

He shoved the rake upward, and the Rottweiler's fangs clamped down on the wood. The dog stumbled against this impediment, momentum carrying him up and over. In a black blur, the body hit the ground and skidded beyond Clay's torso.

Clay clambered to his feet as the dog did the same.

The next attack was a blast of energized fury. Kill or be killed.

Clay drew back the rake, spun its unyielding metal prongs into position, and swung them with every ounce of his strength toward his relentless foe. He alone stood between this creature and a thirteen-year-old boy. He alone recognized that death was here on this early Sunday morning, stalking on paws and four legs.

No room for mercy.

7.1.1.0.4...

"Not today!" he screamed, arching the heavy tool through the air.

The dog's speed was explosive. He came in low, entering the circumference of the swinging rake. The force of Clay's own motion spun him around; in a whirl, he corkscrewed on sturdy legs, a matador avoiding the blood-tipped horns of a bull.

The Rottweiler lunged past. One tooth snagged Clay's skin, tore at his forearm.

He felt nothing. He was in the heat of battle.

To his horror, he watched the animal sprawl on the rain-slick lawn, catch itself with massive paws, then turn its broad head toward a figure in the driveway. The creature had found its original, more manageable target. The throaty bellow of a maniacal murderer could not have sounded more bloodcurdling than the growl he now heard.

"Kenny!" Clay was appalled by the kid's lingering presence. "Get away!"

He couldn't wait for Kenny to respond. He had to intervene. He pursued the accelerating killer across the backyard, but the dog was built for short bursts of speed, and Clay was losing ground. He was running low on options.

In three deliberate, turf-grinding steps, he cocked the rake back over his head and windmilled it forward. The metal tines became predatory claws of a dinosaur. Clumped weeds and roots flew from the rake like eviscerated entrails from its previous feasting.

Down, down, toward the racing animal.

He couldn't let the Rottweiler reach the kid. Kenny would be shredded.

Extending the man-made claw to its limit, he realized he would be short of his target, unable to detain or destroy the marauder. He let the rake fly. It scraped and thudded along the beast's rippling back, producing an enraged yelp and a backward snap of fangs. Fell useless to the dirt.

Kenny remained frozen in the path of destruction.

20

Dog Day Afternoon

Dmitri wiped his greasy hands with a wad of paper towels. He stood over the trunk of the rental car, a white Taurus, and dropped the towels beside his ice chest. Disappointment squeezed his stomach. He had tried to search Engine 418, with less than pleasing results.

Almost a week in Portland? Inactive.

Now this opportunity to further his preordained purpose? Interrupted.

He'd questioned the validity of any old Rasputin curse, but the strange reaction at the fence had convinced him. Lenin himself had left an object on this Finnish locomotive; yet pressing concerns and early successes had distracted the man from later tracking it down. The secret had remained dormant until recent studies brought its existence to light. Without delay, Brotherhood forces had squelched this revelation and schemed to make the object their own.

Dmitri was called forth, delegated, and deployed. An agent of destiny.

I've followed instructions. Here I am, in Junction City, halfway around the globe.

"And a foolish curse holds me back?" He shook his head at this absurdity.

His outburst startled an elderly woman plodding along the sidewalk. She drew her leashed dog near and lifted it to her chest, eyeballed Dmitri as though he were an animal abuser deserving severe punishment.

"I apologize if I frightened you." He reached into the ice chest, peeled a lid from a thin tin can. "Would your pet like a pickled herring?"

The woman's mouth crinkled with cynicism, while the Chihuahua made no attempt to hide perked ears and flared nostrils. It began to whine.

The woman took one step back. "What's that you have there?"

Dmitri relaxed his facial muscles, opened wide his blue eyes—the epitome of a kindhearted dog lover. He moved toward her, herring can extended.

"Your pet is welcome to eat. I wonder…you must know many things about this city. Perhaps you have knowledge of this train engine?"

"Walk by it every day. Have for years."

"Is it true? Rumors about Lenin on Engine 418?"

"Those aren't rumors, my boy. Those are well-guarded secrets. I've been keeping an eye on this train for a long time. For ages, it seems."

———

Astride his mountain bike, Kenny watched Clay's valiant but failed attempt to protect him. He should've run, as Clay had insisted. But how could he leave behind his new companion?

Kenny chose instead to stay. It was what friends did.

Now he realized the foolhardiness of his choice. Too late to escape. If he took off at this moment, he might get twenty yards. By that time, the Rottweiler would draw even with him, clamping teeth into his leg and bringing him down.

Kenny brandished the bike pump. He could use it to swat the beast away. *Yeah, right!*

He dropped the pump, leaned low over the bike, used his thighs to propel him headlong on a collision course with the dog. Better to face his attacker than allow it to catch him from behind.

Speeding forward, he zeroed in on the creature. He heard men's yells, but they accomplished nothing. The dog was still coming at him.

The Rottweiler leaped. Kenny hunched his shoulders, lowered his helmeted head between the handlebars, drove a knobbed front tire into the heaving tan belly. Strands of drool lashed his chin; fur and claws blurred past his face. A crushing weight careened into his back, then tore free on its way down to the pavement.

The bike wobbled and collapsed beneath him.

Kenny, powered by adrenaline, paid no heed to the pebbles in his kneecap and elbow. He scrambled and felt Clay's large hands lift him to his feet.

As he whipped around, he was certain the Rottweiler would be pouncing at his thirteen-year-old throat. He braced himself. Tensed every muscle. His imagination ran wild with movie-generated images as the noise of claws tearing into asphalt awakened primal fears.

He was screaming.

But he was unaware of it until a sound much louder cut him off.

Planted in the neighboring gateway, a man wearing cowboy boots and coveralls lowered a sleek black handgun. He hooked a meaty thumb around a shoulder strap, spit with distaste into the dirt at his feet.

"Friggin' waste of a dog! A full-on, mind-blowin' waste."

Kenny was still wary. He stared at the immobile form.

"Count yourselves lucky," the man grumbled. "I'll never know where she got it, but that dog was born with a mean streak. Woulda killed ya and been downright proud of it." He scratched at his chest. Cursed. Considered the dead animal in the driveway. "Think you two can help lift her into my stinkin' garbage can?"

———

Dmitri Derevenko reevaluated the white-haired woman. "You are...a guardian?"

Standing no higher than his chest, she wore an overcoat, a jewel-encrusted brooch, and a set of silver wire bifocals. Nurse's shoes cradled small feet, while knee-high stockings appeared content huddled about her ankles. Her furry companion was on the sidewalk, lapping sauce from the bottom of Dmitri's fish tin.

In this country Dmitri knew that the woman would be viewed with ridicule and condescension, whereas the matriarchal underpinnings of his country demanded he show respect. He felt an urge to bow.

"A guardian, oh yes. But a cranky one," she confided. "It's a thankless task."

"Who has given you this..." He searched for the word. "This commission?"

She made the sign of the cross, lifted her gaze heavenward in reverence.

"You're doing this alone? Or do you have help?"

"Don't be silly, my boy. I'm old, tired, and impatient." She swept opaque violet eyes across Founder's Park and its environs. "I could not hold them off on my own."

"Who?"

"Not so loud. You can't see them, but they are close."

Dmitri experienced a first tinge of skepticism, mixed with sympathy. He commiserated with her desire for significance and worried that years from now his own lost dreams might push him over the edge into decrepitude. *Da.* It was harsh enough when a body turned on itself, but a mind crumbling beneath the weight of dissolution…

Stop such absurd thoughts, he warned himself. His dreams were close at hand.

"If I wait, will I see them?" he asked.

With a finger to pale lips, the woman leaned forward as though to reveal a mind-altering revelation. "They are invisible."

He decided to play along. "Do they ever go on the train?"

"Of course not. I will not permit it."

"Because you are a guardian."

"One of many jobs I've held. I'm not incapable, you know. Cranky, yes. But I already mentioned that, did I not? Pay better attention, if you will. I say things once, and once only." She gripped her tuft of chin hair, shifted her eyes over Engine 418. "Oh, there's something I'm forgetting. Yes, that naughty little child…Kenny Preston."

Dmitri tucked in his shirt. A man preparing to leave.

"He's unruly, I tell you—climbing on the fence as though it were a playground, gallivanting about the train. Such behavior is prohibited, but he's shown a flagrant disregard for the standard proprieties. Even taken something that was not his."

Dmitri froze. "What's this thing he took?"

"Well, can't say I got a good look at it. But he absconded with it, that he did."

"How do you know this?"

"Because it's gone, of course."

"Of course. And he lives nearby?"

"What concern is that of yours, my boy? Your question is irrelevant, and I would not tell you if he did. Perhaps I've said too much already." The woman gasped, then covered her mouth. Her Chihuahua yapped. "Oh my, now they've seen us."

"They?"

She pointed a pasty, translucent finger.

As Dmitri suspected, the street was devoid of strangers, hostile or otherwise. He turned to leave, saw the old lady's lips twitch with secretive glee. He hoped that, despite her addled state, she had guided him in the right direction.

Kenny Preston. He must find this boy.

———

His mother's calm demeanor surprised Kenny. Was she not seeing, not hearing? His clothes were torn, his knees bloodied, his bike scratched up.

Sure, a route overseer had delivered the rest of his newspapers, but a Rottweiler was dead. Earlier, a stern police officer had stopped by for clarification of the events at Juniper Street. The man in the coveralls was facing questions of animal cruelty and unlawful use of a handgun within city limits.

C'mon, Mom. You're s'posed to freak like never before. You all right?

She had both elbows on her knees, hunched forward on the sofa, warming her hands around a cup of Stash tea. Her light blue eyes blinked behind the steam. Her lips blew softly, cooling the liquid or getting rid of tension. Maybe both.

"Thank you for saving my son's life, Mr. Ryker." She turned her face toward Clay. "I'm glad there're people like you left in this world. Sometimes you wonder."

"I was there and saw the dog get loose. Didn't even have time to think about it."

"No, you're selling yourself short. You didn't have to do what you did."

"Yes," Clay said, "I did."

"Well, it was very brave of you, Mr. Ryker. Really it was."

"Just Clay. Please."

"I'm Kate Preston." Her eyes dropped to his ring, to the bandages that wrapped his forearm and his thigh, then shifted back to the tea. "Kenny tells me you'd like to stick around for the afternoon, keep an eye out for him."

"Uh, well. I'm concerned about him, I guess."

"Might be nice, actually. That officer seemed to think you were an okay guy, and as a mother, I tend to worry myself silly over my son."

"I have a son too. Couple of years younger than yours."

"Well then, you understand. But you've done more than enough already. Look at you. Are you going to survive?"

"What? These tiny scratches? They look worse than they are. I mean, those EMTs acted like they'd been insulted by showing up for such minor injuries."

"Eight stitches." Kenny whistled in admiration. "You're a hero."

When Clay lifted his face, his chiseled cheeks glowed as if he'd turned toward a spotlight. The corners of his mouth stretched into a smile of relief, and he took a deep breath. Chuckled. Kenny reached forward, and they knocked fists together. Clay laughed out loud in the sitting room, a healthy, rippling sound that splashed over Kenny's darkest fears and disappointments.

He liked having Clay in the house. He understood now why his mother hadn't gone ballistic. It was this guy. Here. Within arm's reach.

There was one way to keep this going.

"Anybody for a game of Scrabble?" Kenny submitted.

"Scrabble? With my injuries? You'll have an unfair advantage."

"Yeah right, dude. So whaddya say, Mom? We already missed church anyway. Can he stay, just for a while?"

"For a while?" Kate's eyes glimmered above her smile. "Is that any way to treat a hero? I think he deserves to stay for pot roast and garlic potatoes. But don't say a word about the blackberry cobbler. That should be a surprise."

When Kenny opened the back door and watched Gussy bound back inside to join the party, he thought life couldn't get much better. From one extreme to the other? Within a few short hours?

He poured the Scrabble tiles on the table and wished he could use more than seven letters in a turn. He had a perfect word for the day: *unpredictable*. Too bad the word was a full thirteen letters long.

What a pest this kid had turned out to be. Kids were always a challenge.

Asgoth smiled at Monde's perturbation over the failed dog attack. Hadn't he suggested a simple poisoning? As a killing machine, how predictable was a dog? Plus, you could never guess a human's response to such an assault.

Clay Ryker. He was the obstacle, as well as the goal of this charade.

With him gone, I'll get the key from the train and the funds to go on. I'll buy back my honor.

Asgoth sent Monde on his way, then hurried along the street to the uneven stairs leading up to his place. He had a few props to collect; the day was not yet over.

In his apartment Henna was waiting with candles lit and incense burning. Her tank top was tie-dyed, her skirt thin and cerulean, swishing along the rug as her bare feet danced to Tibetan rhythms and chants. He watched with pleasure the way her hair caressed her shoulders and neck. Although her eyes were half-closed in apparent revelry, he sensed a striving in her demeanor. She was reaching for, but not grasping, something beyond herself.

This was the moment he loved most—her straining, her desire.

"Henna."

"Oh, at last. How long've you been here? I should've felt you in the room."

"We have a few minutes together," he said. "Then I'll need your help."

"My help?" She sounded eager.

"Over at the Preston place."

"If that's what you wish, A.G." She spun once with arms extended, eased into position on the gold shag carpet. "If it means striking back at Clay, I'm open to whatever you have in mind."

———

Through the front window, Kenny could see evening creeping into town. He hoped his mom would let Clay stay longer. She was in the dining room talking with the man, giggling about something, while dishes remained on the tablecloth.

That was a good sign. Very unlike his mother.

Kenny squelched any long-term hopes, though; Clay wore a wedding ring. Would his mom ever remarry? She knew her husband was gone for good. The few reports from Alaska had him involved with loose women and barroom brawls.

I'll kill him if he ever comes back and hurts her again. What'd she ever do to him?

"Going outside," Kenny muttered as he passed through the kitchen. "Gonna see how Gussy's doin'."

"She can come back in," his mom said. "So long as she's settled down."

"I'll throw the ball with her, help her get out some energy."

"Stay in the backyard. Don't be out too long."

Kenny slipped through the door. A storm was gathering, and a breeze rustled the tips of the bougainvillea along the fence. Birds shuffled between trees; moving as one, they dipped and gyrated across the gray black screen of cloud, like a computer cursor in the hand of a preschooler.

"Gussy? Where are you?"

The back fence creaked in the evening wind.

"Gussy, girl?"

The gaps in the fence revealed movement and shadows, and he trembled as he recalled the Rottweiler's attack. He almost turned back inside.

But where was his puppy? With his saved money, Kenny had finished building a doghouse near the garage, and now all it needed was paint. Gussy was nowhere near, though. Had she dug a hole? Found a gap in the boards?

He trotted around to the side gate. This is where he'd packed the newspapers only hours ago. The ground was still soggy. He searched for claw marks in the dirt along the bottom of the wood. Zippo.

Tacked to the inside of the gate, a lavender sheet of notepaper nabbed his attention. He tore it free. What was that smell? Like Cherry 7-Up.

His heart jumped as he read a threat against his missing puppy. There was only one way to get her back, the note said, and that was to shut up, get on his bike, and go to Engine 418.

What was it about that train? Was someone after his discovery?

Kenny crumpled and tossed the note against the house. *Somebody has Gussy!*

He debated going inside for Clay's assistance but decided against it. The note said to tell no one. Kenny had already seen one dog die today; he couldn't risk letting his little girl get hurt—or worse.

Anyway, Clay Ryker had done his good deed, keeping Kenny out of danger. Now it was Kenny's turn to be a hero. For Gussy.

His bike was in working condition, a little scraped, in need of adjustment, but ridable. He eased it from the garage into the street and strapped on his helmet. He looked back once at the front window, at the serene light that glowed from within, then rode into the gathering night.

21

On the Wrong Track

"For real, baby. A girl can't *find* no better sister."

"What time do you plan on getting back, Shanique?" Mylisha cleared glassware from the counter, put a can of Pringles on an upper pantry shelf. "I have classes tomorrow, and I'm behind on homework as it is."

"Be back when I be back."

"I'm not joking. What time?"

"Why you hafta be like dat? You know I can't give you no answer."

"Sure you can." Mylisha turned to scold Tyrone. "Honey, you can't be fiddlin' with my stereo. Tell Auntie what you want to hear, and I'll play it for you."

"Mylisha," Shanique said, "what's wrong wit you? Why you be stankin'?"

She raised a hand. "It'll be all right. Just go."

"I was plannin' on chillin' here for a few, wit you. My big sister."

"I've got my own stuff to think about. Go. Do what you gotta do."

"Well. Tell you right now, I ain't gonna worry *my* black butt over you, that is *for* sure. I ask if you's gonna watch the kids, and you says yes. Now I'm s'posta be all up and feelin' sorry for you. No, girl, that ain't how this gonna work."

"Go! All right? Shake that ghetto bootay, do your thang. We'll be fine."

Shanique looked ready to explode. She cocked her head, then waved off her own emotion. "You know, baby, I ain't gonna let *your* frustration ruin *my* night. This girl's goin' dancin'. You wanna stay wound tight, you do dat. I be krunkin' while you sit 'n pout." She gathered her kids in her arms, planted wet kisses on their cheeks and eyelids. "You listen to yo auntie and be good, you hear? Mama'll be right here when you wake up. Sure 'nuff, do *love* my babies."

Going down the stairs, Shanique's heels clicked with staccato precision.

"Why's my mama leavin'?" Tyrone demanded.

"She has to work, honey. Gotta make money so she can buy you two some new clothes when school starts."

Tawnique's six-year-old smile spread from pigtail to pigtail. Tyrone scowled.

On the street below, the angry sound of their mother's new Mustang faded.

Mylisha set her niece and nephew at the kitchen table with a margarine tub of crayons and a pad of construction paper. She perched on a barstool with a college syllabus in her lap. Hidden between the pages, an astrology chart awaited.

This, she knew, was the reason behind her petulance. So she'd driven off Shanique a few minutes early. What did that matter? She didn't need her sister's happy-go-lucky attitude shoved in her face, and she didn't want Shanique telling her "it's about time you came around" or "I told you so."

Life's a mystery. Least mine is. Just looking for a little direction, that's all.

———

Clay found the wadded note in the grass along the fence.

"His bike's gone," Kate Preston exclaimed from the side door of the garage. "I'm going after him."

Clay clutched the note in his fist and hopped into his Duster before she had a chance to stop him. There was no time. The earlier attempt on Kenny's life had been diverted, but this was an obvious setup. Why else would it be happening today?

He revved the engine and skidded forward on a layer of burning rubber.

7.1.1.0.4...

He angled toward the park. The numerals sloshed over his nerve endings. Eight days ago he'd chased the kid from his parents' front porch, grabbed his arm, sensed the dates on his skin.

Wax...hot and dripping, sluicing over his palm in precise patterns.

No! I'm coming for you, Kenny!

Clay had been wrong to doubt Henna. This seemed obvious now. On the Greyhound she had imparted to him a gift, an ability to discern the parameters of mortal life. So the lady was eccentric, but that was no crime; here, near Eugene, it was commonplace. At the Dixon house he had suspected her, yet even his mother vouched for her innocence. Henna had shrugged him off so he'd accept the gift on his own.

I accept, I accept! I can't just sit by and watch a kid bite it.

As the Duster barreled down Sixth Street, Clay thought of Kate Preston. She was playfully shy and pretty in a natural, no-frills way. Her eyes were pale and blue, marked with the clarity of a person nourished by organic foods and vegetables. She seemed dedicated to her son and dismissive of her husband's philandering, a church-bred woman struggling between godly intentions and human desire.

Back at the dining table, Clay had felt Kate's yearning. He'd soaked up her giving and nurturing gestures, aware of his own similar struggles.

"What's Kenny up to?" he had said. Finding refuge in this concern. An escape.

"Good question," she'd replied. Also using the diversion.

Together they'd searched the backyard, then realized he was missing.

———

Dmitri bemoaned the time wasted on that old woman's guidance. He had tried the phone book, the Internet, the local hangouts...

He still had not found this Kenny Preston.

Did the boy understand the significance of his discovery in the engine cab? Where had he taken the object?

Wandering now, driving the streets of Junction City, Dmitri found himself back on Greenwood. He turned past the Viking Sal, aimed back toward the acclaimed train. For years this town's citizens had functioned without knowledge of the secrets in their midst. How could history remain so quiet in the face of the future's barrage?

Indeed, the Brotherhood of Tobolsk had nearly become a relic of the past; without a burst of fresh wind, their coals might have burned out completely.

We have risen again. Da. A new Tsar shall ascend.

Dmitri liked to imagine he could feel such wind—whispering over his face, assuring him of his place and purpose, nudging him along the correct course.

The flapping of angel's wings.

Straight ahead in Founder's Park, he saw Kenny Preston. Of course he had no guarantee this was the same boy, but he knew it in his bones.

The angel had guided him.

Dmitri watched the child dismount a bike and face a woman with a squirming puppy in her arms. In the darkness they exchanged words. The woman lifted a hand at an awkward angle, and the boy's eyes bulged in horror. Behind the iron fence, Engine 418 stood in silent witness, a ghost eavesdropping over the small boy's shoulders.

———

"Please don't hurt her."

Kenny hated to give in. If he were a real man, he wouldn't let his voice get shaky like this. But what could he do? This woman, the same one who'd given him the note to deliver last week, had a syringe poked at the scruff of Gussy's neck. Between strands of puppy fur, the silver needle glinted.

Oblivious, Gussy wriggled, but she was small and easily contained.

"We know you found it," the woman told Kenny. "Now take us to it."

"What're you—"

"Don't waste time. You know what I'm talking about, the thing from the train."

"Promise you won't do anything to Gussy?"

"Now isn't that a darling name." The woman's thumb stroked Gussy's neck.

"Gimme five minutes, and I'll bring it straight back."

"Nice try, kid. I have a daughter, so I'm more than aware of how your scheming minds work. See the liquid in this syringe? It's a stimulant, designed to reawaken a larger animal after it's been sedated. A lion maybe. Or a rhinoceros. Administered to little Gussy, it'd be like a drug overdose, quick and deadly, frying her little brain."

"What do you want then?"

"I want you to take me to it, your stolen treasure. When it's in my hands, you'll get Gussy back."

"That's it?"

She nodded. "Is it close enough to walk?"

"Uh-uh. It's actually... It's a long walk from here. I didn't want anyone finding it."

The syringe pried at Gussy's loose skin, lifting brown fur.

"Okay," he said. "I'll take you. But can I ride my bike?"

"On foot is better, don't you think? Let's go. You lead the way."

Kenny stared up from under the rim of his helmet. This morning he'd overfilled his cup with excitement. Now, without Clay around, Gussy's survival seemed more important than some old wooden tube and a stone chess piece. What'd it matter if he handed them over?

"Fine, lady, have it your way. Just leave my dog alone."

Kenny saw Clay's car creep around the corner of Sixth and Holly. Yes! He had hoped Clay would track him down, but he couldn't let Gussy's captor catch on.

"Stay back," he wanted to shout. "Don't let her see you."

He ambled across the grass, but his eyes roved the area. On the opposing corner, a white Taurus was pointed this direction, and a large man was getting out. With the blond woman a half step behind, Kenny walked in the direction of the easterly railroad. He'd string her along, then throw her off track.

If he could just figure a way to free Gussy from her grip.

"Kenny Preston."

Spoken in an accent, his name reached across the park to him.

"Kenny."

In midstep, he glanced back to find the man from the Taurus heading his way. Arms bulged under the dude's jacket, and his neck spread down into his shoulders. His hand was a baseball mitt, dwarfing a silver cell phone. He was speeding up.

"You are Kenny Preston? I must speak with you."

Kenny flinched. The blond woman turned, annoyed by the interruption, and she, too, gave a nervous blink. At Gussy's neck, the needle pulled away a fraction.

Now! Be strong and courageous!

In a single motion, Kenny grabbed for his puppy with one hand and jabbed away the syringe with the other. The lady snapped around. In her haste her fingernails dug into Gussy's underbelly, and the puppy yelped. Small teeth flashed as Gussy's blunt head whipped around and clamped jaws into vulnerable flesh.

The woman cried out.

The syringe bounced off the curb, and Kenny saw a beaded strand of pale yellow liquid drape through the air. He heard Gussy's teeth tear at the woman's blouse. Another cry. His puppy landed on the sidewalk in a knot of legs and fur, gathered herself, and sped off across the street.

Kenny chased after her. A protective response. A mindless act.

From the corner of his eye, he noted a black shape, headlights, and spinning wheels. Brakes shrieked. He accelerated, felt the concussion of air as a Ford Mustang skidded sideways and ground along the curb. The door popped open. A black woman stepped out on high heels.

Appearing stunned, the blond woman was glaring at Kenny over the car roof. Farther back, the dude with bulging arms was jogging forward.

"Whatcha all doin'!" the Mustang's driver yelled. " 'Bout ran over you, you hear what I'm sayin'? Buncha crazy white folk tryin' to get their selves killed."

Kenny had seen enough. Or not enough.

Gussy was gone.

He took off, his mind loaded with questions and options and a list of changing priorities. His mother had been drilling into his head that he had to choose what things were most important and deal with them in that order. But how could he prioritize his own safety, his puppy's whereabouts, and the growing number of people who seemed drawn by his secret that lay hidden in the drainage pipe?

His feet slapped the road. He cut down an alley, eyes probing the darkness, every gap and doorway, for his pet. Maybe Gussy was safer somewhere else.

Just stay hidden, little girl. I'll come back for you.

He veered right, back toward the tracks. Shouts chased him along.

Jesus, where do I go? I'm freakin' here!

Behind him another car was coming. He leaned into the storefronts, avoiding the curb and any likelihood of being run over.

Briefly he was out in the open, thudding up the berm to the railroad. Far away the nightly high-speed train whistled. At his back a car horn blared.

Kenny went into high gear, determined to outdistance and outmaneuver his enemies. The spymaster recognized this was no ordinary danger. Vital supplies lay hidden, threatened by Nazi infiltrators and turncoats. His tennis shoes loosened as they ate through weeds and chunks of cracked asphalt. He had reached the tall weeds at the ditch's edge. His laces were coming undone—not that it mattered. This was it. The spymaster was back at the safe house.

The drainpipe was a dark cavern, waiting to hide him. The grass flattened ahead of his flying feet, but his shoes lost their purchase. He landed, bumped down the incline on his backside. Throwing himself forward, he crawled into the pipe, and his helmet bumped the metal. Stones chewed at his knees. He pulled himself deeper into the darkness.

The pipe shivered with the weight of a car overhead. Dirt and dust trickled down. Kenny held his breath. Who was up above?

Never mind, Spymaster. Get the treasure. Lives're depending on you.

Yet this was no childhood game. This was different. What if he did have enemies intent on his destruction? Didn't the Bible warn that Satan was "looking for some victim to devour"? Earlier, had that Rottweiler been turned loose on purpose?

You're my protection, Lord. Isn't that right? My high tower.

The tower… *Hey,* he realized, *that might work.*

He could race back to the JC water tower, spy down on his enemies, and stay out of sight. Looking for a kid, they'd never think to look up. Yeah, he liked it. He could run in a crouch down the ditch for part of the distance, then hop back over the tracks. He'd do it at the last second, letting the passing train cut off any pursuers.

"Kenny, you down there? Hurry, they're headed this way."

"Clay?"

"It's me. Come on out."

———

Clay, from the seat of his car, had watched the whirl of events.

Narrowly missing Kenny and his dog, the black Mustang had slid to a stop—a perfect chance for Kenny to get away. And out jumped Shanique. It had been years since he'd seen Mylisha's sister, but her long legs and flirty fashion were still the same.

He knew the other woman as well. Even as Kenny took off running, Henna tried to move past Shanique and found herself face to face with a fit and street-toughened woman. They were like two old foes. Their voices escalated.

He did not know the man in the European-style jacket.

Clay had an inkling where Kenny might be headed. With the prominence of Engine 418 in these strange dealings, Kenny would be worried about the object he'd found on board. He'd rejected Clay's suggestion of turning it in to the Junction City Historical Society, said he wanted to investigate it himself first. Clay, once an adventurous boy himself, had given grudging approval.

The drainpipe. That's where the kid was going.

So as not to attract attention, Clay fought his urge to punch the gas pedal through the floorboards, chose instead to roll along Sixth Street, a law-abiding citizen.

The streetlights painted the road in yellow green hues. The high-speed train's distant cry was the one harsh note in the town's nightly orchestra of life.

Sure enough, Clay spotted young Kenny sprinting along the sidewalk and over the tracks. *The kid has some wheels on him, that's for sure.*

Clay cruised over the humped pavement, sped down after his charge. He braked to a halt atop the drainpipe. The ditch bristled with crackling weeds and tossed Dari Mart cups. An abandoned shopping cart lay rusting on its side.

He jumped out and crouched above the pipe's opening. He yelled through cupped hands, received a response of relief. Behind him a car was approaching.

"It's me," he assured. "Come on out."

Items clattered in the hollow space, then Kenny's head poked into view. He had the wooden tube clutched in his hand. "They want this. That's what they're after. I don't get it. What's so amazing about some old chess king?"

"You could wait and ask them." Clay jabbed a thumb down the street.

Kenny's eyes widened at the approaching Taurus. In his pupils the railway lights sprang to life, warning of the fast approaching train. Bells rang, and the painted crossing arm made a jerky descent.

The Taurus swerved around it.

"Get in the car, Kenny. We'll lose 'em."

"In this old beater?"

"Hurry!" Clay offered a hand to pull Kenny up and over the drainpipe's lip.

Instead, Kenny pushed forward the carved oak object, and Clay's hand clamped around it, brushing the kid's skin. The confirmation of today's date stamped down into his palm, shooting messages to his brain that he refused to acknowledge.

"You take it," Kenny said. "They'll think I have it."

"What?"

"Go. I'll meet up with you later. Put it somewhere safe."

"Nope, we're not going with that plan." Clay threw a glance back. Behind the windshield of the Taurus, the husky man from the park jounced as his tires clattered over the tracks. "Come on, get in the car."

Kenny took off along the drainage ditch, his helmet bobbing and weaving.

"Kenny! Get back here!"

The kid slithered through curtains of dry grass, loose white laces trailing, arms pumping, feet threading between obstacles of debris and stone. Clay started to hop down after him, then second-guessed the idea. If he pursued Kenny, the man with the European jacket would do the same. They'd be in a footrace.

Clay hitched his legs back onto the pavement, slung himself into the Duster. He jammed the wooden tube into his front pocket, crunched down on the accelerator, felt the car respond and shove him back in the cushioned seat. In the rearview mirror, he waited for the Taurus to pursue him, but instead it slammed to a halt at the drainpipe.

Had the man seen Kenny? Seen his escape?

Clay ran his eyes back along the ditch. Through the thickening darkness, he could make out the kid's head above the weeds.

"No, no-o, *no-o-o!*"

He tapped his brakes, spun the wheel, yanked on the emergency brake. The Duster slid, wobbled, and rocked, then squealed around so that it faced the way he had come. He pressed the gas, but the engine had cut out. He fired the ignition, sped back toward the Taurus. He'd ram the thing off the road if he had to, but he could not let that man reach Kenny.

The train was screaming now in warning. Lights blinked. Klaxons jangled.

Clay saw the man drop into the ditch, and his heart punched into his throat. He threw his car into Park, clawed his six-foot-three-inch body from the seat, clipped his head on the frame.

"Dang it!"

He vaulted after the man. Landed hard on the rocks—twisting. A pain shot through his ankle—burning. He ran on. No time for delays.

Kenny Preston. He's all that matters now.

Ahead, the husky man's elbows churned. In the darkness he was no more than a bisected torso and head floating over the weeds. Why did he want Kenny?

Far ahead, the boy was climbing from the ditch, feet kicking up gravel. He crested the embankment. Disappeared for a few seconds behind a concrete bunker of some sort, then shot into view near the tracks.

The train's whistle was the diving shriek of a thousand birds of prey.

Kenny was the hunted.

The kid hesitated at the railway ties that were thick as his waist, then stepped over the first track. What was he doing? This was no time for fooling around.

"Kenny! Get off there! *Run!*"

Clay wasn't sure if his voice was heard over the blaring dissonance. Did Kenny even see him down here? Was he aware of his other pursuer? The kid remained frozen on the tracks, his face turned into the night train's blinding light.

7.1.1.0.4...

The digits carved and burned along Clay's nerves.

"Don't mess around, Kenny! *Go!*"

The train powered onward, painting Kenny's face in an unnatural light so that it appeared to be floating in place, preternaturally pale, blurred at the edges. His hair lay limp over his head. His eyes were mesmerized orbs absorbing the glare.

The high-speed train had killed others here in JC and in Harrisburg. Most victims were homeless or inebriated; on occasion, fools tried to beat the train across, toying with tons of hurtling metal and steel. During high school

Clay had lost a pair of classmates to such an event. Their funerals were closed-casket ordeals.

"Kennny! Kennnny!"

He yelled the name until he was hoarse. He understood the kid's strategy—trying to lose his pursuer, staying on the tracks until the last moment—but this had reached the point of insanity. The ground shook with the train's sheer weight and velocity. The crossing lights threw shifting shades of color across rock, grass, and pavement.

Was Kenny finally moving? The husky man's nearing shape seemed to stir activity, but Kenny remained in the train's path.

An image of those trailing white laces crossed Clay's mind. Was the kid stuck?

Clay clambered onward. Tears streaked his cheeks. Or maybe it was the rushing wind causing him to tear up, maybe high pollen count. His shoes stumbled over garbage and pebbles. The distance was too great. He was useless.

A final glance provided images that would never go away…

Hollowed by dread, Kenny's eyes turned dark.

Ghostlike, his mouth gaped wide.

The train, unable to stop, blasted through the space where the boy stood as though he was nothing more than air. There was no cry of anguish. No sign of tattered clothes or torn limbs. Nothing. In a moment that came and went, the metal swallowed every last bit of evidence of a child named Kenny Preston.

22

Skin to Skin

Asgoth reveled in the moment.

The kid had played right into his hands, racing through the ditch, dragging Clay Ryker in his wake. On the railroad ties, Asgoth had sprung his trap—with a finishing touch from Mr. Monde.

Now from the other side of the tracks, through the moving frame of the train's rushing wheels, he observed the gray white pallor that permeated Clay's face, as though a bucket of paint had been dumped into his skull. He saw eyes of horror blink with tears, saw trembling arms tighten in a self-preserving embrace.

See now, Mr. Ryker. It'd be so much easier to do as I suggest...

Sacrifice yourself so others might live.

"You are appalling," Monde said.

"Why, thank you."

Asgoth wished the Consortium's other members were present, but with Monde as his partner and witness, they would receive a full report. How could they deny his influence in this town? He was on a roll.

He'd made one mistake, though, which he hoped would go undetected.

"You're certain it'll work, A.G.?"

"What? Now you're questioning my abilities? Look. Clay is devastated."

Once again Clay stood at a calamitous scene, unaware of all that was involved. In some cases ignorance was bliss. In Clay's case it was torture.

"Truthfully," Monde said to A.G., "that ranks as the most horrific scene in which I've seen you play a part."

They stood in darkness, pressed against a factory's corrugated siding. The heat of the day still resided in the metal, comforting, familiar. Storm clouds continued to coil and rumble, as though this summer night was developing a case of indigestion.

On the tracks the night train had finished its transit through town.

Searching in its wake, the large man who'd pursued Kenny picked at stones and dirt, ran his eyes along the street.

"Are you aware," Monde asked, "of this man's identity?"

"The one from the Brotherhood?"

"Dmitri Derevenko, a fourth generation acolyte. He arrived earlier today. Or didn't you see him?"

"He's come for one thing, hasn't he?" Asgoth said.

Mr. Monde nodded. "But after your repulsive display, he'll fear the object is gone forever. Torn from the heart of one train. Cut off by the passage of another."

———

Clay's legs were sodden tree stumps that he dragged back through the ditch. Breathing heavily, he reached his car—his parents' car, technically. Ha. See, this just proved it. The junkyard car served as evidence that his life was a pathetic joke. "Ha!" he said aloud.

He brushed dirt and weeds from his pants, smirked at the husky guy who was pacing the railway on a hunt for things he would not find. The man was in obvious denial. Well, there was no denying what had taken place up there.

Clay's quivering fingers snatched the keys from the ignition, shoved them into his pocket—next to the oak tube. Was this the object of the man's search? Was it worth driving a helpless kid into the path of a train?

With a finger he wrote in the dust on the back windshield: *Steal this car!*

Come on, he dared the man on the tracks. *Search the car. Steal it, for all I care. But you're not getting this! It belongs...uh, it belonged to Kenny.*

He walked back along the street. Avoided the crossing arm. Stepped gingerly over the rails, eyes fixed on a lighted sign a block ahead. His foot stumbled against uneven concrete. He tripped. Laughed out loud.

Okaaay now, Claymeister. Get a grip.

A pay phone caught his eye. Not that it'd do any good, but he dialed 911.

With that superfluous little formality aside, he plugged on to his destination. Just a bit further. He could make it. He'd done his duty, done his best. He was done.

Down for the count... Over and out... Never again... Enough is enough...

A simple little word, so rich with meaning and devoid of confusion.

"I'm done," he called out into the night, convinced for the first time in his life that no one was listening.

Ahead, a sign with a blackbird indicated he had arrived at his destination.

—

"Ryker? Well, of all people."

"Figured I'd drop by."

"What brings you here? You don't look so hot."

"There a rule somewhere says I can't stop for a drink?"

Wendy's laugh was carefree. "Of course not, silly guy. Just didn't expect to see you in this place. Thought you steered clear of the Raven." Free of her Glenleaf Monument garb, Wendy was a different person. Beneath the tavern's haze of smoke, her teeth were radiant, and her hair was pulled up into a bouquet of feminine curls.

"Hey," he said, "I do have a life, you know?"

She cupped a hand to her ear. "What?"

"I said, I do have a life."

"Relax, stud muffin. Wife or no wife, we're just two adults talking at the bar."

"A life!" he corrected.

She winked. "Heard you the first time. Here, belly up."

He threw a leg over a stool. On the Raven's karaoke stage, an overweight woman in skintight jeans and a red Aerosmith shirt belted out a tune. He wasn't sure if her voice was off key or if the low ceiling's acoustics were bad.

Either way, he needed help. He ordered Jack on the rocks.

"Nicely done." Wendy nudged his shoulder with glossy fingernails.

He looked down, worried by the thought of skin-to-skin contact. But, hey, what was one more expiration date? Here a death, there a death, everywhere a...

He accepted the first drink and tossed it back like an alky falling off the wagon. Not that he'd know. The trick, he told himself, was to drink lots of water with a couple of Tylenol before he collapsed into bed tonight. Least that way he'd wake up half alive. Half human.

"Another one just like it," he told the bartender.

The man complied without a glance and left out the whiskey bottle. Clay sipped once, swirled the ice, then swigged down another fiery jolt, courtesy of Mr. Daniel. His throat burned, his insides warmed up, and his tongue probed the space around his teeth.

"Want nachos to go with it?" the bartender offered. "Jalapeño cheese sticks?"

Clay declined. He spotted gray strands woven through the man's slicked-back hair, guessed that each one represented a sob story he'd endured while behind the counter. Clay had no plan of dumping his own woes—not here, not now. He needed sleep. An alcohol-assisted, no-tossing-no-turning, twelve-hour shot of nighty-night.

"Listen, Ryker," Wendy said. "I've worked with you, what, two or three weeks? You're standoffish. That's your business. Got a lot on your mind—that's clear to see. But I can tell there's something else bugging you tonight."

He tapped the bar for another drink. He looked at the lights above the mirrored shelves. Man, was it just him, or was it warm in here?

"Is it just me?"

"Excuse me?"

"Never mind." He snickered. "I interrupted you."

"No, go ahead. Seems like something's worrying you, that's all."

"Me?" A choking laugh. "I got nothing left to worry about."

"What?" Wendy tipped her ear closer, and her hair tickled his cheek.

He said, "There's nothing left to—"

A fist of grief clamped around his neck. He swiveled away toward the stage.

At a pool table, a tattooed man in a dazzling white cowboy hat threw his hands together as his girlfriend took her turn in front of the karaoke monitor. She curtsied, blew him a sassy kiss, then swayed her hips to a Shania Twain hit.

Clay swallowed the remainder of his third drink. Like liquid Drano, it burned a hole through the clogged emotion in his throat. He liked that. He wanted nothing more than a reprieve from his guilt. It'd haunted him all these years, eaten away at his personal confidence and business intuition. In this last hour an even more heart-stopping scenario had flooded over his memories of the river.

See how easy that was? Out with the old, in with the new.

He was d-o-n-e. Time for someone else to shoulder this awful gift.

You hear me, God? Don't need it, don't want it, gonna make a mess of it anyway. Why give me something I can't control?

No answer.

"Whaddya think, Wendy? You think I can control it?" He turned on the stool, and the room stutter stepped to keep up. "Whoa." He snickered again.

"Take it slow," she said. "We've got the whole night ahead of us."

He waggled his finger. "Naughty, naughty. I know what you're thinking."

The bartender caught his eyes, hefted the whiskey. Clay nodded. This guy was good, right on top of it. See, that was how the best ones made their tips. Clay gave the guy a wink of thanks before emptying his tumbler.

"Lookin' nice," he heard himself tell Wendy.

"What?"

"Nice. You. The little skirt and, you know"—he waved a hand over his head—"the hair."

"Really? You like it?"

"Mmm. Definitely."

Was he the only one who thought these lights were turned up too high? Wasn't there a dimmer switch? The music thumped through the countertop beneath his elbows. He held the tumbler to his cheek, relished the condensation's cool drops, and wondered where this encounter with Wendy was leading. He wrapped his right hand around his ring finger.

Why? Was he clinging to, or hiding, this token of marriage?

Wendy crossed her legs and leaned into him.

His first thought was to withdraw. He slipped his hand onto her shoulder, wanting to push her away. Wanting to draw her closer. He'd survived the past few weeks on a strict regimen that denied all human touch, and he longed for it. Desperately. Yet, his lonely bachelor-boy status had made him wary of female contact, and he was familiar with biblical warnings about loose women whose "steps lead straight to the grave."

8.1.0.0.4...

There they were, as expected. Numbers. Wendy's dance card with the Reaper. But why pay any heed? He washed his hands of this.

Hands...touch. Clay craved the comfort of warm skin.

Jenni had turned her back months ago. Filed the papers. Left him on his own. Now the sickness of divorce ate at his soul, gnawing at his moral fiber.

He could feel it: *nibble, nibble, nibble.*

He looked over at Wendy's sleeveless shoulder. Her skin was warm. Before he could lift his chin, Wendy dipped and found his lips with her own. Beneath a hint of barley and hops, her mouth was soft, nipping at his skin.

Nibble, nibble.

He pulled back, chuckling at this image. He dropped his hand to his side. Anyway, it all felt forced. Unnatural. His head was spinning, and heat was burning over his cheeks, down his neck.

"What now?" Wendy tilted her head. "Did I misread your signals?"

"Ummm..."

Was this a trick question? The room seemed to expand, filled with people who waited for his response. He looked to the bar for a clue but found little aid. The tarbender... No, no, the bartender was leaning at a funny angle, filling a glass with ice cubes that clinked louder than normal. Extra-clinky cubes. Now available.

Wendy's eyes begged for consolation.

"Ahhh. Okay, I get it, Wendy. That's what you want, isn't it? You're just waiting for me to tell you, bet you're just *dying* to know." He laughed and slapped his leg. On the job, this dark humor was their common language.

"To tell me what?" She eased away. "Omigosh. You're gay?"

Well, he thought, *that would be a twist.* "Nope, that's not it."

"You're getting back together with your wife?"

"Jenni? She'd sooner slam dunk me through a hoop. Slammajamma!" He held up two fingers. "That's money in the bank! Two points for the home team."

Wendy took a drink, puckered her lips.

"Okay now, don't look so grave," Clay said. "Grave? You get it?" He giggled. "You wanna hear the truth? I know the day you're gonna die."

"Die?"

"You know, as in kick the bucket? We all have to do it sometime."

"Ryker, you're embarrassing yourself. Go home."

"Home, as in to my beddy-bye? Or home, as in…" He widened his eyes and pointed to the floor with exaggerated significance. "Six feet under. In a casket."

"You know, you're a lousy drunk."

"And how would you know?"

"Well, duhhh."

Clay scowled in mock indignation.

"Ryker, you need to get rested up. You have work in the morning."

"What'd I do? All I'm tryin' to say is you should live like there's no tomorrow. Look at the bright side. At least you've got a couple of weeks left. August…uh…August tenth, to be exact."

"Until what?"

He held a fist against his chest in solemn show. "Till you meet your maker."

"That's enough," the bartender said. "No need for threats around here."

Clay saw a waitress brush past, and he grabbed her bare arm. The dates slashed across his fingertips, settled into his palm. He thought of the blank tombstone that had toppled in the shop just yesterday. He shook his head at the craziness of it all. The waitress slipped free and headed toward a hulking figure near the door.

The bartender said, "You owe sixteen fifty. I suggest you settle up."

Clay dug into his wallet; with great attention to detail, he studied a twenty-dollar bill. "Here ya go. Keep the change. Or give it to the waitress that just went by."

"Rhea?"

"Mm-hmm. She's got till the twentieth of this month. Then she's a goner."

"A goner? I doubt that. Rhea Deering's a survivor in every sense of the word."

"Nope. Nothin' you can do about it. Nothin' I can do. Believe me, buddy"—Clay lowered his voice—"I've tried it, and it just don't work."

With affection turning to distaste, Wendy looked him up and down. "Ryker, forget that kiss ever happened. Please. For a guy as tall as you, you're a sad little man."

He was still reeling from her open-handed slap across his face, still trying to set the world back on its axis, when two sets of vise grips screwed into his rib cage from behind. He registered stern words, understood that he was being asked to leave. He'd forgotten how rude these places could be. Smoky little meat markets.

The slap from Wendy? He deserved that.

But couldn't a guy have a drink or two without being harassed? Honestly.

Before he had time to react, rough hands whipped underneath his armpits and knotted behind his neck. He was shoved, stumbling and complaining, out the front door where he bounced up off a knee and turned back to gesture his opinion of this less than stellar customer service.

"I know people who can board this place up! Board it up!"

"Shut your hole, and get off our sidewalk!"

"You hear me? Take your paws off me." Clay stopped. Looked up at the heavyset bouncer. "Man, you're about to die too—same day as that waitress lady. Rhea? Yeah, you might wanna stay away from her, just in case."

Another shove propelled Clay to the pavement. Finding his face near a square of dirt and mulch, he decided it was as good a place as any to purge himself of this evening's ills. Behind him, the tavern's door slammed shut.

He heard steps coming near. A familiar voice.

"Hoo boy. Whatcha doin' down there?"

"Who wantsa know?"

"They weren't akiddin'. They said you called and didn't sound too good." The speaker crouched down on thick legs, folded his arms over his knees. "Well, look at you. That was an understatement."

"You're that sergeant, right? Sergeant Tubby?"

"Sergeant Turney. Rumor has it, you called 911 an hour ago."

"That some kind of crime?"

"Don't know, right off. You tell me."

Clay's intestines clenched and heaved. He used the dirt one more time, then curled into a ball and began to sob.

23

A Pilgrimage

Folded into her course syllabus, the daily horoscope awaited her eyes.

Why, Mylisha wondered, was she sitting through this drivel? At the front of the Lane Community College classroom, an alleged marketing guru—whom she'd never heard of—prattled on about "sales culture." Did he realize most of the students in here had been awake less than an hour?

No, he was enamored of his own knowledge. Although he wore a decent suit and tie designed for garnering customers' trust and money, he seemed wily and insincere. White America, Mylisha believed, had made Mammon and materialism its masters. Revolving credit and high interest rates had become the lashes on lower-class backs.

Not that my people express our freedom any better. We live for the bling-bling and the Paper in My Pocket. Pimpin' it to da limit.

She closed her eyes. Who was she to talk?

She'd chosen a degree that tapped none of her heart's passion. She pondered 401(k) and stock options instead of pursuing filmmaking, which had always been her desire. Even Clay on the phone last week had remembered that much. Sure, she wanted security for her future and for her family to come. But what about her dreams, her passions?

Mylisha opened her syllabus, unfolded today's advice for Pisces. Perusing the words, she latched on to a line that seemed full of relevance.

Old secrets may come to light, but resist the desire to unveil them to others.

Look at that. The timing couldn't be more obvious.

Hadn't she just received Summer's card three days ago, via Sergeant Turney? Hadn't Summer mentioned secrets regarding Clay's past? And hadn't Mylisha dialed Clay's number twice since Saturday, then disconnected before the calls could go through? If she revealed everything to him, it would only bring more pain.

Mylisha refolded and cradled the paper in her hands.

What Mr. Clay Ryker didn't know wouldn't hurt him.

———

Clay awoke to a midmorning drizzle.

He had lost the kid. He had failed.

Refracted by myriad raindrops on the glass, gray light infused the room, and he jerked the blue sheet over his face. In the bed's pastel womb, he spent the next minutes differentiating between his nightmares and last night's events.

His nightmares were less disturbing.

Inside his frontal lobe, sad little men with pickaxes were hammering away. Vaguely he remembered Wendy's insult in the Raven. He'd brought it upon himself, no doubt—touching skin, calling out numbers like a bingo-hall crier.

He lifted himself to an elbow. The bedroom wobbled into focus.

Shoot. Late for work. Mr. Blomberg was supposed to be back this week, which made any tardiness that much worse. Where was Gerald Ryker? Why hadn't he roused Clay from his bed?

As if it mattered.

How could Clay go into the workplace and pretend nothing had happened? By the end of the day, the whole town would be buzzing with details of Kenny's demise. Did Sergeant Turney hold Clay responsible for the accident? Already he'd tied Clay to the other deaths under investigation, but the only correlation seemed to be Engine 418.

He touched his pocket. Kenny's treasure was still there.

What about Kate Preston? How would she react to the news her son was dead? Clay had offered protection that he failed to provide. She would hate his guts.

Clay groaned.

With thoughts of his own son, he read Jason's postcard again. He recalled the dates he'd detected so clearly on the drafted divorce agreement. Based on recent experience, he could only assume that Jason's death was imminent.

Was there a way to stop it? Or would Reckless Ryker screw that up too?

Clay fumbled for the water and aspirin on his nightstand.

Sergeant Turney, he recalled, had provided the Tylenol. Sarge had helped get him home, promising to return tonight for a report. Sarge had spoken with Gerald and Della so that they would not worry themselves over their son, and he might have even instructed them to let Clay sleep in.

Through the window, he saw the Duster parked alongside the garage.

I've got wheels. Sarge must've taken Dad to fetch it last night.

Hoping to avoid either of his parents, Clay moved into the hall. The living room was empty. The TV was dormant, which meant Papa Bear was off to work. He called his mother's name. After three tries, he deduced she was also gone. Shopping? Running errands? Who knew what she did with her free time?

An internal dynamo kicked in, driving him toward a task that he himself could not identify. Time was ticking. Undeniably, he had shoved his secrets down and avoided the past.

No more. He refused to go on as a haunted man.

Bypassing a morning shower, sticking with the same clothes, he whispered, "Let's get this over with. Shouldn't take more than a couple of days."

Sorry, Dr. Gerringer. Guess some things just have no other solution.

He laced up a pair of sturdy work boots, felt his thigh tighten where the Rottweiler's paw had landed. His left forearm was also sore but workable.

He marched out to the garage. Across the rafters, sheets of plywood held boxes filled with photos, yearbooks, his numbered jersey, and a signed basketball from his glory ride to the 3A championships.

Farther back, he found the camping gear. Time to pack for his getaway.

A poke at the automatic door opener allowed the morning's gloom to spread into the garage. Clay half expected to see one of his parents standing outside, arms crossed, eyebrows raised. He didn't know where the car keys were, but a harried search found that they had been stuck under the Duster's floor mat. In JC's rural areas, this was not an uncommon practice.

He popped the trunk, started shuffling supplies from the garage.

A sturdy-framed red backpack and a two-man pup tent from REI…

A Coleman burner with a pair of green propane cartridges, waterproof matches, a multifunctional Gerber tool, collapsible cooking utensils…

A green Kelly sleeping bag rated for zero degrees, plus a flashlight...

Freeze-dried meals, iodine tablets, and two Spyroxene water containers...

Extra clothing, sunscreen, a baseball cap, Gore-Tex hooded jacket and pants...

A waterproof Garmin GPS unit with satellite positioning and compass, a Sony Discman and CDs, a topographical map, a digital camera, and a Shaffer trail guide...

Finally, a folding shovel, Deet insect repellent, and biodegradable toilet paper.

He rolled most of the items in clothing and bedding, then stuffed them into the backpack. In the remaining spaces and pockets, he tucked sealed bags of food, toiletries, a few books, and granola bars. He carried a cell phone and a backup battery in case of an emergency. En route, he'd stop at a bank to empty his newly activated account.

Inside the house, he straightened his old room and left a note for his parents. No need to get them uptight; a brief explanation would allay their concerns for a while.

This was it. He'd dreamed of such an excursion since boyhood, and at one point Bill Scott had planned to join him. They'd done their research. Stocked supplies. After twelve years certain conditions might vary, but the Pacific Crest Trail remained remarkably constant.

Clay climbed into the Duster and fired her up.

This is for you, Bill. Should've done this long ago.

Following Highway 58, he reached the PCT trailhead at Willamette Pass near Diamond Peak. He parked off the road in a gravel lot, unloaded, and locked the car.

From here, he anticipated a five-day trek of over a hundred miles to the rim of Mount Mazama, named by local Indians. Thousands of years ago a violent eruption had decapitated the mighty mountain, scattering white pumice and volcanic ash across the continent. In the collapsed magma chamber, Crater Lake had formed, plunging nearly two thousand feet, making it the deepest lake in the United States.

He would not turn back. This would be his pilgrimage. Once he reached the lake, he would dip beneath the pristine waters in an act of physical and emotional cleansing.

A baptism by immersion.

———

"He didn't have it?"

"Apparently he passed it off."

"That's hard to believe, Monde. I saw him enter the drainpipe to get it."

"But did you watch the child every step of the way? Even a few seconds could've proved critical."

Asgoth reflected on the previous evening. "Okay, I may have missed a step or two. By then I was rushing to our point of convergence on the tracks, intent on my role. You were there too. You can't expect me to take all the blame."

"It's not a matter of blame, A.G."

"Well, when Dmitri Derevenko couldn't locate Kenny, he seemed convinced the object was gone. At least that portion worked in our favor."

"Yes, but possession is everything. It's key that we ourselves find it."

"You think the kid may have handed it off to Clay Ryker?"

"That I don't know." Monde's thin lips curled beneath his long nose. "But I don't mind saying, with a touch of pride, that Ryker is responding as I predicted."

"Where is he now?"

"Packed and on the trail toward Crater Lake."

Asgoth nodded in reluctant approval. "You guessed well."

"Guessed? The human psyche is much like the complicated lock of a safe, and I enjoy the process of cracking it. Probe deep enough, apply pressure to the correct tumblers, and it's only a matter of time until you gain access."

"Too bad you can't use your skills robbing banks."

"Is the irony intentional, A.G.? When we're done with this project, that's precisely what we'll be doing—plundering the wealth of the Romanovs and that devil Rasputin. He could not expect it to stay hidden forever, could he?"

"He hoarded his relics. He believed they held supernatural powers."

"And we're unfit to handle such things?" Monde's voice dripped with derision. "I know you've told me before, but what is the Consortium's stipulation to ensure your commitment in this town?"

"One hundred thousand dollars."

"And in return they guarantee protection and assistance?"

"Plus," Asgoth said, "permanent status as a member."

"If we succeed, that amount of money will be loose change."

Asgoth envisioned living somewhere other than his dilapidated apartment. He deserved marble pillars. Gold-plated faucets. Room to roam. Yes, hand in hand with greed, the entrepreneurial spirit could prove formidable indeed.

24

The Least of These

Clay got off to an undignified start.

Considering the Pacific Crest Trail's legendary romance, he was disheartened by the limited signage along Highway 58. He'd displayed his US Forest Service parking permit in the Duster, and the backpack was now bouncing against his tailbone as he sought the trailhead.

The weight'll settle, he told himself. His muscles would accept their new task.

A pair of freight trucks roared past. Tiny rocks and rain residue spit at his calves, and his Oregon Ducks ball cap whipped from his head. He reached down for the loose item.

Conspiring against him, wind created by a speeding Jeep Cherokee plucked the cap from his grasp, tossed, twisted, flung it into a clump of bunchberries.

He clambered down, shook out the hat, and snugged it back over his hair.

At that moment a pickup hauling a horse trailer rumbled by. The winter months of snow and ice had wreaked havoc on this mountain pass, pitting the road's surface, and the Ford found itself in line with an untended pothole. A small yet significant wave of rainwater fanned across the roadside, lending nourishment to the local fauna and dousing Clay.

He swore. Shook moisture from arms and legs. When at last he picked up the trail, he kissed the signpost in relief.

Shortly, the trail's wooded curves and rising bluffs cut off the last of the noise pollution. The world of convenience was at his back, the world of toil and hard-earned survival before him. His leg wound throbbed, and his arm stitches itched.

Good. Suffering was part of the plan.

At the Eagle Rock Overlook, he found the hike's first reward. He planted his boots on the stone shelf like a man on the edge of the world and soaked in Odell Lake's shimmering expanse, endless Douglas fir forests, and snow-capped peaks that stood as guardians of the Cascade Range.

He removed Kenny Preston's coveted object from his pack. Uncorked, the carved oak tube surrendered its prize into his palm. Sturdy, yet detailed, the stone king wore a black crown with a cross.

Clay rolled the piece, held it up. Around the king's base, thin shadows outlined the etched text. Russian words, if he were to venture a guess.

Who had hidden this on Engine 418? Why hunt down a child for it?

He cinched the pack's strap around his waist and faced his journey of penance.

———

Dmitri angled the Taurus into a Chevron station and headed for the pay phone with a piece of paper in hand. A skinny girl wearing a Bob's Burger uniform cut in front of him. While dialing, she showed him her back.

Dmitri occupied himself with other concerns.

He could not believe he had lost the boy last night. He'd been convinced he would catch him before the train sliced past with an ear-shattering shriek. Despite his exploration on both sides of the tracks, he had found no sign of the child or the object. As though the train had swallowed them whole.

Could the secret still be on the Finnish locomotive?

No. The old woman said Kenny had taken something. He must have hidden it. But where?

Such conjecture was useless. Although today Dmitri had attempted another search of the engine in Founder's Park, he'd come away empty handed. His mind raced with possibilities so that he even questioned the accuracy of the historian's research. Had Lenin truly left something on board?

While standing in this town, he thought it seemed preposterous. Junction City was far too mundane for such matters.

But this makes it a perfect hiding place, nyet? Who would guess?

He read over the paper in his hand, where he had copied down a license plate. Somehow that Duster's driver was connected with Kenny Preston.

"Will you be much longer on the phone?" he checked with the burger girl.

"Why don't you use your own?" Her eyes never lifted, but she indicated the cell phone on his belt.

He set his hand on the converted weapon. "It is… The battery is dead."

"Not like that's my problem. Anyway, this is a public phone. I can talk as long as I—" She turned, clipping her words as her gaze moved from his chest to his face. She cupped a hand near her mouth. "I'll call back later. Okay, sweetheart? No, nothing's wrong. I…I got someone who needs to use the phone. Of course I'm not mad at you. Bye-bye. Okay, bye-bye. Bye."

She tapped at the hook twice, then stepped away and held the receiver for Dmitri. "All yours. My boyfriend's a real control freak. Have to call him like every fifteen minutes, or he thinks I don't love him."

"A control freak? You think this is love?"

"Probably not." Her gaze locked on to his. "Dude, you have seriously blue eyes. Where you from? Germany?"

"Nyet. Russia is my homeland."

"Oooh. Bet it's pretty over there."

"In many places. The Black Sea is nice for holidays."

"I'm Victoria. Just Vicki's fine."

"I am Dmitri." His passport said otherwise, so he had no fear in sharing this.

"Hi." She shook his hand, let her fingers tarry. "How do you say hi in Russian?"

"For friends, we say *privyet*."

"Privyet."

"Very good. Soon you'll speak Russian."

She laughed at that. "You hungry, Dmitri? You like American hamburgers?"

He sensed opportunity, an end to justify the means. With a citizen's help, he might be able to tap this town's hidden currents. He imagined the angel wing on his hip would flap in affirmation of this plan. As a Russian, he was pragmatic but also attuned to life's mystical ties. Such as this.

"I like American women," he replied, willing an extra sparkle into his eyes.

"Oh, you do, do you?"

"Almost as much as American hamburgers and fries."

———

Clay sucked on his water bottle and looked up. Great.

Mount Yoran was jabbing a stony finger at rain-pregnant clouds. Winds from the Pacific Ocean tended to shove the Willamette Valley's cruddy weather eastward, which meant he would have little recourse in the event of a downpour.

Of course, Oregon weather was as hit-and-miss as those horoscopes he'd seen featured on last week's TV show. You could try to guess, try to make the pieces fit, but in the end they did what they were going to do. It seemed that God had set this globe spinning on its axis, then pulled his hands away. Distant. Uninvolved.

Clay draped his Gore-Tex jacket over his backpack, hitched the weight over his shoulders, and wallowed in the horrific memory of yesterday.

Where were you then, God? Answer that one.

Nope, this was Clay's burden, and he'd have to carry it alone. Each step he took, each drop of sweat, each blister and swollen mosquito bite would be a payment applied toward his debt of failure.

Headed south on the PCT, he wasn't running from the past; he was hiking along with it. Feeling each jab of pain.

———

Winding through mountain hemlocks, Clay kept his eyes open for the PCT trail markers. The rain had held off. He had traveled more than thirteen miles, based on the guidebook's markings. Behind him, voices played along the trail's switchbacks.

He skirted Diamond Peak, caught glimpses of its rubble slopes leading to broken tips at over eighty-seven hundred feet. Even here, at seven thousand feet, the thinner air required increasing effort. Clouds raced and peeled apart over the summit, like paper through a shredder. Strong winds carried away the tattered strips, but in the lee of the peak it was quiet and warm.

His neck muscles had become twanging steel bands. He squatted, let his pack rest against a boulder. Water and a granola bar began to grant new energy.

A pair of fellow hikers caught up with him.

"Hey there. How goes it? Think it'll rain?" asked a man with a walking stick.

"Never can tell."

"You from the Northwest?"

"Got web feet to prove it." Clay tipped his Oregon Ducks cap.

The man smiled. "Around here, hiking's a water sport. I've lived here half my life, but I'm from Long Beach originally, born and raised. Surfing used to be my brand of water activity."

"Never tried it."

"I'm too old for it. Haven't ridden a wave in over twenty years. And don't even ask my age."

"He'll lie through his teeth," the other man said. "Like all Californians."

"Hey now. Let's play nice, Sam."

Sam frowned and swiped at his leg. "I told you the shorts were a rotten idea. These mosquitoes are eating me alive."

"Oh, you're so bad." The man slapped his partner's arm. "Here, let me reapply."

Clay shielded his granola bar from the repellent's spray, feeling like he'd been dropped into a *Saturday Night Live* skit.

"Thanks, Lyndon. Let's go on and leave this fine gentleman in peace."

"Maybe he likes the company."

"His body language says, 'It's been nice, boys, but I'll let you go now.'"

Lyndon considered Clay.

Clay snapped the lid on his water container. "Actually, I think I will join you. For a while anyway."

The trail carried them several miles, descending toward Summit Lake. Clay enjoyed Sam and Lyndon's combative repartee and their intimate knowledge of this wilderness area. They'd been traversing the PCT and old Oregon Skyline Trail for years, financing their summers by selling nature photography to postcard distributors.

"Pick up any one of a hundred cards," Lyndon said, "and you'll find us on the back."

"SNL Photography," Sam said. "Nineteen years of business together."

Saturday Night Live...Sam and Lyndon...SNL.

Clay could barely control a chortle.

"You're not the first one who's caught the pun," Sam said.

"Is it intentional?"

"Intentional. Well, that's a good question."

Lyndon looked back over his pack. "Clay, don't you think everything has a purpose, a connection, a reason? Even unintentionally we tap into larger truths. Our spirits are all woven together, which is why it's so important to embrace our differences. Don't you agree?"

Clay placed one boot before the other. Branches creaked overhead.

"Lyndon," Sam said, "that's enough with the philosopher shtick."

"Am I wrong? Tell me I'm wrong. What I'm saying is that hateful words and unaccepting attitudes only harm us all. When we lash out at a fellow human being, we're lashing out at an extension of ourselves. What're your thoughts, Clay?"

"I think your Northwest colors are showing."

Lyndon was in earnest. "You see the truth in it, don't you?"

"I was raised a good church boy, so I'm not sure how it all fits. I know Jesus said that if we do something even to 'the least of these'—the poor, the lonely, the outcasts—we're doing it to him. If he's the one holding it all together, I guess everything we do helps or hurts him on some level."

"Hey. Now that's deep stuff. A command to show love."

"I'm not even sure why I said that. Believe me, I've got my own set of questions and problems. Right now, God and I aren't on the best of terms."

"So then, you're hurting him."

"And yourself," Sam noted.

Clay cleared his throat. Picked his steps through a stretch of loose stone.

"Here's one for you, Clay. You think Jesus would be walking along with two openly gay men?"

In light of the discussion, only one answer fit. "Here I am, aren't I?"

Lyndon turned to face Clay. His camera bag swung from his shoulder, bounced against his hip. "That's the most beautiful thing I've ever heard from a churchgoer's mouth. In my book, you being here is no accident."

"Funny. Besides you two, no one even knows where I am."

"He means here"—Sam extended his arms—"on this planet."

———

Asgoth spent a restless night roaming the streets of Junction City. He stopped at the concrete rail over a duck pond, ignored by a Hispanic couple strolling past. He took a deep breath as he gazed down on the water.

Flashbacks from a previous time and place…

Going under. The biting cold of the river. Hair twining around his face, feet kicking, weakening, hands clawing for the surface that moved up and away from him. Floating. Only moments until the mind would pull the plug. And then, a slow return to the surface. Dead in the minds of many, yet wandering and alive.

Asgoth now found that his shallow gasps matched the cadence of the water sucking against the pond's bank. He watched the Hispanic couple look around, then clasp hands and hurry on toward a better-lit area.

Soon it would be time for the Scandi-Fest. Throngs of people would pack JC. Asgoth knew his strategies for the coming weeks required the assistance of Mr. Monde; there was no choice, if he wanted to win the Consortium's approval. But Monde had exhibited blind spots before; at critical moments his ambition had become a liability.

Asgoth headed back to the lonely apartment.

Never mind the old mistakes. Clay Ryker was on his way out. A sacrifice.

And once he's gone, Henna will be wholly devoted to me—no more schoolgirl distractions. Monde's services will be needed no longer, and I'll be unchained, using my skills to their full potential.

25

Double Meaning

Over Summit Lake Campground, the morning sky was an inverted glass bowl reflecting sapphire waters. Clay waded out to his knees, saw small fish flicker and flash about his shins. Why hadn't he paid for a fishing license? He could almost taste the potential trout fillets lurking further out in the depths.

After muesli cereal and black tea, he broke camp and refilled his water bottles. Unless he went off trail, he'd be without water access until sometime late tonight.

"Good hiking with you guys," he told Sam and Lyndon.

"Clay, tell me you've registered with the Forest Service. As a precaution."

"Don't worry. My parking pass'll give them a general idea of where I am."

"But what if you're injured?"

"Or stranded?" Sam inserted.

"Hey, you can always find friends on the trail. Least that's been my experience."

Lyndon touched a hand to his heart. "I do think he means us, Sam."

"Listen, we'd better stop loitering if we're going to get shooting today."

"Shooting?" Clay didn't think of these two as hunters. "Ah, the photos."

"He's not only friendly and tall, he's smart."

"We're working on a set of historical cards," Sam said. "Points of discovery and what have you. We'll be back up at Emigrant Pass."

"I'll keep my eyes open in the stores." Clay threaded his arms through his pack straps, aware of each aching muscle. "Off I go."

"Remember. No accident."

"I'll be careful."

"No," Sam said. "He means from yesterday—you being here is no accident."

"Gotcha. See ya later, guys."

The first few miles were easy going, threading through trees along Summit

Lake's west shore, then meandering south. The PCT began to climb again, cutting diagonally up an escarpment and bringing sweat to his forehead. He removed his ball cap to mop at thick brown hair.

Should've cut it, he thought. *Buzzed it down to a half inch.*

Nope. He knew from his college b-ball days how itchy a fresh cut could be. Better left as it was. Jenni liked it longer too—used to, anyway.

He extracted his cell phone from a side pouch. To save the batteries, he would use it only if necessary. He noted missed calls from his parents, his work, and another number that might be Sergeant Turney's.

None of it mattered. They would survive without him.

Along the path he spotted deer droppings and tufts of a pelt caught in a ponderosa pine's bark. Hawks patrolled the azure sky. Although bear and cougar sightings were not unheard of, most hikers moved through these woods unscathed.

He greeted fellow backpackers—males, females, groups, loners. Some were on day excursions, while others were long-distance PCT veterans. One man in his sixties claimed he'd completed the entire trek from Canada to the border of Mexico.

"Over three summers," he confessed, but Clay was impressed.

Clay's research reminded him that the Pacific Crest Trail covered more than twenty-six hundred miles. In the 1920s and '30s, the trail's concept grew from passing dialogue into the hobby of mountain clubs. The passion of a USFS regional supervisor carried along the dream, followed by the persistence of YMCA officials and volunteers, but WWII and its aftermath delayed the trail's progress. In '68, Congress appointed an advisory council that had worked with the USFS to map the definitive route Clay was now on.

The scent of berries broke through his recollections.

He located a lode of huckleberries and helped himself to them while his mind pondered the lives of those who had made this trail a reality. They'd gone after a goal and achieved it; they'd created something special.

What, though, had he ever accomplished?

Carry on, Clay. Only a few days left.

Near the saddle of Cowhorn Mountain, he had his eyes down, verifying his position on his GPS unit, when he spotted a flash of color on the path.

Some poor soul had lost a UW cap. Contemplating the rivalry between the University of Oregon and University of Washington, he had an urge to break out his camp shovel and bury this article in symbolic victory.

Anyway, Clay was about ready to find a spot behind a tree.

———

Not a half hour passed before Clay heard plodding footsteps. Hunched under his pack, a man approached with a bright-eyed mongrel panting alongside.

"Hey."

"Whassup?" Beneath a thin beard, the man's face was young. "You seen a hat along the way? Musta dropped it on the ground."

"A hat?"

"Yeah, dude. Like a Washington ball cap. Came back hoping it'd still be here."

"Uh, actually I did find it." At Clay's knees, the mutt sniffed and snorfled. Cute, with gold and white fur, she looked up and begged him to come clean. He coughed. "Hate to tell you this, though. I'm a Ducks fan, so you wouldn't expect me to do something nice to a Huskies cap, would you?"

"Tell me you're jokin'." The man's eyes begged for mercy. "What'd you do?"

"I still have it. If that's any help."

"This is the PCT, dude. S'posed to be lookin' out for your fellow hikers."

Although softened by the beard, the man's face had an odd angular shape, with one hazelnut eye set deeper than the other. He gave the impression of one who'd lived through darker days and had now been granted a fresh helping of grace. He wore green khaki pants, a Scooby Doo T-shirt, and a leather bracelet matching a braided necklace.

"Yeah? Well, uh…sorry." Clay produced the missing cap. "Here you go."

"What'd ya do to it? You tore off the letters?"

"No, no. Nothing that permanent. Just rubbed them in a little berry juice so they'd blend in with the rest of the cap."

"Dude, that's so wrong. I'm not even laughing."

"Trust me. It's better than my original idea."

———

"Dmitri, you better get outta here." A wadded shirt hit him in the chest.

"So soon? Is this what Americans call a one-night stand?"

"Call it what you want, but if my boyfriend finds you here…" Vicki left the sentence unfinished. "What'm I doing? I need to get ready for work. Why don't you meet me later by the Chevron, same as yesterday."

"You must grow tired of keeping secrets."

"You kidding?" She opened her eyes wide to apply mascara. "I live for them. Around here, you take what adventure you can get. Most of my friends never leave the Northwest. Well, maybe a trip to Disneyland, but that doesn't count. If they do leave, they still end up back here. Same old, same old. It never changes."

"You've lived many years in Junction City. You know the town secrets?"

"Oh, I could tell you stories. But you know what, around here it's like a pact—'I won't tell your secrets, if you won't tell mine.' Doesn't stop the gossip, though." Vicki pulled her hair into a ponytail, slipped into work shoes. "My dad, he comes off like some religious nut, but talk about a man who knows the dark sides of this place."

"This is him?" Dmitri tipped back a framed picture on the dresser.

"Mr. Stan Blomberg himself. Dad and I don't get along. As you might've guessed, I'm not the prissy virgin queen he wanted me to be."

"What is his work?"

"He owns Glenleaf Monument Company, makin' tombstones. Pretty creepy, huh? Talk about having a finger on the pulse of the town."

———

"Don't tell me. Are ya headin' south?"

Clay shrugged.

"Is that an answer?"

"You just said not to tell you."

"Mighta guessed." The man put on his UW cap. "Same way I'm headed, my rotten luck. Name's Wesley, by the way. And my dog's Oatmeal."

"Clay."

They shook hands, then turned to the challenge of the trail. They kept pace with one another, held dialogue to a minimum, pointed out vistas through the trees. For a while Clay listened to the band Coldplay on his Discman—upbeat enough to set his pace, moody enough to match his downward spiral of emotion. Occasionally Wesley patted Oatmeal on the head and provided a dog biscuit. Clay and Wesley exchanged snacks of their own, trail mix for fruit leather.

With the sun blazing overhead, they reached Windigo Pass. A nearby parking lot at the trailhead turned this into a busy juncture for both north- and southbound hikers. They marched on without a word.

Ahead they spied the pyroclastic cone of Windigo Butte. Far beyond, snow-sprinkled Mount Thielsen waited to be conquered.

This, Clay realized, was what he had hoped to experience with Bill Scott.

Bill had been his friend during his junior and senior years of high school. A change had come over Bill, though, in those months before the bridge incident. He'd become morose, quiet, more likely to incite trouble with authority figures. He did mean things. His circle of friends tightened into a fiercely loyal, secretive bunch.

Without words being spoken, Clay felt himself being edged out.

When Clay asked what was wrong, Bill snapped at him. "It's this life, this little game they play with us. What do these teachers care, Ryker? Or our parents? They just want to impose their own bitterness on us. We're powerful, young, full of dangerous ideas. And that scares them spitless. Get this—my dad says I should start going by 'William.' More mature, he claims. More likely to score me a job. As if I give a rat's tail about jumping into his world! It's all a big game to them."

For Clay Ryker, jersey number nine, it had been all about the game. On the b-ball court he was a winner, headed for the big time, with nothing to stop him.

Until Bill Scott's death at the river.

How many must die to pay for your sin? Sacrifice yourself...

Wrapped in these thoughts, Clay bumped into his hiking companion's stationary form. Wesley grunted, stepped forward to retain his balance.

"Where'd you learn to drive, Clay?"

"My bad. Didn't see your brake lights."

"S'all right. So what're your thoughts? A night at Tolo Camp?"

"If there's room. Might have to push on to Maidu Lake."

"Late July. Lotsa hikers. Yeah, Tolo might be outta the question."

"What about you, Wesley? You got any specific plans?"

"Figured I'd bum it with you, if that's cool. You're packin' good trail mix, and I've got the watchdog. Not much in the danger department, but Oatmeal's a frickin' awesome early-warning system. Good for chasin' off the critters."

"Critters? Where'd you learn that kind of talk?"

"Raised in Puget Sound, stinkin' Microsoft country. Guess I like anything that goes against the high-tech flow." Wesley flicked at a spider creeping up his pant leg. "So whaddya say? You wanna stick together another day or two?"

"Shoot. I guess I could try taming a Husky."

———

Dmitri carried a mental list of priorities. Near the top he wanted the man's identity from Sunday night's fiasco, the one who had abandoned the car.

He made a visit to the local Department of Motor Vehicles, discovered that Gerald Ryker was the Duster's registered owner. The Yahoo! people search told him where the Rykers lived. During surveillance at the Cox Butte address, Dmitri failed to sight the Duster, but he did see a middle-aged couple exit the house, arguing and gesticulating while climbing into a big Dodge truck.

Dmitri eased away. Still he had not spotted his target.

What was the next step? He'd gone through the motions with Vicki, waiting for the burger girl to bubble over with some relevant gossip or tawdry detail. She'd produced nothing of the sort, nothing about Kenny or Engine 418.

Where was the driver of the Duster? Where had Kenny's adult friend gone?

———

As predicted, Tolo Camp was full. They made the long descent to Maidu Lake, then, with the sun plunging behind the ridge crests, scrambled to set up camp. They'd trekked more than twenty miles. Once Clay had eased out of his pack, he felt weightless, a man walking on the surface of the moon.

The night air turned brisk. Both men warmed their hands with cups of instant Nescafé while stretching stockinged feet toward the campfire. Hiking boots aired out by the tent flaps. Oatmeal curled next to Wesley's legs, eyes reflecting the flames.

"How far tomorrow, Wesley?" Clay was dabbing medicated cream at the stitches on his arm. The soreness in his back and legs gave him a perverse pleasure. A penitent satisfaction.

Wesley groaned. "Can't we talk about it in the morning?"

"I'm thinking of bagging a few peaks. Tipsoo and Mount Thielsen."

"Then what? Head down to Diamond Lake for the night?"

"Why not? Your young legs could use the workout."

"Funny." Wesley twisted his leather bracelet. "Sounds to me like a heck-uva lotta hiking."

"Uh, look around you. We're in the middle of nowhere doing what?"

"Drinking java by the fire."

"Hiking, Wesley. Don't know about you, but it's what I came to do."

Clay disliked the sound of his own sarcasm. His voice had turned snappy, hard edged. He tilted his head back. Above, it looked as though angels had airbrushed the blackness with white glitter and tiny red speckles. The moon was a creamy circular splotch, swirled with wisps of gray.

"Sleep on it," he goaded. "I'll understand if you don't think you can hack it."

"Listen, dude." Wesley pulled his knees to his chest, scratched a hand through his beard. "I used to run cross-country. Back in the day I even held a few records in King County—that's Seattle area if ya don't know—so I've got stamina comin' out my ears. Didn't earn my nickname for nothin'."

"Nickname?"

"Scooter. As in, 'That boy can scoot!' For years that's what they called me."

Clay flicked aside a poking finger of suspicion. "Why'd you drop it?"

"A lot's changed. I've been doing a lotta thinking. Just ready to start fresh. You know what I'm sayin'? Ready to settle my accounts." Wesley drew a hand over his misshapen brow and cheekbone. "See this, the way it's all outta whack? Up till January I was in a full coma."

"Wow. How'd it happen, if you don't mind me asking? Must've been serious."

"Deadly." Wesley rocked with arms still clasped around his knees. "Guess you could say I fell victim to some hard-core poison."

"And you're all right out here? At this altitude? Even after the coma? Wesley nodded. "Don't look so worried."

"Man, forgive my stupid jabs. It was just my competitive nature coming out."

"No harm, no foul. I'm all good, just a little funnier lookin'."

"And slower moving," Clay joked back. "Your nickname could have another meaning. As in, 'That boy's so slow, he just scoots himself along.'"

"S'already got a double meaning. Dude, you need some new material."

"Clue me in."

"My full name's Wesley Scott."

"Scott?" Clay's voice faltered. "Scooter…Scott. Okay, I get it."

You thought you could get off scott-free…

Was the name a coincidence or something more? The hand of suspicion clamped around his lungs, while in his head, misgivings and vague hope jockeyed for position.

26

Bad Call

Clay could barely move. His mummy bag was tight around his ankles, but his trail-weary bones were the real culprit. After a second day together on the PCT, he and Wesley had claimed Tipsoo Peak and Mount Thielsen as their conquests. Tipsoo's glaciated face and Thielsen's needle-tip pinnacles had been well worth the journey, but this morning his body was paying the price.

Carrying my burden. All part of my pilgrimage.

He moaned, then wished he had not.

"I heard that," Wesley said from the neighboring tent.

"Don't even start."

"Thursday morning. Ready to hit the trail again, you peak bagger?"

Clay kicked at the side of his tent. "Shut up."

"I feel your pain. My body's all racked up, like I got beat with a two-by-four."

"Which is what I'll do to you if you say another word."

In the following silence, Clay rumbled over Tuesday night's conversation. There, over the Maidu Lake campfire, his emotions had collided. The fact he was camping with a Wesley Scott seemed unreal, considering he was on these trails because of a dead friend named William "Bill" Scott.

Was the coincidence a gesture of hope from above? An offer to build new friendships while sweeping away the ghosts of Friday the thirteenth, May 1992?

Or was it a sinister sign? A dead man's brother coming for blood?

Clay had made attempts to find out more, asking if Wesley had any siblings.

"Got four brothers," Wesley had responded. "All of them older."

"You grew up around Puget Sound, right? But did any of them live in Oregon?"

Wesley scratched at his chin. "I can't keep track. Sorry, but I was the baby, and we didn't have what you'd call the model family. Pretty abusive, if you wanna know the truth. We get together for two things—weddings and funerals."

There was no easy way to ask this. "Are…all of your brothers still alive?"

"Dude, what kind of question is that?" Aggravation tinged Wesley's words. "What do I care anyway? Been years since I talked to any of 'em, and you won't hear me complainin'. Some things are better left alone."

Clay took the hint. He didn't broach the subject again.

———

Dmitri Derevenko watched Vicki hurry out the door. She was flighty, annoying. After a heated phone call with her "control freak" boyfriend, she'd thrown on her Bob's Burger uniform and muttered something about returning before six.

From the couch Dmitri surveyed the dark apartment with its nicotine-yellowed walls. He had not come thousands of miles from his beloved country for this.

Yesterday he had visited Glenleaf Monument Company on Junction City's northeast corner. He'd entered the single-wide trailer that served as showroom and office, found a buxom secretary tapping an IM on her computer.

She'd turned down her country music station. "Can I help you?"

"This song." Dmitri found a point of connection. "It's by Bering Strait."

"Excuse me?"

"This music group, they're from my motherland. From Russia."

"Yeah? It's a pretty good song."

"You would like Russia. We have many good musicians, da."

"I'm sure I would." The secretary glanced at the monitor's IM window.

"Mr. Blomberg… Is it possible that I could speak with him?"

"So sorry, but he won't be back till tomorrow, and our sales staff's in a meeting." She buffed a nail on her skirt, then fetched a business card from a granite holder. "You can always call to set up an appointment."

Dmitri slipped the card into his pocket. Near the sliding back door, a dry erase board showed names on a weekly work schedule.

"Clay Ryker."

"Excuse me?"

"He works here? He's the son of Gerald Ryker?"

"Gerald and Della. They've been friends of my parents since, oh, way back."

"Perhaps I could speak to Mr. Ryker. One or two short questions."

"The crew's busy and can't be interrupted. Anyway, Clay's been gone since Monday, didn't even call in sick. No one knows what's happened to him." She'd frowned.

Then yesterday evening Vicki had confirmed Clay Ryker's disappearance.

"Guy's lucky he's still alive. Rumor has it he went on a drinking binge, then ran his car off the road into a ditch. The latest is that he's taken off for the mountains."

Today, alone in the apartment, Dmitri considered a personal visit to Gerald and Della Ryker. With some persuasion they would give him the facts he needed to track their son into the woods. In fact, the thought of being out-doors stimulated him; in the forests near Ekaterinburg, hiking and fishing had been part of his life.

Was Clay carrying Kenny's secret? Was he out there intending to hide it?

Dmitri picked up the phone to inform Oleg of his next step. After days without communication, his Brotherhood contact would be worried. He might even suspect Western influences were eroding Dmitri's dedication. It was a prevalent danger.

Before Oleg could answer, Dmitri heard a creak on the landing.

"Astergaisya," he whispered. "Beware."

The apartment door slammed inward. Splinters of wood tore through the air. A burly kid with black shoulder-length hair roared Vicki's name, then came in screaming accusations over the barrel of a gun.

The control freak, Dmitri realized, had lost control.

———

Mako was a bouncer at the Raven. Although boozed-up and flirty women hit on him every night, he reserved his heart for one special lady.

Vicki was a year older than Mako. They'd gone to JCHS together. He loved everything about her, which was why he tried so hard to make her happy—gifts, cards, teddy bears, phone calls, whatever it took to show his love.

But there was just no pleasing some women.

Last night Mako hadn't slept a wink. His eyes were stinging, his temples pounding, his fists clenching in sudden spasms. He faced her apartment building and tried to convince himself the white Taurus must belong to a new occupant. But he had never been a good liar. His aunt used to say he was without an ounce of guile, and he believed her—even though he had no clue what "guile" meant.

He crept up the stairs to Vicki's landing. The gun made him feel powerful.

Just gonna scare her. Let her know I won't put up with this. And if there's some guy in there? Heaven help him!

Mako faced the door, studied its construction. One or two well-aimed kicks—that's all it would take.

His mind flashed back to last Sunday night at the tavern. He'd thrown a tall, lean, drunken fool out onto the sidewalk. A guy named Clay. He'd shoved the guy hard. Sneered. But he could not erase Clay's words: *Man, you're about to die too...*

He hesitated now. Maybe he should back off.

Then he felt the tug, like a finger snagging his chin and pulling down.

There on the landing he spotted Vicki's charm bracelet. The one he'd given her. Paid good money for. Sent with a bouquet of flowers. It was sitting in the dirt like so much trash.

Kur-rashh!

In a burst of wood and popped screws, his boot shot the door inward. He spit out Vicki's name amid a volley of insinuations. Blundering forward, he followed the barrel of his gun, saw a broad-shouldered man with icy blue eyes.

Was the guy just plain dumb? What could a cell phone do for him?

"Too late to call the cops! You think you can waltz in, just take her away?" Mako tried to look past the clothes on the bed; Vicki would never mean to hurt him this way. "She's the only girl I've ever loved. The only one! I'd do anything for her!"

"Even die?"

Mako roared. "You're the one who's going to—"

The bullet burst into his chest with a hot-cold, splashing-shrinking sensation. He stared down. His legs cut out. Crumpling to the floor, he was still baffled by the gunshot's source. He should've listened to the warning: *You're about to die too.*

Coming here had been a very bad call.

———

"Nicely arranged," Asgoth congratulated Monde. "You made it look easy."

"As I said before, it's all a matter of unlocking the human mind. Find the right combination, and the rest is simple. On occasion, though, more drastic measures are needed. Pride, love, hatred, and self-doubt—they can be as effective as dynamite."

"And in this case, the charm bracelet was the fuse."

"I suppose you could say that."

Although sirens were playing in the background, Asgoth couldn't resist. He moved up the apartment stairs, hoping for another glimpse through the open door.

Monde seemed anxious to leave the scene. "I know what you're thinking, A.G. You believe I made errors."

"Did I say a word?"

"Actually I made them intentionally, to attract Sergeant Turney's attention."

"What's the use? He's gone out of town."

Monde's onyx eyes bulged. "Where?"

"I know I'm good, but you can't expect me to know everything."

"Why didn't you mention this earlier? He has a nasty habit of bumbling his way into places I'd rather he ignored."

27

At Long Last

They parted ways at the Diamond Lake guard station.

"Need to stock up at the resort store, make some calls, get a hot shower." Wesley wore a pout. "And try washing the berry stains outta my cap."

Clay forked over a ten-dollar bill. "Here. For the laundry."

"Nah. Keep it, dude."

"I don't need it. Only got one more day before I'm done."

"I'm not takin' your cash. Do I look like a slacker?"

"Then take this." Clay tucked his Discman into Wesley's pack. "I prefer the silence anyway. The sounds of nature."

Wesley's head tilted, and his lips split into a grin. "That's wild, just flat-out crazy. I used to have one of these before my coma. This means a lot, really. Thanks. This is one gift I'll take."

"Good. It's all yours, man."

"But"—Wesley wiggled his cap—"if these stains don't come out, I'll hunt you down. Little Duck better run from mean Husky."

"I'm quaking in my boots."

"Quacking's more like it." Wesley stretched out a hand. "Seriously, Clay, thanks for the company. It's been real. You're a good guy."

Clay avoided the contact. He gave his hiking partner a playful jab in the shoulder, touching nothing more than a tan sleeve. "You're not bad yourself, for a former coma patient. Happy trails, man. It's off to Crater Lake for me. Haven't seen the place since I was a little tyke."

"Think you'll make it there by tomorrow? Without me to baby you along?"

"Nothing'll stop me. I'm dying to do that guided boat ride."

Wesley Scott tipped his cap.

With a wave Clay cut across Highway 138 toward a trail that rejoined the PCT. Through branches of hemlock and lodgepole pine, he saw Thielsen's stony pinnacles slashing at the sky. The temperature was pleasant. According to his Shaffer guide, today's journey would be his least difficult. He would trek past the North Crater trailhead, down along the Pumice Desert, to Red Cone Spring where he'd find water and a campsite for his final night.

Tomorrow he would hike the rim of Mount Mazama.

Step by step. Nearing the point of baptism.

———

Mylisha heard about Clay's disappearance through the grapevine. Through a customer at the Safeway service desk, to be more accurate.

"He's left town," the woman said. "Yep. Couldn't handle it."

"Couldn't handle what?"

"The boredom."

"Was there anything else you needed today?" Mylisha asked.

"Like I don't spend every dime here already. Nope, nothing else. You heard about the other night? I'm only telling you because you and Clay used to be an item. Well, he got drunk as a skunk. That's the way it was told to me. Started mouthing off, grabbing and threatening waitresses. Bouncers tossed him out on his butt."

"We all have our moments. You think he'd want you talkin' about this?"

"Guess he should've thought about that before going into the Raven, eh?"

Mylisha extricated herself from the conversation. She thought she might lose it, give the woman a piece of her mind.

She slipped into her small office area and picked up the newspaper. She knew what she was looking for, although she went through the motions of scanning the latest news—Kobe Bryant trial updates, potential scandal among Olympic athletes, Chechen terrorist threats.

Okay, girl, here's what you wanted. May as well take a peek.

The horoscope column beckoned with bits of humor, sage advice, and projections for the day's events. She knew she should put her trust in God alone. But hadn't God borne witness through the stars before? Bethlehem: perfect example.

Mylisha ran her enameled nails along the page. Twice she read the section devoted to her, seeking parts that fit, finding questions instead.

Hadn't she refrained from calling Clay a few nights ago based on this column?

Now the advice seemed pointed in the opposite direction.

Honesty is the perfume of any friendship. The longer you hold on to secrets and relevant facts, the more likely your relationship will become a real stinker.

Knowing of Clay's recent disappearance, Mylisha now doubted her decisions. Had she misread the signs? What if she followed today's advice, then found that it conflicted with yesterday's? Or tomorrow's? How could she know with any certainty? Shanique never seemed bogged down with such doubts.

Mylisha clocked out for a break, then dialed the Ryker residence. *I hope Clay's mother answers. She might know how I can reach that boy.*

———

"Henna, do you remember Clay's belt buckle?"

"The one you left beneath the Coateses' bedroom window?"

"Yes, that one." Asgoth smiled at the memory. "We need to plant a similar piece of evidence at this girl's apartment, at the scene of the homicide."

"The scene of the crime," Henna corrected. "Mako's not dead yet."

"Give it a few more days."

"I have my reservations, A.G. Your activities keep getting…darker. Are you sure we should be involved in this?"

"We cannot take responsibility for the actions of others. This Russian man has a pattern of violence, and we're merely using his mistakes to our advantage. You know me, Henna. I wouldn't hurt a soul."

"But that paperboy."

"What about him? I didn't break my promise to you, didn't even touch him."

"What do you need me to do this time? What's the objective?"

Asgoth waved at an object on the kitchen's stained wooden table. Left by the former occupant, the table had become a focal point of the apartment's recent activities. Hardened red wax spread tentacles across the pine surface.

"The objective," he told Henna, "is to keep our dear Sergeant Turney busy."

"Aren't there better ways of distracting him?"

"I'll tell you a little secret." Asgoth circled around Henna's back so that his presence hung over her like a cloak. "If you can distract a man through his job, he'll never suspect outside involvement. Human nature longs for meaning, for purpose. A career can become so intertwined with a man's view of himself that he fails to see anything else."

"Clay."

"Exactly. Now there's a man convinced he has lost his purpose."

" 'A child of the earth.' That's what I said to him on the bus."

"And to the earth he shall return."

———

Clay slowed his pace to appreciate the sweeping view. In the future his family might appreciate pictures of these vistas.

He snapped a few photos with his digital camera, thought of Sam and Lyndon. How were they faring? He smiled at the thought of Lyndon's spraying repellent around Sam's spindly legs. Despite his view of their lifestyle choices, he had enjoyed their company. In turn, they had challenged his thinking.

Were they right? Was he hurting Jesus?

I used to think that way, but it all seems so removed now. So distant.

Clay snorted, realizing the words described himself as well.

But why was it that two gay guys could survive nineteen years together, while he and his wife couldn't make it past twelve? When had this world turned upside down and crazy? Why had Clay and Jenni's vows before God fallen apart? Where was the faith to which they'd once held?

Clay crossed a mountain meadow cloaked in wildflowers. He followed a gully, then a gentle slope leading toward the North Crater trailhead and the desolate Pumice Desert.

He signed in at the trail register, then moved across the wide expanse. The going was easy. He picked up and studied bits of pumice and shards of glistening obsidian. The landscape to his right was a lunar setting: barren, wiped out by layers of ash and volcanic destruction. Grouse Hill was a former lava flow, built up on the valley floor.

At Red Cone Spring he refilled his water. Set up camp.

On his cell he had messages from his mother and the secretary at Glenleaf. Mylisha had called as well, but her message contained only brief silence.

He deleted each one in turn.

But the last message sucked the air from his lungs.

Jenni. Speaking her first words to him in months.

"Clay, I hope you get this. Your mother contacted me at work, said she's worried sick and begged that I call you. I know we've had our rough times, and, no, you're not the only one at fault. Do you ever reach a point where you can't turn back, though? As though a part of you has died and you can't revive it, no matter how hard you try. Well that's me. That's the point I'm at.

"We've done enough finger pointing. We have a son…" Her voice broke. "We have a gorgeous little boy who just wants to be loved, and when I look at him, all I can see is you. Is there any chance of us making things work down the road? You tell me."

A bitter little chuckle. "But that's always been our problem. You won't tell me what's going on in your head. It's as though you've locked the door and lost the key. Even after I filed, you sat back as if it was a done deal. Sure, you tried calling, but you weren't going to go beyond surface conversation. You know it's true."

A sigh. "Why am I even wasting my time? I get peeved all over again just thinking about it. You know, my mail still says Mrs. Ryker. Does that mean anything to you? You act as though I should be able to read your mind and be there to hold your hand, be up for you when you need it. You have a son who loves you. You have a wife…uh, a woman who cares about you. But, Clay, whatever's weighing you down, you've kept refusing to let it go. That's why I'm finished, why I don't think I can be part of your life any longer. And if you don't deal with it—through God's help or that Dr. Gerringer guy or whoever—then you won't even have a life of your own."

Clay avoided the other campers in his vicinity.

Dinner. That sounded good.

He fed himself berry-topped pancakes, strips of beef jerky, and a vanilla pudding cup. With a mug of instant coffee, he wedged his long body into the tent. Mesh windows filtered the waning sunlight so that he was able to read a dog-eared paperback. A Louis L'Amour. He hadn't read one in years.

He could hear his dad's voice. *Gotta be a man's man...*

Gerald had read these as well. Father and son finding common ground.

Jason. Clay sank back into the Kelly sleeping bag.

You'll always be a man. Don't let others tell you otherwise. You're a smart kid. Handsome and full of ideas. I'm so proud of you. I tried to love your mother. She's a very special lady, she really is. I think I just kept pulling away from her until she snapped. She couldn't keep giving without getting anything in return.

Jenni. Clay rested the book's open pages over his face.

I'm no relational expert, as you know. But even Dr. Gerringer's not all he's cracked up to be. I'm sorry. For everything. See, I had a hand in Bill's death, and I let it keep whittling me down until I had no confidence left. Now look at me. I've failed at everything, like a disease that keeps getting worse. I tried to let it go, and you're absolutely right, I tried to make you carry that weight with me. Which you couldn't do. I know that now. Well, don't worry. Tomorrow I'm shirking this load forever. And just in case...I'm all paid up on the life insurance. You and Jason'll be able to move on.

As he comprehended his own scheme, Clay stared into the darkening sky, astounded, even amused. No wonder he'd felt propelled along this pilgrimage.

Had he known all along? Or had he hidden it from himself?

Twelve years ago he had caused Bill Scott's death, pushing his friend toward the treacherous river. Days ago he had failed to save a helpless child, thus witnessing a brutal destruction. Tomorrow he would take his own life in Crater Lake's cold depths.

At long last he understood.

Sacrifice yourself so others might live.

28

The Below World

Two chiefs, according to Klamath Indian legends, had been pitted against one another. Llao of the Below World and Skell of the Above World fought a cataclysmic battle, raging with fire and smoke, hurling ashes and stone, until Llao's home of Mount Mazama was destroyed.

Crater Lake was what remained. Evidence of the Below World.

With a brochure describing the conflict, Clay crested the lookout. In an instant he forgot every gripe, every dirty pore and bruised muscle.

He gasped. His mind boggled at the sheer enormity of this natural wonder. Poised a thousand feet above the surface, he gazed upon the nation's deepest lake. If he threw himself over the railing, he would plunge nearly three thousand feet from the cliff's top to the lake's icy bottom. The waters now covering the heart of this ancient volcano shimmered in the sunlight, a mirror of ultramarine blue.

He had never seen anything like it. It dwarfed him. Demanded awe.

To his left a massive lava flow formed the crags of Llao Rock. To his right, Devil's Backbone paralleled Skell Channel, a band of water separating the caldera's cliffs from its unruly offspring known as Wizard Island. The cone was no more than a volcanic youngster, waiting for its turn to blow; tufts of trees sprouted along its neck and pointed chin.

Clay set down his pack. With the GPS unit strapped to his belt, he saved the coordinates. What, he wondered, makes us want to leave our mark?

He locked his arms around the top rail, slipped one leg over the bottom. His foot was dangling over empty space.

"Hold it right there."

Clay gripped the rail tighter. The voice had come from his right.

"Don't move a muscle, Clay. I'm about to shoot."

"Sam? Is that you?" He turned. "Lyndon?"

The Nikon camera whirred and its lens blinked twice.

"Ahhh." Clay slapped a hand to his chest. "You got me."

———

Clay could do nothing but smile at the SNL banter. Sam's Volvo had been parked at the lookout, and he'd driven them to the Rim Village's restaurant near Crater Lake Lodge. By large windows they now waited for their lunch orders.

Lyndon said, "You should've seen the look on your face, Clay."

"Well, put yourself in his shoes, Lyndon. Peering over the lake, nothing but a guardrail to hang on to, and he hears you threaten to shoot. How was he to know we would bump into him out there?" Sam brushed a tidbit of parsley to the floor.

"I saw that, Sam."

"Oh, stop. You know how I despise poor service, and it's plain to see they didn't even touch this table after the last party left."

Lyndon rolled his eyes and looked to Clay for help. "Do you think you could live with a person like this?"

"For hygiene reasons, definitely. For moral reasons, probably not."

"Look at Bible boy climb onto his high horse."

"Hey, I'm not pointing fingers. If you knew my own past, you'd stay far away."

"Let's hear it." Lyndon rubbed his hands together. "No holding back. We want every juicy detail."

"You're a pig," Sam told Lyndon. "You really are."

"You're as curious as I am, just afraid to admit it."

Sam waved off this accusation. "There's a proper way to do things, a time and a place." He leaned forward, propped his chin on folded hands. "Clay, we have no ulterior motives. We made no conscious attempt to arrive here the same day as you. Even if we had, it would've been quite the chore tracking you down at a place as vast as Crater Lake."

"A crazy coincidence, but I'm not complaining. It's great to see you guys."

Although Clay's words were sincere, a portion of him wanted to flee the table. He had a task to carry out, a sacrificial act. He could think of little else.

"It's more than coincidence," Lyndon said. "Don't you remember our conversation the other day?"

"What he's saying, Clay, is that we're here together, talking, baring our souls, because of elements beyond our control. Which brings us back to your past. Despite Lyndon's outrageous lack of manners, we do share a desire to hear more."

"To hear every juicy detail. Why deny it, Sam?"

"It's true." Sam flipped up his hands. "We want to know everything."

Clay grinned.

"Your terrible past, your secrets… Please, what're you hiding from us?"

"In all seriousness," Lyndon said, "you don't have to say a word."

Yes, I do. But it's too late for that now.

Clay took a deep breath. He was in a rustic setting, near a lake of ominous beauty, on the point of confessing his sin to a pair of men many would judge. Lyndon and Sam, like most male roommates, shared rent and space, but according to biblical teaching, they also lived in a specific pattern of wrongdoing.

Don't we all? What makes them less deserving of grace than others?

Clay thought about the lepers of Jesus's day, those whom most religious leaders had dismissed with arrogance and repugnance.

Jesus had reached out to them. He'd walked with them.

Well, isn't it God's kindness that leads us to repentance? Like I can talk!

His guilt yanked him back to that moment on the bridge. It'd been more than a prod. More than a push. In a flash of anger, he'd wanted to see Bill Scott dead, and he'd shoved the kid as hard as he could.

With Sam and Lyndon awaiting a response, Clay mouthed, "Maybe later."

Lyndon sighed.

"Famous last words," Sam said with an air of defeat.

———

"Cleetwood Cove. This is the right place?"

From the Volvo's backseat, Clay saw a marker for the trailhead. "Yep, this is it."

Sam turned from East Rim Drive into the parking lot. "You're sure you want to go down there?"

"I've wanted to do it for a long time."

"Really, Sam," Lyndon chimed in, "I don't see what you're so worried about anyway. Sounds wonderful. A long boat ride around the lake, park rangers in uniform dispensing snippets of little-known trivia."

"And one tiny little boat over four cubic miles of water."

"You're a worry wart—that's what you are. Worry, worry, nag, nag."

"Thanks, guys. Good seeing you again." Clay opened the door, wrestled his pack onto the pavement.

"Clay."

He turned into Sam's slate gray gaze.

"Whatever's gnawing at you, let it go."

"Mm-hmm. Okay."

"You're not alone in this world. There are people who care."

"Thanks, Sam. Lyndon." Clay lifted his load again. "Appreciate the ride."

Without looking back, he took a breath and headed for the ticket kiosk. From there the steep trail carried him down to a rocky shore where tour boats waited for their next loads. He isolated himself from the flocking passengers, stared across the lake's blue-velvet blanket. In this majestic place, it was hard not to think in spiritual terms.

Skell and Llao—warring chiefs of the Above and the Below World.

God and Satan—opponents locked in battle over the souls of mankind.

Or maybe it's all legends and myths. I don't know anymore.

Clay munched on a granola bar. Swatted at a fly. Dug through his pack for Kenny Preston's oak tube. With the cork snugged down, he passed the object from hand to hand. He and Kenny could share this secret in the grave.

When the boarding call came, he shoved the tube into his pants and found a seat on the boat. He set his backpack between his legs, tried to look past those around him. German and Japanese accents mixed with a lone Aussie voice, grating against his crowded thoughts.

Did man's free will prevail here? Clay wondered. Or God's sovereignty?

6.2.1.0.4...7.2.0.4...7.1.1.0.4...and blah-dee-blah.

Had these been arbitrary dates, capable of being shifted? Or had they been set in stone by grand design, beyond mortal manipulation?

He'd tried to intervene. Failed miserably.

8.1.0.0.4...Jason Ryker.

Clay felt a moan well in his throat. He swallowed. If he let the sound escape, it would burst into soul-wrenching wails. The thought of losing his son tore him apart; the thought of being unable to stop it stabbed at his heart. He was done.

In one and three-quarter hours, this boat would return to Cleetwood Cove.

If Clay's free will prevailed, it would be minus one passenger.

———

"The report's just come in," Monde said. Dressed in his corduroy jacket, sporting elbow patches, he could've been an old-time news anchor delivering a story. "One of the Consortium's apprentices has spotted Mr. Ryker on the shores of Crater Lake."

Asgoth's lips twisted into a smile.

"Based on my projections, A.G., we'll soon receive word of Ryker's demise."

"What's to stand in our way? You've been right on the money so far."

Monde's nostrils flared.

"What? Has something gone wrong?"

"Wrong?" Monde weighed the idea. "That may be too strong a word. But there are elements I did not anticipate. Referring back to my lock analogy, even one tumbler out of place could disrupt access to Ryker's mind."

"Are you telling me the plan could fail? The way it did years ago?"

"Let's not dredge that up. Earlier, when Ryker convened with two middle-aged gentlemen near the lodge, it appeared to throw off our timetable. Now, though, they've transported him to the cove, delivering him to the anticipated spot."

"Okay. But you mentioned a tumbler out of place."

"I did." Monde rolled his shoulders. "Given the opportunity, the apprentice was supposed to nab the train's treasure from Clay, but now it's suspected that someone else followed Clay down to the boat."

"Who? The man from the Brotherhood? Dmitri so-and-so?" Asgoth bristled. "I've waited years for this, Monde. We need that item and the riches it can provide. We need Clay to cooperate. He took everything from me, and this is his chance—his duty!—to give it back. If this Dmitri guy steps in, he'll spoil the whole thing. Do you understand? Only a sacrifice will do."

"Of course I understand. Mr. Ryker must believe he's paying for his own sins."

"That's right. A self-sacrifice!"

———

The boat moved through pristine waters, a walnut shell set afloat in a huge earthen bowl. Cliffs encircled the lake, ranging from glacier-carved saddles to ragged lava formations to orange-pumice deposits.

Clay hugged his pack with his knees. When should he do it?

The ranger's running commentary broke through in pieces.

"Nearly five hundred feet below the surface, directly beneath us now, the Merriam Cone is a lesser volcano... Considering Mount Mazama's long eruptive history, scientists predict this area will become active again... Straight ahead, you can see Hillman Peak and the Watchmen... Keep an eye open for the Old Man, an ancient hemlock tree that floats about the lake. We're not sure, but we believe lightning may have felled it. It's been a part of the lake's lore since the 1800s. None of today's tours have spotted him yet, so one of you may be the first."

At Wizard Island the boat released its passengers to a brief period of exploration. Clay wandered without aim. He gazed up, imagined molten lava pouring down the cone's shaved scalp.

Back onboard, the tourists quieted. Couples leaned into one another, while older men rubbed their glasses; some panned the lake with camcorders, while others pulled hats down low in defense against the hammering sun. A large man in a Hawaiian shirt shifted behind him, knees brushing against his back.

Clay was preoccupied. His heart thumped against his chest.

Should he throw himself overboard with his pack on? Were the rangers trained for such emergencies? For insurance purposes he had to be certain it looked accidental. Would it be better to drown in a shallower area, say four or five hundred feet of water? Or would the deepest sections serve best?

As if it matters. Come on, Clay. Just do it!

His eyes pierced the glassy surface. The lake had been stocked with trout. What other creatures prowled below?

Breaking through Clay's fear, the ranger's voice described a nearing collection of lava flows. The tour boat turned so that the eerie formations of Phantom Ship seemed to spring into view. Harbored here indefinitely, this stone vessel rose above them with jagged sails and impregnable gunwales. Clay could imagine, among the crags, ghostly pirates loading muskets and cannons.

Bill should've been here to see this.

Clay flashed to an image of Kenny Preston.

Yep. Kenny would've thought this was the coolest.

Clay shifted his backpack to his knees. How long was he going to put this off? He fingered the buttons of the GPS on his belt, again marking his location. Here's where he would die. His ears burned with his own words from that fateful bridge years ago.

You can't think. You just do it. Just jump.

Around him passengers were shifting and turning, murmuring with excitement. Had he spoken the words out loud?

Following the pointing fingers, Clay saw a timeworn tree hovering in the water. Boosted by the ranger's romantic tales of yore, the Old Man held the crowd's attention.

Clay got his arms beneath his pack, then flipped it overboard.

"My stuff," he cried out. "It fell over."

With the distracted tourists serving as his witnesses, he had to believe that his life insurance policy would cough up a good chunk of cash. For Jenni. For Jason, too—if his son survived beyond next month.

Regardless, this had to appear as an accident, a monumental lack of judgment as he went after his belongings.

His pack smacked the water. He took a deep breath.

Go, go, go...now!

Clay catapulted himself over the side, felt the icy cold rip at his face. He was underwater. His clothes and shoes sucked him down, but he made an effort to reach the pack while air pockets kept it hovering at the surface. All part of the show.

His head burst from the lake. He gulped air. Shouts came from the boat. He clawed toward his belongings, saw them tilt and begin to sink. He porpoised his long body, carved his arms down into the frigid zone, kicked headfirst toward the plummeting pack that had become a specter leading him into the Below World.

Every cell screamed for air. His body resisted this death wish.

Back to the surface? No! Not this time around.

His legs scissored again. Cupped hands pulled him deeper. The pack was nearly beyond the sunlight's reach, a black pebble dropping through cobalt blue gel.

What was he doing? Did this make any sense?

Clay had shouldered his guilt, carried it on this pilgrimage. His sins had dragged him down. Yet now, released from the weight, he was still here chasing after them.

Behind him, far above, water splashed.

He continued his descent. His fingers brushed, then clamped on a strap of his pack. He twisted it around his wrist.

Death's jaws seemed to close around him with each downward inch; the temperature chewed through his clothes; the needle-sharp fangs of oxygen deprivation pumped carbon dioxide into his lungs. Briefly his thoughts snapped into crystalline focus, then they, too, fell victim to the gathering pressure.

God, what have I done? I am unclean. A sinner!

With more than a quarter of a mile to the bottom, he sensed the presence of millions of gallons of ice water shoving him down into the volcano's black heart. Like shattering glass, water pinged and popped in his ears.

He needed air. How long had it been—forty-five seconds, a full minute? Yet the instinct not to breathe underwater overpowered the growing agony in his lungs. The edges of consciousness were shredding. Darkness was closing in.

How pathetic this must seem. Would they find his corpse like some bloated fish? Would they have to keep his coffin closed to spare his family? Clay thought of his parents, of his wife and son, standing over him, staring down.

Would there be tears?

These contemplations joined forces with his base instinct to survive and, in a spasmodic breath that overrode his brain's warnings, his mouth dragged water into his windpipe and flooded his chest cavity. Half-conscious, enfeebled, he turned his eyes to the surface. He kicked once. Tried to rise.

The pack's strap was cinched in a knot around his hand.

He struggled. Panic was his enemy now.

And he was still going down, losing feeling in limbs that weighed upon him like rubber truncheons. The cold water was slowing his metabolic processes. His thoughts were filtering through cold molasses.

So hard to swim. To move.

Below he could see it, shadowy and waiting. Hell. Hungry for his soul.

It's what I deserve… Jesus!

There, carved from the depths, Bill Scott was peering up with vacuous eyes. Then Summer Svenson. Edged in flickering aquamarine, black shapes swirled into a macabre crowd of spectators. They were waiting with yawning mouths, calling to him without a sound, and he was descending to join them.

His body seemed to hover, almost peacefully, in an embryonic state.

Shutting down.

But where was Kenny? The kid was not here among the crowd.

He's not here!

Clay tried again to turn—so sluggish, caught in the grip. The pack slipped free finally, but he was fading into blackness. His lips gaped. Crying out.

A final trail of bubbles, exploding upward…

A silvery telltale chain…

A dying man's desperate prayer…

Oh, Jesus. Hear my cry!

PART THREE

Ghost and fiend consorted with him there....
he walked continually in its shadow,
groping darkly within his own soul.

The Minister's Black Veil, Nathaniel Hawthorne

Everyone must turn
from their evil ways... Who can tell?
Perhaps even yet God will have pity on us.

Jonah 3:8–9

29

Two Things

"Ghosts."

"Shut up. That's not even funny."

"Well, what else could they freakin' be? Listen to that."

The young couple stood in their Junction City apartment, eyes turned upward. Again an object of some sort rumbled overhead, followed by an angry growl. Sheetrock dust and paint chips drifted from the ceiling.

"Usually they're so quiet. I wasn't even sure anyone lived up there."

"This is creepin' me out," the girl said. "Call the cops."

"Like we need that right now." The guy nodded his head at the stash of stolen TVs and DVD players that overflowed from the closet into the hallway. "We look like a stinkin' Circuit City."

"What'd I tell you? We shoulda never moved into this town or this rat hole. You know what they say happened upstairs? Couple months ago some guy got skewered right there in his own kitchen."

"That's a buncha bull. This town feeds off stories like that."

Another low howl conjured images of an animal in pain.

The guy's girlfriend thrust forward a cell phone. "Call somebody; call the apartment manager!"

"But what if he sees—"

"I swear, if you don't do something, I will. Who knows what's going on up there? Somebody could be dying. What if they've got a gun? We could get shot."

"You need to back off the meds, babe. You're trippin' hard."

She punched numbers on the phone, slapped away his hand. He latched on to her wrist. He was not going to let this little tramp ruin what they had going. With sales to scattered pawnshops, they'd be lining their pockets soon enough. Jackpot! He'd buy that Kawasaki he'd seen at the Lane County

Fairgrounds auto show; she'd shop at all those stores that eyed her like she was some sticky-fingered retro rebel.

Well, okay, maybe she was. But that wasn't the point.

"Think about it, babe. Use your head for once."

"Oh, don't even!"

"Listen," he said. "One call and we could lose it all. Every last dime."

Another layer of dust sprinkled between their glaring faces. The guy thought it was hilarious, seeing bits of powder land on the tip of his girlfriend's nose. Knowing her previous habits, he had to laugh.

She socked him in the ribs, then spurted out the door.

Once more the ceiling quaked and fierce wall pounding punctuated a litany of growls. It was getting really annoying. If she didn't come back, he was going to be furious, and he'd blame it on those idiots overhead.

He yelled at the top of his lungs, spitting epithets. "Shut up! You hear me up there? You don't quiet down, I'm callin' the police!"

———

Asgoth paced the apartment, livid and bewildered. After all the planning, how had they failed? Where were the miscues? Clay Ryker had gone on his death march. Yes, he'd thrown himself into the water, relenting to the psychological pressure.

But he survived! And now the treasure of Engine 418 is out of reach.

"Please, A.G., don't do this," Henna pleaded.

He circled her moaning figure. Felt an insatiable desire to grab clumps of blond hair and pull. He wanted to strike out—at anyone, anything.

"Please. We'll make things right."

"You say that so flippantly, but do you know how many years I've waited for this? I might as well be a dead man for all the good it's done me. I've dreamed of this opportunity. With Clay still in the picture, though, I can't even take the next step."

"Maybe I should have a go at him?"

Asgoth churned inside. "What's that supposed to mean? You think I'm inadequate, or do you have a soft spot for him? You have seemed distracted."

"Distracted? No, don't be silly."

"Don't lie to me, Henna. Surely you find him attractive."

"He's always been handsome, I won't deny it."

"Ah! See, there's the reason I can't leave this in your hands. You need me to help carry it out."

"But it's not working."

"There's still time!"

"Aren't the others willing to help?"

"The Consortium?" Asgoth said with disdain. "They'd love to see me fail."

"What about Monde?"

"That fool! He's slipping. He didn't even realize Sergeant Turney was gone until yesterday. I told him, but did he listen? With his purported expertise, he should've anticipated this."

Rage surged through Asgoth's extremities, seeking an outlet. He lashed out. Henna whimpered, hugging herself. When she moved to brush her hair from her face, Asgoth threaded his fingers with hers and pulled back. She emitted a shriek. He followed with a low howl of his own.

Downstairs, the neighbor was screaming empty threats.

———

Clay relived those final moments of consciousness...

His body was on high alert, his mind flipping some primal switch that called for survival at all costs. He was still sinking. The cobalt gel was thickening around him. Frozen muscles and carbon dioxide–poisoned limbs hampered his efforts to claw upward. Shards of light slashed across his eyelids, intensified by the dark waters.

Bump...

It was a creature of the deep.

Bummpp...

Or a malevolent spirit coming to feast upon his soul.

God, I don't want to die! Make it go away. Protect me from...whatever this is.

The thing latched on to his thigh, into his belt, around his chest. It was strong, unyielding. Gathering him in.

Is anyone listening? Anyone there?

He tried to fight, but liquid ice flooded his mouth. No strength left.

Jesus...save me!

The waters folded him up in a cold black bundle.

———

Hands propped him up against cool white pillows. From the corner a lamp poured honey-colored light over the room's sparse furnishings.

"Welcome to the land of the living."

Clay turned toward the warm voice. He was not alone. He was alive.

"For a while there, thought you might check out on us."

Clay blinked against the light. As his pupils adjusted, he saw a patch of short dark hair, wide cheeks, deep chocolate eyes, and a spreading grin.

"Sarge? You again?"

"The one and only."

"Where are we? How'd I get here? Were you there...at Crater Lake?"

"Whoa." Sergeant Turney lifted fleshy hands in surrender. "Hold on a sec, partner. See, we can do this my way: I tell you what happened from start to finish. Or we can try it your way: one question at a time."

Clay sank back into feathery bliss. "I'm so tired."

"You've been snoozin' since yesterday evening. You should be bright as a lark. Heck, by the time I fished you outta the water and flopped your bony butt into the boat, an emergency team was cuttin' across the lake. They performed CPR and all that rigmarole, then shot you off to the nearest medical facility."

In Clay's mind, hazy images supported the sergeant's account.

"'Course, they wanted to hold you for medical evaluation. I told 'em I was in the middle of an investigation, flashed my credentials, promised to keep an eye on you. After a call or two, they handed you over. To be honest, I think they were glad to be rid of you. Bad park publicity—security questions and all that. Sooner you were outta there, the better."

"You dove in after me? You were on the boat?"

"Right behind you."

"Never even saw you."

"Your head was in a fog—that much was obvious. You saw me all right. Just didn't recognize me. Had on a pair o' shades and a baseball cap, jeans and one of them Hawaiian shirts."

"So it was your hands I felt on my belt? Scared me to death. I was praying God would make you go away." Clay's eyes closed as his energy ebbed.

"Thank God for ignorin' that one, huh?"

"I thought I was dead for sure."

"And now you're alive, partner. You've been given a second chance." Sarge rubbed a hand over his cheeks. "The way it looked to me, you went overboard on purpose. Am I right?"

Clay looked toward the window.

"Forget that I've got a badge," Sarge said. "Sakes alive, what made ya think it was time to call it quits?"

With both hands, Clay rubbed his forehead, then closed his eyes. He felt embarrassment and shame, as well as an overwhelming sense of relief. He'd been offered back his life. Free will had been exercised, but God's will had cut in. The life and times of Clay Ryker were not yet over.

"I killed a man."

"You what?"

"Years ago," Clay said. "I killed a friend."

The words of confession were ropes tied to his limbs and pulled in opposite directions. He would be torn apart; he could not survive. Then, as his voice rose and fell, as the full story of Bill Scott's death gurgled forth, Clay felt the guilt ebb away. He'd never told a soul about this, never in full detail.

Sarge met his eye. "You wanted him to die."

Clay nodded.

"Could've been an accident. Those things happen."

"Nope. I know what was in my mind, Sarge."

"Maybe so. But only God knows the intentions of a man's heart."

"Then I deserved to die in that water."

"Don't we all, Clay. So you've been carryin' this around all this time, takin' it out on yourself and those around you? Well, I'd say you had yourself a good old-fashioned baptism in Crater Lake. Time for you to start fresh. As a new man."

"Shouldn't I confess to the police?"

"You just did. And there's really no way of knowin' what caused his death, not one hundred percent. Twelve years—that's a long time. Relax."

Clay eased into the pillows, warm beneath the lamp's honey glow.

He had to ask, though: "Why me, Sarge? Summer's gone, and that old couple out on High Pass Road. Why am I still alive?"

"That's a question we should be askin' ourselves each day. Now listen, you should be countin' your blessings. Think back to those childhood Bible stories, and tell me what kept Jonah from drownin' in the sea. A large fish, am I right?" Sarge patted his protruding stomach. "Well, looky here, you got saved by your very own whale."

———

Located on the North Umpqua River, Steamboat Inn provided the rest Clay needed. Through the windows of the river suite, he watched the rushing waters dip and curl against a backdrop of bigleaf maples and evergreens. The faint noise along Highway 138 reminded him of the outside world, but within the pine-paneled walls he found rejuvenation beyond his physical concerns.

Sarge had paid for two nights here. He'd spread out his stuff on the couch, leaving the king bed for Clay. Clay watched him kindle a fire in the fireplace, cook eggs and waffles in the minikitchen, pour fresh coffee into "Get Oregonized" mugs.

"Ran a load o' laundry for you," Sarge said, pointing at a pile of loosely folded clothes. " 'Course, you're pretty much stuck with whatcha got. Most everything"—he flipped his thumb down—"went to the bottom of the lake."

Clay looked through the stack. His GPS was there, still strapped to his belt.

"Was there anything else, Sarge? A wooden tube?"

"Does an old cork count? Sorry. If it didn't float, it's sittin' down with the fishies."

Without the cork, Clay reasoned, the hollowed oak tube would've sunk like a stone. Did it even matter?

After breakfast Sarge loaded up his fishing gear. "Wanna come along, Clay? Some of the biggest steelhead you'll ever find."

"I'll pass."

"If you're needin' tackle, I've got—"

"No, I'm just not ready to go dipping my feet into the water again. Not yet."

Sarge clapped a hand on Clay's shoulder. "You're gonna be all right."

Clay spent the next hours relaxing. On a private deck, he gazed over the water between sips of coffee and fifteen-minute naps. He tended his stitches, glad to see the skin mending. Trees rustled in the river breeze as passages from the Gideon Bible in his lap began stitching the wounds in his spirit.

Next to the main building, he found the Steamboat Inn library where plush chairs beckoned and vaulted ceilings pointed skyward. In one sitting he read through half a Randy Singer legal thriller—just as Jenni was prone to do.

He considered calling her. Maybe in a day or two.

Sarge returned that afternoon and pan-fried his fresh catch in olive oil. He sprinkled thyme on the thick fillets, served them with broccoli and garlic bread.

"After roughin' it on the trail," Clay said, "this is awesome."

Sarge gripped a fold of his belly. "Yeah, who says we bachelors can't enjoy a good meal? I have been cuttin' back, though. Gotta slim down for the lady in my life."

"Josee, right? How's it working out between you?"

"Wow! Good memory there. Yes sir, things're lookin' up."

The conversation turned from women and relationships to the events of the past few days. With his energy returning, Clay was ready to work through the details.

"Sarge, what led you to Crater Lake? How'd you know to find me there?"

"Trade secret." Sarge winked. "No, you really wanna know?"

"My parents. They realized all the camping gear was gone, right?"

"They did. That's a fact. When they let me know you'd disappeared, it didn't take me long to find out the car was registered for long-term parking up by Willamette Pass. Got worried when I found out you'd drained your checking account. Your mother figured you must be headed for Crater Lake. Told me all about your high school dreams of doin' just that."

Clay speared another bite of fish.

"I had other help too," Sarge said.

"What do you mean?"

"Had someone keepin' an eye out for ya. Kid by the name of Scooter."

"Wesley?"

"That's him. He's a natural at it. Dropped him off at Windigo Pass, had him hike back until he ran into you. Last year he got messed up in some nasty stuff, so this is one way I've helped him stay outta trouble. Good kid at heart. Every now and then he likes to gimme a hand with my investigations."

"He was a spy. That's what you're saying? An informant?"

"He volunteered." Sarge shrugged, sipped at a glass of Pepsi Vanilla.

"So you were watching me the whole time. You think I'm guilty, is that it?"

"I had my questions. Thing is, Clay, it doesn't add up. The nights that Summer Svenson and Mr. and Mrs. Coates died, you were at home. Your parents swear to it. On top of that, the blue paint scrapes at the Svenson scene don't come close to matchin' any of the vehicles you've been drivin'. As for the incident at the Coateses'? That was just one terrible accident. Every bit of evidence says the lady shot him, thinkin' it was self-defense, then died while breathin' in fumes."

"If that's the case, why'd you have me followed?"

"Whoa now. You hiked right alongside Scooter. That was your choice as much as his. And in case you don't remember, he left you a day early."

"At Diamond Lake."

"Mm-hmm. That's when he called. Told me where you were headed."

"But why'd you come?" Clay pushed back his chair.

"Scooter told me how you gave him your Discman. He was worried about you, said you were actin' awful depressed. Guess it was a good thing I was there since you meant to die in that lake. I almost drowned gettin' you out, and now suddenly I'm the bad guy?"

Clay stood and paced in front of the fireplace. "I mean, thanks for saving me. Seriously. Without your help, I guess I'd be fish food two thousand feet under."

"There's something else buggin' ya. What is it?"

"You wouldn't believe me if I told you."

"Try me. I've been through stuff most people would say was crazy. Just ask Josee. She could fill you in." Patient sincerity filled Sergeant Turney's eyes. "C'mon, Clay. Let's hear it."

———

"Expiration dates?"

Clay groaned at the question.

"Lemme get this straight. You think you know when people'll die?"

"I don't just think, Sarge. I know. How else do you explain—"

"Clay, hold up. I'm just workin' this out in my head."

"Sounds like I've lost my mind, doesn't it?"

"How can you lose something you never had?" Sarge laughed and pressed on past Clay's show of indignation. "So the way I figure it, you're like a modern-day Jonah. You've been given the knowledge to help save lives, but you've been more focused on feelin' sorry for yourself. Runnin' from yourself and the past."

"I tried to save one kid, Sarge, soon as I realized what was going on."

"Good. I'm sure that's part of your assignment. God still works through his people, you know."

"Oh, he does, does he?" Clay's voice turned bitter. "Well, guess what. That kid died. He got… He was taken out by a train."

"And that's why you threw yourself off the boat. To pay for your failure." Clay said nothing.

"Lemme tell you something that should bring a smile to that long face of yours. From what I can tell, Junction City hasn't reported a train accident in months. Hasn't reported any missing children either."

"I saw it with my own eyes. You've gotta believe me, Sarge."

"Can't believe everything you see. Don't ask me how or why, but for some reason you've convinced yourself of something that never happened. My investigation has kept connectin' back to Engine 418, so it was only a matter of time till I found out about Kenny Preston's favorite pastime."

"Kenny? Yep, he told me how he liked exploring that engine."

"He told me the same thing."

"Huh?"

"It's true, Clay. Three nights ago I sat and talked with him and his mother. He's got more life left in his bones than you and me put together."

30

In the Bunker

Dmitri lost another ten dollars at the Mill Casino's blackjack table.

This was a poor idea, he scolded himself. He was too distracted to be gambling with Brotherhood monies. Too tired. He felt dirtied by this encounter with greed's ugly stepchild.

"Kak dela?" he heard a voice say. "How's life?"

"Oleg?"

Dmitri turned to find his comrade's shiny face. If the man shaved, he showed no need for it; his skin was oily and without wrinkles. Despite his choirboy look and voice, Oleg Volovnik was a former crime lord from Moscow. His great-grandfather had been one of the Brotherhood of Tobolsk, and Oleg told how he had renewed his own vision for Russian resurgence during the Kremlin's recent exhibit of Fabergé eggs. When he heard that a number of the jeweled artifacts were still missing, he felt it symbolized his country's state of affairs, and he vowed to put things right.

"A nice afternoon. Let's take a walk so we can speak in privacy."

"Da, Oleg. I'm ready to stretch my legs."

Dmitri strolled past a poster advertising an upcoming series of Rick Springfield concerts. Outside, a Coquille Indian totem pole staked tribal claim to the casino's profits, and ocean salt replaced the air's cigarette stench.

"No one knows you are here, Dmitri?"

"No one. After I called you with news of the shooting, I turned in the rental car in Eugene. This casino had a special deal. I took a free bus ride here and also got a weekend in the hotel. I didn't use the passport or my real name."

"Very good."

"But I did lose track of the object from Engine 418. It's far gone, I fear."

"Dmitri." Oleg chortled. "You have already searched, and there was nothing on the train. A little boy's treasure? Bah. More likely a historian's mistake. These things happen."

"The boy may still have it. I chased after him, but a train came, and I could not search until it'd passed. I found no sign of the boy. He escaped with the secret, or maybe he gave it to this man Clay Ryker. I should've followed Clay into the mountains."

"Nyet. We have other matters for you to investigate. We believe we will find the final connection to the Tsars' bloodline."

Dmitri lifted his head. "Are you certain of this?"

"Nothing is certain, comrade. But look at this photo. We believe it's her."

Dmitri accepted the dossier Oleg eased into his hand. He removed a picture and biography sheet, noticed the names and statistics matched those he had coaxed from his Fort Lauderdale victim. This was good; the former Nazi had not lied.

"Gertrude Ubelhaar, she is here? At the women's correctional facility?"

"Da. South of Portland." Oleg looked like a schoolboy delivering an oral report. "Already she is behind bars nine months on charges of terrorist activity."

"Has she told anyone her secret? Maybe she wishes to make peace with God."

"She's not one to worry about God, Dmitri. She's an isolated old woman …babushka. Who would she tell? What for?"

"Because she must surely take great pride in this. She was chosen in secret, because of her ties with Hitler, to mother the descendant of the Romanovs. Her son, may he be blessed, is the very Tsar we seek!"

"Do we know his name? Is he in hiding?"

"We've searched but found nothing. As if he never existed."

"The Tsar does exist. He should be fifty-eight, the age of our fathers."

"Look at these." Oleg tapped at assorted newspaper clippings.

Dmitri removed a paper clip and thumbed through reports of a late-night altercation near an Oregon lighthouse. A photo showed a mangled helicopter, while a corresponding article mentioned a kidnapped woman's harrowing tale, plus a missing man now presumed dead.

"We believe this is the same man. Her son."

"But, Oleg, this man is missing. For how long?"

"Since October of last year. He could be gone for good."

"Dead? I do not accept this. I will not. We must speak to his mother."

"Witnesses saw him that night," Oleg reasserted. "He had a knife, and he—"

"Nyet!" Dmitri slapped the dossier against his comrade's shoulder. "I will not believe this is the truth. You see here?" He folded down the hem of his slacks, jabbed at his identifying scar. "This is the angel we must wrestle. She guides us, leads us to a strong motherland. God has given us this task."

"I, too, bear the angel wing. We are men of destiny, but others make choices that bring us trouble. We must prepare for—"

"Oleg, destiny does not stumble over small obstacles. I will speak with Gertrude Ubelhaar, and we will find our Tsar."

"Da. As well as a portion of the Rasputin fortune." A cherubic smile graced the former crime lord's lips. "You will do this as the Brotherhood has appointed. *Do svidanya.*"

———

Kenny Preston was the reigning spymaster. Strong and courageous.

Jesus, you were with me. I could feel it all the way.

Lying on his basement bed, he grinned and patted the mattress. Gussy pounced up and licked his face, her tongue tickling his nose. His mom kept telling him to "discourage this unsanitary behavior," but he was a thirteen-year-old. What did he care? He loved his little puppy.

"That's right, girl. Wasn't sure if I'd find you again."

Gussy nuzzled his neck with a playful growl.

"You were so pitiful," Kenny said, "huddled in that alley. Can't blame you, not after the lady tried to scare you with that needle."

Had it been over a week already? Eight days since he ditched two grown men along the rail embankment? That Sunday night would stick with Kenny for a long time—the way he'd escaped from the park to the drainage ditch, the way Gussy had bit that lady and almost got hit by the Mustang.

But the night train…

Yeah-huh, that was the best part. Won't ever forget it.

Standing at the drainpipe, Kenny's heart had inflated in his throat. He'd given his treasure to Clay Ryker, then taken off through the ditch. As hoped, that other dude jumped out of the car and started chasing him. For some reason, though, Clay came back. What was he thinking? Kenny wanted to yell at him to get away, to hide the wooden tube somewhere safe. The big guy was gaining. Up ahead, Kenny saw a concrete bunker that he'd explored in the past. On its backside, concealed by thorn bushes, a metal door hung on rusted hinges.

He sprinted up the ditch. Out of view of his pursuers, he shimmied beneath the briers, thankful for his bike helmet's protection. He pulled himself into the bunker's black space, swiped at spider webs on his arms and face. The night train screamed a warning at the shadows along the tracks.

Not like Kenny wanted to get flattened into a pancake, no thanks.

Seconds later the guy with the accent vaulted up the embankment. Amber lights pulsed over the ground. Clay's voice sliced through the chaos, screaming Kenny's name, telling him to run.

Kenny almost obeyed. Almost sprinted from his hiding spot.

But no, why should he? The big dude hadn't seen him.

Through the mess of thorns, Kenny watched the train hurtle by, felt it shake the ground beneath him. A creature scurried over his neck. He flicked it away. Kept his eyes on the man now searching the empty tracks with eyes as intense as the Rottweiler's earlier that morning.

Kenny hunched in the bunker long after everyone had gone.

Boy, talk about a rough day for the spymaster. But he'd fooled them all.

"Then," he said, ruffling Gussy's ears, "I went back and found you."

The puppy shook her head and backed onto his chest, tugging at a button.

"Kenny," his mother called, "come on up."

He set his pet on the floor and dashed up the basement stairs to meet her. She'd been on edge earlier in the week. Although he hadn't told her everything, she knew enough to be worried sick. When an investigative consultant named Sergeant Turney had showed up a few nights back, he'd eased some of her concerns and offered protection. He'd also asked about the locomotive downtown.

"Kenny," his mom was explaining, "you have a visitor."

"Who is it?"

"He's at the table, eating the last piece of blackberry cobbler."

Kenny turned into the kitchen to find a tall man hovering over a slice of week-old pie. He'd made his mom promise not to throw that out. Good thing.

"Guess who?" He tapped the broad back.

Clay Ryker spun in the chair.

"Kenny? Kenny! Oh, man, if you only…if you had any idea."

Clay set his hands on Kenny's shoulders, looked him over, then smothered him in an embrace. Kenny thought it was nice to get this kind of attention, but he had a hard time telling if the man was laughing or crying as the hug tightened.

"I can't believe it," Clay said. "I thought that train took you out. I thought I'd failed in every way. I mean, I watched it happen. I screamed for you to run, but you just stood there. You must've jumped at the very last second."

"Never even went up on the tracks. Just hid in the bunker."

"That concrete thing? But I…I saw you… That was a horrible trick."

"Yeah? Well, I thought you'd disappeared," Kenny said. "Where ya been the last week? Heard stories, but I know most of them were just dog doodie, right?"

"Kenneth," his mother chided from the doorway.

Clay shook his head. "I've been to hell and back, Kenny. What about you?"

———

Clay left the Preston home in a state of joyous disbelief. The kid was alive, flesh and bone. Death had not claimed him. His expiration date had been extended.

At Steamboat Inn, Sarge had commissioned Clay to stop running from this unusual ability, to start using it for others' good. There was a spiritual world, he explained, that impacted things in the physical realm—and vice versa. Clay's task was to release his past burdens and accept God's design for the future.

One thing still plagued Clay. In his mind he could see Kenny's face caught in that night train's light. He winced at the scene's brutal conclusion.

Had his brain lied? Had his eyes deceived him? How could he deny what he'd witnessed?

But of course, he thought. *That must be it...*

In those moments before impact, at that crossroad between life and death, Clay must have projected ahead a few seconds, catching glimpses of what fate had intended for the kid; whereas, Kenny's last-second choices had diverted him from that course.

However it worked, the boy was healthy and breathing. Clay's decision to get involved had reaped the reward of a human life, and relief flooded his soul.

But, he reminded himself, emotions are fickle things.

A sense of regret seeped in as he crested Cox Butte Road, less than a hundred yards from his parents' house. This was a whole different scene. How was he going to explain himself? He was returning the Duster in one piece; that was a consolation of sorts. Sergeant Turney had been kind enough to take him back to the trailhead on Highway 58, and the car had started right up—with a little jumper-cable assistance. On the other hand, Clay had deep-sixed all the camping equipment and lost a week of work.

From the living room recliner, a gruff voice halted him. "The prodigal, eh?"

"Hi, Dad. Is Mom around?"

"Son, you think I keep track of everyone in this family?" With the remote Gerald lifted the volume two more notches.

"I should've called. Let you know where I was."

"Should've showed up for work—that would've been the proper thing."

"Did Mr. Blomberg call? He must be steamed. I'm sorry."

"Sorry? Humph!"

"Well, what else do you want me to say?"

"Nothing. That seems to be your usual tactic."

"Learned it from the best."

Clay stomped down the hall, feeling like a six-foot-three-inch adolescent. In the past few days he'd met new friends, toughened his body and cleared his mind, and had an epiphany in the depths—a full-body, head-to-toe baptism.

And what do I do? I revert to thirteen as soon as Dad's in the room.

Clay thumbed through the mail on his bed. While the entire issue of finances seemed trivial after what he'd experienced, he did feel imbued with a new commitment to do what was right. All in perspective. A day at a time.

"Dollface, you're home."

"Come in, Mom."

Della entered the bedroom, squeezed his arm. "We were so worried."

"We? I find that hard to believe."

"Never mind Gerald. It's just his way. What happened out there, Son?"

"I hiked the trail," he said.

"Just like you've always wanted."

"I was so frustrated with everything here. I'm sorry, Mom. I didn't think I could keep pretending like things were okay, but I should've told you more in the note I left. Please forgive me. Don't know what got into me."

His mother's fingers were still on his skin. The numbers, he noted, had stayed in place—vivid, unmistakable. Yet his previous sense of futility was giving way to newfound assurance. It seemed that some of life's gifts weighed as much as life's burdens; he knew because he'd gone on a pilgrimage, intending to cast this one off.

Kenny's alive, though! I can't explain it, but the kid's still here.

This irrefutable fact filled him with faith, hope, and love. For the future. For a sovereign plan. For humanity as a whole.

Maybe he *could* intervene. He *could* save lives.

"Jenni called," Della said.

"Uh. From Wyoming? When?"

"Early this morning. She asked that you call back between eight and nine." The clock by the bed read 8:52. "Our time or hers?"

"I didn't ask."

Della nudged the door shut. She turned with hands folded in front of her sunflower-print skirt and sleeveless white blouse. "Clay." Questions blinked in her eyes. "You've been through a bad stretch—the divorce, financial struggles, and that Summer girl's passing. A lot to think about. Last week when the sergeant brought you home from the Raven, he warned that you'd become a risk to yourself. I want you to know how much I care about you."

"Things're working out. I'm here now, aren't I?"

"And I'm so relieved. Please don't forget your mother loves you."

"I know."

"Please, dear. If there's anything you—"

"Don't worry. I know I've done some…irresponsible things. But I'll be fine."

"I'll leave you in peace, then."

Clay took a deep breath and reached for the phone. "I'm gonna try calling Jenni."

Okay, boys and girls. Back to reality.

31

Forgotten

Mylisha felt good about this. She closed the office door, punched into an open phone line. She'd checked the daily column during evening break, had even run it by a colleague. Time to do this. She'd call Mr. Clay Ryker, tell him everything she knew about the threats and the link between Bill Scott and Hannah Dixon and...

"Hello."

"Clay? You sound upset."

"Oh. Hi, Mylisha. Sorry, I was just about to...uh, I was calling Jenni."

"I'll call back later."

"No. I mean, go ahead. What'd you want to say?"

"Mmm. Might be better in person."

"Say it." He sounded annoyed.

"Why you have to be like dat? Boy, I'm trying to help you here. I don't—"

"Listen," Clay said. "A few weeks back you made it clear you didn't wanna see me. Now I'm supposed to believe you've changed your mind? For the past year I've been riding a roller coaster, and I'm not anxious to climb back on."

"Let's see, Clay. High school graduation, a final peck on the cheek, a few lines in a Hallmark card... Who took who for a ride?"

"Told you already, I was stuck in my own world back then."

"And now you've changed?" Mylisha asked. "Guess I missed that one."

"Bye, Mylisha. I'm calling my wife."

"You mean, ex-wife."

The phone went dead in her hand. She expelled air. Why had she gone and acted the fool? Why rub salt into his wounds? She was in management at a supermarket, almost thirty, a grown woman. What was she thinking?

Circled and underlined, the horoscope taunted from her desk.

Don't hesitate to realign with estranged friends and lovers. Today is the day. Pick up the phone and watch forgiveness work wonders.

Lotta good that'd done her.

She crumpled the paper and slammed it into the wastebasket beneath the desk.

———

Rhea Deering had the night off from waitressing at the Raven.

And in fifteen minutes she had a date.

She turned on the gas stove, planning to make some tea. Her voice was raspy with nerves. What she needed was some of that herbal, medicinal, antioxidant junk in the little cellophane-wrapped box.

At forty-six Rhea was too old for the bar scene. She'd run into her share of strange cats, the most recent example being that Clay Ryker guy. He'd come in a few days ago, downed a couple of drinks, then grabbed her arm and tried to predict her death. Who did he think he was? What right did he have?

A new job would do her good, Rhea decided. But what else was there for her? She'd smoked since she was nine, having picked up the habit from her older sister. She drank for lots of reasons, and none of them had to do with the taste. She'd gone through three skirt-chasing husbands, all of them suit-wearing stiffs. Just something about a man dressed to the nines.

And dang it, you'd think I would learn my lesson.

So what was she doing tonight? Hitting the town with—you guessed it—another guy in a suit. A star performer. A salesman at Guaranty RV Centers, one of the nation's largest dealerships, located right here at the south end of JC.

The doorbell rang. That was a promising sign. On the first date with her last husband, he'd honked from his Porsche in her driveway.

"Be right there," she croaked.

He was early. That could be a good or bad thing, but she'd decide later.

He knocked this time.

"On my way."

She tossed a leather jacket over her hot pink top, inhaled, then fastened the top button on her trendy jeans with the frayed pockets. Reformed biker-girl chic. The guys in suits seemed to have a thing for it.

———

"Clay?"

Jenni's voice was a crack of light chasing off the darkness. It'd been months.

"Clay, say something please. You're calling back late as it is."

He gripped the drapes of bitterness and peeled them back from the window of his soul. The light was blinding, almost painful, yet capable of life-giving warmth.

He breathed her name. "Jenni."

"I'm not going to bite. Remember, I called first."

"I thought my mom might be lying."

"Della?" Jenni said. "She's been known to be manipulative. But lying?"

"I've had a couple of rough days. Thought she might be trying to cheer me up."

"Yeah, I heard how you vanished. Gave everyone a scare and royally peeved your dad. You did get my message?"

Clay mumbled an affirmative.

"I'll make this quick," she said. "You have a son who misses you terribly."

He grunted. Should he remind her whose fault that was?

"Jason can't stop talking about his trip to see you," Jenni continued. "I've been counting down the days for him with those plastic magnets on the refrigerator."

Clay grimaced. She'd taken the side-by-side Frigidaire when she moved.

"What I'm leading up to, Clay, is that I want to adjust the visitation plans. Now before you say anything, let me explain. I have a family reunion to attend in mid-August over in Bend. I did the math, and instead of separate airfares, it'd be cheaper for Jason and me to drive out together. Due to my schedule, we'd arrive on the eleventh. One day later than the original plan, but Jason could stay with you a few extra days."

8.1.0.0.4...August 10th. What if Jason never gets here?

"Are you there? Have you heard a word I've said?"

He looked at his palm. The numbers were invisible, yet hot and coiling. "Couldn't you get here a few days earlier, Jenni?"

"My clients will be backed up as it is. I can't risk losing new accounts."

"Mm-hmm."

"I've already checked, and the airlines will let us redeem the ticket for some later date. Perhaps during Christmas break."

Clay's eyes clamped down against the thought of holidays divided.

"Well," Jenni huffed, "nothing like the old patterns. I see it's going to be up to me to carry the conversation. You should know that I've changed a lot in the past months—gaining confidence, saving money, building my customer base each day."

"Does this mean less alimony?"

"Is that all you can think about? You probably don't even care that I had one of the Denver Broncos come in yesterday."

"That's amazing. Which one?"

"Clay, I believe client confidentiality's important. This guy—and no, I'm not telling you his name—he says they might need a massage therapist. He's going to speak with the team doctors about having me come down in the preseason to give a hand."

"A hand." His laugh caught in his throat. "I get it."

"Why're you doing this to me?"

"That's supposed to be my question."

"I'm trying to have a nice conversation, Clay."

"Listen, I didn't want this divorce. Or have you forgotten that?"

"What did you want? That's something that still eludes me. You had the Prince Charming act down—tall, handsome, athletic, and motivated. Do you blame me? Is that it? Each year, by degrees, you drew further inward. Like you were hiding from something. Or maybe you stopped loving me and started looking for a way out."

Clay had hoped to tell Jenni of his catharsis at Crater Lake. He'd imagined a moment of reconciliation as he explained the paralysis of guilt that had cut him off from her. Instead, the emotions that'd been shoved into the corners along with his secrets now demanded recognition.

"I'm not the one who filed," he snapped. "I'm not the one who ignores my messages. You don't really wanna know what I'm thinking. You run when I show who I really am."

"That's ridiculous."

"I'm a failure, Jenni. That's what I am! As soon as you began to realize it, you turned away. Didn't even give me a stinkin' chance. When I needed you the most, when everything was falling apart, you left. So my name wasn't on the bankruptcy? Ha! Okay, you can take the credit for that one. At least incorporating SME kept my nose clean, right? Wrong. I have bills coming out my ears. And to top that off, I have these wonderful little things called alimony payments, child-support payments. I'd willingly work my fingers to the bone to take care of you if I could. But that's not good enough. I have to be a show-stopping success, or it's just not worth it for Ms. Jenni Ryker."

For a moment Clay thought she had disconnected the phone.

For kicks he considered spewing more of his thoughts into thin air.

"Clay."

"You're still there? Surprise, surprise."

"Most of what you've said is… I suppose it has some truth in it."

Clay paused. Flabbergasted. He himself didn't believe half of what he had said; he'd been using it to strike back.

"You know something else, Clay? That's the most you've said to me since the morning they towed away my Lexus. That's the day I knew it was over."

"A car. A hunk of metal. That meant more than twelve years together?"

"Clay, you're so thickheaded! No, it wasn't because of the car."

"The house? The SUV? What was the final straw?"

"Your silence! Don't you get it? Are you hearing me? It wasn't over for me. It was over for you. I tried to stand by you, to love you through it all. You were what I wanted most. But you were gone. Not physically perhaps, but you had checked out. When they took our things, they took you along with them. After months of nothing from you—not a word, barely a kiss—I had to escape."

Clay's cheeks burned. "From your failure of a man, huh?"

"No, Clay. From whatever it is that's haunting you."

A tear brimmed on each of his eyelids. She had already cast him in his role as ex-husband, distant father, failed businessman and athlete. He wanted to tell her about Bill Scott, about the bridge and Bill's involvement with Mylisha, about the guilt that had driven him into the depths of Crater Lake.

He could not, however, allow her to add manslaughter or attempted suicide to his list of sins. The list was long enough already.

———

Past midnight. And she could get nothing more than a good-night kiss? A ride into Eugene in a nice car, a fancy dinner at the renowned Oregon Electric Station, a slow dance in the club at the top of the Hilton...

And all he does is ask for a second date. What? Is he low on confidence?

Rhea Deering stood at her front door, key in hand, and watched her date drive away. On the back bumper one of those little fish symbols caught the light.

Was he a do-gooder? Or was his age bracket the problem? These middle-aged guys had loads of emotional baggage, same as she did, and now they thought they could find true love. Well, they'd already blown their good years chasing the pretty young things, never thinking they would be left high and dry once they passed forty.

Welcome to the real world, guys.

Although years of smoking had deadened her taste buds and sense of smell, Rhea caught a whiff of something. She lifted her nose. Turned on the step. Something made her look to her left, where she spotted a figure in an argyle vest skirting the streetlight's glow.

Looks like they've let out the town weirdoes. Gotta make sure to lock my door.

Across the street on her neighbor's porch, an old man and woman were puffing together on hand-rolled smokes. Was that her future?

She dug into her leather jacket, found her keys and her pack of Camels. She pushed inside, flicked her Bic—just like the old ads used to say—held the flame to her cigarette as she moved toward the kitchen.

Billowing without visible form, swelling without a sound, reaching from the forgotten stove burner, the natural gas found the fire at Rhea Deering's fingertips.

There would be no second date.

32

A Lifeline

Clay heard about the explosion from Digs.

In blue uniforms they stood side by side at the sandblasting chamber. Clay had been keeping his gloves on, afraid of what the headstones might reveal. The past two days Wendy had made every effort to avoid eye contact with him, and his other co-workers acted as though his absence had gone unnoticed.

Midweek at Glenleaf Monument Company. Another death, another dollar.

"Woman was a good friend o' mine," Digs said. "Met Rhea at the Raven. Gosh, she's waited tables there it seems like forever." He pulled down a pair of goggles, stood at the Plexiglas viewing slot as he turned on the blaster. "Real heart o' gold."

"I met her."

"You know what I'm talkin' about then."

"Not really. Just bumped into her at the bar one night. She was working."

Clay thought of the numbers, Rhea Deering's expiration date. In his drunken state, he'd called it out irreverently. It matched that headstone he'd brushed with bare hands here in the warehouse a few weeks back. And there'd been that other guy, the bouncer. Same date as Rhea's.

"I...was worried about her," Clay said.

"About Rhea? Ain't nobody worried over her. She was a survivor."

"Is this one of your attempts at humor?"

Digs shook his head, then opened the door into the blasting chamber and removed a headstone. "Wouldn't joke about Rhea." He heaved the stone onto a table, blew away dust with an air hose. "'Specially after two tragedies in the same week. That poor Mako kid."

"Who?"

"Worked with Rhea. A bouncer at the Raven. He caught wind his girl was foolin' around, went to tear the guy up." Digs ran the air hose over his ears, blasted dust from his hair tufts. "Didn't work out. Mako took a bullet in the chest, ended up dyin' Tuesday morning at Sacred Heart."

The news was a stone around Clay's neck.

7.2.0.0.4… Two more deaths while I sat by.

"I'm going to the police," he told Digs.

"Why? You know somethin' about it?"

"I think I do."

"What about the bossman? Blomberg's gotcha ridin' probation already, doesn't he? You'll lose your job, sure as canaries can sing."

"I've got another job to do, Digs. Saving people's lives."

"What about payin' the bills? You got a kid. A wife."

"Yeah."

"Still gotta send off a check, don'tcha? What about their lives?"

"I don't have all the answers."

"Sounds like our boy Ryker is confused. Am I wrong? Lemme ask you this, whassit like out there on the Pacific Crest Trail? What I hear, it's a mighty long haul."

"Only did a hundred miles or so."

"Musta learned somethin' in them hundred miles. About yourself or your family? Maybe God? You tell me."

"I did." Clay mulled it over. "I learned that my time here's not up."

Digs grinned. "Now if that's not the same thing I was just sayin'. There, grab hold o' that end, and help me get this stone back into the blaster. We got work to do. The police, they ain't goin' nowhere. They'll still be there after our quittin' time."

———

"Clay's in there now?"

"Yes, A.G."

"This goes against all we had planned. Do we even know what he's doing?"

"I have theories, but I'll need to observe him further. I would've followed him inside if it weren't for that lady at the front desk."

Asgoth marched higher up the JC Library's handicapped ramp. From this vantage point, he'd be able to see Clay Ryker's departure from the police station. Monde stood below, pensive in his corduroy jacket.

The library door swung open, and a man in a jogging outfit stopped, nose to nose with Asgoth. He blinked, chose to go the other direction down the steps. A moment later a little girl exited. She paid Asgoth no mind. Spreading her arms, she ran with squealing delight down the incline.

Oh, to have that sort of freedom. Henna shows flashes of it.

Asgoth thumbed his tan trousers. He was more than ready for a change. "I thought we had him at Crater Lake, Monde."

"As did I."

"He seemed…very close. Considering your skills, I thought it would be easier."

"The human psyche's not as fragile as one might suppose."

Asgoth tapped against the ramp's railing. "Of course, if Sergeant Turney hadn't snuck into the picture, it might've been a different story. For that, I hold you responsible. Your old nemesis is once again giving you trouble."

Monde stood silent while his black eyes roved.

"You have nothing to say?"

Monde rolled his shoulders back so that his jacket flapped about his angular frame. He snapped his neck one direction, then the other. "This situation requires a revised strategy. Viewed properly, it's not a setback. It's a fresh opportunity."

———

Detective Freeman sat Clay in an interview room. Asked him to write down what he remembered: dates, details, descriptions. Clay fidgeted under hazy memories of his binge at the Raven but copied them down the best he could.

"So you think you can tell when people are going to die?"

"By touching them, yes."

"Touching them." The detective scribbled on his pad. "Explain how that works."

"I can feel…numbers."

"I can see dead people." The man smirked. "Like that Bruce Willis flick."

"For example, if I shook your hand, I'd know the exact day you're gonna die."

Freeman's eyes widened. "Oooh. Scary." He glanced up at the camera fixed in the corner. "I'm going to die. You heard it first from Mr. Clay Ryker."

"Sounds crazy, I know. But it's been right every time." Clay indicated the three pages of notes that'd taken nearly forty minutes to write. "You've already got it on record from the bartender. I predicted Mako's and Rhea Deering's deaths."

"You were pretty well snockered, from what I hear."

"I'm not gonna deny it."

"Maybe you had a hand in their misfortunes. Anything to get off your chest?"

"Your partner just finished questioning me, so you know the answer. I was on the Pacific Crest Trail during the shooting. And I've never even been to Rhea's house."

"Not a pretty sight after the explosion."

"Bottom line is, I'm hoping we can help each other."

"How would that work exactly?"

"I'd warn you in advance, then you'd provide protection for the possible victims."

"Victims. Mr. Ryker, you say that as if we've got a sociopath roaming the streets, as if there's some scheme behind this."

"Well yeah, that's the weird part. So far, all of the expiration dates have added up to thirteen. That can't be mere coincidence."

"Thirteen? Really?" Freeman lifted an eyebrow, then pushed his left elbow across the small table. "What about me? Come on, don't be shy."

"Am I gonna get in trouble for this? Touching your arm?"

"Only if you're assaulting me. The last crackhead tried it. Of course, that voluntary urine test you took will determine whether that's your problem."

"I'm clean. Listen, whatever it takes to convince you I'm sincere."

The detective toggled his elbow, enjoying this masquerade.

Clay let his exasperation take over. He stretched forward, rested his fingers on the ruddy, mole-dotted skin. The numbers transferred within milliseconds. As always.

"The verdict, Mr. Ryker. Let's say it loud enough for the camera."

"You have till the first of August, Detective."

"And then I bite the big one?"

"Not if I can help it."

"Okay then. Am I supposed to carry you around in my back pocket, my own little guardian angel?" Freeman guffawed. "Here's the way I read this, Mr. Ryker. In the past few months you've experienced a bankruptcy, a divorce, and the loss of personal friends. You've exhibited a sporadic work record here in town, been tossed out of a bar, shown self-destructive tendencies. And suddenly you're a superhero?"

"A what? No, that's not the—"

"We all long for purpose, don't we? A natural desire. And you've fabricated this alternate reality to restore meaning to your life."

"Whatever, Dr. Gerringer." Clay pushed away from the table.

"Who? Where're you going?"

"I came in voluntarily, remember? Shouldn't have wasted my time."

"You can't leave now," the detective ribbed. "I'm about to die."

Clay wanted to strangle the man himself. This wasn't how it was supposed to work. If God had a plan, if this was a gift, why was he facing this ridicule? What could he do for those who refused to listen? Maybe free will wasn't such a good thing.

"I'm going to pray for you, Detective Freeman."

"Ah. A praying man."

"Used to be. Trying to be."

"Well, listen to this," the detective growled. He hunched over the table and whispered so quietly that Clay had to lipread to understand. "You tell that God of yours to leave me alone. Got the tests back last month. The doctors say I've got a brain aneurysm, nothing they can do. Only a matter of time— couple days, couple weeks or months at best. In a split second it'll be over. Haven't told a soul."

Clay's faith cowered in a corner of his mind, but he had to offer something. A lifeline.

"Let's pray right now, Detective. What could it hurt?"

"Screw that!" Freeman hissed. "I'd rather die."

33

Preposterous Claims

On Friday, Clay's paycheck came with an admonition from Mr. Blomberg.

"Ryker, I'm not going to belabor this point, so listen and listen close. You skipped out on me once, threw my schedule into a tailspin, and cost me money. That's not something I easily forget, you hear me? Plus, I've got my own troubles on the home front. I suggest you deposit this check, pay off some bills, and lay off the sauce." He held up a hand. "Yes, Wendy told me about your little escapade at the Raven."

"Sir, I made a mistake."

"Sure did, mister. Your father's made it plain that he expects no more favors. You do something like that again, even a minor thing, and you'll be canned."

"That's more than fair. You've got a business to run."

Blomberg combed thick fingers through his red hair. "I still can't figure whether you're a first-class brown-noser or just an ignorant punk still growin' up."

"Still growin' up, sir."

"See now, that's what I'm talkin' about. You think you're some kind of wise guy? You just remember what we talked about a couple of weeks back. God's got a plan. That's a fact. And you'd best get outta the way of it."

"Yes, Mr. Blomberg."

Sitting in the bank's drive-through lane, Clay played over that last bit. Should he be getting out of God's way? He'd tried it for the past few months, and it'd brought nothing but confusion. Maybe the opposite was true; maybe he should be getting in line with God's sovereign design.

Look, I tried doing it my way at Crater Lake…and you sent a whale after me!

In the driver's seat, he signed the back of his check while his thoughts turned from Sergeant Turney to Detective Freeman. And to Jenni and Jason. *Please, Lord. I'm trying to learn how to trust your voice again.*

———

Dmitri Derevenko received word Saturday morning. He was in.

He had sent priority mail to Gertrude Ubelhaar, explaining his need for a visit; with Oleg's help, he had procured new identity cards. Now, as promised, the elderly inmate had submitted a visiting application form for him at the Coffee Creek Correctional Facility.

Dmitri and Oleg drove the distance together.

"Authorities have already screened your information," Oleg said, as they reached the North Wilsonville exit off Interstate 5. "Your ID is good. The man we use is the best in Oregon, a former art-restoration expert from the Ukraine."

"I'm not worried."

"Be careful, though. They will watch as you speak with Gertrude."

"We don't want trouble. I understand, Oleg."

"And she might lie. She's known for it, with many years of practice." Oleg's high voice did nothing to conceal his venomous tone. "She is a blasphemer, same as Hitler, same as Rasputin. She must give back what she took for her own. Our Brotherhood will not rest otherwise."

High barbed-wire fences rose into view, surrounding a complex of flat, tan buildings. Dmitri stopped at the main gate. He identified himself through the speaker to Control Central staff, who told him to proceed to the parking lot.

Dmitri cleared his throat. "Do not worry, comrade. I will find answers. Here." He slipped his Maksalov-modified cell phone across the seat. "I cannot take this in."

After registration forms, a thorough search, and identity confirmation, a female attendant led Dmitri through a series of clanging doors. Cameras scanned the corridors. Sounds echoed with no identifiable source or direction.

In a sterile reception room, he purchased snacks from vending machines before entering a visitation room with a small table.

Two minutes later an elderly lady appeared in institutional garb.

The dossier opened in Dmitri's mind...

Gertrude Ubelhaar, seventy-seven years of age, born in Mosbach, Germany, daughter of a Nazi biochemist. At seventeen inducted into the SS breeding program as a potential mother of Hitler's master race. At war's end US forces falsified her records and arranged for her employment at a military facility in Umatilla, Oregon. In the technological race against the Soviets, the Americans coveted the knowledge of such Nazis. They bent the rules accordingly.

While on the US government payroll, Gertrude Ubelhaar had funneled her anti-American sentiments and post-WWII bitterness into a small group of anarchists. They'd helped mastermind last October's regional terrorist plot for which she was now incarcerated.

Dmitri scooted a Dasani bottle and a bag of pretzels across the table.

Gertrude limped forward in prison slippers and seated herself. "Dmitri, you're a dashing young man," she said, opening the pretzels. "Beautiful Aryan eyes."

"And you're a woman with a dark past, Ms. Ubelhaar."

"Call me Trudi, if you will. I prefer it." On her nearly balding head, wisps of hair played above powdered wrinkles. Her eyes were intelligent, alert.

"We may speak freely, Trudi?"

"Goodness, yes. At my age there's no other way."

"I mentioned in my letter that I've found ties to your son. When you added me to the visitation list, I knew you were curious, nyet?"

"I'm amused by this claim; I won't deny it."

"Where is he? Your son?"

Gertrude gnawed on a pretzel. "Are you inquiring after his soul or his mortal body? We have time to wax philosophical if you so desire."

"But your son is alive," he said. "This I must believe."

"When you say you must believe, it is time to reevaluate. Unshakable truths inspire trust, but they never demand it."

"I don't have time to evaluate such matters," Dmitri said. "I seek the bloodline of the Tsars, and you are the mother to this man. I'm not asking. I know it's the truth."

"Dmitri, you are too handsome for naive talk."

"We've found documents in this evil program's classified records. Hitler chose you. He found the Romanov heir, coerced him out of hiding, and used you to breed a final Tsar as a bridge between enemy nations. He thought such a child would bring the Third Reich favor in Russian eyes."

"You can't believe everything you read." Gertrude laid one wrist atop the other on the table. "You intrigue me with these preposterous claims, but I do admire a healthy imagination."

"Imagination? Nyet."

"You already know the facts, Dmitri. Under Lenin's direction the Bolsheviks set out to destroy the imperial line. In one dreadful week alone, in July of 1918, they killed nearly thirty Romanovs—grand dukes and duchesses, princes and empresses. What is this nonsense about a surviving heir? You are jabbing at an old woman's sorrows."

Dmitri surveyed the visitor area, spoke in hushed tones. "I am from the Brotherhood of Tobolsk. You know this name?"

"I've heard rumors, yes. But it no longer exists, does it?"

"We still wrestle with God, Trudi. This is the mark we bear." Dmitri thumbed down his trouser material to reveal his angel-wing scar. "My great-grandfather, he tried to save the Romanov family. He and others made plans, spoke with British ambassadors and intelligence agents. Across from the Ipatiev house, the British Consulate dug a tunnel to reach the family for escape, you understand. But the Reds suspected trouble and killed the family in cold blood. Only one child survived, protected by diamonds sewed into his vest. Young Alexei. The Tsars' bloodline did not end. This is God's hand showing favor to our Brotherhood."

"A wonderful tale, I'll grant you. Yet it's public knowledge that during an official inquest each of the Romanovs was exhumed and identified. They died in that basement."

"Guards reported so. If they failed, they knew Lenin would kill them as well."

"So they perpetuated this deception to protect themselves?"

"Da. And to this day, falsehoods are told by my government. Leaders in the Kremlin do not want the threat of past royalty. They control news reports so that the country does not question. Trudi, I tell you the truth that Alexei escaped. Our Brotherhood smuggled him from northern Russia through Turkestan and into Shanghai. In early 1919 the British warship HMS *Kent* transported him into hiding on Ceylon."

"So why didn't you pursue your vaunted imperial leader long ago?"

"It's our failure. Hitler found Alexei and swayed him with thoughts of glory. Alexei was a young man, isolated and—what is the word?—impressionable. He felt a destiny to lead, but he was an orphan with sickness in his blood. Hitler promised him a cure, recovered from Rasputin's hidden chamber."

"A brash lie. Hitler did not know the chamber's location."

"But he convinced Alexei to believe. To join with you."

"I was barren, Dmitri. *Unfruchtbar*...unfruitful."

"This is what the SS told you. It's in the records. But Hitler was saving you."

"For an assignment, you are correct." Gertrude's lips twitched with a grin. "You've done your research. Yes, Adolf hand selected me as the perfect Aryan mother for Romanov offspring, a blood link to be forged between empires, to consecrate his Thousand Year Reich. Germany has never conquered Russia's vast steppes. But what if the countries were to be bound together by blood?"

"Madness." Dmitri rose, his knee jarring the table. "My people would not accept this...this link with Hitler. Nyet!"

A guard's head poked through the door.

"He's okay," Gertrude said. "It's these tables. More polish and fewer slivers would be nice, don't you think?"

The guard disappeared.

"So, Trudi." Dmitri felt short of breath. "The Tsar is alive—you admit this?"

"I carried this child in my womb, yes. Hitler, however, was a weak fool, afraid to use the weapons at his disposal. His final cowardice brought the war to an end."

"On this we agree. And you gave birth? You had your son here in America?"

"Yes. I was not so barren as first conjectured, eh? My child was born here in Oregon in early 1946." Her fingers touched her scalp. "I'm an old woman, Dmitri. Does it do me any good to take this secret to my grave? Perhaps my son's time has come. Certainly your visit seems providential."

"I believe so."

"I do not know his exact whereabouts, nor do I know the fabled fortune's location—Tmu Tarakan. If you're willing, though, to do the legwork and report back to me, I'll provide a hint or two. There's a young woman who possesses a vital element. Start with her."

"It is my task. I'm listening."

"Her name is Josee Walker. She has something which is not hers, by rights. Deal with her carefully and do not underestimate her friend, a Sergeant Turney." A chilly expression crept over Gertrude's powdered face and broke it, like cracking ice, into wrinkles and fissures. "They're the ones responsible for my time behind these bars."

———

Monde's report was concise.

"In conclusion, I don't believe Dmitri Derevenko has Engine 418's secret in hand, but we know he wants it as desperately as we do. He'll continue searching, turning over every stone. If we're patient, A.G., he'll do our physical labor for us."

"And you're positive we can get it from him if he finds it."

"Once he finds it." Monde's eyes gleamed. "He is a persistent man."

One of Asgoth's own contacts had delivered news that Clay Ryker was carrying the engine's treasure when he dove into the waters at Mount Mazama. There was no reason, however, to reveal this. Monde was occupied with his own pursuits; Asgoth would use the information for a separate purpose.

He played along. "But we can get it?"

"Yes," Monde said. "Trust my skills for that. Using fear, we'll leverage those around Dmitri until he has nowhere to turn. His Brotherhood believes this secret might help them resurrect the Russian monarchy. They need their

Tsar, and they need Rasputin's legendary riches to finance such a venture. We, on the other hand, want to buy the soul of a town."

"Is that what you'd call it?" The phrasing amused Asgoth.

"Call it what you will. The result is the same. If we succeed—"

"Once we succeed."

"Correction noted," Monde said with a slight smile. "For long enough hell's hounds have been held at bay. Once we get our finances lined up and get Clay Ryker out of the picture, we'll be free to roam."

"Exactly as I've always envisioned it."

———

Mylisha saw the sign while returning from an accounting class at LCC.

Eighteen million dollars.

She pulled off Interstate 5, choosing to pass through Santa Clara on her way home. She stopped at a convenience store. There it was. The Oregon Lottery screen over the ticket machine confirmed the billboard's claim.

She placed her hand over her purse, imagined she could feel the heat of eighteen dollars burning a hole through the brushed, dark purple leather. That morning she'd withdrawn two twenties from the ATM, taken in her car for an oil change, and this was the leftover cash.

Later, in class, she'd read her lucky numbers for the day.

Eighteen was one of them.

Any fool could connect the dots and see the dollar signs.

Somebody has to win. Why not me?

Mylisha vacillated. She didn't believe in paying the "poor tax." Daily she watched Safeway patrons dish out money for scratch-off tickets and reminded herself to stick to her budget—like every good business student should. She laughed at those who rushed to buy tickets when the jackpot bulged into eight figures, as though a measly three or four million wasn't worth the effort.

Eighteen dollars, girl. It's a small investment.

The money was in her hand now.

What was she thinking? If she mentioned this to her instructor as an investment opportunity, he would flunk her on the spot. He would say it was no different than holding a match to the money and watching it go up in smoke.

Eighteen million…eighteen dollars…lucky eighteen.

The machine sucked in the bills and spit out paper tickets in exchange. Mylisha folded them once, tucked them into the front pocket of her jeans. She had a good feeling about this.

———

The good feeling vanished as numbers ticker taped across the TV screen.

Mylisha fell forward onto her lime green beanbag. Groaned. She folded her hands over the back of her neck, embarrassed by her own silliness. Almost twenty dollars. Gone. Consumed by that greedy ticket machine.

She pulled herself up. Turned off the TV.

On a black lacquer shelf, her book of Langston Hughes poems offered distraction. She'd always loved his words, so earthy and empathetic. Mud-covered jewels.

She let the book fall open in her lap. She used to do this with her Bible, seeking the Lord's direction through whichever passage appeared before her. It had even worked on occasion. Overall, though, she had to admit it smacked of desperation. Like plucking at spiritual flower petals: "he loves me, he loves me not."

Mylisha's lips twitched; her eyelids closed.

She knew God's love for her. But what about his plans? Why the silence?

She took her finger and dropped it blindly on a section of the page. Through squinting eyes, she read a poem titled "Acceptance." It spoke of God's infinite wisdom, which foresaw his creation's imminent folly.

She smiled weakly. Leave it to Mr. Hughes to strike the nail on the head.

34

Back for Revenge

Gerald Ryker clomped in from the garage. "Son."

"Morning, Dad."

"Garage's looking mighty bare."

Clay sighed. "Already told you, I'll try to replace what I lost."

"Darn right you will."

Clay opened the Sunday sports section and thought about Kenny Preston. He'd called the kid last night, chatted, drawn encouragement from the high-energy voice.

No doubt Kenny had been out this morning delivering papers in town, and this afternoon he said he was heading to the McKenzie River for some inner-tubing. His mom's idea. Life was looking up at the Preston household.

8.1.0.0.4...

What about Jason, though? In two and half weeks, Jason and Jenni would be traveling this way. Could Clay offer any protection? He could pray, but that sounded hollow in the face of death—especially after Detective Freeman's reaction.

Was there any truth to Freeman's accusations that Clay was fabricating all this nonsense to restore meaning to his life? Setting himself up as an urban hero?

No. Too many had died already—Summer, Eve and Mitchell, Mako and Rhea.

"'Bout done there, Son?"

Gerald topped off the coffee in his blue travel mug and took his seat at the dining nook. Beckoning fingers indicated it was his turn for the newspaper. Clay complied. He placed the other sections back in their original order; with eyes still flitting over the box scores, he folded up the sports pages.

That's when he spotted the envelope poking from the bottom.

"You and Mom have a good time at Mass." Clay slipped the note into his robe. "I'll probably be gone when you get back. Gonna head out for some fresh air."

"We got room in the truck."

"You mean come to Mass with you?"

"Don't have to if you don't want." The blue lid clicked up, down, up, down. Some rain with a chance of clear skies.

"No, I'll come."

"Leavin' right after breakfast. No stragglers."

In his bedroom Clay slipped from his bathrobe. He couldn't remember the last time his father had invited him to anything. He shaved, slapped on some cologne Jenni had bought him ages ago, gelled his hair. From the kitchen the smell of his mother's hash browns and eggs beckoned.

Okay. Let's see what we've got.

He peeled open the latest envelope. Read over the note. Deep in the belly of his nightmares, a theory bubbled up. Far-fetched, yes. But did anything else make sense? How had Detective Freeman phrased it?

...a sociopath roaming our streets, as if there's some scheme behind this.

Clay decided to give Sarge a quick call before breakfast.

———

"Why'd you up and run, Son?"

"Wasn't ready to go through the meet-and-greet line. Nothing personal. These are your friends, not mine."

Clay was standing by the Dodge truck in the parking lot at St. Helen. Although he wasn't much for rituals and liturgy, he had found serenity in the organ's reverential tones and in the sacrament of Holy Communion. He'd reflected on Christ's sacrifice for humanity's sin, and the wine had sent a brief shiver through him.

A moment of cleansing. He knew his price had been paid.

"Doll." Della squeezed Clay's arm. "Please come. Father Patrick's only been with us seven years, and he hasn't yet met you."

"The only polite thing," Gerald mumbled.

Clay tried not to drag his polished dress shoes across the pavement.

Father Patrick was setting things into the trunk of an older Nissan Sentra. Clay felt a tinge of shame. Would the priest see "the sickness" of divorce on him? With a nod and a handshake, they introduced themselves. Father Patrick's voice was rich and clear, his words even and unhurried. Deep grooves in his tanned skin framed a pair of gentle eyes. Everything about the man implied a relaxed demeanor, an uncluttered life, years of ongoing health.

None of which matched the date on his skin.

8.1.0.0.4...

The same as Jason. Same as Wendy.

Clay managed not to flinch as their hands stayed locked in greeting, as the numerals hummed with insistence along his nerve endings.

———

Stretched on a towel at Fern Ridge Reservoir, Henna adjusted her yellow bathing suit. Blond hair cascaded over bronzed shoulders. Sunscreen glistened along her body and gave off a coconut scent. She rolled onto her stomach and tucked her face into folded arms.

"My little sun worshiper, are you deep in meditation?"

"A.G., it's been ages since we were out in public together."

"Have you gone in the water yet?"

"It's so scummy, I'd rather not. I'll look but not touch."

Asgoth's eyes moved over her, producing a wry chuckle. "I understand."

"Anyway, the water scares me. A split second and you can be gone for good."

Asgoth recoiled at the truth of her words...

Shoved. Falling, flailing. Cold depths and deep wounds. Blackness.

He scanned the Orchard Point Marina, where boat masts bobbed like toothpicks thrust into Jell-O. Near the walking bridge, toddlers splashed with their parents, while teens roamed the walkways, scoping out possibilities from behind tinted sunglasses.

The place was pregnant with hazards. *If only they knew.*

"Henna, the Scandi-Fest is coming up. I'm going to need your assistance."

"You know I'm willing. What about the others?"

"They'll get their own sets of instructions. We've had some setbacks, but Monde is revising his strategy. Right now he's tracking a Russian man who might possess the knowledge we need to succeed, but I'd be a fool to trust entirely in his plans. I have an alternative, just in case. It involves Mr. Ryker. Can I count on you being available?"

"Clay Ryker? You've said the magic words."

"Had a feeling that might arouse you."

"Is that a hint of jealousy?"

"He's a physically pleasing specimen, it's true. How can I compete?" A breeze fluttered over the lake as Asgoth touched Henna's hair.

She repositioned her face in her arms, purred with approval. "I'm over him."

"I'll take your word." Asgoth switched to practicalities. "With your connections in JC, do you think you could get a position in one of the festival's food booths? It'd give you access to the backstage areas."

"I'm a vegetarian, so if there's animal flesh involved, I can't do it."

"But it is possible, Henna? You could find a position?"

He knew his own candidacy was out of the question. For the past twelve years, he'd attended the annual event in disguise, unnoticed amid the crowded streets. If his true identity were revealed, it could cause unpredictable reactions, and the Consortium insisted that he avoid such histrionics.

In time, I'll be able finally to show myself.

"Sure," Henna said. "My daughter's working in one of the booths, serving Fri-Jos. I'll speak with her, see if she can put me in contact with the right people. Considering the thousands of attendees, the organizers are always looking for warm bodies to put to work."

Warm bodies? Asgoth liked the sound of that.

"I face the same challenge," he said.

———

Clay gripped the metal bars, dwarfed by the pre-WWI locomotive. One century old, she was a thing of beauty, both fierce and quaint. He knew her history well.

From a Finnish port, Engine 418 had traversed the Atlantic by steamship, then piggybacked across the United States on a Union Pacific flatcar. Twenty-five major cities welcomed her passage. At last the sixty-ton engine reached Portland, Oregon, where she sat neglected for two decades, a target for vandals and thieves. In early 1980 Finnish authorities had intervened so that this historic and valuable relic would be relocated to the Scandinavian-minded haven of Junction City.

Engine 418 arrived on May 5, 1980.

Clay, at five years of age, had joined in the fanfare, while local news crews covered the event. Nobody suspected she had secrets yet to unveil. It had taken another young boy to uncover the hidden wooden tube.

But Kenny Preston's treasure seemed so innocuous.

"None of it makes sense. I mean, how does it fit with the dates or the deaths?"

"Got me on that one," Sergeant Turney admitted. He had joined Clay at the fence. "And maybe we're graspin' at straws. All I know is, Summer visited this train the night she was struck down. And Mr. Coates, he helped paint the engine. The next intended victim, accordin' to the way you tell it, was Kenny Preston. He'd been explorin' this thing and found this mysterious object on board, correct? Did you get a look at it?"

"It wasn't much. A carved wooden tube with a stone chess piece inside. A black king with some writing around its base. Pretty sure it was in Russian. Maybe it's from a set that belonged to Rasputin or the Romanovs. Considering this train's heritage, it's certainly possible."

"And that's it? You know nothin' else about it?"

"Nothing."

Sarge looked disappointed. "But, Clay, you had it in your own hands. Least that's what Kenny said when I met with him and his mom. Did he give the tube to you?"

"He did."

"Why didn't you tell me this earlier?"

"Didn't think it mattered, Sarge. It's gone."

"In Crater Lake?"

Clay nodded in defeat. Then his eyes snapped up. "But we might be able to find it. I had my GPS unit and marked the spot where I jumped in."

"Sakes alive. I'd hafta rescue your butt all over again."

Clay grinned.

"So, kiddo, did this Russian object belong to you?"

"Well, no. I was supposed to protect it."

"From who?"

"The man who was chasing Kenny, I guess. Some guy in a white Taurus."

"A Taurus, you say?" Sarge squeezed shut his dark chocolate eyes. "Boy, it's enough to gimme a headache." He peered up at Clay. "Remind me again why you called me here? It's more than an hour round trip between JC and Corvallis."

"There's something I need to show you." Clay reached into his pocket. "I explained about my friend Bill Scott and about the numbers, but I should've told you about these. Read them for yourself." He surrendered a set of envelopes. "I got the bottom note this morning. Seems to refer to a detective I talked to at the station."

Sarge pawed at the papers while Clay read over his shoulder.

Your days are numbered, like the others.
Even a freeman cannot run from the fate he deserves.

"Detective Freeman?" Sarge pondered the name. "I know of the man."

"His date's coming up. August first."

"We'll give him round-the-clock protection—whatever it takes."

"He's got a brain aneurysm. I don't think it'll help."

"Hmm. I don't like this." Sarge scraped his hand over his short hair. "There's a thing or two I haven't told you yet, either. You already know about your belt buckle they found at the Coates place, but detectives have found a second item of yours." He flipped a sealed Polaroid picture from his pocket so that Clay could see its subject.

"My high school hall pass?"

"Count your blessings. Least it's before the days of photo IDs."

"No kidding. But where'd they find this? I lost it that day at the river. Along with the buckle and the rest of my stuff."

"So what's it doin' at a crime scene off Ivy Street in an apartment rented out to a Victoria Blomberg?"

"Any relation to Stan Blomberg? He's my boss."

"His daughter. You weren't messin' around with her, were you?"

"No! Definitely not. Is she dead?"

"Her boyfriend is. Kid named Mako, a bouncer at a local hangout."

"Died of a gunshot wound. July twentieth. Yeah, he's the one who tossed me out of the Raven. I felt his arm and his expiration date, but I had nothing to do with that."

"Mako took the bullet on the fifteenth. Don't worry. You were hundreds of miles away, stuck up on a mountain trail. Know that one for a fact. Not to mention, a coupla neighbors had noticed a guy with an accent and bright blue eyes. Driving a Taurus."

"A white one?"

"How'd you guess? Same guy is after the item from this train—that's my theory. I've got a couple of leads, some fingerprints from a rental car in Eugene."

"And you think someone planted my ID card and my belt buckle?"

"Startin' to look that way. Like someone's settin' you up, tauntin' you." Sarge studied the notes in his hand. "Where'd you say you found these?"

"One was stuck on the seat of my parents' truck. The others showed up in the *Register-Guard*, one of which Kenny Preston put there himself."

"The same kid?"

"That's how I met him, Sarge. Caught him on the doorstep one morning, and he said some lady had asked him to deliver it."

"Did he know who she was?"

"No, but I do. Henna Dixon. She and I were in school together years ago." Clay looked up. "There's more to it. She'd have to have been in two places at once to do all this, plus she was sitting on her mother's sofa the night I got the note in the truck."

"What're you gettin' at?"

"I think she has an accomplice."

Turney beckoned with his hands. "Let's hear it."

"What if it's Wesley Scott?"

"Scooter?"

"Think about it. What if he was related to Bill Scott? Wesley and William. They could've been brothers. This could be Wesley coming back for revenge." Clay ignored Sarge's raised eyebrow. "Listen. Each date adds up to thirteen, which is just too crazy to be a coincidence. I think somehow Wesley knows what I did on the thirteenth of March at the river, and he and Henna won't stop until they drive me to my grave."

35

Under Observation

Dmitri forked chocolate cream pie into his mouth, then glanced across the plates at his female contact. Svetlana was a hard-jawed woman with dark red hair. Fifteen minutes earlier she had called to arrange this meeting at Shari's Restaurant on the south end of Salem. She'd told him where she was seated and what she was wearing. If she had on reading glasses when he arrived, he was to abort, make sure he was not followed, then head for the alternate meeting spot at a bookstore downtown.

"Are you under observation?" he had asked.

"This I don't know," had been Svetlana's reply. "But I suspect so."

Although Dmitri found her without glasses on, he could tell something was wrong. The eyeliner ringing her eyes only amplified their anxiety. This was not his concern, unless it affected her ability to carry out her duties.

"You are tense."

"They're close by. I can feel this."

He nudged her water glass toward her. "Take a drink. Clear your mind."

"You think I'm making this up?"

"I think you're under stress. This is normal, considering the circumstances."

Svetlana pressed her lips together and tried to smile. "Look at this." She tapped a CD on the table. "The girl you seek is in these photos."

Dmitri unfolded his laptop on the cushioned seat, slipped in the disk. Svetlana's telephoto lens had captured a young woman's turquoise eyes beneath choppy black hair and a silver eyebrow ring. The second jpeg image showed the woman in a long skirt on the front steps of a charming older home. Her shoulders were straight and proud, as though to compensate for her slight frame.

A wooden sign declared: Tattered Feather Gallery.

"Josee Walker," he mused aloud.

"Da. She's a worker at this place. She has a room on the floor above."

"She's an artist?"

Svetlana shrugged. "I went into the gallery as a customer. She was behind the counter, making notes in a book. The store owner is her roommate."

"I need an address."

"It's on Southwest Second Street in Corvallis. Not far away." Svetlana relinquished a slim file containing newspaper articles, one of the gallery's brochures, and a brief biography of Ms. Walker. "She is watchful. You must use caution."

Dmitri nodded. The file held his attention. Was Gertrude Ubelhaar sending him on a fool's errand? Or was Josee Walker an actual connection to the Tsars?

"Svetlana, did you do a search? What does this girl have that is not hers?"

"With the help of others, da, I searched. We found that she has a bank account in Florence."

"On the Oregon coast."

"She received an inheritance from her grandfather. A deposit box. Months ago she signed in at the bank to view this box for the first time. Thank goodness for modern technology, nyet? Motion and heat detectors are used in many vaults, but security cameras are everywhere. You'll find this interesting, I think. It's on a file on the CD."

Dmitri stared down at his laptop. His chest contracted. As his fingers led the cursor to the mpeg file, as it loaded and began to play, the restaurant shrank from view, and the screen became his focus…

Josee, black spiked hair, in a sweater, looking over her shoulder, opening the deposit box on the viewing table, blocking its contents with her back, but allowing a brief peek beneath her arm. Dmitri paused and zoomed in for a glimpse of a felt bag, a twinkle of rose diamonds, a spherical shape.

One of the lost Fabergé eggs? This would be priceless!

"How did you get this video recording?" he asked his contact.

She wrung her hands in her lap. "I cannot give all the details, Dmitri. We had help from a friend of Gertrude Ubelhaar. He put pressure on the new security officer at Bank of the Dunes, and the officer was very relieved when his relationship with his wife's sister remained secret."

"It's not difficult," Dmitri noted, "to find weakness in American homes. Blackmail becomes easy, nyet?"

Without reply, Svetlana whipped her chin over her shoulder. Apprehension sprang into her eyes, and tiny splashes of sweat appeared on her temple. On alert, Dmitri reached for his cell phone weapon and scanned the restaurant, calculating possible threats and escape routes but finding no cause for her dismay.

Perspiration coated Svetlana's forehead. "Can I can go with you to the hotel?"

"Not tonight," he told her.

"But I'm without a home. I'm alone and afraid."

"You live not far away. Enough teasing, okay. I must keep on task."

"Please. I cannot go back." She rubbed her hand over her forearm, let her eyes slide toward the window. "My apartment's in shambles. I found my things torn and thrown on the floor."

"When?"

"This morning. Only hours after we talked on the phone."

"Da, we have enemies everywhere. But this difficulty is only one of many obstacles in our journey. You'll find a new place, a new beginning."

"But my American clothes, my—"

"Enough! You do no good crying now." Dmitri closed his laptop, wolfed down the rest of his pie, rose from the booth, and put money on the table. "Do svidanya."

He left her bent over the table, arms hugged around her waist, muttering prayers in Russian and flinching from the passing diners and waitresses like an asylum patient quarreling with ghosts in her head.

———

Nickel's Arcade was closing down, and the night was robed in black. Clay slouched behind the Duster's steering wheel. He could see the Subaru parked up the street. Henna and her daughter stepped from the arcade. Moments later they were driving up Dane Lane to the intersection with Lovelake Road.

Clay kept his distance on this lightly traveled road. Should he keep following? It appeared Henna was headed home.

As he suspected, the Subaru turned onto the Dixons' gravel drive.

He swept on past, his headlights cutting swaths through dust and darkness. He should've known not to play amateur sleuth. Sergeant Turney thought it might be worth keeping Henna Dixon within eyesight since she was linked to the anonymous notes, but now Clay was questioning his suspicions of her.

Particularly after Sarge had dismantled his Wesley Scott theory.

"Scooter? A criminal mastermind?"

Clay could still hear Sarge's belly laugh. "Hey," he said, "I'm not kidding."

"But Scooter's such a mild-mannered guy—a former pot-smokin', role-playin' slacker, if you gotta know. Is he related to your friend Bill Scott? Doubt it. Does he have some plan for revenge?" Sarge shook his head. "No sir, if that were the case, he wouldn't have called me from Diamond Lake to let me know your next steps. Without him, I would've never been there to yank your sorry bones from the water."

"Didn't think about that."

Clay had too many things to think about. Family. Finances. And fate's agenda in this town he had long ago left behind.

He could relate to Jonah...

I don't wanna be here. I don't want this burden, this seduction of knowledge.

Before reaching the train trestles, Clay made a U-turn, sure that his stake-out of Henna had been time down the drain. As he curved back toward the Dixon property, he spotted headlights. The Subaru was nosing back to the main road.

He punched off his own lights and jerked the car off the pavement. He counted to thirty, then moved back out and tailed her into town from a discreet distance. She altered her route, going down River Road this time. Only as they neared Junction City's heart was he compelled to narrow the gap. Henna was the Subaru's lone occupant; she must've dropped off her daughter at the grandparents'.

So what was she doing back here this late? Almost ten thirty.

On Sixth Street, Henna parked and entered a local video store. Clay passed by, turned onto Holly, kept the engine running while he sat at the curb. From this spot he could see if she used either the front or rear exit.

It was a short wait.

Twenty seconds after entering the store, Henna emerged from the back and jogged up a stairway to a second-story apartment complex. Clay watched her coast along a dilapidated open-air walkway. She hesitated before entering the far unit.

He observed the door number. Counted the seconds.

Once he saw the golden hues dancing behind the apartment curtains, he presumed candles had been lit. He even imagined the sounds of mood music.

His mind played back over his encounter on the Greyhound. That first day back in JC had leveled him. Depressed beyond words, he'd dipped into his dad's stash of Miller Lite. He'd spoken with Summer, felt the numbers on her hand—just as he had on his mother's arm.

And it had all started after Henna's little palm-reading gig.

You'll begin to know things. You'll feel them...

If this was a gift from God, could it stem from that auspicious beginning? And if it was a curse of sorts, why did it keep prodding him along with the sense he could save lives? Regardless of the answer, it seemed that someone had tried driving him toward his own grave, playing the guilt card that had been dealt years ago.

Was Henna at fault? What else had she said to him?

That whole thing about the first seduction. In the Garden of Eden.

At the apartment window, a shape moved. Clay pressed back into the shadows of his car, barely breathing. It was time to curtail this clandestine activity. If he pressed too hard, he might alert Henna to his presence and forfeit his chances of tracking her to her accomplice. Who, he wondered, lived up there? Was it her partner in crime?

Maybe this was nothing but Clay's paranoia talking.

For kicks, during a break at work tomorrow, he'd make a routine phone call to quell his suspicions.

———

Those were Henna's footsteps coming up the stairs.

"I need you now," Asgoth spoke into the apartment's stillness, and the hallway swatted the words back in an indecipherable echo.

He was beginning to question her loyalty. When they were together, her eyes seemed to wander, her mind felt closed to his advances. And at this late date, as the festival crept closer and the Consortium awaited results, she had the gall to gather solace from another source. This morning he'd seen her enter a low building at the edge of town where a chiseled lawn sign advertised acupuncture treatments.

"A.G.?" Henna cooed. "Are you there?"

She oozed into the apartment. The front door creaked as she pushed it back into its heat-warped frame. Through a gap in the bedroom door, Asgoth watched her.

"No need to be jealous, A.G. I've been tense. Just needed to unwind."

"Here I am." Asgoth slipped from behind the door, moved toward her. "Why'd you go to him this morning?"

"I should've known you'd be watching. That's not very civil of you."

"He's a charlatan. He can't do the things I do."

She lit a row of candles on an upturned crate, hailing the benefits of acupuncture, flaunting her disloyalty with no regard for him as her host. He could appreciate her need for stress release, and he knew she was drawn to the respectable doctor types, but this was annoying.

Much more of this and she'll think she no longer needs me.

Henna peeked through the curtain. "As I thought. There he is."

"Who?"

"Clay. He's down there in his car."

"What's he doing here? Have you been meeting with him as well?"

"I bumped into him at the arcade. That's it," she answered. She rolled her neck. Slipped out of her sandals. "A.G., help me relax. I've been so tight recently."

Her words stirred his doubts into a desire to wrest control. As she stepped toward the hall, he enwrapped her body and grabbed her blond hair with his free hand. He could smell her oregano scent, plus a mixture of foreign oils— from her treatment, most likely. The thought enflamed him.

"Do you want me?" he said.

"A.G.," she cried.

"Or have you begun fantasizing about Clay Ryker again?"

"He was the first man I ever loved."

"So you have been thinking of him."

"Only when necessary for the sake of our plans."

"Listen, Henna. I'm the only one for you. Oh yes, you have a soft spot in your heart for Mr. Ryker, but who has stayed by your side?" He drove her down to her knees, tugging back on golden locks. "Who loves you?"

"A.G."

"Who?"

"Asgoth!" she called out.

"So if you know the answer, why, may I ask, do you look elsewhere?" He kneaded the bleached handful, let his words trickle down that beautiful neck. He was in command; he was the dominant one here. Then, slapped anew by the possibility of her betrayal, he found himself moaning into her hair with the awkwardness of a teenage boy thwarted by love.

"Why?" he managed to ask.

Henna shook her head. "I'm sorry. Please, I don't mean to hurt you."

"How do I know you won't close me off?"

"You're the only one," she said. Her eyes were wet, sparkling in the candlelight. She was a woman reconfirming the vows of a religious order. "I won't let anyone else in my heart."

"I hope not. Or we're through."

Asgoth spoke the words with more acid than he felt. He knew he was lying, because he needed her more than she would ever need him. Wasn't that the way it always worked? When it came down to it, he was limited without her.

36

Three Numbers

Guns firing, tires screeching, cries of pain… What was going on?

Jiggling the controls of a video game, Tyrone and Tawnique startled Mylisha into awareness. She muttered, tucked herself tighter into her sister's couch. She needed to shave her legs; she could feel them bristle beneath the multicolored throw blanket. The digital readout on the DVD player said it was not quite seven o'clock. Two hours before she had to get ready for work.

Where was Shanique? She'd been staying out longer each night.

"Ty."

Her nephew was engrossed in the mayhem on the screen.

"Tyrone. Tawnique."

They didn't budge. "We playin' a game," they replied in unison.

On the screen a roadster careened into an enemy on foot, and the body somersaulted back out of view. The image disturbed Mylisha—stirring thoughts of Summer Svenson, awakening slumbering suspicions. Something Clay had told her on the phone a few weeks back…

Who would've wanted to kill my friend? It's so wrong.

She turned to the kids. "I don't think your mama wants you playing that game."

"But we just started," Tawnique said.

"Mama ain't even here," Tyrone snapped.

That did it. Mylisha wrenched herself up, stumbled to the PlayStation, hit the Power button. "Please, I don't need attitude to start my day. Your mama left me in charge, so I'm enforcing her rules while she's gone."

"She's always gone," Tawnique bleated.

"I know, honey. I feel you. You think I like sleeping on the couch all night?"

"Why isn't she here? She forgot about us."

"Tawnie, that's just not true. She's doing what she thinks she has to do."

"She did forget." Tawnique pointed to the kitchen. "We outta Cocoa Puffs."

Before Mylisha could respond, her niece burst into tears and pattered down the hall. The lock clicked on the bathroom door. Tyrone slammed his game controller to the carpet, crossed his arms, threw his body into an over-stuffed chair.

Mylisha felt an urge to turn on the PlayStation and wreak some violence of her own. Instead, she flopped back onto the couch and snuggled in the throw blanket.

Shanique showed up soon after, smiling but puffy eyed. "I needs me some sleep, for real. Thanks, baby. Kids were good for ya?"

"They miss you. They need time with their mama."

"True, dat. They's sweet as can be." Shanique wandered off toward the whimpers in the bathroom. "Baby doll, talk to me. Wha's wrong?"

Mylisha gave up the charade of sleep, skimmed through her collection of Hughes poems. One that was titled "Frosting" brought a smile to her face with its exhortation to find freedom by taking action, by learning how "to bake." For a long time she'd found meaning by serving others, which wasn't a bad thing. She had chosen the easy road, though, steering away from God-given goals for safer destinations. Why had she never got to the business of "baking" in her own life?

God's will, she believed, led to true freedom. He had a plan.

Her eyes ran to the newspapers on the table, to the star charts she'd been searching for guidance. Straight up, she had turned to things created when she should be turning to the Creator. God had sent his Son, and Jesus had freed her. In the Good Book, in his own words, he no longer called her a servant but a friend.

It's time I start walking in that freedom.

Mylisha set aside her reservations, placed a call to the Ryker home.

———

Clay had done his detective legwork the night before. In his wallet he had three numbers to call. Aware of Mr. Blomberg's disapproval of cell phones on the job, Clay waited until his ten o'clock break to dial the first.

Mrs. Dixon...

Her voice was pleasant, businesslike.

"Oh, yes, you're Della's boy. We used to come out to watch your ball games, Clay. My husband's a JC alumnus himself."

"Appreciate the support. Go Tigers."

"You're almost like family, Clay. Practically watched you grow up. So things didn't work out for you in Wyoming?" Her innocent curiosity, Clay knew, was a trap for catching tidbits of gossip. "I suppose you're glad to be home, eh?"

"I guess."

"Just not the same, is it? After a...separation."

Clay expected this sort of nosiness and told himself to remain detached, to feel nothing at all. Instead, he blurted out, "Jenni and Jason are coming for the Scandi-Fest, Mrs. Dixon. Things aren't over till they're over."

"Oh. Forgive me, Clay. It's not my place to pry."

"S'okay. Actually, I was calling about Henna. How's she doing?"

"Hannah, you mean? I've never quite adjusted to this New Age nonsense of hers. 'Henna.' Nothing wrong with the name in and of itself, but she sees it as a means of bringing herself into 'alignment with the collective conscious-ness.' Or some such notion, which I'm quite sure she'll snap out of. I think Hannah's a beautiful name. But then I'm just a doddering mother, so what do I know?"

Clay said, "I'm thinking about changing my name."

"Oh dear, have you talked with Della yet?"

" 'Red Rock.' Sounds okay, doesn't it?"

Mrs. Dixon giggled at that.

"In all honesty, though, I need to ask about your daughter. You remem-ber how I barged into your Avon party? I know I looked silly, but I...I was worried about her."

"Worried?"

"Not to upset you. In fact, I'd rather you not say anything to her about this."

"For heaven's sake, what is it?"

"I've seen her around town a few times, bumped into her here and there.

In this close-knit community, it's been hard to ignore her new set of, uh…acquaintances. I'm not saying she and I were close friends in school or anything, but—"

"You would've been, Clay, if she'd had any say. She had quite the crush on you."

"She did?"

"She even dated your friend Bill Scott for a time—"

"I thought she was just bummin' with him."

"She was using him to get close to you, if you want the truth. Anyway, their relationship was short-lived." Mrs. Dixon paused. "Oh, forgive my poor choice of words. Bill's accident was a terrible misfortune, and the police showed little concern for your feelings through it all, did they? But at least that's all water under the bridge." She gasped at her second faux pas.

"Don't worry about it," Clay told her. "I'm trying to let it go."

"Maybe you should speak with my daughter. You're right. She has been out and about lately, keeping strange hours and providing flimsy excuses. She drops Serene here, expects me to fulfill my grandmotherly duty. Not that I mind, but I did raise my daughter to take care of her own. It's a sad thing, actually."

Clay tamped down thoughts of his own son.

Not much longer…8.1.0.0.4

"Hannah just won't let it go, I suppose," Mrs. Dixon went on. "She was young, susceptible. After Bill's accident, she changed. She still keeps some of his notes to her, but I think she fantasizes that they came from your pen, Clay."

He shuddered. Did this explain it? Was Henna acting alone as his tormentor, punishing him from her twisted sense of loss and unrequited love? If so, her actions were even creepier than Mrs. Dixon's willingness to reveal them.

"Why are you telling me these things?" he inquired.

"You could've been my son-in-law. The thought did pass through my mind years ago, and I even discussed it with your mother at one point. Those days are gone now, aren't they? I hardly recognize my little girl anymore. Oh, she still calls this home, but she spends many of her nights elsewhere. I often wonder where I went wrong with that one. Hannah's always been something of a troublemaker."

Clay breathed deeply. "Try not to worry, Mrs. Dixon, and don't say a word about my call. I'll keep an eye out for her. I'm sure she'll be all right."

"Really? That means so much. I've always hoped to hear you say that."

Clay hung up without saying good-bye.

——

On his lunch break Clay made the second call.

Detective Freeman...

"Sir, this is Clay Ryker. We talked the other—"

"I know who you are. I'm on duty, which means you're interrupting me in the middle of writing reports."

"Sounds like work."

"You hit it on the head."

"Uh. I've been thinking about what you said when I offered to pray for you. You can laugh, but I was serious about the numbers I told you. That's only days away."

"Five."

"Yeah. So do you wanna figure out a plan? Maybe we can—"

"We can what? Tell me, Mr. Ryker. Do you have a way to stop the inevitable? When it's your time, it's your time. Not a dang thing you can do about it."

"Maybe there is. I've already helped protect one kid."

"Just as I thought. A superhero. Were you wearing your mask and cape?"

"All I did was get involved. It seemed to change things somehow."

"Ah, even better. A modest superhero."

"I know your circumstances are pretty grim, Detective Freeman. I'm not denying it. What can I do that a doctor can't?" Clay drew in air. "Here's the deal. I think maybe God's given me this ability so he can be given a chance to step in."

"You already tried to do your little prayer thing. Now what?"

Good question. Where am I going with this?

Clay covered the cell phone's mouthpiece, lifted his eyes upward. The fast-approaching first of August caused his heart to pound. Death was nearing, so impersonal, so inexorable. Was there a way to override another individual's choice?

"Bye-bye, Mr. Ryker." Freeman's tone was snide.

"Wait! Hold on. I don't expect you to buy what I'm saying, but what if God's just waiting for you to give him a chance? Maybe I sensed the numbers so you could live a little longer. Like an early-warning system. The Bible says it's 'destined that each person dies only once.' But it doesn't say that date is written in stone. In fact, there are times God held death back. Times he seemed to change the plan."

"And he'd do that for me?"

"There's only one way to find out."

Detective Freeman sniggered. "You're a real nut case, you know that? I've lived my life, made my choices, and I don't need some religious caped crusader swooping in to save the day. I became a detective to bring justice to this world, but you know what I've found? There's no such thing. Life's one huge septic tank, a godforsaken mess! And yes, Mr. Ryker, you can quote me on that."

"Godforsaken, huh? Even though he's trying to reach out to you?"

"You get more delusional by the minute."

"August first, Detective Freeman."

"Tell 'em to bury me with my eyes open. You can tell 'em I saw it coming."

———

After conversations with the unnerving Mrs. Dixon and the irascible Detective Freeman, Clay was ready for a straightforward call.

The Holly Street apartment manager…

"Yeah, I'm wanting some information. Rates, move-in dates, and all that."

"Don't got any places available." The voice was male, thin, and feeble.

"Popular place, huh?"

"We make do. I can give ya a number to call, place on the north end o' town."

"Actually, I had my eye on your second-floor apartment, the one on the corner." Clay recited the number. "View of the park. Close to the video store. Private."

"You know how to pick 'em, don't ya?"

"Is it taken?"

"Did I say that?"

"If you give me the renters' name or number, maybe I could talk to them about a roommate situation. Shared utilities, phone bill, whatever." Clay realized the manager was no longer listening. To go along with the man's muffled chuckles, Clay visualized an age-marked hand over colorless lips. "Did I say something funny? People make arrangements like that all the time."

"It's not that," the manager said. "I take it you haven't been in town long."

"Grew up here actually. Just moved back from Wyoming."

"You missed all the hubbub then. Still under investigation. You're not one o' them cops, are ya? They told me to keep my gums from flappin' and let 'em know if I heard anything, anything at all."

"About what?"

"You are a cop, I can tell. Well, good try there. Guess we're done talkin'."

Clay stared at the disconnected phone in his hand. By degrees, his day had gone from abnormal to bizarre. Welcome to his world.

At home that night he found two new bills and a phone message from Mylisha. For dinner his mother served a homemade Bartlett pear and Gorgonzola cheese pizza—not bad at all. Della explained her baking stone's benefits while Clay thought about the coming days. The coming deaths.

Gerald rescued them both by demanding Clay's help in clearing leaves from the gutters. They worked together, their words never moving beyond the chore's logistics.

After a shower Clay called Mylisha back. He told her he was ready for real conversation and feedback, and she agreed to join him for a hike on his next day off.

Sunday. August first.

Even a freeman cannot run from the fate he deserves.

Clay shoved aside his frustration with the detective. Although he remained concerned, he could not take on the responsibility of those who refused to listen; he must keep up a buffer, dulling his emotions for what lay ahead.

37

The Color of Blood

The Tattered Feather Gallery had aged with dignity. Situated on Southwest Second in Corvallis, the old two-story home featured local artists, and it appeared that the curator took oil paintings and sculptures on consignment. Myrtlewood clocks and carvings filled one wall; genuine Indian art pieces graced another, with a selection of dream catchers dangling in the front windows.

Dmitri filed these observations within seconds of crossing the threshold.

As a Russian, I appreciate fine works of the imagination. We lead the world in classic literature. We boast the Hermitage Museum in St. Petersburg.

The strident cry of the front door's electric eye did not surprise him. Art was worth protecting. He smiled at the lady behind the long glass counter, let his eyes linger on hers. He was here to find Josee Walker.

"I'm looking for the last Tsar," he could say. "Please point way to the treasure."

But of course that would never do. Americans were too self-absorbed to believe such a statement, and even if they did, they were too self-seeking to offer advice without reward.

He let his hand brush against the cell phone on his belt.

Cleaned, checked, loaded. He might have to do today's work the hard way.

"Come on in, come on in," said the lady at the counter. "I'm Suzette Bishop. Feel free to look around."

"Spahseebah… Thank you."

"You're Russian? Oh, I do love the accent, love it. Are you a fan of Kandinsky, per chance?"

Dmitri Derevenko let his smile widen. This might not be so hard after all.

"I'm a fan of the Fabergé eggs. Do you have anything like this? Any replicas?"

"How odd that you should ask that. My assistant's been engrossed with the same thing of late. Have you met Josee yet?"

Clay peeled off his gloves. His skin was damp with sweat. He ran his wrist down his cheekbone, swiped it across his blue canvas pants, looked both ways along the workbench. Digs was rolling a new stone toward the sandblasting area; Wendy was etching out a line of letters; Brent was loading blank slabs onto the hand truck.

Why worry? They would have no idea what he was doing.

Still, he felt the need for secrecy. As though he were about to peer into the crypts of the tombstones laid out before him.

He had to know. His fingers hovered over the first. Dropped down.

Clay recoiled from the distinct row of numbers, but they clung to touch receptors beneath his skin, shot off messages to his brain. He blinked once, reached for the next stone. More numerals. He checked his palm, but there was nothing to see. Cut by an invisible blade, each number throbbed below the surface. Who would believe him? Why should anyone listen?

He touched another slab. Another and another.

The third, fourth, fifth, and sixth—they were all the same.

A coming Tuesday... *8.1.0.0.4*

That was impossible. The date was already taken by Jason, Wendy, and Father Patrick. In a town this small, what were the odds of so many people dying in one day? There must be some mistake.

Clay pushed his fingers back into the gloves, continued his work.

Lunch break brought Wendy and him together at the time clock.

"Hi," he said. "I don't blame you for avoiding me the past few days, but I want you know I'm sorry for the way I acted in the Raven."

"Just two adults sharing drinks."

"I was rude, Wendy."

"And I was a flirt, but it didn't mean anything. Liquor can make a person do silly things."

"Do you remember what I said to you?"

"Oh, I see. Gonna act like you forgot, Ryker? It's the oldest trick in the book."

"No tricks. I just want you to...be careful. Take it easy. Watch your step."

"You're making no sense."

"On August tenth. Isn't that the day I mentioned? I'm trying to protect you."

"Stay away from me." Wendy elbowed past him. "I heard what you said to Rhea and Mako that night, and look what happened to them. I don't know what your trip is, but I'd feel more comfortable if you kept your distance. You hear me?"

"I hear you."

Digs caught a ride with Clay to the corner market.

"What's goin' on?" he asked. "You got Wendy rattled."

Clay shook his head, said nothing.

"You like drivin' with those gloves on, Ryker? Can't say that I've ever seen them come off. Must be a fixation with canvas, eh?"

Clay ripped them free, dropped them on the Duster's seat.

"Okay, I might be a white-haired fool, but I can tell when a man's all twisted up. You don't hafta carry your burdens alone." Digs shook his head. "Life ain't a one-man show, you know?"

"Lot on my mind. I know you're just trying to be a friend." In a show of nonchalance, Clay threw out his hand and clapped Digs' bare forearm. He mumbled a thanks, but his mind was focused on the results.

Skin to skin. Numerals…*8.1.0.0.4*

Now I'm convinced of it. The numbers must be wrong!

For whatever reason, it appeared they had locked up, jammed on one date in particular. Or maybe his ability had departed altogether, leaving only a residue. Yep, that must be it. What else made any sense?

He parked at the market. "What're you having, Digs? I'm buyin'."

"Now there's a quick turnaround for ya. Let's see, how 'bout a Butter-finger."

Clay left his gloves in the car, hesitated at the beer cooler, chose an Arizona Iced Tea instead. He collected a few other snacks and plunked them on the counter. He was feeling expansive. He was free from worry. Now that the ability had taken a nosedive, he realized the amount of pressure it had been exerting on him.

"How goes it?" He nodded at the teenage girl behind the counter.

"Okay. Yourself?"

"It's a great day." Clay handed over his cash, made a purposeful effort to let his hand touch hers. He had nothing to fear, no responsibility and no worries.

But he was wrong. Her expiration date was over two years away.

Which meant the numbers were not stuck; they had not malfunctioned. The other dates must be as accurate as ever, precursors of doom and destruction.

August tenth was going to be a very bad day.

———

Asgoth patrolled the streets, gauging, plotting. Soon festival booths on these sidewalks would channel thousands of pedestrians from fried delicacies to crafts to clog dancing and face painting. On the Scandi-Fest's edge, the Finnish locomotive would stand watch.

Just as I will. Watching. But no longer waiting.

For twelve years he had labored in this obscure principality. Few of these citizens knew he still walked among them, but they would find out soon enough.

Yes, one bad worm could work its way through an entire barrel.

He wondered how things were going north of here in Corvallis. Screws were being tightened, and it was only a matter of time before secrets came to light. With the Consortium's aid, Monde was shadowing the Russian and others in the Brotherhood, and his latest message had confirmed the location of a woman Monde knew all too well.

Josee Walker. She'd caused Monde trouble before.

Let Mr. Monde deal with her while Asgoth pursued a strategy of his own.

———

"Josee's a feisty little character. She's lived and worked here with me for less than a year, but what a true gift she's been. A fine employee, as well."

"So she also has interest in the Fabergé eggs?"

"Yes," Suzette said. "Quite definitely."

Dmitri made appropriate sounds as Suzette Bishop showed him around her art gallery, pointed out trinkets, thumbed through clothbound catalogs that creaked with age. In a circular case, jeweled Fabergé imitations—"Fauxbergé," some called them—sparkled on fabric beneath a band of lights. One or two bore marked resemblance to the genuine *objets de luxe,* demanding a second look. Was it possible? Nyet. This would be silly for Josee to hide her treasure in the open rather than in a locked vault.

"Why is she so curious, do you think?"

Suzette's nose twitched at the question. Between long, limp curls of hair, her eyes were almond shaped and pretty. "Well, Josee's naturally inquisitive, and once she sets her mind to something, it's not easy to pry her away."

"Like a bulldog."

"Yes. But a cute bulldog."

"Forgive me, it was an improper joke of mine."

"You're fine, you're fine." Suzette giggled as she moved back behind the glass counter. In a bowl of Nez Percé pottery, ivory business cards sported maroon calligraphy. "Perhaps it was an inquiry by one of our customers that set Josee on her search. She's been preoccupied with it, that's for certain."

"As a Russian, I also have much interest. The Fabergé treasures were made special for the Romanov family, Easter gifts each year for three decades. They are important to my people, Mother Russia's glory and past."

"They're exquisite, from what I've seen of them."

"But foreign money has stolen many away. King Farouk of Egypt, J. P. Morgan, and Dr. Armand Hammer, even your President Roosevelt—FDR, I think you say—they have owned our treasures. For us, it's a national shame."

"That's so sad," Suzette commiserated. "I've never thought of it that way, but I can understand that you'd have a sense of loss."

"Our people are torn. We have many troubles already, with Chechnya and terrorists, crime, inflation. I hope to bring change."

"Oh, Dmitri, you're right, you're so right. We have it easy here."

"You see now why I need to know."

She wrinkled her eyebrows. Again her nose twitched.

"I need to know," he said, "where is the missing Fabergé egg?"

"And this search brings you to Oregon of all places? How strange."

"These are symbols of new life, rebirth. It is what my country needs. After the young Tsarevich, Alexei, was discovered with a blood defect—"

"Hemophilia."

Dmitri nodded. "When this happened, Tsar Nicholas and Alexandra turned to Rasputin for a cure. He placated them with brief breaks in the disease's symptoms. Miracles, he claimed. He misguided them on the political path, causing rumors and shame. The blood defect brought distorted thinking to the Tsars, and later Lenin took advantage of this unrest. Alexei's illness opened the door for revolution."

"I've heard that said before. The Romanovs' story is indeed a tragic one."

"So, Suzette." Dmitri set his cell phone on the counter's wood molding. "I seek a particular egg from 1917. It bears rose diamonds, indicating that it's one of the last gifts created."

"As an art lover, I adore such details. Tell me more."

"After the discovery of Alexei's condition," he explained, "the color of blood was not allowed on Fabergé's imperial creations. Red was forbidden since it could bring anguish to his parents. This rose-diamond egg proves what has been suspected, that Rasputin believed he had obtained a true cure at last."

She held up a hand. "But he died in late 1916, if I remember correctly."

"Poisoned, shot, and drowned."

Suzette gave an involuntary shudder and took a step back.

"Rasputin gave an idea to Fabergé's work master, Henrik Wigstrom. In the design he included the forbidden color. It was a surprise for the Romanovs, for the coming Easter celebration. He would present this gift along with the cure for Alexei."

"Yet they never received it. Is there any happiness in this story?"

"Nyet. The egg disappeared, Bolsheviks killed the imperial family, and my country still mourns." Dmitri straightened his jacket. "Do you know when Josee will return? I wish to speak with her about such matters."

38

Downriver

"Now this is scary, Clay."

"Scary how?"

He held the passenger door for Mylisha French. She settled into the Duster with a daypack on her lap. She looked good in her dark green sweatpants and T-shirt, Nike hiking shoes, and one half of a "Best Friends" necklace. The other half, Clay felt certain, was with Summer Svenson beneath the headstone he had prepared.

"Hard to believe this thing's still running, that's how."

Behind the wheel Clay pumped the gas twice and turned the key.

"We had our first date in this, you remember?" She patted the dash. "Guess it outlasted us, hmm?"

No suitable comments came to mind. Clay didn't trust his mouth at this juncture. A friendship, he reminded himself; that's how their relationship had started, and that's how it should remain. Before God and family he had made vows to be a faithful husband. That hadn't changed yet. Not irrevocably.

The Duster carried them out of town. Clay was glad to see a clear sky overhead, a perfect Sunday afternoon for their hike at the falls. With the window down, he adjusted the side mirror and noticed a vehicle trailing them toward Monroe.

"You think you're ready for this, Clay? You up for a good hike?"

"It was my idea. You'll be wishing you could keep up."

Mylisha chuckled into her hand. "Can't fool me, boy. Straight up, we're both older now. And the way I hear it, you've been a desk jockey. Is that true?"

"Yep. Had my own business, a satellite mapping service."

"Act as if I don't have a clue."

"Uh, basically, you establish the coordinates of any given location by using a grid of GPS dots, global satellite positioning. When you translate and lay it all out, the information has numerous applications, especially for emergency services. If they need to pinpoint where a hunter's disappeared, for example, these maps can save a life."

"What got you into it?"

"Wish I knew." Clay noted the car still behind them. "When things didn't work out with my b-ball career, I finished up at college, then moved with Jenni and Jason to Cheyenne. I borrowed money from my grandfather, leased a new car and an office on the second floor of a building downtown, hired a secretary. Tried to make a run at it."

"You always did have ambition."

"Well, it never got off the ground. Couldn't compete with the bigger guys."

"So here you are."

Mylisha's statement held no judgment. True to form, she went straight to the issue—he was here and that was what mattered. He focused on the road. Two more miles to their turnoff. In the mirror the trailing car was growing larger.

"What about you, Mylisha? Summer told me you haven't had any real serious boyfriends. Is that true?"

"She said what?"

"The night I got into town she stopped by to chat. Didn't stay long, though."

"Mm-hmm, my girl had a thing for you. Thought you were a regular hottie."

"Nothing happened, if that's what you're wondering."

"Not like it's my business. But yeah, she told me it was all innocent."

"How'd she do that?"

"In a card, which she must've written minutes before the accident. They found it in the glove box." Mylisha's head swiveled. Lustrous and shiny, her permed hair draped over her eye. "You know where it happened?"

"It was a hit and run, right?"

"Yeah, but you know where?"

"In town, wasn't it?" When Clay saw grief curl her lips into a sneer, he realized he was slipping up. "Uh, I don't know."

"Outside my own apartment!"

"On Maple? Where I picked you up?"

"Yes, Clay. Why're you asking stupid questions? She was right outside, and I didn't even know it." A tear splashed onto the leg of her sweatpants. "If I'd been out there, maybe I could've done something. Instead I ended up next to her hospital bed for three nights. She was pretty well gone, but I sat there praying she'd come back. Told her I was sorry, that I hoped she knew the Lord as her Savior, that I should've been a better friend."

Clay considered putting a hand on her shoulder but stopped himself.

I'm not ready to deal with Mylisha's death date on top of everything else.

"It was the hardest thing I've ever done," she continued. "Waiting in that hospital room, feeling so useless. You know how that feels? Do you have any idea?"

"I know exactly." He locked eyes with her. "It sucks."

Mylisha cracked open her window, and the perfume that traced across the front seat teased him with her nearness. Although this was a bad time for it, he wanted to spill all, to tell her about his theory of the numbers, about Summer and the Coates couple. He'd intended to bring her into his confidence, but she had toils of her own; she didn't need to be dragged into his nightmare.

A turn in the road led him over railroad tracks toward the falls, and Clay's surreptitious glance told him that the trailing vehicle had continued on in the other direction. So he'd been acting paranoid—surprise, surprise.

"Hey, you know what?" He tried to sound lighthearted. "You never did answer me on the boyfriend issue."

"Clay." She pursed her lips. "Now you're just talkin' silly."

"See? You're trying to avoid the question."

"Not avoiding it. Just don't see how it's your concern. No, I haven't had any boyfriends. For real. I'm taking classes a couple days a week and working salary at Safeway, which means whenever and however long I'm needed."

"But that's just it, Mylisha. You are avoiding stuff, and you know it."

"Like me not calling you? If that's what you're thinking, that just goes to show how self-centered Mr. Ryker's little world has become."

"I'm talking about your world. I know you. Since when've you cared about business degrees or doing time on the corporate level?"

"Called paying the bills," she said. "Helping my sister, watching after her kids."

"I saw Shanique."

"Not at the club, I hope."

"Huh? No, it was a few weeks back, downtown JC. I don't think she saw me. She almost ran into this kid—it was his fault as much as hers—then she got out and started yelling at Henna."

"Who?"

"Henna Dixon."

"Hannah? As in, thin with dark hair? She was a few grades behind us?"

"That's her. She's a fake blonde now. I hardly even remembered her. You know how it is when you're an upperclassman—no time for the little people."

"Hmm. I'm supposed to talk to you about that."

"About what?"

A baby blue envelope rested on Mylisha's knee. She curled it, slid it back into her purse on the floor mat. "It'll wait. We have our own catching up to do."

"There you go, avoiding the question again."

"Clay?"

"Yeah?"

"Talk to the hand."

———

Detective Freeman launched his boat after setting his bike in the hull. He weighed anchor, then splashed back through the shallows to park and lock his truck. He winched in the heavy-duty boat straps. Made sure he had his ice chest of food, his bucket of bait and tackle.

Fishing wasn't the point. Drifting downriver? Now that was a day off.

He set his things in the aluminum boat, hitched himself over the lip onto a bench. With oars fitted into the locks, he rowed out into the current. The McKenzie River prodded, tugged, twisted the vessel around. His dipped oars made adjustments.

Sizzling on his neck, the sun followed him beyond the rapids, past a spot where a trio of inner-tubers waved and hollered in greeting. He looked at the boy on the lead tube and was reminded of himself as a youngster. Oh, to be carefree again.

Detective Freeman didn't wave back. He wasn't here to socialize.

With the riskier stretch behind him, he pulled his fishing hat down over his eyes and let the river have its way with the boat. He thought about eating the egg sandwich he'd packed in the ice chest. Considered the chips and cold cola. But he was too tired to lift a finger.

A shadow moved across the sun.

He opened his eyes and saw he was passing beneath a bridge. Usually right about here he shifted over into the deeper pools and dangled a line. The fish liked hiding in this section beneath submerged boulders and tree stumps. After an hour or two, he would tie the boat at the next landing and cycle back to get his truck and trailer.

The thing that really killed him about all this was how tense he felt.

Sunlight, nice breeze, beautiful river, and solitude... Some called it God's country.

And I'm wound tighter than a kite! Darn Ryker and his dreams of being a hero. I don't need anyone but myself.

Detective Freeman's boat popped out from the bridge's shade, and the sun stabbed him in the eyes. Pain detonated behind his retinas—sharp, yet short lived; like an itchy finger on a hair trigger, it fired off the fatal aneurysm in his brain.

His boat made a lazy, uncorrected circle and continued downriver.

———

They parked, then stepped into the forest's leaf-filtered heat. As they neared the rocks, the water's minty breath greeted them in a frosty rush. Clay bounded from one rock to the other, bobbled, then pounced on the opposite bank. Mylisha, with a raised eyebrow, folded her arms and cocked a hip.

"You need a hand?" he goaded.

Now that he had succeeded, he knew she'd make it across; she was no slouch, and her female pride would heighten her determination.

"Oh no you didn't. Mr. Ryker thinks I need his help?"

He eased up. Walking a delicate line between friendly concern and confidence in her athleticism, he turned his back and followed the path through the trees. He heard a splash and a grunt, and soon Mylisha trotted up behind him with a show of energy. He pretended not to notice that her sweatpants were wet up to the knees.

During the next two hours, Clay caught up on old news and shared the basics of his courtship with Jenni, plus the escapades of young Jason. Mylisha was a gracious listener. She probed only so far, allowing him to expound as he wished.

With the trail as his focus, he grew less aware of her appearance and more attuned to her attributes as a friend. Mylisha was more introspective than she'd once been, yet she was much the same woman who had attracted him years ago.

The trail crossed back over the river and returned them to Alsea Falls.

"Ready to eat?" he asked.

"Thought you'd never ask."

Within the spray of cascading water, a flat rock acted as their table. Mylisha stretched out on the bank and leaned back with her face lifted to the sun. Clay joined her, and they unpacked the snacks. Cold drinks never tasted better.

"Clay, I'm sorry about my reaction in the car."

"Which one?"

"There he goes again." Mylisha dipped a hand in the water, flicked her nails at him. "I mean the envelope I was carrying. It's a card that Summer wrote me. There are things she wanted me to pass on to you."

Clay was munching on a handful of Doritos.

"You know what? She accused me of letting the Lord hold me back."

"You, Mylisha? That's hard to believe."

"She was right. I've been waiting since high school, maybe longer, to know God's will. I prayed for a scholarship, but then Shanique got the free ride to UCLA. I was stuck here, wondering where I missed my cues. Did I do something wrong? So I kept on praying, which turned into wishing, and then it became nothing more than a daydream now and then." She flicked a half-nibbled chip into the riverside undergrowth. "And nothing's changed."

"Timing's everything, right?"

"I'm in my late twenties, Clay. Still taking classes at the community college… Now *there's* a quick road into the world of indie filmmaking! And worst of all—"

"There's more?"

"Boy, now you're mocking me."

"Only trying to liven things up and put a smile on your face."

She gave him a closed-lip grimace. "See, that's what I'm talking about."

"You lost me."

"I am boring. It's like the kiss of death."

"No!" Clay said. "Don't even joke about that."

"But Summer was right. I've been waiting for God to do something, and in the meantime life's been passing me by. So recently I took matters into my own hands, started checking into astrology." Mylisha set her forehead against her crossed arms. "I don't mean to unload this on you. What with Summer's funeral and you back in town, just seems I've been doing a lot of thinking. Maybe I've been acting the fool."

"Mylee."

She turned her head, rich brown irises glowing through long ebony hair.

He said, "I've always admired your belief in God. Seems so real to you."

"Mmm. Well, look at me now."

"Look at us. A recovering stargazer and a soon-to-be-divorcé." He could add other things to his own list, but he refrained. "God's latest poster children."

"Two more people in need of his healing, dat's the truth." Mylisha sighed. "I know I've been wrong, won't even debate it. Just tired, I guess. Weary of trying to do the right thing."

"Is that any surprise? I mean, nobody finishes a race without getting weary."

"Listen to you, Clay. Glory hallelujah! We's havin' church now."

Clay let out a laugh.

With dialogue flowing and snacks depleted, he sensed she was ready to dip into Summer's well of secrets. To push now, though, would be to close her off once more. He restrained himself, and within a minute his strategy paid off.

Mylisha French began to share. Clay Ryker stared into the distance with mounting horror.

———

On the way back to the car, Clay's mind reeled.

"Clay, watch out for—"

A tree root snaked from the forest floor and ensnared his boot. Stopped cold in his tracks, he dropped to his knees, felt something dig into his skin.

"Shoot, what an idiot!"

"Tried to warn you," Mylisha said. "You did that with true white-boy style."

"Hey now. No racist remarks."

"By the looks of it, boyfriend, you've lost what little coordination you had."

"Please. Enough." Clay extricated his foot. "How much to make you stop?"

"How much you got on you?"

"What if I told you there were no empty seats for the ride home?"

Mylisha wagged her finger. "Oh no, that ain't right." She dropped the finger to point at his knee. "Look, you're bleeding."

"It's nothing."

She snorted. "You haven't changed, Clay. That's a fact." Before he could rise, she had a leaf in hand and started brushing dirt from the abrasion. "My dad used to do this with a square of sandpaper. Said it cleaned up the wound so it'd scab faster."

"No thanks." Clay tried to stand. "It'll heal on its own."

Back away! The twelve-inch rule. Please, don't touch me.

Her fingers slipped into his, pushing down. "Stay put, Mr. Ryker, and let me finish. What now? Please tell me it's not sprained. Where does it hurt?"

His groans, however, were expressions of something deeper. He snagged his hand back, angered by his verbal reaction. He should know better. Time to shut his trap and inject himself with a full dose of detachment.

Mylisha French…August 10, 2004.

"You can do away with the tough guy act," she said. "I know you're in pain."

He pulled himself upright. She was wrong. He felt no pain, felt nothing at all.

39

Clay's Choices

A key jiggled in the lock. Henna, no doubt. Asgoth knew she was one of the few with access to this place. He waited at the kitchen table in the dark blue shadows of dusk and watched her slip inside.

"A.G.?"

He noted the renewed timidity in her voice, a schoolgirl's desire to please.

"I'm here," he said. "What'd you bring me?"

Henna moved forward and spread her findings over the table's spilled wax ridges.

"You couldn't find his GPS unit?"

"I tried," she said. "I did what I could with the time and privacy allotted."

"We need that absolutely. At Crater Lake, Sergeant Turney turned in a piece of cork he found, which tells us the object went down. That GPS is our one link to its position."

She set her hands on the wood, closed her eyes. "Please, can I get a little positive feedback?" She rolled her neck in a circle, moaned in appreciation as he applied warm pressure to her muscles. "Ah, that's better. I should do more of these deep breathing exercises. All my stress seems to go to my back."

"What else did you find, Henna? Anything we can use against him?"

"Piles of bills. Mr. Clay Ryker's in a financial bind."

An idea stirred Asgoth's zeal. "So far Clay's choices have caused us delays. What does history tell us, though? Money, or the lack thereof, can be as dangerous as a loaded gun. The fall of the stock market, Japanese business failures, the era of the Great Depression—they've all provoked suicides in high numbers."

"Self-sacrifice," Henna said.

"We can't wait for Monde any longer. I say we channel our energies to this situation. Clay's proven he's no fool. But didn't your mother say that his wife and son will be heading this way for the festival? He'll be more prone to depression."

"Let Jenni die, for all I care."

"Exactly. We'll tighten the screws, and I'm sure Clay'll see what must be done."

———

Gerald's Miller Lite called out from the refrigerator. Clay stood in the kitchen doorway, eyeballing his options while refusing to dwell on Mylisha's spilled secrets. As a means of reciprocal healing, he'd shared with her most of his own recent quandaries.

Hoping to expel the junk. To cleanse his system.

Mostly he wanted to forget.

After walking Mylisha to her door, he had found a voice message on his phone in the Duster. Local police. Could he stop by at ten in the morning to discuss Detective Freeman's death? The man had been found floating in his boat on the McKenzie.

A random accident? A sovereign act?

With taste buds anticipating his first cold swig, Clay set his hand on the fridge's handle, but a swish of cloth turned him back toward the hallway.

"Dear?"

"Mom, you're still up."

"Is everything okay?"

"Yep. A-Okay."

"You've been out most the day. I was beginning to worry."

"I'm a big boy, remember?"

"But you're my big boy." Della's hand stroked his upper arm. "And you've given us a few scares of late."

He rolled his eyes, turned back toward the fridge. Pretenses were pointless. He snapped a beer can from the little plastic thingamajig, ready to weather his mother's protests. In the morning it would all be but a dream.

Row, row, row your boat, gently down the stream...

Della clasped her arms around her waist. "You're acting just like your father, Clay. You clam up, then shut out the women who truly love you."

He went through the motions of pouring himself a drink.

"By the way, Jenni called for you again."

Clay's longed-for inebriation crashed to a halt. "Today?"

"While you were out, yes. I hope you don't squander these last chances to set things right."

"It takes two, Mom."

"Precisely my point."

Clay tossed the empty can into the recycling bin under the sink.

"You also missed our afternoon visitors," Della said. "Mrs. Dixon and her daughter stopped by to say hello. Henna says you need a woman around. She thought your room was a horrifying mess."

"You let her go in there? Mom!"

"No, not exactly. Her mother and I were looking through the new Avon catalog, and I believe Henna just poked her head in on her way back from the ladies' room."

Revulsion welled in Clay's throat. He swallowed against it.

"Eat, drink, and be merry," he said with a caustic chuckle. He sipped at the foam in his glass. "For tomorrow we die."

"Please get some sleep, doll. I know you've had a lot on your mind." Without waiting for a reply, Della strode back to the room at the end of the hall.

Clay's cell phone vibrated on the counter.

"Mylisha, whassup?"

"You'll think I'm a pest soon enough, but I had to share this with you. Actually, I got a sense—from the Lord, I think—that you should hear this right away."

He swirled the glass, creating a frothy whirlpool.

"I told you about the Langston Hughes poems I like to read. Listen here. This is from one called 'Little Old Letter.' Made me think of those notes you've been getting."

"Mm-hmm."

"Says that you don't need traditional weapons when you've got the power of pencil and paper to issue threats. As a whole, I know the poem refers to my people's history, full of racial threats and violence, but I think it applies to your situation too."

"Go on."

"Don't you see, Clay? If Henna is the writer of those notes, she's using fear as a tactic. Using pencil and paper to goad you on. You were the man she always wanted for her own, but she lost out. So now she's pushing you to the edge, hoping you'll make that final jump. The incident at Crater Lake? That was by design."

"Almost worked."

"Since she can't have you, she's trying to make sure no one else can."

"Jenni." Clay's throat squeezed tight. "She'll be coming in a week or so."

"I'd keep an eye on her, if I were you. You're still here for a reason, boy. I suggest you don't waste it."

"I'm so tired of this."

"Nobody finishes a race without getting weary, Mr. Ryker. Sound familiar?"

"Okay, okay. I deserved that one."

They ended the call. He stared at his drink and slurped once more at the foam.

Like you have time to drink, Claymeister. You've got people's lives to consider.

He tipped the glass into the sink and watched amber liquid spiral down the drain.

———

As a habit, Dmitri did not remember his dreams; when he did, however, they flowed with symbolic and prophetic meaning.

He tossed one leg from the Best Western bed and pushed himself into a seated position. Other than the air conditioner's purr, the morning was still. He considered his dream's images. Horses. Snakes and skulls. Monochromatic charcoal gray panels.

Dmitri recognized certain elements...

In Russian folklore, a soothsayer had once told a man named Oleg that his horse would be the cause of his demise. Thus warned, Oleg never rode the horse again. When at last his horse died, he stamped scornfully on its skull, but a snake that nested within struck back with poisonous fangs. Oleg died as had been foretold.

Here in the present, Dmitri's partner from the Brotherhood bore the same name.

What did this mean? Was the cherub-cheeked man courting death?

At the bathroom sink, he splashed water over his face and rubbed away thoughts of the dream with a towel. On his hips, his angel hovered with spread wings, ready to guide and protect. Assuring him of preordained success.

———————

"Thank you for coming in, Mr. Ryker."

"My boss wasn't too thrilled," Clay said, "but he'll survive."

Oops. Better leave the dark humor back at the job.

The blue-uniformed man said, "I'm Officer Kelso."

They shook hands, then both men let their arms drop with looks of sudden comprehension. Kelso's eyes slid past Clay's shoulder, his unspoken question hanging over the interview room.

"Don't worry," Clay reassured the man, "it's not anytime soon."

"I wouldn't want to know. So it's true? With just one touch, you can tell?"

"Yep, seems that way."

"We have it on tape, your conversation with Detective Freeman." Kelso whistled. "Especially eerie the way you predicted that one."

"Not sure I'd call it a prediction."

"Call it what you will, but all of us here at the station sat up straight after watching that clip. Not one of us knew about the detective's condition. He was a straight shooter—no bull, just the facts—so most of us are convinced there was no trickery in the exchange between you two. A few don't know what to think."

"Put me in that second group."

"But you were on the money. On top of that, we have signed affidavits from people down at the Raven who heard you foretell Rhea Deering's and Mako's deaths." Kelso propped himself on the edge of the interview table.

"Which means we have a dilemma. Understand this, if we try to use your… psychic powers—"

"No, not psychic. I'm not into that stuff."

"Alien telepathy, Nostradamus channeling—whatever term you use, it's categorically spooky. We'd cause a panic if we unleashed you on the townspeople. Some would want to hang you, while others'd want to bronze you and kiss your feet."

Clay pointed. "Mind if I sit down?"

"Sure thing." Kelso rubbed his hands against his uniform. "Do you see my point? If we don't say a word and we let someone die, we might be held responsible. On the other hand, if we do say something and it provokes extreme or negligent behavior, then we'll face another sort of liability."

"These things've been running constantly through my mind."

"I'm sure they have, Mr. Ryker. You a religious man at all? Maybe the higher power's got his hands full, and now he's doing a bit of micromanaging, using you to spread the load. Or maybe there is no such power."

Clay squirmed in the wooden chair. "If there's no God, how do we explain this?"

"Chance. Sheer dumb luck. Chaos theory."

"And if there's no such thing as good or evil, what does it matter? A negotiable moral code, based on the needs of the moment and the individual?"

"Hey, let's not get too deep with this."

"Deep? You have no idea, Officer. My mind's been racked with this stuff for weeks now. We're barely scratching the surface."

"Not my cross to bear, buddy."

"Try this on," Clay snapped. "I know at least a half-dozen people who are going to die a week from Tuesday. I don't know how, when, why, where— nothing. Just that their dates have come up. Time to kick the ol' bucket."

Officer Kelso pushed a legal pad across the table.

"What's this for?" Clay said.

"Give us names and dates. We'll make a concerted effort to intervene."

"I hope you're not just messin' with me. I took off work to come—"

"Not at all, Mr. Ryker. We're taking this seriously. Although we don't like to make a fuss of such things, the department's used clairvoyants in the past."

"Clairvoyants? Do you see me wearing a turban or swami robes?"

Kelso forced a smile. "You'd be surprised. Some of them dress much nicer than you. And believe me, when it comes to missing children, we're willing to resort to such measures. In the world of law enforcement, we rub shoulders with the paranormal quite frequently, good and bad. If pushed, most of us will admit we've seen inexplicable things. Blame it on what you will—the occult or the divine, drugs or faith healing—but the stuff's out there. An unsettling reality."

"I can't argue. The Bible describes a struggle between darkness and light."

"If it works for you, stick with it. In this case, Mr. Ryker, we have the chance to effect a positive change. That's not always so. We're willing to give it a shot this one time if you're willing to work with us and keep it strictly confidential."

For a moment Clay felt possessive. This was his gift, his obligation. Could he risk involving others? What if they failed?

August 10, 2004...Jason, Digs, Wendy, Father Patrick, Mylisha—who else?

"We're as nervous as you are," Kelso confessed. "If this doesn't work, the department'll wash their hands of the deal. Bad press? We can do without it. This town's been under enough scrutiny already."

Clay stared at the blank legal pad. The rows of lines begged to be filled, and he wondered what would happen if he strolled the streets—touching, detecting, recording.

Would it matter? Death was inevitable. At some point it swallowed everyone.

Sure, he'd challenged God's hand in the past. He'd even convinced himself that if he were in charge, if he were omniscient, he would step in at every point of personal tragedy to create a world of never-ending tranquillity. When laws were broken, when rights were violated, he would administer quick and fair punishment. Where inequality and greed abounded, he would scatter the wealth to be shared by all.

But of course, not everyone could have his or her way. It would become a mess.

Maybe it's better not knowing. Walking blindly. By faith.

In the Garden of Eden, yes, the knowledge of good and evil had seduced humanity's mother and father. Their eyes had been opened—a backlash that continued to this day. They had succumbed to their desire to be like God.

Satan's same pitfall.

Clay thought first of Detective Freeman's refusal to receive help, then of his own prostrate form, vomiting into the dirt outside the tavern. He could see his hands shoving Bill from the bridge in rage and later pulling his own body down into the hellish depths of Crater Lake. How could he deny the results of mankind's first seduction?

Good and evil—they're on practically every corner. We each have a choice.

He looked at Officer Kelso. "I'll do it."

40

Up the Crooked Stairs

Dmitri watched from across the street. He'd been told Josee would open the shop.

On Monday, he had found the art gallery closed. He'd passed the day at the Corvallis Public Library, pleased by the selection of Russian classics. He'd spent many similar hours in Ekaterinburg among Belinski Library's fifteen million volumes.

Today, however, he was ready for action.

In the mirror he admired the way his morning shave seemed to brighten his blue eyes; his hair was combed back; he wore a belt with loose-fitting trousers and a white tank top beneath a light tan jacket.

On his hip the Maksalov VI cell phone was a comforting weight.

He took another bite of the bread from a local bakery. Nibbling, he saw a station wagon bearing the Tattered Feather's logo pull into the driveway.

Out jumped Josee Walker, keys dangling from a wrist strap.

He'd seen her photos, watched her on the vault videotape, but in person she looked smaller. Baggy corduroys swirled around her legs, while a sweatshirt with cutaway seams disguised her shape. A silver hoop clung to her eyebrow.

He gave her a few minutes to settle into her routine, then moved across Southwest Second and up the gallery's steps.

———

Clay was back on the roller coaster. He'd left a message yesterday at Jenni's office in Cheyenne, but she hadn't called back. Was she ignoring him? Should he wait? Try again?

Nope. He refused to come off looking desperate.

He swigged from a fruit juice bottle and settled into the break room's sofa. "Still no luck?" Digs plopped down beside him.

"She's the one who called. But hey, I'm not lettin' it get to me."

"That so? Well, Ryker, I'll buy that the same day I buy tickets to the moon."

"Look who's bugging me now," Clay said, but without malice.

"You need a diversion, somethin' to take your mind off the women in your life."

"I'm open to suggestions."

"Next Tuesday," Digs said. "C'mon down after work, shoot some pool with me. Place over in Harrisburg, they got a little tourney goin' on. Think on it, and let me know."

"I'll do that."

At the moment Clay was more concerned about letting Officer Kelso know. He'd agreed to collect information on August tenth's potential victims, including their activities for a week from today, travel arrangements, companions, work schedules. Local detectives were making inquiries as well, establishing possible connections between those on Clay's list.

"Ryker, you awake? Got a woman on hold for ya. Line four." Digs wiggled his furry white eyebrows.

Clay dashed to the phone between the trailer's drinking fountain and rest room.

"This is Clay."

Jenni's voice was warm, compliant. "Sorry I missed your call yesterday. Had to drive down to Denver. Is this a bad time? I was trying to catch you on your break, but it sounds like you just ran in from the shop."

"It's you, Jenni," he said. "You always take my breath away."

Extra cheesy. What am I thinking?

The distance stretched along the phone lines, but Jenni's soft laugh erased it in a moment. "That was goofy, Clay."

"Yeah, I thought so too."

"I'm glad we're speaking. That's a good thing. For Jason's sake especially."

"And for our sakes too. Twelve years together. We can't make that disappear."

"Do I like your assertive new approach? I don't know. What're you aiming for, Clay? We're only a few signatures from putting those years to rest once and for all."

"That's what you said a few months ago."

"Your point being?"

"Maybe we're not supposed to do this. I still think about you, about us." Clay leaned his forehead into the wall. "I've been weighing a lot of things lately. I deserve most of the junk you wanna throw my way, the late hours and the loneliness, the…" He closed his eyes. "The things I couldn't provide."

"I don't hold that against you. Didn't I try to tell you that last time? You held it against yourself, then made Jason and me pay for it."

"How?" he barked. "Tell me how Jason paid? I never did anything to—"

"Exactly. You were so busy trying to punish yourself, you had no time left for your son. Playing Xbox once a week doesn't qualify in my book."

"Ask Jason if it qualifies. He complains that you never play it with him." Jenni heaved a sigh into the phone. "Now we're exchanging insults."

"You just don't wanna hear it, do you?"

"Clay. Listen. I still care for you."

"And vice versa," he growled.

"We're two wounded people. It's normal to strike out in self-protection."

"Is that so? Boy, you're good at this psychoanalysis. Where were you when I was paying for visits to Dr. Gerringer? You could've saved me a bundle."

"You're underlining my point."

"What is the point again?" Clay painted the picture in his mind: Jenni's soft freckles scrunched together beneath green eyes, her left cheek puckered as she chewed on her mouth in thought.

"I'm bringing the settlement papers. I know I could send them, but honestly, I'm not sure I'd get them back in an expedient fashion. And"—she gathered her breath—"I'm going to be a little later than planned. Jason and I won't be leaving until the tenth, which means we'll arrive on the twelfth."

"Here a number, there a number. What do I care?"

"I knew you'd be upset."

"Please, just promise me you won't drive on the tenth. You know I'm not usually superstitious, but it's a bad feeling I have. Maybe you could lock your-selves in a bed-and-breakfast somewhere. Relax, stay inside. But don't go swimming, I beg you."

"Clay, I need to run."

"Yeah, same here."

"If you'd like to call Jason, we'll be home the next few nights."

"And you'll let him pick up?"

"He needs to hear from his daddy."

Clay gave a tight-throated affirmative.

———

As Dmitri walked through the gallery's door, Josee Walker glanced up. Her greeting was dispassionate, but he could feel her earnest scrutiny, the way she took him apart and put him back together again.

Damaged idealists were good at this, he thought. Cynically intuitive.

I, too, use high ideals to purify my actions.

He made a circuitous approach, from one art display to the next. Her feline presence demanded that he give her time to adjust. At the counter he kept his head down and asked if the gallery carried any Russian artifacts.

"Got anything specific in mind?"

"Fabergé. You know this name?" Dmitri turned his eyes upward, intend-ing to weaken Josee. He faltered instead as her eyes absorbed the sparkle in his own, taking on a deep shade of turquoise.

"Heard of it," she said.

"The store owner said you have studied the Fabergé eggs."

"Suzette said what? Okay, yeah, they intrigue me. Not that it's an obses-sion or anything."

Dmitri had to break away his gaze. "Perhaps I misunderstood. Suzette insisted that you could help me find information on the imperial treasures. I was born in Ekaterinburg, the city where the Tsars were murdered, so this is also intriguing to me."

"You grew up there?"

"Da. It was a lot of history for a young boy."

"Have you been to the Cathedral-of-the-Blood?"

Dmitri gave a knowing nod. "You are a history buff, I see. As a child I also saw the House of Fabergé in Moscow, with granite pillars and much— what is the word?—opulence. Do you know this? There are still twelve eggs missing from the collection. Some of the creations no longer have hidden treasures inside. They've disappeared over the years, stolen or lost."

"You seem to know a lot about them."

"It is Mother Russia's pride and joy. My heritage."

"Well. Maybe you can help me. You can read Russian, right?"

"But of course. What is this help you seek?"

Josee folded her arms on the counter's wood molding, her eyebrow ring shifting as she leaned toward him. "I'll tell you a secret, but I swear, if you whisper a word of it, I'll have to hurt you."

Dmitri waited. His pulse throbbed in his temples.

"I think I might have an original," she said. "Dated 1917."

"A Fabergé? Here?" His eyes darted around the showroom.

"No! Do you think I'm whacked in the head? Not here, but not far. I have questions about it, things that aren't recorded in any of the official records. Maybe you could fill in some of the blanks. Do you think you could take a look?"

He shrugged in a show of mild interest. "If you'd like, da. I can look."

"That'd be cool."

"Where is it?"

"You think I'd tell you? We're talking about a stinkin' gold mine."

"Very valuable," he agreed. "We can do it now if you'd like. I am free."

"Hmm. I'm on shift. Fridays, though, I don't have to be here till two."

They made arrangements to meet, with Josee warning Dmitri to keep it between the two of them. On the way to the car, he touched his hip and whispered thanks to his angel for directing his steps so favorably.

———

I should've checked this out earlier, Clay scolded himself.

After a long day at Glenleaf and a short phone conversation with Jason—

it was bedtime in Wyoming—Clay changed into dark clothes and grabbed a flashlight. He parked his Duster in the Dari Mart parking lot, jogged across Ivy, and cut over to the bank on Sixth and Holly.

From the back corner he spied the apartment Henna had visited a few nights ago. The windows were dark this evening.

Was Henna Dixon up there? With her unidentified partner?

Clay decided he should stroll up the stairs to the dilapidated walkway. He could listen at the door. If it opened, he'd move on quickly as though headed for a friend's place down the way. Better than sitting out here as a mosquito snack.

He moved up the crooked stairs on the backside of the video store, his adrenal glands kicking into overdrive. Henna was not to be taken lightly. She was a woman scorned, ruthless and conniving, according to Mylisha's account.

At Alsea Falls, Mylisha had jolted Clay with details from their shared past.

Years ago, as a freshman, Henna had dated Bill Scott in an attempt to get closer to Clay. When that failed, she had tried to break up Clay and Mylisha's relationship by convincing Bill to get his own little taste of brown sugar. More than willing, Bill had cornered Mylisha against the lockers and tried to make advances, which she resisted with a knee in the groin and a fist to the gut.

It did not end there. Some of Mylisha's account Clay refused to dwell on.

Bill had begun leaving threatening notes. Predatory. Lecherous. He'd taunted Mylisha. Then to poke at her weak spots, he began messing around with Shanique. With the help of an adult supplier from the nearby lumberyard, he funneled drugs to this girl who had no means of paying for them.

At least not with cash. But Shanique found other ways.

Desperate, Mylisha worked longer hours after school to cover Shanique's debt. She made Bill swear to leave her sister alone once the money was paid off. So it was, on a particular weekend, she went to his house to buy back her sister's soul.

As arranged by Henna through Bill, Clay showed up minutes later.

At the top of the crooked stairs, Clay now revisited his rage...

He was a senior. Walking into Bill's family room. Finding his friend and his girlfriend in one another's arms. Hearing Bill's chuckles amid Mylisha's cries of innocence. Some freshman chick was also in the house, one who'd been hanging around Bill a lot. She tried to offer Clay her own brand of comfort. He turned without a word. Closed the door softly. Drove to the gym, where he shot three hundred jump shots before collapsing in his bed that night. The next day Bill gave a joking apology. And Mylisha swore nothing had happened. Clay said it was no big deal, but his anger simmered, building beneath the surface.

Until that fateful day on the bridge.

A prod…a push…a shove.

They were all really the same, weren't they?

———

The stairs ended in a pool of darkness. Clay curled around the railing to face the far corner unit. He saw no signs of life, no flickering candlelight.

Nothing to fear.

His footsteps brought harsh protests from the weatherworn walkway. On the road below, trees swayed, and a streetlamp thrust daggers of light between the rails.

Clay checked his perimeter. He saw no movement in either direction. He tilted his ear to the apartment door until his thick hair was pressed against the painted wood. In his hand the flashlight waited for duty. He could hear nothing but his own breathing. He stood straight again. Caught by a loose numeral on the door, a hair twanged from his scalp, and he tried to hold back his reaction.

Still no movement or sound or light or any apparent reason for concern.

Clay gripped the doorknob. Turned it. The unlocked door squealed as he pushed inward. He stretched his long legs inside, snapped the door shut. He wasn't sure how he would explain himself, but now that he had entered the space, he intended to explore.

With his hand over the lens, Clay flipped on the flashlight. Turning on the apartment lights was out of the question, certain to alert those on the street below.

His senses embraced their detective work—tasting stale smoke in the air; smelling incense and candles; sighting gold carpet that looked dingy in the pale illumination through the curtains.

He turned along the wall, adjusting to the darkness, listening for anything other than the faint voices downstairs and a slow water drip from the kitchen area. He bumped into a wall clock. On the window sill, his fingers found ashes, incense sticks, strands of melted wax. In the middle of the living room, his light revealed a bundled blanket, a group of folding chairs, paper plates.

No furnishings or decorative elements.

The hall, the bathroom, the bedroom—they all lacked signs of long-term occupation. This renter lived a grim existence.

Why, he wondered, would Henna waste her time here?

The kitchen was a black cube, split by the light that chopped through the window. Spots on the walls indicated spattered cooking grease. Red candle wax fingers reached across the dining table and curled over the edges. As Clay leaned closer, one of the fingers poked at his leg. He flinched.

Etched into the wax, six letters formed a word. A name.

Asgoth.

As Clay's flashlight panned further down, he thought his heart would punch the eyeballs from his skull. Beneath the table, a jogging shoe rested on the tiles.

An Osaga KT-26.

The Osaga athletic company had folded years ago, but Clay would never forget the last time he'd seen this product on a person. Twelve years ago. At the riverbank beneath the bridge. Clay had yelled and pounded his chest, then shed his shirt and shorts for the coming plunge into the Willamette. Bill Scott had done likewise, tossing old and weary Osagas onto their pile of discarded clothes.

PART FOUR

He looked up to the sky, doubting
whether there really was a heaven above....
"My Faith is gone!" cried he..."and sin is but a name."

Young Goodman Brown, Nathaniel Hawthorne

"Just kill me now, LORD!
I'd rather be dead than alive...."
Then...he waited to see if anything would happen to the city.

Jonah 4:3, 5

41

No Physical Proof

Clay Ryker was afraid to touch it.

Crouched in the dark kitchen, with his shoulder butted against the wax-entangled table, he stared at the prodigal shoe and deliberated. Under normal conditions he would've discounted its presence as a coincidence or strange twist of fate. Tonight, however, the circumstances prompted wild speculation.

After tackling and tossing aside theory after theory, Clay ran headlong into one that refused to go down. This idea had wriggled about in his mind for weeks now, but the shoe gave it the courage to walk out into the open.

What if Bill Scott had survived?

What if his friend had been severely injured and floated to the surface in an unconscious state, kept alive by a trace of a pulse?

Clay thudded his forehead against the table's edge.

But I watched him go under, saw his bloodied body. I ran for help.

Clay bent low, stretched his fingers to grab the Osaga. He drew it across the kitchen tiles and noticed a rolled white envelope tucked down inside.

———

"As usual, Sergeant Turney's making a nuisance of himself."

"I fear he's connecting the loose ends, A.G. He was at the rental car place in Eugene earlier today. After that, he visited the FBI office."

Mr. Monde and Asgoth watched Sergeant Turney hitch up his pants, tuck in his shirt, and walk across the Blombergs' driveway. Out of sight they trusted the night to protect them, but the big man turned as though alerted to their nearness. He clamped a hand over his upper arm, muttering fervent words. A prayer of protection.

"Surely he can't see us," Monde whispered.

Asgoth remained frozen beneath the juniper branches.

Turney swung around to ring the doorbell. He coughed, hitched his pants again, and tightened his belt a notch. He looked back over his shoulder, deep-set eyes raking the shadows. Only the sound of an automatic garage door diverted his gaze.

Light crept over the driveway as the door lurched upward. Behind it, two cars and a motorcycle were at rest for the night.

"Yvonne, whatcha think you're doing? Close that thing, you hear!" A large, red-haired man stood with hands braced on his hips, stock-still until the garage door came down. A half minute later, he reappeared at the front screen door. "Who's there?"

"Good evenin'. Sergeant Turney, but just Sarge'll do."

"We got people trying to sleep, so I don't much appreciate you showin' up on my doorstep unannounced."

"Stan Blomberg?"

"That's right."

"You got a daughter stayin' with ya? Name of Victoria?"

"Vicki. Yeah, she's here."

"I'm sure she's upset, what with her boyfriend's passing and all."

"Whaddya know, Sarge? You're pressin' on some sore spots."

"I know losin' a loved one's hard on the emotions. Sometimes it helps just knowin' that what you say can make a difference. I'm here in the role of investigative consultant. Not makin' any arrests, nothing like that. Just need to jot down some info. Was hopin' you could help me out."

Blomberg's shoulders fell and his belly extended. "Can't it wait till mornin'?"

"It can, I s'pose, but I'm closin' in on the person responsible. I need to verify some details with your daughter. We'd hate to let him get away."

"Five minutes—that's whatcha got to work with. C'mon inside."

At Asgoth's side, Monde gave a nervous twitch like a bird ruffling its feathers.

—

Twelve years ago Clay had attended William "Bill" Scott's memorial service. There had been no viewing of the body, no physical proof of death in the form of a corpse. Yet to think that his companion could've pulled off such a hoax…

It was mind staggering. What about Bill's parents? And the local law?

What about me? I touched his cold skin!

Clay sniffed foot decay and shoe leather as he lifted the Osaga's tongue to remove the envelope. He unfurled the white generic paper. Although the inclusion of his name was superfluous, it confirmed that his visit here had been anticipated.

The handwriting matched the others, as did the vanilla and cherry scent.

You look tongue-tied. Have you lost your sole?
To reunite as a pair, you'll have to hit the trail.
Love comes at a price!

He folded and slipped the envelope into his back pocket, chewed on the words, mumbled them twice into the kitchen's stillness. Was the note issuing a threat against his relationship with Jenni? What was the price?

Clay fell back against the wall, shuddering at this latest development. He was worried about the note's meaning but equally concerned about its form of delivery.

Henna's writing…her Avon pen…a note stuck in one of Bill's old shoes. Was Bill Scott alive?

Clay cupped his hands over his eyes. He must've been avoiding the truth all this time. Must've been blind. The more his mind pushed at this mystery's elements, the tighter they came together. The puzzle was becoming complete.

Henna Dixon…a jilted high school girl.

Bill Scott…a victim of Henna's ploys and Clay's jealous rage.

The pair must've heard of Clay's divorce and impending return to JC, then plotted revenge by arranging deaths on dates that added up to thirteen— matching the date at the river, Friday the thirteenth.

They'd conspired against him. They wanted him to pay by doing himself in.

Clay shook his head, his breath pressing through his lips in short gasps. He'd faced determined foes before, on the basketball court, in the business world, and elsewhere. Loss was part of life; no one was immune to its anguish or rejection.

But this was vindictiveness at a level beyond his comprehension.

Perhaps Bill was alive but severely handicapped. Or disfigured. Perhaps he was nursing a bitterness that had grown into demonic proportions. What lengths of reprisal would Clay go to if a friend had pushed him toward his death?

A sudden scraping sound told Clay the front door was opening.

"Junction City Police! We're coming in."

He turned to see a pair of policemen entering the apartment, side arms drawn.

"Officer Kelso." Clay held his hands up. "I'm in here."

"Keep your hands up, and don't move!"

A beam of light cut across the living room into the kitchen. Officer Kelso came to stand over Clay while his partner moved down the hallway. He called back that the rest of the place was clear. Clay knew it would be useless to mention the note or the Osaga's past owner. He would sound nearly as crazy as he felt.

"What're you doing in here, Mr. Ryker? We received a call that someone was breaking in." Officer Kelso flipped the switch on the wall, but nothing happened. His flashlight combed the table, counters, floor. Paused, then moved past the old shoe.

"The door was open," Clay said.

"And that gave you the right to enter?"

"I was trying to find out who was up here. I wanted to talk with him. I, uh...I might've gone to school with him."

"With Mr. John Doe? You're the first person who's claimed to know him."

"John Doe? He could've picked a more original name."

"It's far from humorous, Mr. Ryker." Kelso aimed the light at Clay's face.

"That hurts, Officer. I can't see."

"Apparently not. You may have the ability to see into the future, but you certainly can't see into the past. This place hasn't been lived in for months. Not since the unsolved homicide of our John Doe, which happened here on this very table. Those aren't grease spots on the wall, you might be interested to know. We found a knife, but no prints, no solid leads. As if a ghost slipped in and carried out this savage act."

Clay's mind reeled. *A ghost is right! I thought my friend was dead.*

Bill Scott couldn't be the victim, John Doe. He would've been identified.

Bill, however, could be John Doe's killer. No one would ever suspect it.

This was lunacy. Who would believe such a theory? How, Clay wondered, would he stop a man who was able to murder with impunity? As far as this town was concerned, Bill Scott was in the grave, dead and gone. Twelve years and counting.

———

In the research forest north of Corvallis, Dmitri Derevenko was target practicing with his Maksalov cell phone. Lacking any barrel to speak of, the weapon was built for short range. Accuracy was paramount.

"I cannot let you go alone, comrade."

"You do not need to worry." Dmitri said. At his back Oleg's car lights provided illumination for the impromptu firing range. "Josee is small woman."

"I do not worry about Josee Walker. I worry about you." Oleg poked his joined and steepled fingers into Dmitri's chest. "If true, if she has a Fabergé egg, how do I know you will bring it back to me?"

"It is not for you, Oleg. It's for the Brotherhood and for Gertrude Ubelhaar. We want her to speak, to tell us where to find the Tsar. Or have you forgotten this?"

"You're right, Dmitri. But this one treasure, it alone is worth millions of rubles."

"You think I might steal it?"

"The Brotherhood is concerned. They've asked me to keep an eye on you."

This lack of trust incensed Dmitri. He fired a shot into the paper target on the tree. "Oleg, you are *neudachnik*!" He triggered a second shot.

"I am a loser?"

"Da. I work for a new day in Mother Russia, the same as my father, grandfather, and great-grandfather. It's a deep insult that you carry no trust. When I go with Josee on Friday, I will bring back the Fabergé egg. It will provide finances and bring about Ms. Ubelhaar's cooperation. That's more valuable than millions of rubles."

"What if Josee tries to stop you? You have not killed a woman before."

"It is no different. If necessary, she will die."

42

Tmu Tarakan

The headstones faced Clay with insolent indifference. He stared back.

"You with us this morning?" Digs asked.

"Yeah, I'm fine."

"I dunno, Ryker. Gonna take a little more convincin' than that."

Clay used a pick to peel lettering from the marker on his bench. "Digs, how would you handle it if you could foresee bad things?"

"Still wrestlin' with God, eh? Wonderin' about his plans in this world?"

"It's only natural, isn't it?"

"There's your problem in a nutshell. It ain't about natural. It's supernatural."

"Just trust and obey, you mean? Blind faith and all that."

"You tried doin' it the other way yet? On your own agenda?"

Clay nodded.

"Me, too," Digs said. "Took years in the state pen to cure me of it. Let's hope you learn faster than this white-haired fool. Don't always got the answers, don't even understand, but I do know God is good. That's money in the bank."

Since the discovery in the apartment a few nights back, Clay's racing mind had caused him to sleep restlessly. What was the latest note's meaning? Would August tenth be a day of disaster? How should he intervene? Was Jenni now a target too?

Thankfully, Officer Kelso had released him with a warning to avoid further late-night escapades. The officer knew nothing about a Mr. Bill Scott and laughed when Clay tried to indict Henna for visits to the same unit.

"Henna Dixon? We'd expect to find her up here," Kelso had said. "She's the one who first found John Doe. She does the majority of cleaning at the complex."

"She's a maid?"

"'Interior overseer' is her official title. The whole thing shook her pretty badly."

"Yeah. I bet."

Clay left it at that. He had nothing incriminating to present. Some vaguely threatening notes, yes, but little to suggest malevolence on Henna Dixon's part.

———

"If we get split up," Josee said, "just hit Highway 101 and head down to Florence, Bank of the Dunes. It's on the north end of town."

"I'll meet you there," Dmitri agreed.

"Hope you're not wastin' my time. I'm ready for some answers."

"I know much about the Fabergé creations. You'll be pleased."

Josee's turquoise eyes considered him from beneath a tuft of chopped black hair. Her fingers twiddled at her eyebrow ring. "Okay, let's do this."

Dmitri watched her climb into a red VW Bug with original hubcaps. The rear bumper dragged on the passenger side, creating occasional sparks as it struck the pavement. Keeping track of Josee would be easy. He set his cell phone on the seat of his rental car, followed the VW into early lunch traffic, and adjusted his mirror while trying to determine which car Oleg was using to tail them.

Horses, snakes, and skulls. The dream images returned.

Dmitri pictured Oleg's choirboy face and his criminal background. The man was a walking mystery. Superb organizational skills, yet questionable allegiances.

In the forest Dmitri had feared Oleg might lash out at him for his words. Neudachnik? Da, it was the truth for any man who did not trust him. He was a man appointed by the Brotherhood of Tobolsk, by the Almighty himself.

Be careful, Oleg. Try to stamp on my head, and a snake will strike!

At that moment Dmitri spotted his comrade in a Chevy pickup, three cars back and one lane over.

"Did he take the note, A.G.?"

"He did, but he left the jogging shoe."

Henna peered into the kitchen where the Osaga remained beneath the table. "Those shoes always did stink. No offense, but it's the truth."

"I refuse to take the blame."

Henna folded herself into a lotus position on the living room carpet. She closed her eyes, her nostrils inhaling the aroma of sandalwood incense.

Asgoth admired her beauty but suspected her thoughts were somewhere else. On someone else. From the start he'd known of her obsession with Clay Ryker and used it to his benefit. Full of scorn cloaked as independence, Henna acted as though she had no more feelings for the man; yet all these years later, her willingness to take this course of action suggested a strong undercurrent of emotion.

"If given the choice," he asked her, "would you select Clay over me?"

"What?" Henna's eyes popped open. Her trance was broken.

"Forgive my insecurities, Henna. I shouldn't push."

"You always want more. That's my main complaint. When it comes to a woman's spirit, it's better to simply enjoy what she gives you."

"I'm impatient, it's true. It's a fault of my species."

"Yeah, why is that so?"

Asgoth pondered. "We're afraid you'll see through us, I guess. We're always concerned that you'll close us off if you catch a glimpse of who we really are."

"One little glimpse. Is it really so horrifying?"

"You tell me."

"You're a gentle spirit, A.G. You have your dark side, but who doesn't?"

"Are you ready to tap into yours? We have only a few days until Jenni Ryker arrives. I'm sure you'd love to arrange something special for her."

"It'd be my delight. What about Monde? Have we heard from him?"

"He says not to worry. He's stirring up troubles between Dmitri and friends. It's always fun to watch havoc ensue. Of course," Asgoth said, "we'll have to include Clay in Jenni's 'welcome home' plans. We'll wait until after the tenth, though. Clay's been visiting with the JC police, and I think he's enlisted their help in protecting the targets. Poor officers. They're going to be very disappointed in him."

———

Against the natural backdrop of windswept sand dunes, the Bank of the Dunes looked small. Josee parked off to the side, but Dmitri selected a spot near the entrance, ready for a getaway. He clipped the cell phone to his belt.

"Come on." Josee knocked on his window. "You look pretty enough already."

Dmitri gave an obligatory smile.

Together they entered the bank. To the left, wing chairs faced an accounts manager at a polished desk. Near the doors, a hefty security guard greeted customers on their way in and out.

"Give me a minute," Josee said.

Dmitri stood to the side as she approached the next available teller. He saw her produce ID from a pouch suspended around her neck. He noticed also a wooden crucifix and a necklace of braided twine.

"Okay, Dmitri. All I have to do is sign in, and we can have a look."

The security guard joined them, smoothed a leather-bound register on a podium near the vault. "Here ya go, ma'am. Print and sign." He winked and held out a pen.

Dmitri watched her spell out the name: Josee M. Walker.

"And this gentleman's going in with you?" the guard inquired.

"I hope that's okay. I asked him to come."

"It's your deposit box. Got your key on ya, Ms. Walker?"

"Right here."

"Lemme see. Number 89."

The guard's shoes clacked on marble as he led them past a door of reinforced steel bars into the vault's tomblike space. A gun poked from the holster on his hip. At the correct box, he inserted his master key into the left slot; when Josee did the same on the right, the door clicked open.

"All yours, ma'am. Be right out here when you're done. Just holler."

Dmitri made sure they were alone before turning to Josee. His hand brushed his cell phone. He angled himself so that he would be less identifiable in the camera peering down over the viewing table. Josee had the safe-deposit box open with her hand already dipped inside.

"I have it here." She hesitated. "Why am I doing this? I hardly know you."

"You can trust me. We are safe here in the vault."

"What if this thing's a fake? I'd almost rather not know."

"We can look another day perhaps. No need to hurry, Josee." He shrugged, hoping she was deaf to the thumping of his heart against his rib cage.

"No. I'm not gonna wait any longer. Get over here."

He stepped to the table. Josee removed a felt bag. Her fingers loosened the drawstring so that he saw clearly a golden eagle stamped beside the Fabergé name. Without warning, a groan escaped his lips as she brought the jeweled egg into view. Translucent turquoise enamel covered the exquisite object. Above gold cabriole legs, rose diamonds formed a glittering band around the four-inch oval shape. A garnet-encrusted stem bore the initials *H.W.,* while other symbols marked the base.

"You think it's the real thing?"

"Very real."

"Tell me about it, whatever you know."

Dmitri quelled a rush of exuberant pride. Outside, in all likelihood, Oleg was waiting to see this prize.

He will see he can trust me. He'll have no more words to say.

Dmitri directed his energy to the task of identifying and cataloguing the treasure's specifics. With Josee's permission, he lifted it and pointed out assay marks engraved into the bottom. He explained St. Petersburg's city of origin symbol and the numbers which represented the gold's *zolotnik,* or carats. He told her the stem's initials stood for Henrik Wigstrom, Fabergé's work master at the time of the Bolshevik Revolution, and he detailed the enamel process that had been unique to the House of Fabergé.

"Don't most of the eggs contain hidden things?"

"Da. Many are ingenious, Josee. Very crafty."

"Well, I must be freakin' stupid. I've tried, but I can't get it to open."

"May I try?"

She nodded.

Dmitri studied the jeweled surface, enamored by its coolness in his hands. Gertrude Ubelhaar had spoken the truth. From Russia, through the hands of the Nazis and a greedy American soldier, this object had ended up here. Nearly eighty years old and still magnificent.

He tried pushing, pulling, poking at the creation.

In the vault's even light, he detected Cyrillic letters, hovering, almost invisible within the translucent turquoise shell. He swiveled the egg. Spelled the Russian words in his head, but they offered no obvious clues.

"What is it?" Josee asked.

"Words. You see here, very faint. They say, 'Tmu Tarakan.'"

Even as the phrase left his mouth, the solid garnet stem seemed to loosen between his fingers. He moved with it. Guided and twisted it.

...k-r-i-k-l-i-c-k...

The sound was barely audible. The stem slipped up into the egg, and the cabriole legs flattened on hidden joints. The section seated above the rose diamonds lifted upward on the center stem as four golden miniatures eased outward. They sparkled, boasting tiny diamond eyes. Yet they were somehow disturbing.

"What are they, some sort of bugs?" Josee whispered.

Dmitri furrowed his brow. "Tmu Tarakan. Some say it as one word, *tmutarakan,* referring to one of Russia's remote medieval regions. Others use it to mean 'Place of Darkness' or 'Kingdom of Cockroaches.'"

———

During lunch Clay hurried to the downtown police station. He and Officer Kelso referred to the August tenth targets, creating diagrams of each person's anticipated patterns. Kelso said he was in contact with the police department in Cheyenne, Wyoming, to see what they could do about Jason. Here in JC, the police had been checking residences and job sites, fleshing out details, but at this point they'd made no specific connection between the targets. Nevertheless, an officer would be assigned to cover each individual.

Wendy, Digs, Father Patrick, and Mylisha...

"Time and money," Kelso said. "That's what we're investing."

"The lives of four citizens are at stake. Maybe more."

"And that's why we'll give it a shot, Mr. Ryker. Let's hope it's energy well spent."

As he drove back to Glenleaf Monument, Clay dialed Jenni's number. The other night he had caught Jason on his way to bed, and even though this call would be abbreviated as well, Clay wanted to hear his son's voice again.

Jenni's in-home day-care provider answered. "Mr. Ryker? Jenni said you might call. Hold on one moment. Jason's eating a corn dog and watching SpongeBob."

"Daddy!"

"Jason, little buddy. How you doin'?"

"Good."

"I wish I could be there to watch the show with you. I haven't seen that one in ages. Not since…well, not since I moved here. I'm living with Grandpa and Grandma Ryker now. They're not big SpongeBob fans."

"When you movin' back?"

"Uh, that might be a while."

"You can bring the bus. Mommy says it's better when husbands and wives are together. Like Adam and Eve. Not good 'for the man to be alone.' "

"She said that, huh? Were you guys talking about me?"

"I dunno. I guess so. Me and Mommy's comin' next week."

"Can't wait to see you, buddy."

"Me too."

"I'm gonna take you to the Scandi-Fest. There's lots of food and costumes and dancing. Mommy's been there before."

"She told me. She says it's fun."

"Listen, Jason. I love you. I have to get back to work, okay? See you soon."

"Love you too."

"You listen to your mother and don't do anything too crazy."

"I'm a big boy now."

"Yes, you are. Bye, Jason."

"Bye, Daddy."

43

The Switch

"Cockroaches?" Josee shivered in the vault's cold space.

Dmitri lifted the Fabergé artifact. The four golden cockroaches were like points of the compass, projected outward by the garnet stem's smooth cork-screw action. Each bore a mark. A single word on its back. Dmitri swiveled the egg, reading each in turn. Once again, the ingenuity of Henrik Wigstrom's works impressed Dmitri. He cradled the long-lost treasure with the wild-eyed look of a man possessed.

"What do those words mean?" Josee's question snapped him back.

"Four words...'Black King Is Key.'"

"Who is the black king? What's he the key to?"

"I don't have an answer," Dmitri lied. He knew he should hurry this up. He needed to escape from this vault with the 1917 Fabergé egg in hand, and only Josee Walker and the bulky security guard stood in his way.

With gentle pressure on its turquoise point, Dmitri brought the egg's halves back together. The golden miniatures retreated into the shell, the stem twisted downward, and the cabriole legs stood straight once more, forming a delicate base. Beneath the translucent surface, the ten letters still floated. Still taunted.

Tmu Tarakan... With this, I'll track down Rasputin's priceless relics.

Dmitri set the object back into the felt bag, grasped the drawstring. With the hand hidden from Josee, he powered up his cell phone and slipped it into position.

"I will take the egg now," he said.

"What? No, that's all the help I needed. Thanks, though, I appreciate it."

"I am not asking permission, Josee."

"But I don't want it leaving this vault. It's safe here."

"Nyet. It is not safe, and you also are not safe. I have a gun, you see? This cell phone can fire four bullets. With only one, it can kill you."

Josee's eyes flickered toward the vault's entryway.

In one motion Dmitri lifted his knee onto the viewing table and launched himself upward, thrusting his fist into the watching camera; he did not need witnesses to this theft or to the murder of a young woman. The device tilted. His finger hooked a cord on his way down and sparks arced from the connection.

Josee clutched at the bag. Yelled out.

"Sarge!"

Dmitri held tight, bringing his loaded phone toward her forehead.

Pain slashed through his arm as Josee's fingernails dug into his skin. Her other hand flew to his hair like a vicious claw. With a hollow detonation, the Maksalov weapon fired a round, hitting the vault's corridor wall. Josee drove her head up into Dmitri's chin so that his teeth clamped into his tongue and colors burst before his eyes. His grip on the bag loosened.

He had never fought a woman. He did not expect such tactics.

He yelled. Then pistoned his knee into Josee's midsection.

She fell away with a gasp, a muffled cry. And a handful of his hair. His scalp burned. He kicked at her again. She was huddled on the floor, her arms drawn in, and the felt case was nowhere to be seen.

"Sarge!"

"Give it to me!" Dmitri shouted, convinced she had it beneath her. "Or I'll kill you!"

With one thrust, he flipped her onto her back.

"Okay," she sputtered through her pain. "Take it."

He snatched the bag, but the security guard was coming straight for him, gun drawn, deep-set brown eyes assessing the situation.

"Don't move," the guard said.

"You're a fool to stand in my way."

The guard aimed his gun, but with Josee on the floor he looked unsure about using it. His eyes moved to her. "You okay, kiddo?"

"He kicked me." She winced. "No big deal, Sarge. He's a wuss."

"Give the lady back what belongs to her."

Dmitri lifted the Fabergé bag. "This? Nyet. It belongs to me."

"My grandfather gave it to me," Josee said.

"But it's property stolen from the Romanovs. I'm from the Brotherhood of Tobolsk."

"Who?"

"We were commissioned to protect our rulers. We failed once. Not again."

"The Romanovs are dead."

"Their bloodline still flows. Here in Oregon, a descendant of the Tsars lives!"

"You're whacked," Josee said.

"Do you know this name? Gertrude Ubelhaar?"

Sarge and Josee exchanged glances.

"Da. You do know it." Dmitri inched toward the vault's marble passage-way. "She's the mother of the last Tsar. She carried a child as part of Hitler's strategy to unite nations. I will find this man and usher in a new era for Mother Russia."

"Sarge, what's he talking about? Does this have to do with Stahlherz?"

Dmitri came to attention. "Stahlherz? Who is this?"

"Gertrude Ubelhaar claimed he was her son," Sarge said. "The man joined her in her terrorist plot, but they failed. Not more than a couple of miles from here. Before it was all over, Stahlherz slit his own throat."

"Nyet!" Dmitri hugged the felt bag to his stomach.

"But I think good ol' Ms. Ubelhaar's misled you. Stahlherz wasn't her son, a Tsar, or anything close. He was the blood brother of my friend Marsh Addison."

"You cannot prove this. These are lies."

"I found official documents," Sarge said, "in the wreckage."

Josee's eyes cut to the sergeant's. "Really?"

"Sittin' all this time in the mangled helicopter. Right where Stahlherz left them."

Dmitri shook his head to clear away this nonsense. He was weary of these lies, these attempts to dissuade him from his purpose. He edged along another few inches. Lifted the cell phone.

"Watch out, Sarge! That phone's his gun."

Dmitri said, "I'm a man of honest intent. I will not kill you if you let me go now. If you do not…that is your choice."

"We will let you go, but—"

"No, Sarge! We can't. That's my inheritance he's got."

The sergeant raised his hand. "Dmitri, you can go. But ya might like to know a thing or two first. I've already turned in evidence to the FBI, talked with a field agent. You left fingerprints in Junction City and in your white Taurus rental car. Got sloppy, I guess. Figured your fake ID would protect ya."

Dmitri chuckled at this turn of events. "You are better than I expected."

"And," Sarge carried on, "they're linkin' the ballistics from the shooting in JC to homicides in Fort Lauderdale and Orlando. Been a busy man, I take it."

"I have a task to fulfill. For Mother Russia. For Almighty."

"Hmm. Guess that's where you messed up. When you came trippin' into my girlfriend's gallery, didn't take me long to put the pieces together. 'Specially after you tried to get Russian artifacts from that train in Junction City."

"Engine 418."

"You're all outta luck, partner."

"I am going now," Dmitri said. "I am not stupid. Surely you've pressed an alarm and wish me to talk until more police come."

"You're free to go."

With his cell phone aimed at the sergeant's head, Dmitri eased on by. He clung to the felt bag. Small backward steps carried him along as his eyes shifted over his shoulder. He had what he wanted; he would not risk further confrontation. In the bank's lobby, he saw worried tellers duck behind their counters. Customers crouched in wide-eyed horror; no doubt, words of a robbery and a gun had buzzed through here.

Dmitri tucked the Fabergé bag and sprinted out the bank's doors.

Leaving behind the lies. The falsehoods.

I must keep the faith. It's my destiny. And I have the Fabergé egg!

———

Tyrone and Tawnique were at the gumball machine, inserting coins and squealing over the assorted colors that dropped into the chute. Shanique's head was turned, rested on her hand, so that her smoke-scented hair hid her face from Mylisha.

"You okay?"

Shanique's head bobbed twice.

Mylisha gazed at the beach scene painted on the wall of Johnny Ocean's hamburger joint. She wished she could step onto the sand and run away. Instead, she bit into an old-fashioned burger and chased it down with a thick strawberry shake.

"You remember Mama bringing us here, back in the day?"

Shanique nodded again. Sucked at the straw in her chocolate shake.

"So you gonna punish me the rest of the morning?" Mylisha asked.

"Oh, don't even. Mylisha, you's the one punishin' me, and don't I know it."

"I love you, Shanique. I just need to start living the life God gave me, you know what I'm sayin'? And you need to live yours. Ty and Tawnie, they need you. I can't be the one to take up all the slack, enabling you each step of the way. You love them, for real, but they'll be all grown up before you know it."

"Okay, dat's how it's gonna be? Yeah, I see. Point da finger at li'l sister."

"I'm pointing the finger at myself as well. High school hurt us both in different ways. You jumped into life, the good and the bad. I chose the side-lines, figuring I'd be safe if I stayed away from the action. But I was wrong. Living safe is just dying slow."

"And I be dyin' fast? Hmm? Dat whatcha think?"

"Girl, would you stop it. I'm talking about me, not you."

"Sure 'nuff, I believe dat." Shanique dipped a finger in her shake and licked it.

"You want me to talk about you? Okay, let's do that. You already know what Mama thinks about your job. Daddy doesn't even know. It'd kill him, straight up. You're a smart girl. Maybe not book smart, but head smart. And look at you, with your long legs and your neon smile. Like Daddy used to say, you're as 'pretty as the day is long.' But it's eatin' you up, girl. Little by little."

"You don't know nothin'.." Shanique's chin jutted forward. "I got *cash* to watch after my babies, a place o' my own, a new *ride*. I be krunk."

"And when gravity kicks in, what then?"

"Surgery, baby."

"Shanique, here's what I'm sayin'. I care about you. Don't wanna see you chewed up and spit out by the nightlife. We grew up together, had our ups and downs, but we've always been there. You feelin' me?"

"Mm-hmm."

"I'll still help with the kids. You know I will. But I've gotta make some changes."

Shanique blew air from the side of her mouth. She leveled her eyes into Mylisha's. "You a good sister. You just don't know nothin' 'bout my life, do ya? Ain't so easy as you say. But you do whatcha gotta. I be awright."

She stood, tossed a twenty on the table, called Tyrone and Tawnique to her side as she marched out the door.

With eyes on the wall mural, Mylisha sighed. She knew it was time to make the switch. Earlier this morning she'd peeked at her horoscope, but even then she'd known changes were in motion. For years she'd moved barely an inch, waiting for direction, for some sign in the sky. She'd prided herself on this patient faith.

Stepping out blindly, though? That was a different sort of faith.

Faith in a pair of walking shoes.

Lord, I'm scared. Can't see what's ahead, but I'll take that first step. Please just let me feel you at my side.

She finished the last fries in the burger basket. Pulled a brochure from her purple brushed-leather purse. Started planning an escape from the safe life. Back at home she solidified her intentions by dumping into the trash her old shoebox of Clay's letters and cards. It was the first step.

———

Dmitri could taste blood in his mouth. That stupid girl, Josee.

He clipped his phone to his belt, jumped into the rental car with the felt bag in his lap. Even as he turned the key, he played over the scenario.

Sarge had tracked him down, he'd planted himself there as a security guard, and Josee Walker had led Dmitri into the trap.

I won't make that mistake again. I'm too close now to finding the Tsar.

Dmitri slipped the car into reverse. He looked over his shoulder and in one moment made two new observations: one, Oleg's Chevy pickup was parked on the lot's far end, and, two, Oleg's shiny, stubble-free face was rising from the seat behind him.

"Oleg!"

Snaking over the seat, the crime lord's arm clamped on the buttons of Dmitri's phone. The first bullet carved through Dmitri's hip, tearing at his angel wing.

He arched back. Screamed.

Sirens sounded in the background, but he was a momentary prisoner to his pain. His wounded leg jammed down on the accelerator, and the car lurched backward. He was in no position to fight Oleg, but he could use the automobile to throw off the man's weight. He pulled on the wheel, bringing the car around in a tire-screeching slide.

The heavy front end's momentum whipped it into a parked vehicle.

Metal shrieked. Glass crumbled in jagged sheets.

Somewhere between the violent snap of his head and the second fiery bullet trail—this time through his abdomen—he realized his angel had for-saken him. Dmitri Derevenko had walked destiny's path. He'd wrestled with angels.

The demons had come for him nonetheless.

Cackling, Oleg shook glass from his hair. He plucked the bloodstained Fabergé bag from Dmitri's lap. "Spahseebah. Thank you for the treasure, Dmitri. You've been good to find it for me. We are not so different. Money is my god, and the Tsar is yours. But I'm afraid the Tsar is dead."

A curtain of red was falling over Dmitri's vision. Sirens were wailing.

Oleg's voice hit a piercing note. "Nyet! What did you do with it?"

Dmitri registered the man's words but had no strength to respond.

"It's a trick! This is not the real egg!"

Sprawled back in the driver's seat amid glass and blood, Dmitri's last liv-ing memory involved a whisper of felt and an oval-shaped object dropping onto the seat beside him. As part of her subterfuge, Josee Walker had managed to make the switch, most likely while huddled on the vault's marble floor.

This was not the Tmu Tarakan egg.

This, according to the sticker, was a "Fauxbergé" priced at $89.99.

44

Midnight

"Eight ball." Digs pointed with his cue stick. "Bank shot, corner pocket."

"Look at the champ go."

"No gripes, Ryker. I'm kickin' in for pizza afterward."

With marked enthusiasm, Clay accepted his loss. "Bank it in! Go, Digs."

Earlier here in the Harrisburg billiard hall, Digs had worked his way through the tourney's entrants to claim a purse of five hundred dollars. With white hair glowing beneath the neon beer signs, he'd chalked his stick and called his shots, shown finesse and power, used English to twist the cue ball to his will.

"Ain't half-bad for an ex-con, eh?"

"You learn to shoot like this in prison?" Clay asked.

"Nah. Learned from my kid sister. She hustled her way through Cal Berkeley."

"You're just full of surprises."

"Most people are by the time they reach the big five-o. Life fills up your plate in a hurry. That's a fact." Digs dismantled his personal cue stick and laid the pieces in a case. "Let's go. This old man's ready for some grub."

"Is there anyplace still open?"

"Right next door. They're open late 'cause of the tourney."

Midnight was only ten minutes away. August tenth was almost in the bag.

8.1.0.0.4…

Six hundred seconds to safety.

Throughout the day, Clay had prayed like never before. He'd even stopped in at St. Helen after a long day at Glenleaf and knelt between the pews in petition.

With his cell phone, he had tracked Jason and Jenni from this morning on. They had packed, then left Cheyenne with french toast sticks from Burger

King. Jason told Clay about crossing the Continental Divide and about a dead cow he saw on the side of the road. Once evening hit, they holed up at a Holiday Inn, and Jenni agreed, with mild protests, to keep Jason from going to the swimming pool.

With the time change, Clay had confirmed their safety less than an hour ago. They had survived. Clay had rushed into the billiard hall rest room and splashed water over his face to disguise the sudden tears of relief.

Jason was safe. His son had made it into another day.

Officer Kelso's updates assured Clay the local targets were unharmed as well.

Wendy, after a day of work, had stopped by for happy hour at the Raven, dropped in at Safeway for groceries, locked herself in her home for the night.

Mylisha, after a morning class at LCC, had run by her apartment, re-appeared in her Safeway uniform, worked at the customer-service desk, dealt with a disgruntled employee who refused to mop the recycling center's floor.

Father Patrick, after morning Mass at St. Helen, had studied in his parish office, heard confession, gone into Eugene for a visit to Pier One Imports, come home, and settled himself on his back porch, comfortable in his new wicker armchair.

"Pizza sounds great," Clay said. "With your prize money, heck, you could feed us all for weeks."

"Don't push your luck, Ryker."

On the way out, Clay nodded at the undercover officer at the bar. He was grateful for the officer's presence—for Digs's sake and for his own. Clay could do without the entire burden of other people's lives.

No thanks, God. You can have this job.

———

"It feels like home," Asgoth said.

Henna was settled, with blond hair fanned across her pillow. She still used this pink canopy bed from her childhood. She looked like a princess in repose, waiting for the prince and fairy-tale life that would never be hers.

Serene, her teen daughter, slept in the next room.

Asgoth circled Henna's bedroom on Lovelake Road. Although he'd been comfortable at the downtown apartment, this was a safer option. Since Clay's intrusion, that place had become a hot zone.

"With the Scandi-Fest opening tomorrow, it's better not to take any risks. Not when we're so close to our goal. Even now, Monde is fine-tuning the plans, and one of the Consortium will be arriving in the next day or two."

"Will I have a chance to meet them?"

"I'm sure you will."

"Well," Henna said, "you know they're welcome here. With me."

"Right this minute I need you to make a trip over to Harrisburg."

"Now? It's almost midnight."

"It's only a few minutes away, a quick trip across the bridge and back. It'll be an opportunity to see Mr. Clay Ryker. Doesn't that stir your little heart?"

She pulled herself up. Ran self-conscious fingers through her hair.

———

One hundred and eighty seconds to go.

"Relax, Ryker." Digs shook his head. "Pizza's on its way."

"I'm fine."

"You been checkin' that clock like a man sittin' in Ol' Sparky."

"Say what?"

"The electric chair."

"Oh." Clay grimaced.

"First piece o' pizza's all yours. How 'bout that?"

"Appreciate it, but it's not necessary."

One fifty, one forty-five, one forty…

"Probably be about ten minutes till the food's done," Digs said. "Think I'll take me a walk down by the river, get some fresh air."

The river? Death could be prowling anywhere along its banks.

"I'll go with you," Clay said.

"Nah, gimme coupla seconds alone. Been quite a night."

If only you knew. Just two minutes left!

Digs set down his billiard bag. "Mind keepin' an eye for me?" He turned to go.

"No, wait!"

Clay was beyond the point of worrying about appearances. The old guy could think what he wanted, but Clay needed one hundred and twenty seconds. After that, Digs could swim across the river in concrete boots. Whatever. Just so long as Clay could see him through to the stroke of midnight.

"You don't last long without food in your belly, do ya?"

Clay shrugged. "It's a weakness of mine."

"Noticed you laid off the bottle tonight. Good man."

"A slow learner, but I'm tryin'."

"Not much for the booze myself," Digs said. "Used to have me a li'l drug problem, but that's been behind me for years. Which is why, Ryker, I like gettin' a bit o' fresh air every now and then. Bein' alone for a spell." He patted his case on the table. "Back in a few."

Ninety-nine seconds, ninety-eight, ninety-seven...

Clay thrust out his hand. Grabbed his work partner by the arm.

The presence of numerals on Digs' hairy skin was no surprise, but the fact that they had changed rocked Clay back on his mental heels. He jerked his arm away. Shook out his hand as though to rid himself of this new data.

"Wait!" he exclaimed. "This isn't how it's supposed to happen!"

"Whatcha rattlin' on about?"

"I can't believe this."

"Do I get an explanation?"

Clay closed his eyes, inhaled. "Sorry. Go on, I'm not stopping you."

"You need to get somethin' off your chest, you let me know. Be back in a jiffy. If the pizza shows up, don't wait on me. You jump right in."

Clay nodded, peeked at the clock. Digs had made it to day's end. Only problem now was the old guy's expiration date had shifted to this coming Friday.

The door chimed as Digs headed outside. Clay stared at his palm.

8.1.3.0.4...

Friday the thirteenth.

"Midnight. We made it without losing a single one."

"Thank you, Officer Kelso. I appreciate all you've done."

"Had a close call, but otherwise it was a routine day for four relieved officers in plain clothes." In Clay's cell phone, Kelso's voice was buoyant with celebration. "I'm not certain the threat was genuine in the first place, but either way, we did our duty. And more important, it worked. We thwarted the accuracy of your psychic touch."

"It's not psychic—"

"Call it what you will."

"And I don't think we thwarted it. Not totally."

"Come again, Mr. Ryker? Line's breaking up."

"I think, uh...well, I think I was off. I think the numbers were off."

"Or you were simply wrong."

"That's not what I'm saying. I think something changed."

"How so? Has that happened before?"

"Uh, no."

"Listen, nobody died. That's a good thing. Who knows, maybe their survival shifted everything. Were you conjuring all this up for attention? I don't know. Frankly, I don't care right now."

"Why would I conjure it up?"

"You tell me." Kelso cleared his throat. "Here's my suggestion. Go home, prop up your feet, rest in the knowledge of a job well done. That's what I'm going to do. Sure, the chief'll want some justification for the monies assigned to our shenanigan. But after what happened to Detective Freeman, I feel better about it. Don't you?"

"Officer, don't shut me off. Digs's date is this Friday."

"Digs? The one you work with?"

"I touched his arm a moment ago, and that's what the numbers matched with."

Kelso paused. "But that's not right. Add 'em together, and they equal sixteen."

"I know, but—"

"What happened to your unlucky thirteen theory?"

"Don't you see?" Clay tried to keep his voice below a shout. "Friday the thirteenth. There it is. The rules've changed, but it's the same game."

"Mr. Ryker, go get some sleep. This is one game I'm done playing."

"Shouldn't I check the others? What if—"

"No. We're not doing this. At some point fate steps in, don't you think? Are we intended to run around obeying your every whim, saving people's lives until they're well into the hundreds? What if our attempts at intervention are the very things that trigger a fatal chain of events? Have you considered that?"

"Yes, Officer. But these numbers were as clear as ever."

"You sound like that guy Jonah."

"Excuse me?"

"I'm not a religious man, but isn't he the one who predicted everyone would die? Then when God had mercy, Jonah whined and moaned about it." Officer Kelso found humor in the story. With laughter still trickling from his words, he said, "Go home, Mr. Ryker. It's been a long day."

"Just this one last time. That's all I ask."

"Good night."

"Just this Friday."

"Good-bye."

———

Oleg dabbed a cloth at his facial cuts. Even days later these wounds stung, and he suspected a glass chip remained buried in his cheek.

Dmitri Derevenko was dead. The newspapers had confirmed it.

What did Oleg care? Dmitri had been duped; he had failed to secure the Fabergé egg. Oleg, bloodied and sore, had escaped from the scene only moments before the first City of Florence Police vehicle caromed into the lot.

He bandaged his wounds and settled onto the bed of the Portland hotel.

The world was no place for idealists. Decades ago the Brotherhood of Tobolsk had pursued dreams of a restored monarchy. A dead cause. In this era of pragmatic realities, it was no wonder the globe's longstanding monarchies had fallen within a short time of each other—the kaisers, the Tsars, the royals of Great Britain.

Times had changed. The world's citizens were more urbane than in days of yore. They expected to rule themselves. And why shouldn't they? The heavy-handed abuse of sovereigns had gone on far too long.

A righteous ruler? A fair ruler? A loving ruler?

Bah. Such a one does not exist.

Of course Lenin had been right, destroying churches and murdering acolytes by the thousands. Religion was the "opiate of the masses." Those who clung to their ancient customs and guilt-driven beliefs were the ones standing in the way of progress.

Da. That's why it's a good thing Dmitri is dead.

Oleg bandaged his wounds and returned to his late-night research.

The more he studied, the more he was convinced Gertrude Ubelhaar did not have a biological son. She had claimed one as her own, a man named Karl Stahlherz. Stahlherz, however, had died last year, and according to documents recently recovered by Sergeant Turney and made part of the public record, the man was the brother of Marshall Addison—both of them genetic offspring of Virginia Addison.

All this gave substance to Oleg's theories. He believed Gertrude Ubelhaar, ward of the Coffee Creek Correctional Facility, was after Rasputin's fortune. She, too, wanted to slap the world into awareness. She wanted the reins to the riches represented by Josee Walker's Fabergé egg.

In other words she was hungry for money, power, and control.

Oleg liked Ms. Ubelhaar already. He would have to pay her a visit.

———

"Mind if I join you, Clay?"

"Henna?" He stared up from the table. "Surprise, surprise. Don't tell me it's coincidence to find you tramping in here after midnight."

"Is that a yes? I was hoping you'd be pleased to see me."

Clay took a steaming pepperoni slice from the deep-dish pizza on the table. "Sit down. But the pizza's off-limits." He took a bite.

"You should be glad that none of your precious charges was harmed. In fact, we had to divert one of them from a dangerous situation. Just in case."

"Am I supposed to thank you?"

"Would you rather they had died?"

Clay's eyes shifted toward the front counter. "Can you keep your voice down?"

"You're in no position to ask favors, dear heart. Do you know where your wife and son are at this moment? Asleep in their beds at a Holiday Inn off I-80."

Clay slammed down his pizza slice, causing red plastic cups of Coke to jump.

"You leave them outta this!"

"Please." She winked. "Can you keep your voice down?"

"Henna. Forgive me. You were a underclassman, and I'm sorry I didn't notice you more, but that's the way life goes. You brought trouble to Mylisha and Shanique. You tried to manipulate things in your favor. Real love doesn't work that way."

"And you're the expert, Mr. I'm-Going-Through-a-Divorce?"

"In this life we don't always get what we want. We move on and take what God provides. He 'causes everything to work together for the good.' We have to trust that."

"The rest of that cute little verse says for 'those who love God and are called according to his purpose.'" Henna lifted her hands, palms up. "Which eliminates me, doesn't it? I choose to love myself. I don't need your outdated religious nonsense."

"Whether we like it or not, we're all part of his plan."

"Not so, Clay. We can choose our own plans. Make our own paths."

"Tell me what you want. Why're you here?"

Henna grinned. "I thought you might like to speak to your high school pal, the one with the missing shoe. Keep Thursday night open. We'll arrange a reunion."

"As a habit I don't talk with my dead friends."

Through the front window, Clay saw Digs heading back.

"For Jason's and Jenni's sakes, I'm sure you'll make an exception." With care, Henna wrapped a piece of pizza in a napkin. "It might also be wise to start pooling your resources—that is, if you'd like to 'reunite as a pair.' If you hope to see your wife again, I'll need your GPS unit and a hundred thousand in cash."

"Dollars?"

"Love comes at a price!"

Clay let out a snort. "If you could see my bank statement. That's impossible!"

"Weren't you the one just quoting scriptures? 'With God everything is possible.'"

Henna brushed past Digs on her way out.

"My eyes deceivin' me, Ryker, or did that blonde just swipe some o' my dinner?"

Clay dropped his head into his hands. One hundred thousand dollars? Henna was insane. At the present rate that was more than he'd make in the next four years. And the GPS? Apparently she was after Kenny Preston's treasure from Engine 418. But where was it? At the bottom of Crater Lake.

"What's eatin' at ya now, Ryker? You are one ball o' nerves."

"I'm done. I give up."

"After only one piece o' pepperoni? You're a lightweight."

"This is so stinkin' ridiculous!" Clay shook his head. "I mean, what would you say if someone told you they needed a hundred grand within forty-eight hours?"

"I'd say ya better start talkin'. Tell your pal Digs what's goin' on."

"As if you need my burdens. What good'll that do?"

"Try me." Digs folded two pizza slices into a hearty deep-dish sandwich, took a bite, washed it down with a swig of root beer. "Done said it yourself, Ryker. I'm just full o' surprises."

45

In Touch

While waiting at the toaster that morning, Clay tried reaching Jenni and Jason. The hotel room phone rang without response, then rerouted him to the operator.

"I'm sorry, sir. Would you like to leave a message?"

"My name's Clay Ryker. Tell them to call me ASAP. It's an emergency."

"An emergency? I can have one of our staff go to the room."

Clay insisted on it. He waited, tapped the end of his butter knife on the counter, deflected Gerald's stern stare from the dining nook with a stare of his own. He was buttering the second piece of toast when the operator came back on.

"Thank you for your patience, sir. I'm connecting you now."

"Clay?"

"Jenni. Thank God you're there."

"Where else would I be? It's only eight in the morning here, which means seven your time, am I right? Gosh, I'm tired. I drove most of yesterday."

"Sorry to bug you."

"They said this was an emergency. Are you okay?"

"Yep." Clay coughed. "I'm heading to work soon, but I...I wanted you to know I love you. I love Jason."

"That's very sweet. We luvya too."

"Do you, Jenni?"

"Please. Don't try to make me feel guilty."

"No, what I mean is, do you still...care about me? After everything I've done?"

"And not done."

"Yeah, rub it in."

"Of course I care, Clay. But let's leave it at that. We'll only stir up old emotions, and I haven't even had my coffee yet."

Clay pictured her curled up on the bed; he recalled their mornings together. Usually he had awakened first. Oftentimes he had watched her sleeping form—tousled sandy blond hair; strands that curled against parted pink lips; lean legs that had never lost the baby dimples on her knees. Although he would think of cuddling next to her, his insecurities and guilt had held him back. He didn't deserve her. He never had.

And in the past two years, his failures had mounted like evidence against him. Triggered by the incident at the bridge.

Friday the thirteenth.

Only two days remaining till this came full circle.

"Clay. What's the emergency? Or did you just say that to get me on the phone?"

"Be careful," he said. "Even if it takes a little longer, choose a different route. Shoot, that might be the best idea. Show up a day late, if necessary."

"First you try to sweet-talk me. Now you want me to stay away." Jenni's chuckle held no humor in it. "Brings back memories."

"This'll sound crazy, okay, but I think someone might be planning to kidnap you."

This time her laughter was real. "If it's money they're after, good luck."

"I'm serious."

"Clay, have you found a girlfriend? Is that what you're trying to hide?"

"Don't be silly."

"Mylisha. What about her?"

"What about her?"

"When we went to the Scandi-Fest a few years back, she was there. She still cares deeply for you. That was obvious in her eyes. Girls can tell these things."

"Jenni, I'm still wearing my ring. Is there any reason we can't keep it that way?"

Her silence was pregnant with regrets and unresolved issues. "Clay, we'll talk more about this when I get there. I promise. But for now, please try to stop worrying. And don't make up any more emergencies to get my attention. Depending on which route I take, we should arrive sometime Thursday. I'll get hold of you then."

"If I call your cell, please pick up."

"No, Clay. I'll be driving. Praying. I'll need the time to think things over."

"You have to promise me. You can't—"

"I'll tell Jason you love him. I'm going back to sleep. See ya soon, Clay."

———

Clay cradled the dead receiver in his palm. Banged his head on the cupboard twice. Turned, thrust the phone back onto its hook.

Over the *Register-Guard*, his father was glaring at him.

"Don't even say a word, Dad."

Gerald's chair hit the wall as he stood. He had his travel mug in one hand; with the other he nabbed a sheet of paper from the stack beside his checkbook. Slapped it on the counter so hard that Clay's toast jumped. With a stubby finger, callused by years of lumberyard work, his father poked at a circled figure on the paper.

The telephone bill. Totaling over one hundred dollars.

"*My* phone," Gerald said. "Take care of *my* stuff, or you'll be out on *your* butt."

Clay stared down. His hand moved toward the bill but came in contact with his father's arm. Numerals shot through his skin. Uninvited. Deep and tenacious.

8.1.3.0.4

Gerald shook him off in a show of disgust. Snapped the lid from his travel mug and dumped the contents down the drain.

———

On his morning break at the monument company, Clay dialed Officer Kelso. The result was no worse than expected.

"You want me to do what?"

"My wife and son are in danger. Is there a way we can arrange some sort of police protection?"

"You mean, is there a way I can arrange it?"

"Well, yes."

"Listen, Mr. Ryker, I was tired last night, and I'm man enough to admit it. I was curt. Maybe even snide. Please, though, tell me this isn't another fabricated attempt to prolong your moment in the spotlight."

"This is serious, Officer. Please don't shrug me off. My drug test came out clean, didn't it? So put me on the lie detector if that'll convince you."

"Let's skip the red tape, shall we? Two questions for you. Are your wife and son still out on the road between here and Wyoming? If so, that presents a logistical problem, does it not? And what gives you the idea they are in danger? I thought we'd made it over your little hurdle of August tenth."

"I told you. The numbers have changed."

"Oh, of course. I let that slip my mind."

"Somebody threatened me, Officer. And threatened my wife and son."

"You have proof of this?"

"It was verbal."

"Ah."

"No, wait! I have a note. Written with an Avon pen."

"The plot thickens."

"Henna Dixon," Clay said. "You might like to question her about it."

"The same one who cleans at the apartments. Is that what we have—a squabble between the two of you? Are you in a relationship with her?"

"Definitely not!"

"You say that with a good deal of emotion. So tell me, what does this note say?"

Clay ran the words through his head, realized how foolish they would sound. He chose a different approach. "I found it up in that apartment."

"The one you broke into."

"Uh-huh."

"So let's get this straight. You do a little B & E at a vacant apartment, but the nonexistent resident knew you were coming and left you a note. Or maybe it was the cleaning lady, is that it? She invited you to join her for dinner there in the darkness, then had the gall to leave you a little threat. Written, of all things, with an Avon pen." Officer Kelso's sarcasm oozed through the phone. "Sounds like we need to be keeping a closer eye on those shifty door-to-door saleswomen."

"Thanks for your time, Officer."

"If it puts your mind at ease, I can tell you from experience that most of the clairvoyant, paranormal crowd tend to exaggerate their own abilities. Comes with the territory, I suppose. We don't hold it against your type. I'm sure it's easy to lose touch."

"I wish."

"Excuse me?"

"I'm more in touch than ever before. It's not a weight I'd wish on anyone."

"Rest, Mr. Ryker. I suggest you get lots of it."

"How can I sleep when my wife and my son are out there?"

The police officer was undeterred. "As for these phone conversations, interesting as they might be, I ask that you discontinue them. The department will have its hands full enough with the Scandi-Fest opening tomorrow and running through the weekend. Being a local boy, you know how it is. With all the out-of-towners, this place'll be a zoo."

"That's what I'm worried about. Friday's a big day down there."

"Is this another of your harebrained predictions?"

"Good-bye, Officer Kelso."

This time Clay had the pleasure of ending the call.

———

Clay kept his Garmin GPS unit in his pocket. The thing had become vital.

At Glenleaf Monument Company, he found the same numeric results as at his house. With Wendy, he made an excuse to help at the air compressor, then touched her hand while forcing laughter over her latest version of the mummy joke. With Digs, he helped load grave markers into the sandblasting chamber, then brushed his forearm in a charade of bumbling awkwardness.

Both co-workers shared the revised digits. Converted from the previous set. *8.1.3.0.4...* Friday the thirteenth. The high point of the Scandi-Fest.

And the same set of numbers was present on headstone after headstone.

"Remember what I told ya last night," Digs said, cutting through Clay's despondency. "You'll let me know if ya need my help, won'tcha?"

Clay bobbed his head.

"Be my pleasure, Ryker. Seems to me someone's lookin' out for ya."

"Wish I had your confidence. But, yes, I'll let you know. Thanks."

"Me and Wendy, we'll be gone the rest o' the afternoon. Got rehearsal."

"At the festival?" A question spilled into Clay's mind.

"Don'tcha say a word. I happen to think my costume's snazzy."

"Hey, if you've got the ability to dance in public, more power to ya."

———

"What does he see in her?" Henna wanted to know.

"Don't start now. You're cranky after a long night's drive."

From the Subaru, Asgoth could see Jenni and Jason Ryker at a window table inside an Idaho diner. The tourist spot was run-down, with tumbleweeds surrounding the modular building like regulars at a bar. A hand-painted plywood sign leaned against the fence: Biggest Burgers Within a Hundred Miles.

Thanks to the Consortium's network, Asgoth had never doubted his ability to locate Jenni and Jason. When mother and son deviated from Interstate 80 earlier in the day, they did so before watching eyes.

"I'm serious," Henna persisted. "Am I missing something here?"

Asgoth watched Jenni's hair part around her fingers, liquid gold in shiny waves. Light freckles danced across her nose. No wonder Clay was upset about his divorce; this was a nice little specimen of a woman. She reminded Asgoth of licentious moments in his past.

"Beauty and brains," he said. "That's what she has."

"Like I said, what's she have that I don't?"

Asgoth took this opportunity to stir up emotion. "She has Clay's heart."

"Then we'll have to cut it out."

"First, get ahold of young Jason, and don't let him run off the way Kenny Preston did. That's why you brought the handcuffs. Once Jason's secured here in the car, Jenni will do anything we ask. We'll lead her to our friend's trailer in central Oregon, where we'll keep the two of them locked up until our plans on the thirteenth."

46

The Backseat

Clay had suspected this would be the case. Despite numerous attempts Wednesday and today, his calls to Jenni's cell had gone unanswered. He wanted to know his wife and son were safe. He tried dialing from a pay phone at the Chevron station so that her caller ID wouldn't recognize him. Still, she never picked up.

Was she there? Ignoring him? Or…

Stop. Don't even think about it, Claymeister.

Getting ready for work, Clay tucked his phone and GPS unit in his work pants. He expected a call from Henna. Tonight he was to meet with her.

And with Bill Scott.

It was a mind-twisting concept that went against the memories he'd experienced, catalogued, and avoided. He considered calling the Scott home. Mr. and Mrs. Scott might be able to give him insight.

No. He screwed his eyes shut against the idea. What would he say? "Hi, this is Clay Ryker, the one who was drinking and bridge diving with your son. You know, the last one to see him alive. Sure it's been twelve years, but I think Bill's back in town. Has he contacted you?"

Okaaay then. They would think I've gone psycho.

Clay faced the time clock, breathed a sigh, and punched in for the day. On the corkboard to the right, fliers and handbills advertised local restaurant specials and upcoming events. He tugged a pizza coupon from its pushpin, and a tan brochure dropped free as well. He bent to retrieve it.

Skin to paper. A fresh tattoo with the latest refrain…*8.1.3.0.4*

Who was the victim to be this time?

He walked to his workbench. Pulled on his gloves. With his fingers, he flattened the brochure and found the name of Kenny Preston's mother printed across the front. Kate's church was coordinating a weekend retreat along the McKenzie River, and newcomers were welcome. Kate was listed as the information person, with a phone number that looked like a church extension.

Was this what she did for a living? Or was it volunteer work?

Clay told himself it wouldn't matter if she didn't live past tomorrow.

———

Trolls and farmers and Scandinavian lovers. Asgoth liked this tale. He'd seen "Hardanger Wedding" performed here before.

He and Monde wove themselves among the crowd of parents and performers. Portable bleachers faced the Festival Park Stage, where Scandinavian-garbed dancers of all ages twirled and stepped to traditional folk music. Starting today, they would put on their show for standing-room-only crowds.

The Scandinavian Festival was in its final preparations.

"Here we have our lovely pairs dancers," Monde said.

Asgoth peered around a knot of gossiping mothers. "I see them."

Digs and Wendy dipped, stepped, dipped, and spun. Following them across the stage, Father Patrick and Mylisha mirrored the choreography.

"They're all healthy as can be. I liked the bait-and-switch idea, Monde. I'll give credit where it's due. I do think we've got Clay Ryker flustered, but we can't let him survive like he did at Crater Lake. I need him. He's the signature on my paycheck."

"Rest assured, Dmitri Derevenko will present no complications. Like so many dreamers, he viewed himself as indispensable. Now he's dead, shot by his partner Oleg. And of all things, Sergeant Turney and his girlfriend lent me a hand. Unwittingly, of course."

"Turney? Your hated foe?"

"They fooled Dmitri. Now Oleg's off on a hunt of his own."

Asgoth hushed him. "More later. This is one of my favorite scenes."

Against the painted backdrop of deep blue fjords and jagged crags, the young lovers pranced over a makeshift bridge, unaware of the lurking troll beneath.

"If I had to guess," Monde said, "I'd say this is where you stole your idea."

"Nothing wrong with a little inspiration."

"It does fit nicely."

Asgoth found his gaze sweeping along the stage, the props, the performers' exit points. The lurking troll here in his scenario would be of a more explosive nature.

He was confident in Henna's ability to penetrate this low-security area; he had other friends who would execute their duties, but she would be the fire to the fuse. The Oklahoma City bombing had demonstrated the staggering destruction of a homemade device consisting of, in part, standard fertilizer ingredients.

In a rural community such as JC, there had been little difficulty obtaining the correct components. Rigged properly, the Festival Park Stage would erupt in a superheated blast.

During Friday night's nine o'clock performance, if all went as scheduled.

"Look," Asgoth whispered. "One of them's arrived."

Monde followed his partner's gaze to a red-nosed individual who waddled along on hoglike legs. The tailored suit and silk tie only distorted his size.

"Is he with the Consortium?"

"He is. Come on, Monde, I'll introduce you."

———

Clay slipped into St. Helen on his morning break, peered about the empty chapel area. Votive candles and holy icons graced the walls. A reverential silence blanketed the pews, providing cool yet detached comfort.

Was God here? Was he personal enough to meet one frantic soul?

I used to believe it.

Although raised Catholic, Clay had taken his father's lead and held faith at arm's length. Della displayed her devotion, but it seemed more sentimental than heartfelt. In Wyoming, Clay had surrendered to a relationship with a personal God. He and Jenni had attended an interdenominational church that encompassed Protestants and Catholics alike in loving, corporate communion with Father, Son, and Holy Spirit.

Like his old man, though, he had started to distance himself.

How could he come boldly into the presence of the all-knowing God?

Here now in St. Helen, he found himself on his knees with hands folded over the back pew. *You know the things I've done. You've seen my anger, my pride, my lust. Well, here I am. Take a good look. I need you, Jesus. I can't do this on my own, and now I'm stuck without a wife. I've tried paying for my own sin...and even failed at that!*

He thought of Sergeant Turney. His rescuer. A whale sent to save him.

God had extended forgiveness and a second chance.

A whisper of feet caused Clay to lift his face. Father Patrick stood above him, set a hand on his. Clay tried to keep from recoiling, but his skin burned with the tattoolike etchings of five numerals.

Tomorrow. Father Patrick's date had also shifted.

"You're welcome to stay. You're Gerald and Della's son, is that right?"

"That's me."

"I'll be gone most of the day, but don't let me stand between you and God."

"Where are you going? I mean, not that I'm trying to be nosy."

"The Scandi-Fest. Opening day. I'll be dancing on the Festival Park Stage."

"You?"

"Is that a problem? I'm already accustomed to wearing robes."

They shared a moment of laughter.

"From what I understand, you used to be...good friends with my dance partner."

Clay's cheek twitched. "Oh yeah?"

"Mylisha French. A beautiful young lady. Please don't accuse me of trying to fit her into a box when I say she has more rhythm than the majority of us on that stage."

———

As a festival participant, Mylisha had requested time off from Safeway. After speaking to her LCC guidance counselor, she headed from Eugene to the Scandi-Fest.

En route, an automated billboard flashed the lottery's latest jackpot amount. She shook the temptation from her head. Things were looking up. Changes were in store.

In the backseat, a leather camera case provided evidence of that.

She pulled into a parking spot at Ralph's Drugs and trekked across the main thoroughfare to the changing rooms at the Festival Hall. Amid pale Danes, Swedes, Norwegians, and Finns, she was hard to miss in her bonnet, apron, and dress, but she'd earned her place with the dancers. She heard few complaints.

None to her face, anyway. Nobody was that stupid.

"In half an hour," her director called out, "the cloggers will be rehearsing on this stage. This is it, folks. Our last practice. Let's work out the kinks, shake off the nerves. That's right. Loosen up, and let's have some fun."

Mylisha gathered with her troupe. Took her place beside Father Patrick.

She was touching down her foot, starting to spin, when she spotted Henna.

The blond woman was on a top bleacher, outfitted in bracelets and a shawl laced with shiny threads. Her eyes were closed. Head back. Mouth parted.

Mylisha stopped in midstep. She came down squarely on both feet. With the sun beating down on the bonnet, she stared at this woman who had brought such pain. She thought of Shanique. Of Summer Svenson. Of Clay Ryker. In a blur her thoughts and emotions spun, then came to an abrupt halt, with the fabric of deceit swishing about her in the same manner as her Scandinavian gown. Cringing, her head filled with the image of Clay's dad, Gerald Ryker.

He was there! He knows what happened. Why didn't I think of him weeks ago?

Mylisha decided it was time to contact Sergeant Turney.

Her thoughts cleared in time to see Henna staring at her. Henna's smug expression was that of a woman guarding dangerous secrets, and the cell phone she lifted to her ear was her co-conspirator.

Clay peeled off his canvas glove and answered on the second ring.

"Clay, I hope I'm not interrupting anything."

"Oh. Hi, Henna."

"You sound disappointed."

"I was hoping it was Jenni."

"Your ex? You still talk with her? My understanding is that she's not returning your calls of late."

Clay's ribs formed a fist around his lungs. He could hardly breathe. Through clenched teeth, he said, "Do you know where she is?"

"Obviously you don't. If you did, you wouldn't need to ask."

"Are we still meeting tonight, Henna?"

"I certainly hope so, for the sake of your loved ones."

"Just tell me where. I'm too tired for innuendos and threats."

"My place. On Lovelake."

Clay saw Mr. Blomberg striding his direction across the warehouse floor. He held the phone against his shoulder, slipped his glove back on. "I don't get off work till six." He leaned down, pretending to be focused on the headstone before him.

"We'll be waiting for you at eight. No sooner. And don't worry about bringing the items I requested just yet. We'll save that for later. This will be our excuse for a friendly reunion, nothing more or less."

Blomberg slapped a meaty hand on Clay's shoulder. "I'll be waitin' for you in my office after lunch. That is, if you're not too busy yakkin' on your blasted phone."

"Yes sir."

The big man shoved his way through the exit.

Clay lifted the receiver again, gathered strength. "Tell me. I've gotta know. Did he really survive, Henna? Is Bill Scott alive?"

"Hmm. That's a relative term, is it not? After what you did, he has no life."

———

Digs saw Clay's approach, lifted his goggles so that white eyebrows sprang free. Sweat droplets outlined the ring of granite dust around his face. He studied Clay's face. Wrapped an arm over his shoulders. Drew him to the far end of the sandblasting hut.

"You don't have to do this if you don't want," Clay told him.

"That's about enough o' your nonsense. Ain't one person I'd rather help."

"Sure it won't get you in trouble?"

"At my age? With my past? Nah. Won't be no trouble at all."

"Hey, Digs, you could come with me."

The man pursed his lips, spit dust on the floor. "Now who would Wendy dance with if not an ol' codger like myself? My schedule's plumb full. This one's all yours, Ryker. That's the way of it." He pulled a pencil from behind his ear, scrawled a line of numbers on a notepad, double-checked it before delivering them to Clay.

"These're the right ones?"

"Been, oh, a coupla years, but that's them, all right." Digs tapped his head with the pencil's eraser. "Got 'em locked up tight in here."

"I might not be back."

"Don'tcha be talkin' like that."

"I mean, I might not be back here." Clay frowned. "Blomberg wants me in his office after lunch. I think today's my last day on the job."

"Your last day, eh? You shoulda told me you were dyin' to get outta here."

Clay groaned. "That's not even funny."

"Hmm. Well, sometimes there ain't nothin' ya can do but laugh."

———

8.1.3.0.4... Wendy, Digs, Mylisha, and Father Patrick.

Tomorrow four people within his circle of acquaintances would be joining the festivities downtown. Each was marked for death. Each was scheduled to dance in the "Hardanger Wedding" evening performance.

Nine o'clock at Festival Park Stage. Friday, August 13. What were the odds?

Then of course there were his son and his own father.

And Kate Preston. Where did she fit in?

Clay swallowed a dry bite of a ham and cheese sandwich. He fished in his wallet for Sergeant Turney's number. It'd been a week since they talked. On his cell Clay caught the sergeant waiting for a courtroom appearance. Apparently, he had to testify regarding events surrounding Dmitri Derevenko's death.

"The big guy?" Clay said. "White Taurus? One who killed Mako?"

"That's still to be determined. But the Dmitri fella was found dead in a rental car, two bullets in him. Shot by his own gun, a little thingamajig that looks like a cell phone. Made in Croatia."

"Scary the stuff they come up with."

"Tell me about it."

"Was it suicide, Sarge?"

"I'm not s'posta be talkin' about it too much. Be under oath in a few minutes." The investigative consultant cleared his throat. "But it looks like someone else was involved. Good thing is, me and Josee are fine. She's sportin' a coupla bruises."

"Josee? Your girlfriend? How'd she get tangled up in it?"

"You've gotta meet her. Tell ya right now, partner, she gets tangled up in everything. One free-spirited woman."

"So it's all good between you two?"

"Gettin' better by the day."

"What about Summer Svenson's death? Any word?"

Sergeant Turney's voice turned husky. "I'll always care about the Svensons. They're good people. Can't rightly tell you that I understand God's plan, but I do know he works things out. One day at a time. The way Josee tells it, our job's to just walk on."

"But did they find out who ran Summer down?"

"Roundin' up a suspect as we speak. Or haven't ya heard?"

"Heard what?"

"Talk to your friend Mylisha French. Or call up your old man."

"I'll have to check into it later, Sarge. Right now, I'm supposed to go throw my butt in a sling. I think I'm about to get fired."

—

"Dad?"

"Son, grab your stuff."

Clay had finished his lunch and clocked back in, figuring he might as well get paid for the time it took Mr. Blomberg to rake him over the coals. He sauntered up the single-wide trailer's back steps, braced himself for the inevitable reprimand, shoved his way into the lobby.

Nothing looked right. The secretary was huddled over her desk, blubbering into a wad of facial tissue; the front door was wide open, wasting coveted air conditioning; two patrol cars faced the railed entryway, lights spinning.

"What's going on?" His question to the secretary caused her to burst into fresh tears. "Who's in the backseat? Did they arrest someone?"

At that moment Gerald Ryker came from Blomberg's office, followed by two cops. His face was grim. He looked like a man ashamed, but oddly proud, of what he had done. He was telling Clay to grab his stuff, but Clay was still reeling.

"Can someone tell me what's happening?"

Gravel churned in the parking area. Heads turned, and Clay watched Mylisha French hop from her car, march to the back of the first patrol car, and slam clenched palms against the glass. Angry tears ran down her face. Years of pent-up pain and regret.

"You killed my friend!" Her palms punctuated her words. "You aimed right for her, didn't you? *In cold blood!* Trying to cover your tracks, you self-righteous piece of dirt! I hope you rot, you cold-hearted freak! Are you listening to me?"

Clay suddenly understood.

"Hold on there," one of the officers said, trying to coax Mylisha from the car. "You may have every right to be mad at Mr. Blomberg, but you're going to hurt yourself."

"He killed her!"

"That's for a judge to decide. Thank you for your call to Mr. Ryker. He's explained it all to us."

Clay wondered why he had never pieced it together. He could feel Mylisha's conflicting emotions as she turned. She looked pitiful with tears and dirt staining her Scandinavian dress.

She faced the hard stare of Gerald Ryker. Unrestrained, she came up the stairs. Stopped a foot from the man who had made it clear years ago he disapproved of his son's interracial relationship with her. Her deep mahogany eyes had roots somewhere deep in her soul, in her ancestral heritage. Those same roots had drawn up water many times, only to discover the burn of acid rain.

Here though, in this scenario, Gerald Ryker had backed her up.

"Thank you, Mr. Ryker," Mylisha said. And threw both arms around his chest.

Clay's only clue that his father was not carved from granite was the single blink of Gerald's eyelids followed by the twitch of his lower lip.

47

Speaking to the Dead

Clay digested the news with doubt, bewilderment, then outrage.

"So Mylisha called you. At work?"

"Got my attention."

"I'm surprised you gave her the time of day."

"Think what you want, Son."

"So she told you what Blomberg had done. But what made you listen?"

At the dining nook, Gerald explained how he and Stan Blomberg had once worked together at the lumberyard. Blomberg was a religious zealot who formed no specific ties but preached a gospel all his own. Pulling verses from the Bible and blending them with his own prejudices and vices, he ostracized himself from his co-workers. Eventually he left the yard to take over Glenleaf Monument Company.

But he still owed Gerald a favor. For Gerald's silence.

During Clay's senior year, Gerald had complained at work about his son's relationship with a black girl. He felt uncomfortable with it. Small-town Junction City was unprepared for such dilemmas.

Blomberg, without permission, took it upon himself to cleanse the town of this abomination. He believed he must fight fire with fire. Evil with evil. In his own mind, he justified the sale of drugs to a minor and the use of violence to purge the depravity.

Hannah Dixon and Bill Scott were his selected implements of punishment.

Mylisha and Shanique were the offenders.

When Gerald realized Blomberg's involvement, he threatened to turn the man in. Blomberg swore he had done it for Gerald's good. He agreed to curtail his extracurricular activities and to leave the lumberyard but told Gerald to keep his mouth shut, or Clay would hear how his father had ordered this round of heavenly wrath.

A lie, Gerald now assured Clay. Yet one that would've been hard to disprove.

Blomberg and Gerald forged an uncomfortable truce. Silence for silence: *You don't tell my secrets, and I won't tell yours.*

Clay's recent return had given Blomberg a chance to pay off the owed favor.

It'd also brought to light Summer Svenson's knowledge of Blomberg's deeds. In the past she had been known to use her secrets for mild forms of blackmail, but she crossed swords with the wrong man in Stan Blomberg. He was the avenging blade of the heavenlies. And in this case, his blue Dodge Intrepid was the weapon of choice.

He drove it through Summer, convinced it was for his greater good.

Death was his business—tombstones and graves. It had been thus ordained.

According to Gerald, Blomberg had stuttered at his desk this afternoon when Gerald walked in with the two cops. He'd been out of town much of the past few weeks, hoping to avoid questioning or confrontation. But he had slipped up by telling Clay about Summer's head wound. Mylisha had realized the mistake when she checked the local papers and found that none of them divulged such information. Blomberg had also left tread marks and paint chips as evidence, which Sergeant Turney had sent in for analysis. Mylisha's calls had linked the separate clues, and Turney's recollection of a glimpsed Ford Probe in the Blombergs' garage added the final nail.

The police had means and motive, evidence and witnesses. A judge had signed the warrant. A blue Probe was being towed off from the Blomberg's garage even as Stan Blomberg was being hauled in.

"You did a good thing, Dad."

"Not lookin' for approval."

"Thanks, though."

"It was the right thing, Son."

"I agree."

"Hafta find you another job. The Ryker family is done workin' anywhere near that man." Gerald stared down into his emptied travel mug. "As for me, I'm 'bout tired of tourists crawlin' all over town during the festival. I'm takin' tomorrow off."

"You? A day off?"

Clay's palm throbbed with a searing reminder of Gerald's expiration date. He glanced down, felt the numbers coursing along his skin, following whorls and lines. His father had twenty-four hours to live. Unless Clay could step in.

"Going fishin'," Gerald said. "That spot o' mine up the McKenzie."

"Hey. Looks like I'll have the day off too. What if I—"

"No, Son. My thinkin' time. I'll be doin' this alone."

"But I—"

"Man's word is his word. Not changin' my mind."

Acting in her self-appointed role as a buffer, Della slipped into the dining area. "Clay, I've just spoken with Mrs. Dixon. She tells me you're paying her daughter a visit this evening. To be honest, I have mixed emotions about you going over there."

"Join the club."

———

Downtown Junction City was closed to automobile traffic. The festival would be a pedestrian event, with police sawhorses and orange reflective barrels marking its boundaries. Already, nearby businesses were preparing to cash in on coveted parking spaces; along Greenwood Street, booth operators stocked supplies and arranged displays; setup crews ran electrical cords and strung lights for the hot summer nights.

Asgoth and Monde paced beyond the perimeter, past the fire station to the lawn beneath the water tower. Workers were battening down a canopied expanse over the wine terrace. By tomorrow evening the place would be a lively attraction.

The Consortium's obese representative joined them on the grass.

"Monde, meet Mr. Gerde." Asgoth had always found the name effeminate, yet fitting.

"Mr. Gerde." Monde bowed his head in respect.

"Thanks for coming," Asgoth said. "We hope to make an impression."

"And I'm sure you will." A wheezing hiss accompanied Gerde's words. "Whether it's positive or negative rests entirely upon you. Let's not beat around the bush. The Consortium has bigger goals than this piddling place. You tried here on your own twelve years ago, and it was a fiasco. That was your second failure, am I correct?"

"Sir, it's hardly fair to—"

"Don't interrupt, Asgoth! If you fail a third time, I'll personally demote you to mindless minion in some backwater town. Yes, you went through your initiation, providing us with the death of John Doe, so we know you're serious. However, to invest any further in this area, we need the hundred grand and the assurance that Clay Ryker has been persuaded to leave the picture. Permanently? That'd be best."

"Believe me, Mr. Gerde, I want nothing more."

"You were careless twelve years ago, allowing hard work to go to waste. This time, if Mr. Ryker discerns your identity, he might once more jeopardize everything you've striven toward. Already he seems impervious to your cat-and-mouse tactics."

"The screws are tightening. Another day or two—that's all I ask."

"If you fail to come through—with the money or Mr. Ryker—we'll pull you out."

"Absolutely, sir. That's been clear from the start."

"And if you trigger any premature destruction, you'll face consequences of a most severe nature. The last thing the Consortium needs is the undue attention of a bomb. We have pressure enough as it stands, without inciting a public backlash. When it comes to conquering a population's will, violence is always a delicate balance."

"I've worked hard to coordinate this explosion. I'd be disappointed if—"

"This has little to do with your disappointment or personal animosity toward this town." The porcine face grew larger in Asgoth's vision. Stench-laden tendrils coiled along in the draft of Gerde's breath. "It has everything to do with avoiding a repeat of your incident at the bridge. Have I minced my words?"

"No, Mr. Gerde. This time I'll do as you've stipulated."

"A.G., I have to believe," Monde interjected, "that I've played a signifi-cant role in your preparations. I don't think it's too bold of me to say so."

Mr. Gerde leaned back, arms folded over his bulging waist. "I'm glad to see two partners dedicated to working as a team. It's much rarer than you might suppose. Succeed or fail, your fates are now intertwined. Whether it's sink or swim, you'll do it together."

Asgoth exchanged a glance with Mr. Monde.

Sink or swim? Hadn't they been through this before, many years ago?

———

Oleg had submitted his request to visit the Coffee Creek Correctional Facility. This evening, at last, he was walking through the screening area. With his papers cleared, he entered the visitors' room and joined Gertrude Ubelhaar at a table.

"Where is Dmitri?" the old woman inquired.

"My comrade has returned to Mother Russia. He has not the patience for this task."

"And which task is that, might I ask?"

Oleg leaned forward. "Finding Rasputin's treasure." He opened a folder of newspaper articles. "We both know you gave lies to Dmitri. Nyet, you have no biological son. It is a documented fact that Karl Stahlherz is dead."

Gertrude smiled. "But you are wrong. Oleg, is it?"

"I have proof here. These papers."

"Stahlherz was my adopted son, my tool. He is dead, yes. I do have another son, though."

"I should believe this? You're using lies to keep me searching for the hid-den chamber."

"You're right about one thing," she acknowledged. "I am interested in the fabled treasure, only because the Tsar deserves all that is rightfully his. My son deserves it."

"Is this true? Hitler's attempt to forge ties between our countries?"

"Der Führer commissioned me personally."

"So, Mrs. Ubelhaar. Where is this Tsar?"

"That is my final secret, Oleg. Until my son's fortune is recovered, it is pointless to reveal his whereabouts. In Rasputin's chamber lies his proof of identity."

"You and I are alike. We can form a good team, da?"

"You want to cooperate with an old German woman?"

"Bah. I do it for myself, for riches, but we need each other to make it work."

Gertrude Ubelhaar considered Oleg from beneath thin silvery hair, then, seeming satisfied, she said, "Tmu Tarakan. To proceed, we must find its location."

———

Clay felt inadequate. He circumvented the festival traffic, followed High Pass to River Road to Lovelake Road. He was going to meet a woman who nursed an old obsession and a man who was dead and gone in most people's minds.

Henna Dixon and Bill Scott.

In what way was he prepared? How would he confront this? He had no idea.

Jenni still failed to answer his calls. He wished he had a way to express emotion through each push of a button so that she could hear his desperation. Where was she? Where was Jason? They should've made it into Idaho by Wednesday; earlier today they should've crossed into eastern Oregon. Jenni had said she would call when they arrived Thursday.

Still no word.

The sun was sinking behind the coastal mountain range; shadows stretched their fingers into the road's dips and hollows. But Clay hardly noticed. His phone was idle in his pocket, and his hands moved with the steering wheel in mindless routine. He knew these roads, knew this landscape.

But what did he know about human lives and the paths they took? *Knowledge,* he told himself, *is a seduction. Rooted in pride.*

He played over the series of deaths. Perhaps he had been reading too much into all this. Maybe Henna's words and his own need for purpose had inflated the threats around him.

Summer Svenson, June 21... Hit-and-run victim. Blomberg under arrest.
Eve and Mitchell Coates, July 2... Victims of a tragic misunderstanding.
Kenny Preston, July 11... Apparent victim of a train collision. Still alive.
Mako, July 20... Gunshot victim of a lovers' squabble. Dmitri also dead.
Rhea Deering, July 20... Victim of an accidental gas explosion.
Detective Freeman, August 1... Dead from a diagnosed brain aneurysm.
Mylisha, Wendy, Digs, and Father Patrick, August 10... All unharmed.

Which left him with tomorrow's list of potential targets. What was he afraid of? Going over the mental list, he could unearth little evidence of foul play. The sensation of the numbers and the sum totals of thirteen might indicate a paranormal element, but they didn't warrant a state of full-blown panic.

His heart crept into his throat as he pulled into the Dixon driveway. The motion-activated lights came on so that he could see the same spot where he had watched Henna park her Subaru at the Avon party.

On this very property, someone had slipped an envelope into the truck. While Henna Dixon sat innocently indoors.

———

"Clay Ryker, what a pleasure."

Clay's eyes roved the living room behind Henna's mother. Where was Bill?

"I must say," Mrs. Dixon told him, "I've always hoped to find you standing on my doorstep. Hannah's been waiting for this day."

She ushered him in. Offered him coffee and tiny cakes that creatures from a fairyland might have made. On an antique bureau sat stacks of Avon order sheets, sales catalogs, and items to be delivered. In cellophane wrappers, a cluster of pens waited to accompany the orders. Complimentary. Nothing out of the ordinary.

See, he had read far too much into all this. Henna's delusional hope had infected him with suspicion and fear. There was nothing to fear but his own thoughts. His past guilts were running wild.

"Clay," Henna greeted him. "I see you made it right on time."

"I try."

She moved close and whispered, "My mother's bound to dawdle and then pass along every juicy detail. Follow me. Let's take a walk out by the pond."

They stepped through the backyard's dry grass until reaching the lusher patches around the pond's perimeter. The sun was almost out of view, flinging its last drops of orange and deep red across the rural landscape's black purple shade.

"Where's Bill?" Clay demanded.

"He doesn't want you to see him," Henna said.

"What? You brought me out here and—"

"Don't overreact, please. He will talk to you, Clay."

"When?"

"Now. In a moment. But you'll have to sit here"—she indicated a flat rock at the pond's edge—"while he speaks from back here."

"Is it really Bill Scott? From high school? I've gotta see him for myself."

"You can't. Not yet."

Clay plopped down on the stone. A grasshopper flung itself into the grass. *Fine, I'll play her little game.*

"Clay Ryker."

The male voice behind him sent a stream of chills down his neck. He had last heard this voice at the bridge over the Willamette. A nervous tone still ran beneath its husky pubescence.

"Bill?" He started to turn.

"Don't look back. Face the water."

"Do you look…different?"

"You may not recognize me. But you do remember? After what you did?"

"Bill, I was wrong. Yeah, I'll admit I was angry with you—after the way you treated Mylisha. I didn't mean for it to happen, though. How did they revive you?"

"Are you disappointed?"

"No! Of course not. I just know what I saw. You weren't moving. I don't even know how long you were under." Clay would have disbelieved this, except the past weeks had prepared him for such a moment. And he could not deny Bill's voice. This was no recording; he was speaking to the dead.

Or one I thought was dead.

"You left me wandering, Clay. With no place of my own."

"Your parents don't know you're back? Does anyone know?"

"I have no parents."

"He's telling the truth," Henna said. "Why do you think I've opened my home to him? Most people ignore him. Others fear him. He just wants a place to call his own."

"Does he look...deformed? What's going on? Let me see him."

"What do you say, Henna? Should we let him turn around?"

"I suppose." Henna giggled. "But I don't think he'll understand."

———

Mylisha had an uncharacteristic flutter in the pit of her stomach. She was costumed and stretching for the Thursday night premiere of their performance. Bright lights pointed across the stage, and scents of cinnamon and baked goods hovered over the audience. Despite the setting, her thoughts hopped back to the scene at Glenleaf, to that look of surprise and support on Clay's face. His care for her had been evident.

Clay Ryker? What's that boy doing in my head again? Not now!

The day had been an emotional ride. Blomberg's hypocrisy had been exposed, along with his self-inflated sense of destiny. And the process of washing away her years of violation and oppression had begun. She felt free.

Clay? No, he's got his own life, and I've got mine. Time I started living it.

Shaking off her musings, Mylisha fastened a bonnet on her head. Time to go on stage. Tonight's show would be a warmup for tomorrow's larger crowd.

Again Clay's face popped into her mind.

Okay, she knew this must be a good time to pray for her friend. That's what this was all about—hearing God's still, small voice, carrying on a daily relationship with her Maker.

God, you are good. If you're prompting this girl to pray, that's what I'll do.

———

Turning on the pond's flat rock, Clay found himself facing the backside of the Dixon residence. He tried to prepare himself for a horrendous disfiguration but saw nothing. Dry lawn stretched in both directions; rhododendrons circled the house; fifty yards away, a barn sheltered farm equipment and supplies.

Only Henna stood before him. Too slight of frame to hide a man at her back.

"Where is he, Henna?"

"He's not here. Not in the way you think."

Clay started toward the house. He'd had his fill of this ridiculous charade.

"I'm right here, Clay."

Clay froze at Bill's voice. Very close. Within arm's reach.

"Yes, right in front of you," the voice said. Coming from Henna's lips.

Clay stumbled back, almost tripped. Choked for air.

Henna's mouth opened again, moving in a manner discordant with her own form. Bill Scott's voice was issuing from her, as though she were a life-size doll programmed with the wrong speech commands. "Did you really think I was Bill? How touching."

"This is sick, Henna! You are not funny."

"I'm not Henna. Though I do feel very connected with her."

"Who are you then?"

"You saw my name at the apartment, where she'd carved it into the wax. An act of devotion that I found touching."

Clay's mental gears whirred. "Asgoth?"

"Yes, but it's only an acronym. Unscramble the letters and you'll understand."

Clay could barely think of his own name.

"A-s-g-o-t-h. Do I have to spell it out for you, Mr. Ryker?" Asgoth's voice was mocking, enjoying this moment of exposure. "Turn it around… A-g-h-o-s-t."

"A ghost."

"That's right. You pretend to know bits of the Bible. Do I need to refresh your memory? It says that an evil spirit 'leaves a person…goes into the desert, seeking rest but finding none… So it returns…finds seven other spirits more evil than itself, and they all enter the person and live there.... That will be the experience of this evil generation.' "

Clay had an urge to flee this perverse scene. He felt sick to his stomach, but he braced himself and said, "You're Bill Scott's ghost?"

"More or less. His demon, to put it more accurately. I worked with him, cultivated him, softened him for my purposes...and you stole him from me! You ruined my chances of success. Your little shove put an end to all my work in him. Of course, my goal for my friends is death anyway, but I seek it on my terms. Self-sacrifice."

"Suicide?"

"That's right. It's our ultimate laugh in the face of him who sacrificed his Son for all. It's my blood money. If I can't convince my human friends to do themselves in, I don't get my full share in the market."

"The market?"

"This town. Junction City. The market of souls. Call it what you will."

48

Digging Deeper

Clay's skin crawled at the vehemence trickling from Henna's lips. By her own volition, she'd given this demon freedom to manipulate her vocal cords to his purpose. Her face twisted into a mask of unnatural contours.

"I've been waiting for this moment, Clay."

"What've you done to Henna? Henna? Can you hear me?"

"Oh, she hears you. But I've taken over the reins. When she discovered you were coming back to town, her obsession with you fired up all over again, and I promised to help her get to you. I have my own reasons too, as I've shared."

"This is sick. I'm outta here."

"No!" Asgoth whipped Henna's hand forward, and it clamped with unnatural strength onto Clay's shoulder. The deep voice continued to generate from Henna's mouth. "I've anticipated this for too long to have you walk away. You need to hear this."

"Please let me go."

"You don't know the turmoil you've caused me. Shut up and listen."

"I'll pass." Clay's heart had turned into a lump of motionless tissue. "Please."

The voice grew snide. "Clay, I know you humans fear us, and well you should. Think about it. Only a third of the angels were thrown from heaven, which means we demons are the minority. Yet look at all the havoc we cause. Lies and deception—they're our trade craft. If we can get you peeking under every bush, fearing us more than you fear God… Ha! That's the ultimate thrill."

"So you're behind this? You gave me this ability to sense death dates?"

"Through Henna, yes." Henna Dixon's eyes were glassy, her lips moving with numb disconnection from her jaws. "She's been a willing tool of mine."

"You can't work without her, can you? You need a…a host."

"A host for a ghost?" Asgoth's chuckle turned hollow, as though rising from a cavern. Henna's limbs quivered, went limp, and she slumped to the grass. From her side a shape moved under night's cover. Wispy and without depth, Asgoth rose tall in Bill Scott's clothing. He was missing a shoe. Bill's voice became strained.

"It takes energy to show myself. I prefer a host, but it's not mandatory."

"You don't look right," Clay said. "You look...shallow."

"Usually only my victims get to see me—as I draw on their last traces of energy. You're right," Asgoth confided. "Bill's clothes aren't my style, but they're what he left me at the riverbank. I never could find his other shoe, so I've had to hobble around in this foul thing."

"You took his stuff?"

"Didn't get an option. Few of us do. But at least I'm not tortured by corduroy jackets with elbow patches, like my partner Monde. He got stuck with the attire of a man who died on the cliffs at Heceta Head Lighthouse last winter."

"Monde?" Clay turned the word in his head. "You mean...demon?"

"Aren't you clever."

Clay began muttering prayers as he twisted free from Asgoth's grip. Here in the Dixons' yard, at the edge of a pond in the darkness, he was facing a spirit that had plagued him for the past few weeks. One that had tormented his high school companion. Did this creature know the whereabouts of his wife and son? In hopes of unearthing a clue, Clay decided to poke at this demon's pride.

"What's with the silly names?" he jibed. "Couldn't they give you something spooky or ancient? 'A ghost.' You sound so...generic."

"I don't have to justify myself to you, you runt."

"You don't have a real identity, do you? Without stealing one."

"You have no idea what you're talking about." Bill Scott's shape wavered, opaque and without substance. "You're an ant in the grand scheme, Clay. An ant!"

Clay was trying to piece it together. "You took my belt buckle, didn't you?"

"And your ID. I had Henna plant them for me. Our little attempts to drive you to the brink."

"So you've been orchestrating the deaths to match the numbers?"

"One of my favorite pastimes."

"But I've disrupted a few of them at least."

"Did I say they were foolproof? We should never have overlooked Summer Svenson's connection to Sergeant Turney. What a nuisance he's been! But Blomberg was easy to exploit. Of course, people are always doing their own thing, stubborn little sheep that they are. The gift of human free will is a source of constant upheaval, and I don't understand why the one who sacrificed his Son for all ever gave such a thing."

"So you planned this all out? Summer and the Coateses? Rhea? Mako?"

"All my doing. Though Monde might try to take some credit. We've used any and all means at our disposal, some of them manufactured, some already set. Detective Freeman's condition, for example? Worked like a charm."

"What about Jason? Jenni? Is there a specific plan for them?"

"Nice try." Asgoth wagged his finger. "I wouldn't want to ruin the surprise."

Clay could feel arrogance emanating from the vaporous being, could almost smell its desire to boast. Clay continued to prime the pump with questions. "What about my mother's numbers? They're years away."

"I used hers to throw you off balance, to keep you guessing."

"Kenny Preston. He broke your string, didn't he?"

"He hid and survived. Don't you just love kids? I'll remember him in the future."

"It's not right to pick on a child."

Asgoth's mocking laugh caused his form to undulate, to dissipate. He kicked his one shoe at a dirt clod, lifting a few motes of dust and nothing more. "Since when have I agreed to play by the rules?"

"Why'd you choose Kenny anyway? Just an innocent kid."

"Exactly. That's why he was able to find the key."

Clay thought of the chess piece in the wooden tube. "You mean the king."

"Same thing. I've tried taking hold of it, but our heavenly rivals have been guarding the train for years. They're like a curse! One even comes disguised as an old woman, just to taunt me."

"You're talking about Engine 418?"

"What else? Of course you have no idea why I should care, do you?"

Clay shook his head. Under his breath, he was petitioning God for help.

"I'll have to hold on to a few of my secrets, Mr. Ryker." For a fleeting moment, black caftan robes seemed to envelop Asgoth, but they washed away in the moonlight. "Don't forget, my other goal with Kenny was to drive you over the edge. With some quick thinking, I used a shadow of Kenny's form on the tracks to deceive you. You should've seen your face. So horrified! Monde is fairly adept at bird sounds, so he provided the shrieking whistle of the train."

"I thought the kid was a goner."

"And you were too caught up in self-pity to catch my mistake."

Clay dredged up that macabre image. He saw the hollowness in the eyes, the lifeless pallor of the face, the unreal aspects of the temporary apparition.

"Kenny's bike helmet," he said. "You forgot to conjure it."

"Ah, you figured it out. Finally."

"And everyone who survived through August tenth, they were just decoys, weren't they? Throwing the police off so I'd be on my own for Friday the thirteenth."

"Can you think of a more fitting date? You're next, Mr. Ryker. Save me the trouble, and take your own life."

"You tried this once already, didn't you?"

"No. You tried. And you failed."

"I think God intervened."

"Or maybe you simply failed again, as you do with everything. Business. Marriage. Can't even kill yourself properly." Asgoth shook his head. "This time I've got to have results. For the Consortium's sake."

"The Consortium?"

"The seven others. Smug, condescending creatures. They think they're better than me. Well, I intend to prove them wrong. Once you're gone, I'll be free to go where I will. The floodgates'll be opened."

Clay had an urge to grab this demon, to shake it by the throat. But hadn't he seen a train shoot right through it? He had no doubt Asgoth would dissipate in his grip. On a deeper level, one he'd tapped while on his knees at the chapel this morning, Clay felt an impulse to cry out a name. The same name he had called on in the black watery depths. The name above demons and ghosts, spirits and death.

It was a whisper. "Jesus."

Gathering force in his throat. "You are Lord."

Clay let the truth seep deep into his soul. "Jesus. You're the only sacrifice!"

On the grass, Henna's entire body jerked. Her mouth was a contorted shape, sucking in the blackness, providing a place of dark retreat. Asgoth's specter shrank within Bill Scott's clothing, whirled, then rotated into a funnel of soundless shapes and shadows that disappeared down the drain of Henna's cavernous throat.

———

Henna smoothed her blond hair. "Did you speak with him?"

Clay stared at her. "With Asgoth? Yep, I sure did."

"He's a gentle spirit, isn't he? A spirit guide, as some say. I may not see him directly, but I'm always aware when he enters a room. As I told you on the bus the day you arrived, 'God works in many different ways.' "

"You're very confused."

"Enlightened," Henna replied. "I don't expect you to understand."

"Where's Jenni? Where's Jason? I want my family back."

"Have you forgotten what I told you? What Asgoth had me write in the note?"

"I know, I know." Clay's legs were weak. "Love comes at a price!"

"So true, don't you think?"

"How do I know you have them? Maybe you're bluffing."

"After all that you've seen us accomplish, you still doubt us, Clay? Call her now. She's with some of our…friends. They've been told to expect a call anytime after eight. Go on. She'll pick up."

Clay tore the cell phone from his pocket, hit redial. Before the second ring had sounded, Jason's voice came on.

"Daddy!"

Then Jenni's voice. Indignant. Full of fear. "Put him down!"

Clickkk... Someone hung up on him.

With every ounce of his strength, Clay resisted the depression lingering over him. He bit back the rage rising in his throat. "I'll have your money, Henna."

"I doubt that, Clay. We created these stipulations knowing you couldn't meet them. Which means you'll be responsible for their deaths. Tell me, where're you going to get a hundred thousand dollars?"

"I'll have it."

"If not, your wife and son will die. Churches aren't the only places that solicit donations to fund their outreaches. We need money to carry out the wishes of our spirit guides."

"You're opposing God."

"We're all one with God, Clay. Each of us is a god or a goddess."

"So that gives you the right to decide between life and death?"

"It's a position of great responsibility."

"Yeah? What if another 'god' decides it's your time to go? Your logic breaks down on so many levels."

"Clay, I don't expect you to understand. Just bring the cash—if that's possible—along with the GPS unit. 'To reunite as a pair, you'll need a spring in your step.'"

"Okay, would you just tell me what that means?"

"A quiet little spot up the McKenzie River. We'll meet at Belknap Springs. Keep an open mind, if you would. For years I've waited for you to pay me any heed, and I don't want it to be a wasted opportunity."

"I want my wife," Clay said. "And my boy."

———

Clay checked his bank account on the way home. The ATM receipt told him he had negative seventy-three dollars and change. Tomorrow's paycheck hadn't come soon enough to cover the bills he'd sent out on Monday.

Am I surprised? That's what I get for trying to pay my bills on time.

He sped back to his parents' place. Snatched the change from the candy bowl atop the refrigerator. Rummaged through the garage, found his flash-light and camp shovel. Loaded the stuff into the Duster's backseat.

In the glow of the dash, he powered the GPS unit and cradled it in his lap.

The horrendous confrontation out on Lovelake Road, the sheer depth and depravity of one demon's schemes had left him spiritually exhausted.

It had also filled his heart with a renewed sense of protection and provi-dence. Despite the hardships and rough spots in his journey, Clay Ryker understood he walked with a God who was skilled at piecing together life's puzzle. God had a plan—adjusting and strategizing, working with people's choices, absorbing the grief and anger humans directed his way when their own decisions backfired.

God was history's storyteller. A master novelist. A craftsman of suspense.

He never stopped working toward a good ending, but his chapters were cliff-hangers, and his twists and turns could take one's breath away.

In Junction City the usually subdued streets still bore festival goers and late-night revelers. Clay stopped to fill the Duster with as much gas as his fist-ful of change would permit. He sent up a prayer—for angels to watch over this old beater. Then he headed south.

Highway 99 took him to Beltline Road, which joined him with Highway 126. Even now God's hand was at work. Clay was forging ahead on the very road Gerald would be using for his McKenzie River fishing trip. Only hours would separate them, giving Clay a chance to anticipate Asgoth's designs. Clay was also taking the route required to reach Jenni and Jason. In three hours, according to Henna's instructions, he was to meet her at Belknap Springs off Highway 126. He would turn over the hundred grand and the GPS unit; in exchange, Henna would release his wife and son.

Henna didn't know of Gerald's fishing plans.

Gerald didn't know of Henna's schemes.

Neither of them knew of Clay's own reason for heading this way. Years ago his friend Digs had earned a nickname without cognizance of the role he would play in today's events. August 13, 2004.

Failure's no option. It seems obvious God's shifting these pieces into place.

Still, he decided, it wouldn't hurt to have some backup. He dialed

Sergeant Turney's number to tell him about the encounter at Lovelake. Turney brushed aside any concerns about sleep and agreed to keep an eye on Henna's movements.

———

On her beanbag Mylisha laid out the components of her Beaulieu Super 8 sync sound camera. More than one independent movie had been filmed successfully in this format. Oliver Stone had even used it in one or two high-budget movies, preferring its grainy and more realistic style.

She'd spoken to the school counselor; starting next week, she would audit introductory filmmaking classes. She'd bought the camera on eBay, as well as a Sony DAT recorder and an EWA Super 8 backwinder.

She had to start somewhere, sometime—and this was as good a start as any.

Dipping into her savings account had been tough.

But it's the right thing—that's a fact. Clay helped me face it.

Mylisha spent two hours going over the camera's instructions. Tomorrow she would give it a trial run. In between the morning and evening performances on the Festival Park Stage, she would roam the streets and capture on film the struggles many faced in breaking free from fear and insecurity.

It was the tension of small-town life. Earth's tension between heaven and hell.

She already had an idea for a title: *Living Safe, Dying Slow.*

———

The Garmin GPS unit was pointing Clay south along Cougar Reservoir. He verified each digit, reassuring himself this was right. He had little time to kill.

The Duster led him to a bridge, which carried him to the reservoir's other side. The car chugged a bit harder as it skirted the water on a rising face of dirt and stone. Evergreens and an occasional redwood sprouted on either side of the narrowing road. He found it difficult to keep the GPS unit visible while bouncing over summer-hardened ruts, while shutting vents against billows of dust.

Distance: *1.2 miles.*

The unit was homing in now. This should be it coming up.

Clay proceeded a bit farther, then stopped as far as possible off the negligible dirt road. The unit's arrow pointed east. On foot, with shovel and flashlight in one hand and GPS in the other, he strode beneath the forest canopy. Brushed away spider webs and briers. Crested a natural berm. Discovered a hidden lake, just as Digs had said.

Distance: *0.3 miles.*

He wandered in zigzagging patterns, trying to follow the satellite's positioning as it triangulated upon this spot. The air was brisk, blowing across the nearby water. The morning was coming to life with the first sounds of wildlife.

384 feet, 376, 357…

Clay knew from experience that GPS coordinates could be off by a few feet, even a couple of yards—particularly since it had been three years since Digs had come out and marked the spot with outdated equipment. Earth and stone could shift and slide. Rain could conspire against him.

What had Digs said? Something about a boulder tilted against a fallen trunk. Lots of moss. Insects. Roots and dirt.

Here. This must be it.

Clay stuck the Garmin unit into his pocket. Started digging.

Within twenty minutes he had cleared out a hole and uncovered bugs and centipedes but nothing else. He dug deeper, and a second hole exposed equally unsavory creatures while also revealing a silver garbage bag. The shovel blade snagged on the plastic. Clay freed it, then dug out a military-style ammunition box.

Inside the box Clay found Digs's share of a bank robbery.

Digs had been one of three armed robbers. Within days they had been caught out in these woods by undercover agents who raided their tent site and delivered them to the courts. During the course of the robbery, one of the thieves had shot a bank customer, making Digs and the other man accessories.

The state pen awaited. Digs did his time.

Years later he came back on his own to relocate and label this spot. For old times' sake. A symbolic keepsake of the life he had left behind.

What good would $101,000 do him? he had asked Clay. It was all marked anyway. Long ago, news sources had reported that a bank teller broke open an invisible ink pack within the cache, staining the bills until the day some fool tried to use them and left an obvious trail for law enforcers everywhere.

49

Collision Course

"A.G.?" Henna sat up, pulled the pink bedspread around her. "Are you back?"

Asgoth warmed to the sound of her voice. "I'm here."

Earlier he had left the Dixon home by attaching himself to the roof of Clay's car. It was worth a shot—a free ride to the Belknap Springs site, a clandestine opportunity to ensure Clay's compliance. At the gas station, however, Clay had called upon angels for protection. In a flash heavenly beings revealed their locations, and a ring of white fire encircled the ramshackle old automobile as though it'd become a golden chariot.

Asgoth shot from the roof, incensed by this intrusion.

What right did they have? It was disgusting, really. For years guilt had weakened Mr. Clay Ryker. Now, after a silly little rescue at Crater Lake, the man was growing steadily stronger, once again recognizing the touch of his Creator.

This nonsense would have to stop.

"We need to go," Asgoth told Henna.

She stretched. "It's finally time?"

"Friday morning, almost sunrise. We're running late."

She swung her legs over the side of the bed, stood to fetch her clothes. After peeking into her daughter's room and finding Serene still asleep, she followed Asgoth's lead outside to her car. They loaded the trunk. From the rearview mirror, a large crystal dangled on a beaded strand, and she rubbed it between her fingers.

"Let's hurry," Asgoth prompted. "While you're meeting with Clay, I'll be arranging his father's last breath."

"First, I'll be rekindling the fire in Jenni's heart." Henna flicked a lighter so that flame danced at its tip. "She'll be hot for her husband all over again. Hot and crispy."

———

With the ammunition box in the trunk, Clay threaded his way back down to Cougar Reservoir. The trees parted so that he spied water and sunlight giving each other good-morning kisses.

See, he told himself, this is what it's like to live within the palm of God's hand.

Why do I ever doubt?

His finances were still a wreck, and his marriage was still in question, yet he saw glimmers of hope. Kisses throughout creation.

Not five minutes later the clouds swept in, dumping rain at the feet of the Cascade Mountains, shoveling gloom and fog into the valleys and river bends. The Duster shivered, its balding tires working extra hard for purchase on slick pavement.

So sure of his divine place, Clay failed to notice the gas gauge.

Not that he could've done a thing about it. He was broke. Penniless.

With nary a whimper or a gasp, the faithful car lost all power in the middle of a steep incline. Clay was able to work his way over to the guardrail with the remaining momentum. What to do now? His wife and son would be waiting for him; his father needed his protection.

And here he sat. Useless.

His mind washed first one way, then the other. Any assurance of godly interaction seemed empty. He stared at himself in the rearview mirror, hating the doubt, despising the resignation that drilled deep into his pupils.

———

From the backseat, Asgoth had been caressing Henna's blond locks as sunrays splayed through the crystal and swept over her cheeks. Now Highway 126 led them beneath heavy clouds, and Henna's face darkened in the mirror. Rain struck the windshield in a sudden downpour, delivering doubts.

He tried to hide his concern. "Are you ready, Henna?"

"Honestly, you should know the answer. I've been waiting twelve years for this."

Asgoth thought he saw a vehicle on the highway's narrow shoulder, but it was hard to tell through the sluicing rain. He knew steep cliffs cut down from this mountain pass. These roads could be dangerous. Ahead, he spotted a logging truck, and he nudged Henna's shoulder. "Here's where I get off. I'll see you back at the Festival Park Stage tonight. Soon Junction City will be our marketplace."

Asgoth oozed through the glass, crouched, then pounced upon the passing rig. His hands and feet hooked into rough bark as he clambered over huge tree trunks, his form flapping in the draft of the speeding vehicle.

———

Clay ducked his head into the neck of his shirt and climbed from the car. He'd turned on his flashers to indicate he was experiencing trouble. Surely someone would be kind enough to pull over. He had twenty-two minutes left until the rendezvous.

As if in a conscious attempt to increase his frustration, the rain came down harder. He yanked open the trunk and removed the ammunition box so he could snag the dirty silver garbage bag. Clumps of worm-filled mud dripped on him.

He growled. Frustrated with his own fickle emotions. And with the Lord. *Why let it rain now of all times? Why let me run outta gas? What's going on?*

Clay stripped off his soaked shirt, tried to keep himself covered with the garbage bag while waving with the heavy cloth. Passersby stared at him through rain-drenched windows as though he was a lunatic. As though he meant to run out of money and gas and good luck on this awful section of the highway.

On the guardrail's other side, a cliff plunged toward the McKenzie River. Trees perched perilously on the slope, stabbing upward to impale anything on its way down.

Down...

The word brought back thoughts of Crater Lake. It mesmerized him with a sense of uselessness. How easy it would be to say good-bye to this spinning globe.

No. Jesus, help me. I don't wanna listen to those types of thoughts.

A pair of semitrucks screamed past with tires blasting water and pebbles and cold air. Clay shook his head. He wanted to holler at the top of his lungs, but that was out of the question. No reason to waste his breath. He was numb, going through the motions. What was the point of Digs and his buried money if Clay could get no farther than this treacherous hill?

Are you taunting me, God? Is that it?

He moved into the upward bound lane. He waved his shirt back and forth. A vehicle was approaching. He could tell because a pair of blurred head-lights was swimming back and forth through the currents of rain. An SUV flashed past, doused him once again.

What did it matter? Maybe it was all one big game.

I'm going to wave the next person over—or die trying!

After a moment of shivering beside the Duster, Clay saw another set of lights lurching through puddles and road ruts. He squinted through the slash-ing rain and planted himself in the middle of the lane. With both hands he whipped the silver bag to and fro over his head.

He had no hope of making eye contact with the driver. In this deluge it was impossible. He did exaggerated jumps. Waving. Kicking.

But the vehicle was not slowing. It was a light fuzzy shape coming at him, a white phantom coming to steal away his soul.

Jenni and Jason will die if I don't make something happen.

The driver hit the horn. It blared at Clay through the downpour.

Do or die!

"Stop!" He yelled at last, without budging an inch. "Please *stop!*"

He realized the driver was not honking at him but at the logging truck coming down the hill in the other lane. The big rig was on the edge of con-trol, hurtling along, swerving across the middle line. In a prolonged low tone, its air horn burped.

Clay took a step over but kept his basic position.

The rig slipped farther over, loaded with gigantic Douglas fir trees.

———

The logging truck was a medieval steed. Armored and trained for war, the truck relied on horsepower to make its charge at the enemy. Riding on its back upon a saddle of chains, Asgoth was a knight shrouded in ghoulish wisps and Bill Scott's argyle vest, guiding the stripped tree trunks like deadly lances toward the oncoming vehicle.

Of course, the rig's real driver was in the cab: Darnell Rigsby. According to the airbrushed name on the driver's door.

Like most humans left alone for hours at a time, Darnell had latched on to a vice or two. This made it easy. Asgoth had hopped from Henna's car onto this truck going the other direction and, within moments, devised a distraction. He'd harnessed his energy for a brief knock against the glove box, which released the hatch and dropped a stack of Darnell's adult magazines onto the passenger seat and floorboards.

"Not again," Darnell grumbled. "Somebody's been messin' with that latch."

His eyes darted over. Swiveled down. Hovered over the splayed pages.

This is too easy, Asgoth thought.

Darnell pulled his eyes back to the road, saw how far he'd veered off course. He shouted as he tried to bring his vehicle back under control on the wet descent.

———

Clay needed transportation, or his family might be gone forever. He waved and yelled. In the uphill lane, the smaller vehicle materialized, a white and glistening pickup with probing headlights and thrashing wipers. A face moved behind the glass, turned up toward the logging truck. With no room for escape along this narrow mountain road, a collision seemed inevitable.

The pickup fishtailed, and Clay heard brakes stuttering. He scrambled away, felt water whip his thigh as the vehicle slid diagonally, riding rain-slick asphalt.

Clay was on his knees. The logging rig plunged past.

Beside him, the smaller vehicle rammed its nose into the Duster's back fender.

In one tortured movement, Clay's old beater crunched into the guardrail, side panels scraping, glass and fluids spitting. The white pickup plowed it forward so that it climbed over twisted metal, then dipped down as if for a peek into the gorge. The back end flipped free, and the Duster somersaulted from the precipice.

In a slow uphill slide, the pickup also reached the edge. Three tires clung to road and rail, while one stretched over space in a farewell wave to the car. Across the steering wheel, the driver was sprawled in an awkward position.

Clay ran toward the driver. The logging truck had almost killed them both.

If it weren't for my car sitting here, this guy would've gone over the edge!

———

Asgoth bellowed. How had Clay known to park his car at that spot?

Furious, he rose into the wind-swept mist, dashed forward along the rough spines of the fir trees. He dove over the top of Darnell Rigsby's cab and clasped the driver's side windshield wiper. Drawing on his last dregs of physical substance, Asgoth resisted the mechanical motion so that raindrops slathered over the glass.

Darnell was flicking at the wiper controls. Cursing.

His loaded trailer was jackknifing across the highway. Twisting over. Grinding onto its side. Chains snapping like rubber bands and logs bursting loose.

The cab also flipped onto its side. By the time the trailer piled into a mound of moist earth and gnarled roots, Darnell was curled into a protective ball. He would walk away with only bruises.

But the oncoming Nissan was no match for fourteen tons of rolling Douglas firs.

The female driver was killed instantly.

Although unplanned, the moment worked in Asgoth's favor. From the car's description, he realized the driver was none other than Kate Preston, which left her son, thirteen-year-old Kenny, all alone.

Asgoth watched the wreck for confirmation. Waited.

From the crushed car, a wisp of light ascended and fluttered heavenward. Repentant or otherwise, all souls made the same initial journey that would take them before the One who had sacrificed his Son for all. Would this woman find her name already inscribed there on the Son's nail-scarred hands?

Kate Preston...

Barely a whisper in the wind.

Joining the whisper, sounds of a far-off, joyous celebration gave Asgoth the answer he'd feared.

———

The rain clouds were moving away. Through thinning sheets of moisture, the white truck's driver was groggy, half-conscious, yet easily identifiable through the side window.

"Dad?" Clay tried the handle, but it was jammed. "Dad, can you hear me?"

From the Dodge pickup's deployed airbag, Gerald Ryker lifted his face. Dazed. Still breathing. His stern jaw could not hide his expression of relief.

50

Water and Flame

Clay tried the ignition. The Dodge rumbled, hissed, and fumed. Came to life. With his dad's pocketknife, he cut away the spent airbag. With a hand on the emergency brake, he shifted into reverse. The guardrail tried to hold its captive, but the four-wheel drive kicked in, yanking the truck back until the suspended tire was on solid ground once again.

"Front end's a mess," Gerald said. "Radiator's leaking."

"Think we're good to go? For a couple of miles at least?"

"Hard to say. You'll have to drive, Son."

"I should take you somewhere, to a hospital or a clinic."

"We're already late, Clay. And your son's safety is at stake. My grandson."

Minutes earlier Gerald had hobbled from the truck, braced his arms against the side to gather his bearings, refused to give voice to his obvious pain. Traffic had continued in both directions, with drivers slowing to gawk. Two had offered assistance, but Gerald had declined after hearing of Clay's dilemma. Years ago, through Mr. Blomberg, Gerald had become aware of Henna's behavioral aberrations, and he knew this situation was no joking matter.

"This yours?" Gerald rounded the truck's nose, set a green ammo box on the passenger seat. "Found it on the ground between the tires."

"Yes!"

Clay flipped open the lid, saw the cash was still inside. He moved his GPS from his pocket into the box. With these items, he'd make the exchange at Belknap Springs.

The dash clock told him he was already twelve minutes late.

——

"They'd better be here," Clay said.

Steam hissed from the truck's overheated engine as they coasted into the lodge's parking area. He spotted a Subaru in a parking lane. Was it Henna's?

"Twenty-six minutes late."

"Thanks, Dad. As if I don't know that."

Clay was familiar with Belknap Springs Lodge. As a kid, he'd been here with his family on a number of occasions, as well as on a high school senior skip day. The property included a number of campsites and cabins clinging to a hillside, a beautifully renovated lodge with animal carvings guarding the perimeter, and an assortment of tended gardens. The chief attraction, however, had always been the natural hot springs, which were piped into a fenced, man-made pool facing the river.

Early Friday morning... *8.1.3.0.4.*

Aside from thick vapor floating above the pool, the place was still.

"I'm supposed to meet her in there. By the pool."

"It's closed, Son. Locked. We'll have to check at the front desk."

"No. They'll make us wait until it opens."

"I'll see what they say."

"Sure. Fine." Clay watched his father shuffle toward the grand front entrance, shook his head. His old man could be so stubborn, so unfeeling.

Clay clipped his cell phone to his belt. He grabbed the ammo box and circumvented the lodge. He could see a footbridge spanning the McKenzie River, casting a deep green shadow upon white-capped currents. Through a wire gate around the pool, mist seeped outward and blocked any view of the heated surface. One hard rattle proved the gate was locked.

"Henna?"

The clouds were dispersing before the rising sun. Warm rays slipped over the hilltops, between the tree branches.

"Henna, are you here?"

A bird chirped from the opposing bank.

"Jenni? Jason?"

A breeze coursed down from the mountains, tracing the river's path, churning the steam above the pool. Clay peered through the mist. Saw two gray garbage bags floating in the water. Tied off at the ends, cumbersome and misshapen, they looked as if they contained human bodies—one medium sized and one small.

He screamed out the names of his wife and son. He dropped the ammunition box, clawed his way over the wire fence, and barely noticed the metal end that gouged at his thigh and tore away his cell phone. Adrenaline, keeping pace with his fear and anger, raced through his limbs. He dropped to the concrete. Fully clothed, he dove into the pool.

———

Asgoth was depleted. Nothing but a ghost wandering the wastelands. With the last of his strength, he'd latched on to a car heading over the pass. He had let the wind carry him from there until the gruesome accident scene was out of view.

Now, miles away, he faced a scene just as horrific.

In fact, the fires engulfing the trailer home before him were but a glimpse of his own irreversible destiny. Hell…Gehenna. A punishment without end. Death would be welcome, yet unattainable, in that place.

The trailer's front door popped open. Asgoth flinched at the sight of a charred body curled into a fetal position on the bubbling tile floor.

He'd had no doubt of Henna's ability to carry out this deed. She had stopped by here to secure her victims before setting the place ablaze; she had welcomed the idea of watching Jenni "burn" for her soon-to-be ex-husband. Clay's wife and son had been here since yesterday, held captive by two heroin-addicted roughnecks who'd given themselves long ago to the Consortium's desires.

How sad. Jenni and Jason were nothing more than kindling now. The authorities would shake their heads. Another matchstick home gone up in flames—a dropped cigarette, a miswired baseboard heater.

Or arson, initiated at the feet of bound hostages. Whatever.

His smile froze. The form in the doorway was twitching. Dead? Absolutely. But reacting to the extreme heat. Nothing more than a bacon strip in a frying pan.

Again Asgoth cringed at the thought of his own impending doom. A macabre fascination pushed him forward, and within yards of the inferno, he noticed something amiss. What had gone on here? He moved closer, with a need to know for sure. In the ceiling, wood snapped; from the walls, metal pinged.

He slithered beneath coils of blue-tinged flame, his tired shape passing the corpse in the doorway before reaching the smaller form on the kitchen floor. Both bodies, to his dismay, wore heavy, mud-caked logging boots. And both held firearms in their gnarled hands, bolstering Asgoth's theory that drug-induced suspicions had sparked a bloody confrontation between these two roughnecks.

So typical! But where are Jenni and Jason? Did Henna change our plan?

Asgoth's howl rose through the roof, a shriek from the fire's throat.

———

The pool's heat burned along Clay's skin. His hands clawed upward. Brought him back to the surface. He grabbed at the plastic bags, snagged both, dragged them toward the side. Their weight resisted him. He heaved and rolled them one by one up over the pool's edge.

He would not let his emotion take over. Not yet.

"Leave it all behind, and come with me," a female voice crooned.

Clay spun to see Henna through the mist, on the other side of the fence. "What're you talking about?" He pawed at the rope, then tore instead at the plastic where the faces should be. Trapped oxygen and earthy decay rushed up into his nostrils. Apparently the bags had been airtight, kept afloat despite their burden of moldy potatoes in dirty sacks.

"Where are they!" He clung to the side of the pool. His clothes were heavy, pulling on him.

"They're already dead."

"You're full of it!"

"We could start fresh, Clay. You and me, the way it was supposed to be."

"I wanna see my wife and son."

"Are you sure about that? A trailer home fire is never a pretty sight."

"Where? Tell me!" He climbed from the water.

"What do you think?"

"About what? Stop playing games, Henna."

"About us?"

"You're outta your mind. Where's my family?"

"Your loss, Clay. Thanks for leaving the money and GPS. I appreciate that." Henna was holding the green ammo box. She gestured at his feet, at the torn plastic and waterlogged cords. "You know, this would be an ideal time to use the leftover rope. You've refused to recognize me all these years, so now let my face be the last one you see. Here's a suggestion. Tie yourself to the bags and throw yourself into the deep end. The pool's closed. No one's out here to spoil things. Do it right this time."

Clay attacked the fence. "Where are they!"

Henna shrugged, then disappeared around the lodge with the ammo box.

———

Riding thermal waves produced by the smoking conflagration, Asgoth floated around the trailer and caught sight of two more bodies, sixty yards back at the edge of the trees. Kneeling over them, Sergeant Turney was giving them long draughts of water from a bottle. He'd spread wet blankets over them, no doubt soaked in the nearby tributary of the mighty McKenzie.

Why him again? Why here of all places?

Asgoth swooped down toward Turney. Before reaching him, Asgoth found himself facing a husky, bearded individual who looked supremely uncomfortable in a logger's plaid shirt and blue jeans.

This was no logger; that much was obvious.

Behind the creature, Turney continued ministering health to Jenni and Jason. They looked weak from smoke inhalation; their eyes were swollen, their faces grimy with sweat. But they were alive.

"You have no authority here," said the bearded being. The voice was a hammer, nailing deep its words.

"Step out of my way!"

The being remained rock steady. "We've met before, haven't we?"

"I don't know what you're talking about."

"I'm sure you do. Decades ago you sauntered about in black robes with a blasphemous cross about your neck. You were one of an entire legion, you and your friend Mr. Monde—and still you could not protect the man whom you possessed. Oh, you tried. In the end, though, Rasputin died like any other mortal."

"And I was sent into exile, halfway around the world. Can't you let me be?"

"You also lost the right to open Rasputin's hidden chamber."

"If we ever do open it, your kind will feel the sting of our revenge!"

"It'll never happen. Your hopes've drowned along with the men you possessed."

The statement injected Asgoth with melancholy. He relived those final moments—sinking into darkness, gulping water, fighting poison and the bite of bullets.

The icy depths of the River Neva.

Later the murky waters of the Willamette.

"Leave!" the angelic creature commanded. "You have no place here."

Asgoth saw an ethereal light seeping through the lumberjack facade. He knew that for the moment he was impotent to counterattack. Already exhausted, he felt the being's syllables pound into him and drive him away.

———

Wet and breathless, head spinning from the temperature difference between the pool and the outside air, Clay gathered his dropp ed cell phone, then pulled himself to the fence top, where metal tines scratched at his stomach. He edged a toe into the wire and hefted himself over.

His shirt caught. Ripped across his face and over his head.

He was half-naked. Bleeding. Running.

His characteristic despair was a familiar spirit, hovering, haunting his thoughts. Although he refused to accept that his wife and son were dead, Henna and Asgoth had shown themselves more than capable of arranging such a thing.

No! Jesus came to "destroy these works of the devil."

His feet scrambled in pursuit. At the front of the lodge, Henna hopped into her Subaru and peeled toward the winding exit road.

Clay saw coolant and water still dripping beneath his parents' Dodge truck; regardless, he jumped in, turned the key. The engine ignored his fist pounding and yells. The truck was lifeless.

God, please! Why can't I get a miracle? How hard could this be?

Gerald limped from the lodge's front doors. "Forget it, Clay. Won't work."

"Come on! She's already out of sight. I'm losing her!"

"Who? Henna?"

"She took the money and the GPS. She says Jenni and Jason are dead."

"Henna was out by the pool?"

"Didn't you hear me yelling?"

"The guy at the front desk, he has the morning news turned up loud. He said no one's allowed in the pool till nine o'clock."

Clay kept trying the ignition. Nothing. Nothing, nothing, nothing...

Gerald stood at the passenger window. "Clay."

"What?"

"It's dead. Overheated."

"No, we've gotta go. Jump in."

"Clay, the water pump's shot. Forget it."

Clay slammed both palms down on the steering wheel so hard that the repercussion traveled back up his arms into his chest. He could try pursuing Henna on foot. Or try stealing a car. Or borrowing one. Deep down, though, he knew he had already lost her. She could've turned either direction on Highway 126. She was gone.

"Son."

Clay closed his eyes, shook his head.

Gerald cleared his throat. "Son, thanks for helpin' me. Back at the cliff. I thought I'd punched my ticket, thought I was goin' over that cliff for sure."

"I ran out of gas."

"At just the right spot." Gerald removed his hand. "An act of God, you think?"

"I don't know what to think."

Accepting the good and the bad was no easy task, but Clay had learned it was the best option. He had to believe that the master storyteller was still writing the tale, that the climax would justify the heartrending moments that preceded it.

Numb inside and out, wet and shaking, Clay took a deep breath.

God is good.

He took another breath.

Nothing in all creation will ever be able to separate us from the love of God.

Silently he made his commitment of faith; yet there was no feeling behind it, no emotion. The words spiraled through his head.

And then his phone rang with a call from Sergeant Turney. "Hello?"

"Clay?" The connection was poor, but Sarge's concern was evident. "Are you…Belknap Springs?"

"Sitting in front of the lodge as we speak. Henna was here, and she—"

"I can't…losing you…the lodge, you say?"

"I'm right out front."

"Don'tcha move…muscle."

Clay heard the line disconnect. He dropped his head into his hands and stared at the pool water still dripping from his jeans.

———

"Daddy!"

Jason's compact body hurtled from Sergeant Turney's car. His hair was matted and smelled like smoke—the most beautiful smell in the world. Clay could only imagine Turney's part in this reunion.

"Jason. Man, am I glad to see you!" Clay caught up his son in a hug.

Peering beyond, he saw Jenni step into view. Did he dare perceive her grin as anything personal? Could he risk a moment of hope? Physical and emotional numbness threatened to bog him down; he could feel them like weights on his limbs.

"Jenni." He resisted an overload of reactions. "Are you okay?"

Her voice was rough. "I can hardly talk…the smoke."

"Smoke?"

"We have a lot to tell you."

Clay cringed at the thought of detecting any more numbers, but he could not let this moment pass. He would not. With a hesitant smile, he held out his arms and gathered her in so that the three of them were mashed together in a soggy embrace. His hands ran through her hair. He flinched as his fingers brushed the soft skin along the back of her neck.

At first he felt nothing.

And then he felt everything.

A Confession

Scandinavian Festival, August 2004

With Jason's hand firmly in his own, Clay jostled through the Friday night crowds. He greeted old friends. Nodded. Waved.

He wished he could have his wife at his side, but Jenni had opted for a quiet evening with relatives in Eugene. Despite mutual words of reconciliation, he knew they faced a long road ahead as a couple—rebuilding trust, opening new lines of communication, dealing with past rejection. At least she was willing to give it a chance.

By God's grace. After twelve years of detachment, it's more than I deserve.

"Can we buy one of those?" Jason tugged at Clay's arm.

He noted the long line for the perennially popular hollow pancake balls. He watched a server add cinnamon and sugar. "You betcha, Jason. We can't come to the festival and miss out on aebelskivers."

"Can I give the lady the money?"

"Whatever you want. You're getting to be a big kid."

Waiting to order, he could not shake his despair over Kate Preston's death. He'd heard about it only hours ago. Young Kenny had been at his uncle's house while his mother went on her weekend retreat, and according to an officer's report, the news had torn the boy apart. At least he had nearby family; for now, he'd remain under his uncle's care. Still, Clay knew he would need to go visit first thing tomorrow.

Maybe Jason can befriend him. They might do each other good.

Clay turned his concerns to the upcoming performance on the Festival Park Stage. Half an hour from now he would meet with Sarge and Josee for the show in which Mylisha, Wendy, Digs, and Father Patrick would all be dancing. Any sort of disaster could wreak havoc; along these constricted walkways, chaos would rule. To contact the police would be counterproductive. After the fiasco of August tenth, they would only scoff at Clay's interference.

What's to stop Asgoth from trying something? He could be here. Now.

With Scandinavian desserts in hand, Clay led Jason through a group of craft booths displaying red vests and knitted sweaters, plastic Viking helmets and Nordic jewelry. One booth boasted nature prints and a swivel rack with an assortment of postcards.

Clay stopped. "You've gotta be kiddin'."

He picked out a card with a photograph of cross-country skiers in Norwegian garb standing before a sparkling snowbank along a cabin at Odell Lake. On the backside in neat print, he saw the words: SNL Photography.

Spinning the rack, he found seven more postcards produced by Sam and Lyndon, his friends from the Pacific Crest Trail. Each card was startling in its clarity and beauty. The guys were talented, no doubt about it.

Clay bought every card available—hey, what were friends for?—investing in Sam's and Lyndon's earthly existence while depositing a prayer for their eternal ones.

———

Clay took Jason along side streets to avoid the crush of pedestrians. Muffled by buildings and trees, the sounds of partying and music seemed vacuous, as though the festival was a charade of good cheer meant to fool the outside world. Clay sniffed at the air wafting from the beer garden. He shook free of it and held tighter to his son's hand.

At Fifth and Holly, they found the Finnish locomotive standing sentinel.

"You remember this train?"

"Mm-hmm." Jason chewed on his aebelskiver.

Outlined by the festival lights, Engine 418 was an ominous reminder to Clay of all that had gone on in recent weeks. He wondered if Henna would ever find the wooden tube and the black chess king lying at the bottom of Crater Lake. She had the GPS coordinates; nevertheless, a salvage operation would be expensive.

Would such an endeavor be worth it?

Of course, odds had it that soon Henna would be in police custody—as soon as she began leaving a trail of marked fifty-dollar bills.

From the stage area, traditional Norwegian music kicked in to indicate the play's opening act. Amid melodious chords, Clay thought he heard a soul-wrenching scream.

———

Asgoth's remaining time in JC was short lived. He had failed. Clay Ryker was still alive, and Henna Dixon was hiding out with over a hundred thousand dollars and a Garmin GPS unit. According to Consortium informants, she had "given up the ghost."

The phrase brought a wry grin to Asgoth's mouth.

What do I have to lose now? I'll go out with a bang!

He meandered unseen through the crowd, reached the Festival Park Stage, where crew members were taping down a cord before the grand performance of "Hardanger Wedding." He ducked through an access panel into the darkness below the stage. He would wait another ten minutes or so until the show started. Until families and friends filled the stands in colorful displays of their Scandinavian roots.

The carnage would be beyond anything this city had experienced.

"I know what you're thinking, Asgoth."

"Sir?" Asgoth jolted at Mr. Gerde's sudden appearance.

"It would be a temporary setback at best," the Consortium member emphasized. "Unless timed perfectly, violence tends to unite humans and redirect their attention to spiritual matters. Is that what you want?"

"I wasn't thinking of doing anything."

Gerde's fleshy features nearly hid his piggish eyes. "Then why're you crouched beneath this stage?" The demonic breath came in gaseous waves.

Asgoth diverted his gaze.

Gerde gestured toward shadows where cobwebs swayed over coiled electrical lines. "It's time for these good sirs to deliver you to your new wandering place."

Claws dug into Asgoth's ghostly fabric, although he could see no sign of his captors. Overhead, shoes clomped on wood, and klieg lights sliced between the boards while dancers moved into position. The crowd noise dropped to a murmur.

"You've been a wretched failure, Asgoth, botching your opportunities with Rasputin, Bill Scott, and finally Clay Ryker. This town could be useful to us, but we've learned more subtle methods than those you seem to favor. You've been nothing but a nuisance to the Consortium. You'll be receiving that which you deserve."

"What about Monde? Shouldn't he get the same treatment?"

"How very noble of you, turning against your partner."

"Where're they taking me?" Asgoth's struggle was in vain.

"Hell's Canyon." A wheezing laugh followed Gerde's words. "It's in eastern Oregon, near some old Indian burial grounds. You'll be miserable. I guarantee it."

The play's soundtrack kicked through the speakers, muffling Asgoth's scream as infernal claws took hold and whisked him away.

———

Clay and Jason had squeezed into saved bleacher seats beside Sergeant Turney and Josee. They enjoyed the play's drama and humor but especially the dancing. At the conclusion, their enthusiastic cheers brought smiles to the troupe's faces.

Clay let his eyes meet Digs's, and he gave his co-worker a slight nod.

Digs nodded back.

Clay then smiled at Mylisha. She reciprocated, her face golden and vibrant under the stage lights. She seemed infused with fresh energy. Spinning around, she exited the Festival Park Stage with a sense of purpose in her step.

The crowd began to disperse.

"Clay," Sarge said, "you gotta meet Josee."

"So you're Josee."

"The one and only."

"Sarge's told me about you."

"Better have been good." Despite her tough exterior, Josee's words were playful. She wore her black hair short and choppy; a silver ring hung from her eyebrow, and a vial dangled from a string necklace. Her turquoise eyes hinted at wisdom and pain beyond her years.

"He didn't tell me you were so short," Clay said.

"Hey now."

"Then again, everyone looks short to me."

"Guess I'll let you slide this time," Josee said.

In loose black jeans and a buttoned striped shirt, Sarge looked more relaxed than Clay had ever seen him; even at the Steamboat Inn, the investigative consultant had been focused on the job.

Sarge slid his hand into Josee's. "How 'bout we all get somethin' to eat? My treat. I bet our buddy Jason here is ready for some food."

Jason perked up. "Food? Yeah!"

"You two've had a rough day."

"A rough year," Clay amended. "I'm just glad to have my son with me. The good thing is, it's finally over."

"Hmm, maybe not." Sarge winked. "Let's walk on over to DQ and find ourselves a place to talk. I've got a confession to make, and Josee's got something to show ya."

Once they had ordered and settled into a booth by the back door, Clay instructed Jason to wash up in the rest room. With his son out of earshot, Clay surrendered to his curiosity. "Okay, Sarge, let's hear it. What's going on?"

"Well, this ain't easy to admit."

"Come on. No stalling."

"You remember your dive into Crater Lake? 'Course you do. Afterward you wanted to know if I'd found a wooden tube, the one from Engine 418."

"Yeah. You asked me if an old cork counted."

"That's right, I found a cork. But I must've forgotten to mention that the cork was attached to the tube you wanted."

"Forgot? You mean you lied to me."

"I just left off some of the truth." Sarge shrugged. He glanced across the Dairy Queen lobby, then tugged the smooth, carved wood from his pants pocket. "Just tryin' to protect you, partner. Plus, I knew this artifact might be directly linked to an item of Josee's. As it turns out, I was right."

Clay took hold of the object, removed the cork. He found himself transfixed anew by the black king that slid onto the table. Tall and distinguished, the chess piece had an ornate cross atop its crown and Cyrillic text etched into stone.

"What does it say? Do you know?" he wondered aloud.

"Tmu Tarakan," Josee replied. "It's Russian, meaning a 'place of desolation.' We think it refers to a chamber where Rasputin hoarded ancient relics."

"I've heard rumors of such a place. Does anyone know where it is?"

"Not yet," Sarge said. "But we have some solid clues locked away in a vault."

Josee spoke in a whisper. "The black king is key."

With the chess piece at his fingertips, Clay felt a tingle brush over his skin.

"Hey, Dad, that's cool." Jason slid in beside Clay. "Where'd you get it?"

"Did you wash your hands?"

"Yep." His son turned up his palms for inspection.

"Good job. Here, have a look." Clay scooted the chess king toward his son. "A boy about your age found it. We're gonna go visit him tomorrow."

"You think it's worth money?"

"Could be."

Jason's interest swerved toward an approaching teen girl in a DQ cap, his eyes widening at the fast-food delicacies on the red plastic tray. Clay uncapped his butterscotch sundae, Josee spread out a napkin and dumped out her fries, while Sarge acted as though his salad was the epitome of indulgence.

Sarge took a bite, then pointed to the black stone king. "I get the feeling there's more to it than just cash, don't you?"

Josee's eyebrow ring swayed with the nod of her head.

"After all that's gone on in the last few weeks," Clay said, "I can't put a lot of trust in my feelings. But yeah, in this case I'd have to agree."

"Well then, I hate to say it."

"Say what, Sarge?"

"It's not over yet."

Josee's fingers slipped around the big man's elbow as he rolled his neck like a prizefighter prepping himself for another round. Clay could relate. He thought of the work ahead and sucked in air to combat his weariness.

It's your story, Lord. Do with it what you will.

Acknowledgments

Dudley Delffs, Don Pape, Carol Bartley,
Michael Warden, and the incredible crew (WaterBrook Press)
for personalizing this industry, showing care for art and artist alike.

Dave Robie (Big Score Productions)
for meeting me early on, knocking on doors, and getting replies.

Ted Dekker and Randy Singer (award-winning authors)
for slicing fact and fiction into manageable bites.

Cindy Martinusen and Tricia Goyer (authors and sisterchicks)
for encouraging e-mails, Austrian tales, and a sisterchick pin of my own.

Barbara Guise, Blanche Monaghan,
Lynn Frost, Jacquie Manning, and numerous others (unofficial publicists)
for going out of your way to help me on mine.

Shaun Wilson (brother and lifelong friend)
for leading me along the Pacific Crest Trail, despite snow up to our knees.

Scott Shelton (scholar and gentleman)
for pointing to Hughes's poems and Hawthorne's short stories.

Johnson "Jay" Bell and Robin Taylor (coffee moguls in their own right)
for flexibility, sincere friendship, and the caffeine to fuel creativity.

Tim Stone and the FedEx Kinko's crew (West End, Nashville)
for paychecks, helpful schedules, and a copy of the last draft.

New River Fellowship (Cool Springs, Tennessee)
for spiritual nourishment, connection, and creativity joined with integrity.

Bill, Shannon, and Caleb Cushman (family friends)
for laughs, long-term hospitality, and inspiration in the "blue room."

The Connollys, Firas, Griffins, Hahns, Howes, Langs, McClendons, Ogles,
Surratts, and many others (friends and spiritual family)
for meals together, tick-infested hikes, advice of all sorts,
and shared war stories.

Rick Moore, Charliy Nash,
Brian Reaves, and Sean Savacool (fellow writers)
for encouraging words, inspiring articles, and books in progress.

Chuck at Café Coco (Nashville location)
for a spot to plug in the laptop while writing and people watching.

Temah and TraVonda (friends and co-workers)
Temah, for sharing your art; TraVonda, for sharing your name.

Elena Gadomski (Russian translator/advisor)
for keeping a straight face while correcting my mistakes.

Corporal Larry Larson (Junction City Police Dept.)
for investigative insights, despite any of my oversights.

Edmondson, Hermitage, and Donelson Public Libraries (Nashville, Tennessee)
for great service, selection, research tools, and enthusiasm.

Coldplay, Skillet, Jeremy Camp, Superchick, Thousand Foot Krutch, Toby Mac,
Pillar, Grits, and Chevelle (recording artists)
for chasing away my lethargy with sonic and spiritual energy.

Readers everywhere (fans new and old)
for delving with me into the mysteries of life and death...
May you, too, reach out to feel God's hand of providence!

I welcome your feedback at my Web site or e-mail address:
wilsonwriter.com
wilsonwriter@hotmail.com